Shot Through Velvet

"First-rate ... A serious look at the decline of the U.S.
textile and newspaper industries provides much food
for thought." —*Publishers Weekly* (starred review)

"Great fun, with lots of interesting tidbits about the history of the U.S. fashion industry."
—*Suspense Magazine*

"A thoughtful mystery with an energetic, very likable
heroine that will attract new readers to this established
series." —The Mystery Reader (four stars)

Armed and Glamorous

"Whether readers are fashion divas or hopelessly fashion challenged, there's a lot to like about being *Armed
and Glamorous*." —BookPleasures.com

"Fans will relish *Armed and Glamorous*, a cozy starring
a fashionable trench coat, essential killer heels, and designer whipping pearls." —*Midwest Book Review*

Grave Apparel

"A truly intriguing mystery." —Armchair Reader

continued . . .

"A fine whodunit . . . a humorous cozy."
—The Best Reviews

"Fun and enjoyable . . . Lacey's a likable, sassy, and savvy heroine, and the Washington D.C. setting is a plus."
—The Romance Readers Connection

"Wonderful."
—Gumshoe

Raiders of the Lost Corset

"A hilarious crime caper. . . . Readers will find themselves laughing out loud. . . . Ellen Byerrum has a hit series on her hands with her latest tale."
—The Best Reviews

"I love this series. Lacey is such a wonderful character. . . . The plot has many twists and turns to keep you turning the pages to discover the truth. I highly recommend this book and series." —Spinetingler Magazine

"Wow. A simplistic word but one that describes this book perfectly. I loved it! I could not put it down! . . . Lacey is a scream and she's not nearly as wild and funny as some of her friends. . . . I loved everything about the book from the characters to the plot to the fast-paced and witty writing." —Roundtable Reviews

Hostile Makeover
Also a Lifetime Movie

"Byerrum pulls another superlative Crime of Fashion out of her vintage cloche." —Chick Lit Books

"The read is as smooth as fine-grade cashmere."
—*Publishers Weekly*

"Totally delightful . . . a fun and witty read."
—Fresh Fiction

Designer Knockoff

"Byerrum intersperses the book with witty excerpts from Lacey's 'Fashion Bites' columns, such as 'When Bad Clothes Happen to Good People' and 'Thank Heavens It's Not Code Taupe.' . . . quirky . . . interesting plot twists."
— *The Sun* (Bremerton, WA)

"Clever wordplay, snappy patter, and intriguing clues make this politics-meets-high-fashion whodunit a cut above the ordinary."
— *Romantic Times*

"A very talented writer with an offbeat sense of humor."
— The Best Reviews

Killer Hair
Also a Lifetime Movie

"[A] rippling debut. Peppered with girlfriends you'd love to have, smoldering romance you can't resist, and Beltway insider insights you've got to read, *Killer Hair* adds a crazy twist to the concept of 'capital murder.' "
— Sarah Strohmeyer, Agatha Award–winning author of *Kindred Spirits* and the Bubbles Yablonsky novels

"Ellen Byerrum tailors her debut mystery with a sharp murder plot, entertaining fashion commentary, and gutsy characters."
— Nancy J. Cohen, author of the Bad Hair Day mysteries

"A load of stylish fun." — Scripps Howard News Service

"Lacey slays and sashays thru Washington politics, scandal, and Fourth Estate slime, while uncovering whodunit, and dunit and dunit again."
— Chloe Green, author of the Dallas O'Connor Fashion mysteries

"*Killer Hair* is a shear delight."
— Elaine Viets, national bestselling author of *Pumped for Murder*

Death on Heels

A CRIME OF FASHION MYSTERY

Ellen Byerrum

AN OBSIDIAN MYSTERY

OBSIDIAN

Published by New American Library, a division of
Penguin Group (USA) Inc., 375 Hudson Street,
New York, New York 10014, USA
Penguin Group (Canada), 90 Eglinton Avenue East, Suite 700, Toronto,
Ontario M4P 2Y3, Canada (a division of Pearson Penguin Canada Inc.)
Penguin Books Ltd., 80 Strand, London WC2R 0RL, England
Penguin Ireland, 25 St. Stephen's Green, Dublin 2,
Ireland (a division of Penguin Books Ltd.)
Penguin Group (Australia), 250 Camberwell Road, Camberwell, Victoria 3124,
Australia (a division of Pearson Australia Group Pty. Ltd.)
Penguin Books India Pvt. Ltd., 11 Community Centre, Panchsheel Park,
New Delhi - 110 017, India
Penguin Group (NZ), 67 Apollo Drive, Rosedale, Auckland 0632,
New Zealand (a division of Pearson New Zealand Ltd.)
Penguin Books (South Africa) (Pty.) Ltd., 24 Sturdee Avenue,
Rosebank, Johannesburg 2196, South Africa

Penguin Books Ltd., Registered Offices:
80 Strand, London WC2R 0RL, England

First published by Obsidian, an imprint of New American Library,
a division of Penguin Group (USA) Inc.

First Printing, February 2012
10 9 8 7 6 5 4 3 2 1

ACKNOWLEDGMENTS

Sagebrush, Colorado, does not exist, except on the page, though it may resemble a town or two out West and incorporate a memory or two of my own. I am indebted to several people who helped me bring this fictitious town and its people to life. The name *Muldoon* comes from *The Solid Muldoon*, a freewheeling and spirited newspaper in Ouray, Colorado, in the late 1800s, but nearly forgotten today.

I owe a debt of gratitude to legendary cowboy Monty Sheridan and his gracious wife, Ruth Sheridan, for sharing tales of ranching in northwest Colorado and giving me insights into the daunting and challenging life of a modern cowboy. My thanks also go to David Blackstun of the Bureau of Land Management, who was very generous with his time and information.

My husband, Bob Williams, has been by my side through the entire process: from walking with me through miles of dusty sagebrush to get a feel for the territory, to proofing, copyediting, and challenging me every step of the way on this manuscript. *Death on Heels* wouldn't be the work it is without him. Thanks are never quite enough.

As always, any mistakes in the book are mine, or possibly, creative acts of fiction.

chapter 1

"Dying with your boots on is a point of pride in the West, Vic. But these women died barefoot," Lacey said. "And that grieves me."

Digging around the bottom of her small closet, she hunted for her cowboy boots. Lacey wasn't going to be caught unaware and unshod. Not like those three women.

Colorado rancher Cole Tucker had been arrested for murder, so fashion reporter Lacey Smithsonian was heading back to the last place on earth she swore she'd ever return: Sagebrush. That meant she would need, among other things, her best, dandified, make-a-statement cowboy boots. And more than a little guts. Lacey was afraid she was really going to stick her foot in it this time. She needed the most fearsome footwear she owned to wade through all the mud. And the mudslinging.

Tucker can't be a killer, she kept saying to herself. *I loved him. That cowboy wanted to marry me.*

"Where are you going?" Her current boyfriend, Vic Donovan, was right behind her at the closet door. "Is there a secret passage in there I don't know about?"

Lacey crawled farther into her closet on her hands and knees, into that dark limbo where old clothes went in disgrace, until they might be useful—or fashionable—again. Vic watched her, fidgeting. It wasn't like him to wait behind, but there wasn't room in that dark recess for him. There was barely enough space for Lacey. She stretched full length on the floor and finally felt her fingertips brush one of those half-forgotten boots, tucked into the farthest corner. *I must have been crazy when I bought these,* she thought. However, the boots were surprisingly comfortable, with their stitched, pointed toes and two-inch stacked leather heels. Lacey loved the lift they gave her. And maybe they would also give her courage to—

"Darn it! Where's the other one?" She looked at the single boot in the light and tossed it furiously over her shoulder. "I hate this closet!"

Vic Donovan dodged the boot. "Really, sweetheart, I don't think you ought to be going back to Sagebrush anyway—"

She ignored him. Somewhere in that cramped cave was her other boot: handmade, calf-high, Western-style, pale green and golden brown leather, with elaborate green and gold stitching that resembled filigree. Showy and cowgirly, they were just worn enough to pass out West for serious boots. Lacey hadn't tried them on since she'd left that shabby Western boomtown for a better reporting job in Washington, D.C.

The boots had nothing to do with Cole Tucker's arrest, and yet somehow they were a tangible link to her life back then. They were solid, stylish, American-made reassurance in tough times. Like Cole. He was a rancher who knew his way around horses, and boots. But not murder.

Lacey threw more shoes over her shoulder in Vic's general direction, high heels, sandals, pumps. Vic caught one red high-heeled shoe by its slender leather strap and stared at its worn-down heel.

"Lacey, you are death on heels, you know that?"

"Hilarious. I'll show you death on heels if I don't find my other cowboy boot. I'm wearing them on the plane tomorrow. Both of them." She blindly chucked another red shoe. Vic ducked.

"About that plane flight," Vic said. "It doesn't make any sense for you to go." He surveyed the mess of shoes and boots on her bedroom floor and ran one hand through his dark, curly hair. He dangled her one cowboy boot in the other hand and fiddled with its loose bootheel like a nervous little boy.

"I'm going. I have to be there for the arraignment on Monday." She stood up and faced him, wiping her hands. "Besides, you're going."

"That's different. I was Sagebrush chief of police when Rae Fowler disappeared. I have to talk to the prosecutor. He wants all his ducks in a row and he might call me to testify. When Tucker goes on trial."

"For murder." Lacey gazed mournfully around her bedroom. It was a mess, but there was a bigger one waiting for her in Sagebrush.

A copy of the Associated Press report on Tucker's arrest lay on the bed. Lacey picked it up. Pictures of the dead women. A picture of Tucker, taken at some rodeo, looking very dashing on his horse. The headlines about the murders had popped up on the Internet when Lacey was at work at *The Eye Street Observer* that morning. The photos jarred her memory back to Sagebrush. She'd called Vic at his office. He'd just heard the news himself.

Only seventeen years old, Rae Fowler was the first alleged victim, found strangled on a lonely country road in Northwest Colorado two years ago. The first of three murders now suddenly charged against Cole Tucker, Lacey's once-upon-a-time, almost would-be, but never-was, fiancé.

Rae Fowler was a runaway from Denver, pretty and baby faced, in too much of a hurry to start her adult life. She made her way across the state to Sagebrush, where she lied about her age and waitressed in a bar for a few weeks. Then she disappeared.

When her body was found, no one could pinpoint how long she'd been dead or how long she might have been in the company of her killer. The police thought the victims were held captive somewhere, perhaps for as long as a week.

For Sean Victor Donovan, the Fowler murder had been one of those cases that haunts a cop. Even though he left the law enforcement world behind and turned to the more lucrative business of private security in Northern Virginia, he'd be tormented by Rae Fowler's murder until it was solved. And now it looked like it was.

"You are over Cole Tucker, aren't you?" Vic asked.

"This has nothing to do with that."

"Cole Tucker's accused of killing three women, Lacey. Three. Not just Rae Fowler. And she was murdered two years ago."

"Did you know the other two victims?" Lacey leaned against the bed, happy Vic was there, but slightly irritated with him. It was complicated.

"I used to see them around town. By the time Ally and Corazon disappeared, I had moved on to the Steamboat PD, you know, and then back here to Virginia. Nursing my broken heart and all. Surely you'll recall my broken heart? All your fault, if you remember."

"Then why was Tucker arrested now? Today?"

"Darlin', you know after the first forty-eight hours, a typical murder case is colder than Sagebrush in December. Unless the cops find new evidence or—"

"Unless someone talks," Lacey completed his thought. "Who talked?"

"No idea. They're keeping it quiet. One of the sheriff's deputies apparently caught the tip." Vic moved closer to her. "He told the sheriff, who called the CBI, who alerted the FBI. That's where the AP caught the story."

She simply didn't believe Tucker did it. It wasn't possible. Lacey read the story again. "It says the bodies were all found partially clothed. All were barefoot. Stop playing with my boot, Vic."

Vic shifted the boot from hand to hand. Lacey grabbed it from him and set it on the bed. "When we found Rae, she was mostly dressed. No shoes. But she'd been out there in the wind and rain for a while. Hard to say what condition they were in when they were dumped."

Ally Newport was the second reported victim. At thirty, she was older, presumably wiser, but not quite as pretty as Rae Fowler. Yet dishwater blond Ally was "the belle of the ball," according to those who had known her. Lacey stared at Ally's picture: a rather plain face with blank round eyes, but a wide smile softened the effect.

Vic took the AP wire story and glanced at it. "When Ally hit Sagebrush, she was still acting like she was homecoming queen."

"She must have grown up the prettiest girl in a very small town," Lacey said. "Even smaller than Sagebrush. Any boyfriends?"

"Plenty. But nothing serious, and no suspects panned out. This was after I left, you know. Hearsay."

"And Corazon Reyes?" Lacey pointed to her photo. Corazon was the standout beauty in that unfortunate group. Petite and fine boned, Corazon had long, black hair and dark, almond-shaped eyes that twinkled, even in the smudged copy. "What do you know about Corazon?"

"Not much. Other than she was dating Cole Tucker."

"What?" Lacey snapped to attention. *My Cole?* "That's not in the news stories!"

"No. But it's probably common knowledge in town. Brad Owens, the prosecutor, mentioned it when he called me."

"The story says Corazon's body was found nine months ago! But they arrested Tucker this morning?"

Vic picked up Lacey's boot again and absently wiggled the bootheel. He was worrying at it like a loose tooth. "Takes time to put a case together. New evidence apparently came to light. Owens said some things of hers were found out on Tucker's property."

Lacey was dizzy at the thought. *Did I ever really know this guy?* "Three women have been found. You think there are more out there?"

"God only knows, darlin'. Big county, size of Connecticut. Good place to hide a body. Five thousand square miles, a lot of it pretty desolate. Bodies don't always get found. Some turn up a hundred years later. Course, in that case, they go to the state archaeologist, not the cops."

By then, they'd be mummies, or bleached bones, like the carcasses of dead cows Lacey had seen on the Western Colorado landscape.

"The wire story says the women were strangled," she said.

Vic nodded. "The hyoid bone was crushed in each case."

She closed her eyes for a moment. "That's a horrible way to die." It was intimate and ugly. Lacey pictured someone's hands around the women's necks. But then the killer might not have used his hands. *Maybe a rope, or— Stop, Lacey,* she told herself.

Rae Fowler, Ally Newport, and Corazon Reyes. Their murders rocked that little Colorado town with a ripple of horror that grew with each death. In a small town, everyone's private business seemed more immediate, Lacey knew. In a small town, the news was always personal, from the high school sports to the newest business in town, to random acts of graffiti. The locals took a personal interest in the news. *And there's little enough of interest in Sagebrush anyway,* Lacey thought.

She recalled her Sagebrush reporting days. People thought nothing of stopping her in the grocery store or at the gas station to offer their personal and sometimes vivid commentary on her news stories. They told her when she got it right or wrong, they told her when they had something to add, and they told her what they thought even when they had nothing to add. It was exhausting.

Murder was not common in Sagebrush, and when it did happen it was most often a domestic dispute gone bad or a bar fight. Lacey remembered only a few murders in the entire county in the two years she had lived and worked there. It wasn't like Washington, D.C., where murder was so routine most killings didn't even make it to the pages of the major newspapers. Not even her own paper, *The Eye Street Observer.*

In Sagebrush, anyone who ever met Rae or Ally or Corazon—or Tucker—would have a story to tell. Everyone in town would be touched in some way.

"Tucker couldn't have done this." She took her boot away from Vic again and set it down on the suitcase to await its mate.

"You have to remember, Lacey, cops don't arrest people without evidence. Not even small-town cops. I was a cop. I know. Cops hate to end up looking like idiots, believe me." Vic reached out for her.

"Most of the time."

"Lacey—"

"Don't 'Lacey' me, Vic Donovan! I dated this guy for two years. Two years! If Cole Tucker is a killer, then I don't know anything about anybody. I don't know anything about myself. Or even about *you*. If I'm wrong about Cole, then I'm wrong about *everything*. I'm going to Sagebrush and I'm going to get to the bottom of this."

chapter 2

"And I'm still missing a boot. Damn!"

I should know how to pack by now, she thought, *so why is this so hard?* She'd even written about how to pack for a weekend getaway, sarcastically of course, in her Fashion Bites and Crime of Fashion columns.

But when it came to preparing for a return trip to Sagebrush, she was at a loss. She was no cowgirl. She picked out jackets, a skirt, some jeans, her faux-fur-lined leather jacket. Her cowboy boots, as soon as she found the one that was MIA. And she had carefully laid out on the padded bench at the foot of the bed a new, yet vintage, outfit.

Something else to give her a shot of strength.

Her great-aunt Mimi had selected the pattern in the late 1930s, and even cut out all the pieces: a bolero jacket in green and gold shot velvet, and a moss green velvet skirt. Lacey's favorite seamstress, Alma Lopez, had finished it, but Lacey hadn't worn it yet. She found a soft gold sweater in a delicate knit to wear with it. The outfit would go with the cowboy boots; at least Lacey thought it would. The green would enhance her eyes, the gold her highlighted hair. She planned to wear it to the arraignment of a man she once loved, now arrested for murder. But she would accessorize the outfit with the gold Cupid pendant Vic had given her.

Clothes shouldn't matter when it comes to life or death, Lacey told herself. But clothes were her armor. Makeup was her war paint. She would need that armor in the coming days. That's why she needed the vintage outfit. Her insides might be torn up, her emotions a mess, her imagination full of murdered women; still she had to put on a brave front. At home she always had Aunt Mimi's trunk to run to for inspiration and consolation. She would have to pack a little of Aunt Mimi with her.

She caught sight of herself and Vic in her dresser mirror. He was dark and angular and she was light and curvy; he was tall and she was petite. He was strong and protective; she was—*what?* she wondered. *Impulsive? Sentimental?* But they fit together well, she thought. And not just physically. The attraction was magnetic. However, at times like this, when they were butting heads, it was a magnetic storm.

Lacey moved the clothes to one side and flopped down on the bed. The fragrant breeze from the open window tickled her nose. It was one of those deceptively warm March days, teasing the Nation's Capital with the promise of a spring that was still weeks away. Lacey knew she would much rather enjoy springtime on the Potomac than head off to that still-frozen little Colorado town, far west of the Continental Divide.

"Please don't go." Vic looked troubled, his green eyes serious, his jaw tight. "It's going to get ugly before it's over." He brushed away the dark brown curl that fell over his forehead.

"Too late. My ticket is bought," she said.

Vic pulled her up and held her. "It's really not a good idea."

Lacey laughed, a little ruefully. "Maybe not, but when has that ever stopped me?"

"When have *I* ever been able to stop you?"

"You wouldn't want to, Vic. You have way too much fun telling me 'I told you so.'"

"There is that." He kissed her hair.

"Tell me. Was Tucker ever on your suspect list when you were in charge of Rae Fowler's disappearance?"

Vic took a deep breath. "No. Tucker's name never came up. We focused on a couple of guys. Nothing came of it." He crossed his arms and frowned.

"Who were they?" *Maybe the cops missed something*, Lacey thought.

"One was a coal miner. The only connection was that he left town right after Rae went missing. Never came back, never located him, never turned up in the system. Then there was Zeke."

"Zeke? Who's he?"

"Zeke Yancey. He was the go-to guy whenever I had a bar fight or a drunken brawl in town. Beer, weed, and busted knuckles? You could bet Zeke would be involved. You probably saw him around town back then. He's a Sagebrusher, born and bred."

"Okay, the local knucklehead. How was he with women?"

"Mostly they stayed far away from him. Had a history of domestic violence with girlfriends. He was seen bothering Rae on several occasions. Yancey called it flirting. But we couldn't prove our suspicions. Last I heard he was banned from the Sundance Kid."

"One of the bars where Ally Newport worked?" The Sundance had a pretty rough reputation, at least the last time Lacey was in town. "Banned for what?"

"Ugly behavior. Zeke is rude, crude, and socially unacceptable."

"Any official complaints of sexual assault or harassment?"

"Nothing that ever went to trial. I booked him into a cell on many occasions."

"Did he have a girlfriend?"

Vic thought for a moment. "Jillie Maycomb used to put up with him when no one else would."

"Jillie Maycomb? Any relation to Aggie Maycomb, the old bartender at the Little Snake Saloon?"

"Aggie's daughter. Looks just like her mother." He winced.

"That's a shame." Lacey remembered her. Aggie was skinny and bitter and tough as nails.

"Anyway, when Zeke got kicked out of every other bar in town, he'd crawl back to the Little Snake and hook up with Jillie again. For a week or two."

"A match made in heaven?" Lacey stretched her back and started refolding her clothes.

"More like drunk-tank hell. I don't think they even liked each other."

"What does Zeke look like?"

"Like a drunk. Big, sloppy, week-old stubble. You remember the type."

Lacey wrinkled her nose. "Blue jeans, flannel shirts, stench of beer?"

"That's Zeke Yancey."

"So he was your prime suspect? Not Tucker?"

Vic raised one eyebrow, the one Lacey usually raised at him. "Then there was Muldoon."

"Dodd Muldoon! Are you serious? My old boss?" Dodd Muldoon was the editor, publisher, and resident maniac who ran the Sagebrush daily newspaper.

"Don't know why you're surprised. You suspected him of all kinds of skullduggery."

"But not murder! And you never told me?" She leaned against the wall, her head reeling.

"Didn't come up. Muldoon always seemed to know too much about that murder, information that was never released."

"As terrible a journalist as he was, Muldoon probably had sources."

"He was up to his eyeballs in dirty business. He was even named in a couple of assaults."

"Assaults?"

"No one ever pressed charges. He has friends in high places, you remember. He became a real nuisance in the bars later on, trying to pick up women, usually very young women."

She remembered a puffy middle-aged man with a talent for making her snarl. Lacey nodded slowly. "Muldoon tried to put the moves on women at the paper. But never me."

"You have that endearing way of sending out death rays from your eyes, sweetheart."

"Blame the nuns. I don't know about Muldoon. He can be sleazy, but a killer?" She found the idea unsettling. She knew once the seed had been planted, she would worry it into a full-blown tree of suspicion. "But I could believe that before Cole Tucker."

Vic shrugged. "Well, the prosecutor believes otherwise. Lacey, I don't want you there. You're too emotionally involved to be objective about this." She scowled. He sat down on the bed, still holding her boot. "It isn't because you're still in love with him, is it?"

"I'm not in love with Tucker. But a part of me will always love him." *But if he was a killer?*

"What if he's still got a thing for you?" Vic started fiddling with the loose heel again.

"Got a thing for me? Yeah, right! That would explain why he married someone else six weeks after I left town. Six weeks to the day, Vic. And, adding insult to injury, on Valentine's Day! Because he adored me?" The whole episode still made her cheeks burn.

"Darlin', you don't understand men. It was a grand gesture. He couldn't marry you, so it didn't matter who he married. And see how long it lasted? Divorced in a year."

The first time Lacey Smithsonian saw Cole Tucker, he ambled through the newspaper offices to buy a legal notice for his ranch, buying or selling some piece of land. He was all cowboy charm and sinewy muscles, wrapped snugly in tight, faded jeans, a fur-lined jean jacket, and beat-up cowboy boots. He was the Old West come to life, with a swagger that was electric.

Tucker had honey-colored hair and deep brown eyes. He stared straight at Lacey with frank appreciation and interest, yet he seemed a little shy too. But before he left, the cowboy tipped his hat to her and said he'd get back to her later. They dated for almost two years, until she couldn't take Sagebrush for one more forty-degrees-below-zero winter's day.

She could not remember her first kiss with Cole Tucker, and that bothered Lacey. *You're supposed to remember the first kiss, aren't you?* What she remembered best was the very first time she saw him, when their eyes locked. That moment was stronger than a kiss—at least Cole's kiss.

Vic and Lacey's first kiss, on the other hand, was something she would never forget. It was her last New Year's Eve in Sagebrush. Lacey had just that day said no to Tucker's marriage proposal and he didn't take it well. He had to take care of business out on the ranch, instead of taking her out that evening for the last night of the old year. So Lacey headed to the biggest local nightspot, the Red Rose, with a girlfriend from work. She didn't intend to dance, but she wasn't about to stay home on New Year's Eve and cry over Cole Tucker. And that handsome chief of police, Vic Donovan, was there.

Vic had asked Lacey out so many times she'd lost count. It was a running joke between them, Vic asking, Lacey turning him down. For good reason. One, she was going out with Tucker. Two, Vic was still technically married, and Lacey had always been a stickler for details. Three, because she was afraid she wanted to say yes to Vic just a little too much. And four was more than a technicality. It would be a colossal conflict of interest for a reporter to date the chief of police, and cub reporter Lacey Smithsonian had ethical standards. So the answer was no, again and again.

But at midnight that New Year's Eve, the dark-haired, green-eyed Sean Victor Donovan somehow materialized right in front of her on the dance floor at the Red Rose. In the clamor of bells ringing and horns honking and the country band playing "Auld Lang Syne," Vic reached for her and kissed her, and he drove all thoughts of Cole Tucker from her mind.

"You could have had me," Vic interrupted her thoughts.

"You were married."

"Separated! I was getting a divorce." He waved her one found boot in the air for emphasis. "You ever heard of it? D-I-V-O-R-C-E."

She gazed up at Vic's handsome face. "Didn't matter. I'm Catholic."

"Lady, you are the toughest grader I've ever known."

"Again: blame the nuns," she said. "You're just lucky you got married in some drive-through wedding mill in Vegas."

"It wasn't a drive-through. Not quite. Still, it doesn't count in the church." He was a Catholic boy and he knew his ecclesiastical loopholes as well as she did. "What happens in Vegas, stays in—"

"And what about Montana?" Vic's bleached-blond ex-wife, Montana McCandless Donovan Schmidt, was a sore point for Lacey. Montana had made a last-ditch effort to win Vic back less than a year ago, right in Lacey's face, and on Lacey's turf. She'd failed, but Lacey would never let it go. *One of my flaws.*

"Montana is history. You know that."

"Ha! You think I'll rest easy knowing your ex-wife is lurking around Sagebrush, ready to pounce on you like a hungry lioness and drag you back to her lair?"

Vic chuckled and tossed her boot from hand to hand. "I'll never even see her. She's living in Steamboat. A million miles from Sagebrush."

"More like fifty, Chief." Though the chic upscale ski resort of Steamboat Springs did seem a million miles and several decades distant from Sagebrush. "And your man-eating ex will hear about your arrival. On the neighborhood tom-toms."

"Lacey Smithsonian, you are ridiculous, but cute. Besides, I'm sure Montana is busy hooking some other poor fish."

The bootheel was looser; he had made it worse with his worrying. "You're the prize marlin, sweetheart. And I'm going," she said. "Now where is my boot?"

"Lacey, about that boot of yours— Where do boots always go to hide over at *my* place?"

"Under the bed!" She dived to the floor and shoved aside the small mountain of shoes she'd excavated from her tiny closet. She crawled halfway under the bed and Vic heard her victory whoop. Lacey emerged flushed and grinning, triumphantly holding aloft the other cowboy boot. "I knew I asked you over for some good reason."

Vic was still frowning. "That's the other thing—" He held out both hands, the boot in one hand, the heel in the other. "Oops. I broke off your bootheel. Sorry."

Lacey grabbed the two pieces out of his hands. "Oh, Vic! Don't talk to *me* about being death on heels! You— you *boot breaker.*"

chapter 3

"Look what you did to my boots!"

"I'll buy you some new boots. You can use them to stomp all over me."

Lacey glared at Vic. "Don't tempt me, and I'm still going to Sagebrush tomorrow." She hugged her boots to her chest, one boot with a heel, one without.

Vic reached out for the heel. "Maybe I could fix—"

"Drop it right there, mister. Do not touch one more thing." He backed away, hands in the air.

Lacey and Vic stared each other down. They carefully sat on the floor in her bedroom, surrounded by shoes and clothes and boots and Lacey's half-packed suitcase. He put his arms out for her in apology and she relented, snuggling into his embrace.

"I have to go. I already told Mac I needed some time off. He was grumpy about it, but I promised to write him a feature. On Western wear or something." Lacey sighed. For a Westerner she realized she didn't really know much about Western wear, aside from her cowboy boots and owning a couple of snap-front shirts.

Fashion reporting for *The Eye Street Observer* was not exactly Lacey's dream job. Writing for a second-string D.C. paper might not give her access to the New York or Milan fashion shows, but at least she could more or less create her own beat and follow her nose for news. Nevertheless, her editor, Douglas MacArthur Jones, balked when she asked for an immediate leave of absence.

"What? Are you crazy?" His trademark bushy eyebrows were saying NO, NO, NO. Light bounced off his dark balding head, distracting her. "And you really went out with this guy in Colorado? I don't know, Smithsonian. You've never had to leave the East Coast to find a killer before," Mac said.

"There was Paris. And New Orleans." Lacey moved papers around so she could sit down for the argument.

"Okay. That time. But aren't there enough degenerates in the District to amuse you? You have to go running off to—where the hell is this place? Purple Sage, Colorado?"

"Sagebrush. Thanks for your support, Mac. I know this guy. He's not a killer."

"Ha. You say that now. You involved? He's a killer." Mac shifted in his chair and reached for a brownie decorated with bright green shamrock icing.

Lacey had personally snagged Mac one of these rare delicacies from the paper's food editor, Felicity Pickles. Lacey even presented it to Mac on one of Felicity's shamrock-festooned paper plates. The brownies looked nauseating to Lacey, but they were undoubtedly gooey and delicious. When Mac had something sweet to eat, he was sweeter to deal with. Usually.

"What I'm saying, Smithsonian," Mac continued after a large bite, "is that you keep running into trouble when you least expect it, and now you want to run off to the ends of the earth to see a man who's already been arrested for murder. This is asking for trouble, isn't it? This is a good idea *why*, exactly?"

"Sagebrush, Colorado, is not exactly the ends of the earth," Lacey protested, though it certainly felt like that to her. And *maybe* she had once or twice *happened* to say something like, "I used to work in this little town at the ends of the earth." How dare he use that against her?

"You're chasing trouble, Smithsonian. You *know* there are murdered women. You *know* this guy could be their killer. You know and I know you're going to get into some kind of mess. This is way off your beat."

"Cole is not a killer. And I'm not going to get into any

trouble. I just want to be there for the arraignment. I'll grab some interviews with the sheriff and prosecutors, I'll try for an interview with Tucker, and then I'll come back and, um, write something about it."

Mac cocked one bushy eyebrow, a warning sign over his scowling café au lait face.

"Convince me you *need* to do this trip, Smithsonian. We are a local newspaper, you remember? We cover the Nation's Capital, not every crime and criminal to the very ends of the earth."

"I'm owed the time, Mac. I have leave coming." She paused. "How about a feature article? Subjective, interpretive journalism. Something like 'Cowboy Justice in the West.'"

The bushy brow softened with editorial interest, but not quite soft enough. "What about your Crimes of Fashion column? And your Fashion Bites?"

"Cowboy clothes," Lacey said, thinking fast. "And you keep telling me to take some time off, Mac. Mostly when you're mad at me, true, but couldn't I do it now, before you get mad at me again?"

"You're getting there," Mac growled. "I suppose you'll have to go." Out came his best martyr impression. "We're short staffed, you know. Hiring freeze." Then his exaggerated sigh. "Send me some column inches when you have a chance. If you're not in some damn ridiculous fix. Or in jail." She rose from her chair to leave quietly. Saying one more word might be pressing her luck. "And Smithsonian—"

"Yes, Mac?"

"First sign of trouble, you call me. You hear me? Don't cowgirl off alone on one of your nutty adventures. Danger is not in your job description. You write about shoes and purses and dresses. Hats and haberdashery." He picked up some brownie crumbs lingering on the paper plate. "Write me something about—cowboy hats."

"Cowboy hats? Like Stetsons?" She thought she must have misunderstood.

"They're classic, don't you think?" He stared off into space, somewhere out on the range, far beyond the Beltway. "Had one when I was a kid. You could call it cowboy couture." He smiled at his own cleverness.

There had been black cowboys ever since there was an American frontier, but even though Douglas MacArthur Jones grew up in California, Lacey couldn't see her African American editor riding the range. Not any range, anywhere. All he ever rode was the copydesk. And his reporters.

"I'll see what I can do, Mac. And really, I don't foresee any trouble."

"Then you've got your eyes closed." He scowled. "Get out of here. Stay safe."

"Just for the arraignment, right?" Vic's words broke into her reverie, and his hands began an all-too-brief massage of her neck and shoulders, easing the tension that had settled in like a long-term leaseholder. "You're not going to stage a jailbreak or picket the courthouse or something, just because you think Cole's innocent, are you?"

She threw him a give-me-a-break look over her shoulder. "Why, sweetheart, you're the only man I'd stage a jailbreak for."

Vic kissed her. "I've been waiting to hear you say that. You're my Get Out of Jail Free card."

"Don't stop rubbing my neck. You missed a spot."

Vic stopped anyway. He grabbed his black leather jacket and headed reluctantly toward the door. "Gotta go. My flight leaves in a couple of hours."

"I wish we were going together. I'll see you Sunday." She opened the door for him. He paused, and stroked her face.

"You got your way with Mac. What about your friends? Stella's going crazy with that wedding thing. Think she can do it without you?"

"She'll live, and I'll have a blessed break from talk of tulle and ruffles, or whether it's the leather bustier or the velvet corset for the wedding."

"And Brooke?"

"Busy with work. Can't get away. You know I love them, but . . ." She let out a deep breath and glanced at her watch. "Anyway, I have a powwow with the Pink Collar Posse in an hour. I'm sure I'll get my last-minute instructions."

"This crazy mercy mission of yours couldn't come at a worse time," Brooke said, slinging her bulging briefcase into the booth at the restaurant. "My caseload is full. Stella is up to her bustier in strategizing all things wedding. What if you need us? What if I need you because Stella is driving me crazy?"

Stella gave Brooke The Look. Brooke Barton, Esquire, was Lacey's sometime attorney, full-time friend, and longtime Washington conspiracy theorist.

"I'll be fine," Lacey said. "So will you. And Stella."

Stella frowned. A look of pique crossed Brooke's face. It was eight o'clock on Friday night and Brooke still wore a sleekly tailored pin-striped suit of indeterminate color, somewhere between taupe and gray. Her long blond hair was twisted back in a tortoiseshell clip, strands escaping picturesquely around her face. Lacey knew this was Brooke's hey-it's-the-end-of-the-day-and-I-don't-know-what-to-do-with-my-hair look.

The third member of their group was Stella Lake, Lacey and Brooke's loyal friend and fabulous-yet-opinionated hairstylist, who was at the moment planning her nuptials and more crazed than ever. Stella wore a tight purple sweater with deep-dipping décolletage, a short, tight, red miniskirt, and purple-and-white-striped tights. Her eyeliner and mascara and currently chestnut-colored cupid curls made her look like a naughty Raggedy Ann doll who had lost her way.

Lacey wore old jeans and a soft, deep turquoise sweater. On her feet were comfortable low-heeled boots, not cowboy boots, and her hair was free. She felt a little subdued next to Stella, but a lot more comfortable than Brooke.

Stella tapped her purple fingernails on the table, drawing their attention to her irritation, and to her engagement ring, which sported a large diamond solitaire.

"I'm with Brookie," Stella said. "This trip is totally rotten timing, Lace. Like, I know you gotta go. But to be honest, it kinda feels like you're abandoning me. Us."

"Hey, I'm not abandoning anybody. Life doesn't run on schedule. Don't worry, Stella. I'll be back in time for your wedding." *And in time to wear whatever scary brides-maid dress you finally decide on.*

Stella's choices for dresses had been all over the map, from Renaissance Goth Princess to Judy Jetson high on rocket-fuel fumes. Lacey shuddered at every new idea, each a little further over the top than the last. At least there was no time now for custom-made dresses. They'd have to buy them off the rack. Lacey just hoped the rack wasn't at the costume shop for *The Rocky Horror Picture Show.*

The trio met for a quick dinner at the Southside 815 restaurant in Old Town Alexandria, instead of someplace in the District. It was two blocks from Lacey's apartment, and she was still dithering over last-minute details. They ordered the Southern-style appetizers, crab and corn fritters, fried green tomatoes, barbecued shrimp, sweet potato biscuits, and corn bread. Stella was grooving in grits heaven. Brooke was delicately diving into the bread basket. But Lacey only picked at her food.

She had toyed with the idea of not telling her friends she was leaving town and dropping them an e-mail after the fact, but she couldn't deal with the hurt feelings. After all, the three of them had been through a lot together.

Stella, who had been in physical therapy since her leg cast came off, was now proudly hobbling around. Devastated that she couldn't wear high heels yet, at least not *two* of them, Stella was determined to wear her highest heels for her wedding to the semi-dapper Nigel, a scamp of an Englishman who had stolen her heart—and, Lacey hoped, nothing else. Lacey still didn't trust Nigel completely, but he was growing on her. Nigel called himself a "professional stolen jewel retriever," but he was in fact a semi-reformed jewel thief turned some kind of shadowy insurance investigator. Lacey thought he had a little too much interest in shiny baubles. *Most likely why he's attracted to Stella. She's nothing if not a shiny bauble of a person. With a heart of gold.*

"This is my hour of need," Stella whined. Brooke and Lacey rolled their eyes in unison.

"We can't all have our hour of need together at the same time," Lacey said.

"I didn't mean it like that. Exactly." Stella fiddled with a chestnut brown curl. She was the manager and head stylist at Stylettos Salon in Washington's Dupont Circle neighborhood, and she was fighting the urge to do something radical with her hair before her wedding. But for the sake of her friends, and the wedding pictures that future generations of her progeny would see, she was restraining the impulse. Lacey could see self-control was taking its toll. "I just meant that I'm swamped at the salon or I'd come with you."

"No thanks, ladies. The Pink Posse can sit this one out."

"Sure, you say that now, but when you're up to your ass in alligators, or alligator pumps, you'll be sorry," Stella said.

"No alligators of any kind in Sagebrush," Lacey assured her. "Just rattlesnakes and other assorted wild critters. Coyotes. Pronghorns. Jackalopes. You know."

"What's a jackalope?" Stella asked.

Brooke handed Lacey her own copy of the Cole Tucker story, with annotations. "And when you need a lawyer, who are you going to call, way out West?"

"Really, guys, you're very sweet to worry about me, but I'll be fine. Vic will be there." Lacey tried to shift the subject. "Frankly, I'm surprised you two don't have dates tonight."

"Ha! Who says I don't? I'm seeing Nigel later," Stella said. "We have to discuss ushers, and he still hasn't picked a best man. I suggested Vic."

"My Vic? Vic Donovan? Really? You're kidding, right?" Vic and Nigel had a history, from prep school on down to the present, and it wasn't friendly, though their diplomatic relations were now thawing a bit.

"Funny, that's what Nigel said. But he's got to have a best man. And he hardly knows anyone here. Any other guys, I mean."

"How about Kepelov?" Lacey was being facetious. Gregor Kepelov was supposedly an ex-KGB spy, and Nigel's sometime partner in the soldier-of-fortune business. And sometime mortal enemy.

"Yeah," Stella said dubiously. "He's, like, semi-under-consideration too. Sort of."

"And you, Brooke. Working late tonight?"

"Unfortunately. It's going to be a long weekend too. But I might see Damon in the morning for coffee."

Stella batted her eyelashes. "The romance of the century. Skyping at two a.m. to keep you warm."

"That's right, Stella, the twenty-first century." Brooke was very fond of Damon, her boyish cyberspace muckraker. "Truth, justice, and the American way. And Skyping."

Stella dismissed Brooke's romance with a shrug. "And why haven't we heard about this killer before, Lacey?"

Why indeed? Lacey wondered. She was beginning to feel ganged up on. "He didn't kill anyone. And he was just—a boyfriend. He just, um, never came up in conversation. Till now." They looked unconvinced. "Come on, Stella, your past conquests could probably fill several New Jersey phone books. Not counting the unlisted ones. Have you told us about all of them?"

Stella harrumphed. "You dated this guy for, like, *how* long and he, like, proposed to you and now he's been arrested for murder? We shoulda known! You have totally been holding out on us, Lace. Ask me anything. I'll tell you whatever you wanna know, even up to and including Jared Goodman behind the bleachers when I was in seventh grade. He was in the eighth grade. Jared was, like, this total middle school rock star, see, and I was, like, his groupie, and we used to—"

"Too much information," Brooke interjected.

"Too much is never enough, Brookie," Stella shot back. "Now *your* private life is like the Book of Secrets, ya know?"

The pin-striped attorney blushed pale pink. "My only Book of Secrets is a law book. There's hardly been time for anyone. Certainly not in middle school!"

"Till Damon Newhouse," Lacey reminded her.

"Yes, there is Damon." Brooke allowed herself a small angelic smile. "But no secret there. You both know all about him."

"And he knows too much about all of our secrets," Lacey interjected.

"As an investigative cyberjournalist, it's his job to know." Brooke smiled.

Damon ran the Conspiracy Clearinghouse Web site, also known as DeadFed dot com, a forum for fringe conspiracy theories of all kinds, including such ever-popular mysteries as who was *really* behind the global recession, toxic chemtrails, killer vaccines, CIA mind control, and the brain-eating zombies who secretly run Congress.

Some journalist, Lacey thought. *Damon's a berserk blogger with an Internet bazooka.* But she held her tongue and merely groaned delicately.

"Speaking of Damon, he's not going to believe this one," Stella cut in. "And you can get yourself into more trouble than anyone I know, Lace."

"Check a mirror, Stella. Really, you guys. My trip won't interest Damon. There is no global conspiracy angle. No aliens, no leaked documents, no strange creatures out of time and space," Lacey said.

"You don't know that until you get there, now do you?" Brooke said. "Speaking of strange creatures, what is a jackalope, anyway? And what if you happen to need legal advice?"

"Why would I need legal advice?"

Brooke and Stella shared a look and broke out laughing, as if on cue.

"'Cause you always get in trouble," Stella said. "Duh."

"I do not." Lacey seemed to remember that Stella had been in trouble quite a lot recently, and surely it must be Brooke's turn.

"Yes, you do. And we'd be right there with you,"

Brooke said. "If only this stupid case I'm on hadn't been continued, I'd be free to explore this legendary Sagebrush of yours."

"It's too gritty for our favorite Gucci girl, Brooke," Lacey said. "There's no Burberry for two hundred miles. Well, at least fifty."

"I'm sure I'd bear up sans Burberry."

Stella gazed at Tucker's picture in the news story. "He looks hot. I love cowboys. So was he good, I mean as in really *good*? You know, like, tall in the saddle?"

"Oh, Stella. He was a good guy, if that's what you mean." Lacey knew it wasn't at all what Stella meant. "The cops got the wrong guy this time."

"And you're going to find out who really killed those women?" Brooke asked, now at full attention. Stella's eyes lit up with interest. "That's what this is all about, isn't it, finding the real killer?"

"I'm going to Sagebrush to assure myself he's not a killer," Lacey said. "I'll let the law do its job. If Tucker's innocent, he's got nothing to worry about. Right?"

" 'If'? You mean you're not sure?" Brooke leaned forward.

"Of course I'm sure," Lacey said.

"That's what Bluebeard's wife said," Stella added. "Just before she opened the forbidden door. And found the rest of Bluebeard's wives. Dead, I might add. Totally dead. And blue."

"They were not blue!" Lacey sputtered. "You're a comfort, you know that, Stella?"

"I try." Stella stabbed a piece of corn bread with her purple nails. "Gee, I wish I could come with you, Lace."

"If you're so busy at Stylettos, how come you were able to meet us here? I thought you might have to work tonight," Lacey asked.

"I had to cut back my hours. I can't stand a full shift on my leg until it's, like, totally back in shape. Good thing I've decided to wear a long wedding gown."

"And you can always wear low heels if nobody's going to see them," Brooke pointed out.

"Bite your tongue, Brooke Barton!" Stella was so aghast that Lacey laughed. "I am not wearing some nightmare orthopedic clodhoppers."

"Low heels do not mean orthopedic clodhoppers."

"Tell that to the jury, Miss High-Power Pumps," Stella shot back.

"You could always get some fancy lace-up, high-heel boots, maybe in white leather," Lacey suggested.

Stella nodded. "You're talking about high heels, pointy toes, cute laces? That might be cool. Maybe some crystals, or pearls. Or at least rhinestones."

Of course they would have rhinestones, Lacey thought. "And they'd support your ankle."

"But nothing orthopedic."

Lacey was pleased the conversation was safely back in the land of sugarplums and wedding gowns. Considering how sick she was getting of the whole wedding planning rigmarole, it was surprising how comforting it could be.

Suddenly the memory bubbled up of Cole Tucker's long-ago wedding proposal and what it might have been like to get married in Sagebrush, Colorado. In January. At forty below. A sudden chill went right through her, and she waved at their waitress for hot coffee. Stella and Brooke were still deep in Wedding Dress Land.

At least I won't have to explain what a jackalope is.

FASHION BITES

The Higher the Heel, the Harder the Fall

Every shoe, like every woman's dating history, has a heel. They may be tall, short, thin, thick, stacked, or see-through, chunky or stiletto, kitten or Cuban. But *high* heels are in a class by themselves.

With the ability to lift you to new heights, to wound you, to pinch you, to squeeze you, and to bankrupt you, high heels are like a certain kind of man we all know, also known as a heel.

Your foot has a heel. So has your shoe. A shoe may also have a tongue, a vamp, a sole, and a shank. But it is the heel that has seized the imagination, as it sashays through our thoughts and words. Has any other item of apparel achieved so much versatility in our vocabulary?

When someone is "nipping at your heels" or "close on your heels," you're being pursued. You can be "head over heels" in love, but you may have to "cool your heels" and wait. Someone with "round heels" is said to be promiscuous. To be "down-at-the-heels" is to be shabby, and to be "well-heeled" is to be well-off. Basically, we all want our shoes to be well-heeled and keep us on our toes.

And we want more. We are all subject to fashion fantasies and lies. And we might be foolish enough to believe that bows on the toes or bright red soles make all the difference.

If only I had those powerful red peep-toe platforms, I'd win that job.

If I had those darling pink slingbacks, I'd live a magical life.

If I had those sexy glass slippers, I'd catch the eye of Prince Charming.

But really, the most you can hope for in a pair of heels is that they complete your outfit, add sizzle to your figure, and won't injure you by the end of the evening. Or cut your foot when that glass slipper shatters.

Sadly, certain heels—once reserved for those ladies of the night who ply their wares on street corners—have been flogged into a fashion obsession by designers who apparently want to cripple women. Stilettos on steroids with five- or six-inch heels and towering platforms have become the Monster Truck of shoes, something the Bride of Frankenstein might wear to hobble down the aisle. But when heels are so high that fashion models topple while strutting the runway, the shoes are too high, too ugly, too dangerous, and *too stupid* for you!

So a few pointers for the next time a pair of Garden-of-Eden-apple red, snakeskin stilettos whispers your name. Go ahead and try them on. But be aware of their pitfalls:

- If there is an inch of space between your heel and the back of the shoe, cramming your toes into the pointed end as you lurch along in your sky-high heels, something is wrong. What could it be? They don't fit.
- The skinniest heels may call to you, but if you wobble instead of waltz and find yourself stuck in street grates like a deer in a steel trap, close your ears to their flattery and walk on by.
- Treacherous cobblestone and brick streets, as found picturesquely in our Nation's Capital, are the mortal enemy of high heels. You'll need the grace of a ballerina to navigate these rough surfaces without falling.
- Extremely pointed and allegedly fashionable shoes should be reserved for Aladdin and his

genie, and for witches trapped under falling houses. You might put somebody's eye out with them, but you should not wear them. The truth about extreme pointy-toed heels is that they will go out of style someday. Soon. And when they do, we will all wonder, "What on earth was I thinking?"

- Remember the pumps that you wear all the time, tall but not too tall, the ones that slip on and comfort your feet? They carry you faithfully to the office and the cocktail party after work. Kind of like your favorite guy; he really doesn't care what you wear on your feet. He thinks pink Reeboks go everywhere. He is wrong, of course, but adorable. When the shoe (and the man) fits, you can frolic happily down the street, past all those poor women staggering on their sky-high, skinny, strappy sandals.

So beware of killer heels: The ones you wear and the ones you date. Choose high heels that fit and lift your spirits, and kick those other heels to the curb!

chapter 4

The phone began ringing insistently the moment Lacey let herself into her apartment. The number told her everything she needed to know.

"Lacey? It's your mother."

As if I wouldn't recognize your voice. "Mom."

"You heard the terrible news, I suppose," Rose Smithsonian said.

"News? What news?" She shrugged out of her coat and sprawled on the blue velvet sofa, part of her inheritance from Aunt Mimi.

"Don't be cute, Lacey. Your old boyfriend was arrested in Sagebrush today. For murdering three women."

"Oh, that news. I heard." It was never smart to say too much too soon to her mother. Her mother would eventually say *everything*. Lacey adjusted a pillow beneath her head.

"Did you see this coming?"

"How could I see this coming? I haven't seen Cole in years. I might not even recognize him."

"When exactly are you coming home?" Rose asked. "You are coming to Colorado, aren't you?"

Lacey stared at her suitcase, standing ready by the door. "I'm not sure."

"Does all this hesitation mean you think he *is* a killer?"

"Cole Tucker is not a killer. He's a rancher." *I'm not up for a long chat, Mom.*

"In other words he kills cows, not people, but never mind," Rose said. "What are we going to do about it?"

"'*We*'?" Lacey's voice rose. Rose Smithsonian and Lacey's sister, Cherise, had discovered an unexpected taste for crime fighting when they visited Lacey the previous fall, and now they were proving entirely too willing to help out as freelance crime solvers. Lacey loved her mother and her sister, but they could be so *enthusiastic* about things. So perky, so exhausting. Although their last visit had turned out surprisingly well, Lacey didn't want to jinx it. "*We* are not going to do anything."

"You're not coming to Colorado to get to the bottom of this? That doesn't sound like you. Do you want people to think you dated a maniac?"

"I have dated maniacs. Tucker wasn't one of them. Trust me." Her mother waited. Lacey sighed. "I'm flying to Colorado, but I'm just going to Sagebrush for the arraignment. I'm going there *alone*. To assure myself that he's innocent. The law is going to handle this one. I'm not getting involved this time. I'm serious, Mom."

Her mother was silent for a moment. "But you *are* stopping in Denver first, aren't you? There are no direct flights into Sagebrush. We can spend some time together. You could borrow the station wagon. I'm sure it will make it over the mountains. Pretty sure."

Dad's old Oldsmobile station wagon? Across the Continental Divide? I'd be better off in a covered wagon.

"I've already rented a car."

"We *will* see you, then? Good! What an unexpected pleasure!" Rose purred with satisfaction.

"Yes, Mother." Lacey groaned silently. "You'll see me. Briefly."

"You don't need to drive to that awful place until Sunday anyway, so you can spend the night here. Won't that be fun?"

Lacey closed her eyes. "Fun. Of course, I'll stay one night, Mom."

"That's wonderful. Your room is all ready, and Cherise said she'd come over. It'll be fun. Just us girls."

*She already arranged everything before she called.
Naturally.* "What about Dad?"

"Oh, he's around. Somewhere," her mother said
vaguely. "He's fine. He said to have a safe flight."

Lacey said her good-byes and hung up. *Some things
never change. Mom. Dad. My sister. And the station wagon.*

Lacey always seemed to forget how drab the Colorado landscape was in winter, at least the dusty High
Plains side of it. She already missed the green of Virginia, even though the snow-capped Rockies on the horizon were stunning in their drama. Lacey retrieved her
little econobox rental car—the rental agent swore it would
make it over the mountains—and wondered again whether
she'd made the right decision to travel here. She ticked
off the miles as she drove over the brown and yellow
plains east of Denver, past the steel and glass skyscrap-
ers of downtown, and finally down the Valley Highway
and Speer Boulevard to the middle-class neighborhood
where she grew up.

The family manse, a brick midcentury ranch-style
house with a "modern" vibe that had been gussied up by
some wacky would-be architect, looked the same. Her
parents loved that house. They'd been living in it since
Lacey was a little girl, even before Cherise, her little sister, was born.

Lacey never warmed to the house, never liked it. The
architecture was chilly, all sharp angles and harsh lines,
with a preposterous roof that met at a peak in the middle and swooped over the rest of the house and the car-
port like black-tiled bird wings. A row of windows under
the roofline let in too much light and too much cold. The
house was poorly insulated, hot in the summer and cold
in the winter. The thrifty environmentalism of her parents prohibited one and all from ever turning up the
thermostat. And forget about air conditioning. It simply
wasn't *green.* The Smithsonians had been discussing so-
lar panels on the roof for at least ten years, but had yet
to take action.

As a child, Lacey lived in fear that the house, with its

winged roof, might really be a spaceship, though not the flying saucer kind, which would take off in the middle of the night for another galaxy, never to return.

When she was five or six years old, Lacey came to hate the glass block windows in the bathroom. In her nightmares a monster with an extraordinarily long neck would crash through the glass blocks with his head. It didn't matter how often her mother said it would be impossible for a monster to crash through the thick block windows. Monsters can do *anything*, Lacey would remind her.

Last, but not least, Lacey suspected the crawl space, with its tiny door hidden in the bottom of the linen closet, might lead to another dimension entirely, just waiting to pull her in. Rose Smithsonian told Lacey she had a too-active imagination and she would grow out of it. But in the meantime, no more late-night television for *you*, young lady.

The floor-to-ceiling windows in the living room and dining room were another source of anxiety for young Lacey. There weren't enough walls. People looking in could see everything, and Rose liked to keep the sheers open to let in the light. Not to mention the stares of curious neighbors. The one floor-to-ceiling brick wall had an opening at the bottom that they called a fireplace, though no wood was ever burned there, which frustrated Lacey no end. She would have given anything for a two-story, center-hall colonial, roaring fireplaces with ornate mantels in every room, and bathrooms with actual curtains over the windows. And no glass blocks to tempt the monsters.

Then there was the furniture. The weird furniture that changed with Rose's redecorating schemes. It always seemed to be square or angular and made of blond wood (except for her chrome-and-glass phase). It was never comfortable. Lacey didn't care if it was an authentic Eames chair if you couldn't sink down into it. Rose adored the modern, the new, the hard-on-your-bottom. That may have been why Lacey loved visiting Aunt Mimi in Washington, D.C., where there were comfy plush velvet couches, deep-pile colorful Chinese carpets, and a traditional dining set carved out of splendid dark cherrywood.

It was funny how her parents' house now looked harmless and much smaller than the one that loomed in her memory. Lacey pulled the rental car to the curb. She wasn't out of the door before Rose and Cherise came racing out of the house to greet her.

Cherise grabbed her bag and Rose gave her a quick hug. The three evaluated each other in a split second. Lacey assumed she passed muster or they would have said something. Or they were saving it for later.

Her mother was fit, trim, and attractive. Her dark hair had grown out a bit since Lacey had seen her last, just a few months before. Rose was wearing purple corduroy pants and a baby blue V-neck sweater. She looked like anybody's semi-harmless mother. Prettier. But with a suspicious gleam in her eye, full of questions and curiosity.

Cherise was younger, taller, skinnier, and about three hundred percent perkier than Lacey could ever hope or want to be. Cherise rocked on the balls of her Nike-shod feet as if ready to take off on a marathon. She wore tight, faded blue jeans and a pink turtleneck. Her blond hair was in its inevitable ponytail.

"I just painted. I hope you like it," her mother said.

"I'm sure I will," Lacey said, trying not to sound either sarcastic or amused. She and Rose disagreed on so many things, and décor was just one of them. Rose loved projects and painting and improving things—things like her daughters. However, Cherise, a former high school cheerleader, was light-years ahead of Lacey in the mother-pleasing category. She needed less improving.

In her spare time, aside from golf and tennis and improving her daughters, Rose devoted herself to her home, which Lacey felt didn't deserve all the attention. But there was only so much that could be done with a dumpy midcentury modern ranch-style home, even one with their house's odd architectural quirks. Lacey didn't know how she had lived through Rose's Neon-Orange-

and-Lime-Green Phase, the Eye-Popping-Primary-Colors Assault, and the Dismal-Eggplant-and-Ochre Period.

Lacey took a deep breath and stepped into the living room, gazing at the carpets and the half wall dividing the living and dining rooms. "Mom? It's—wow."

"I'm glad you like it. I thought you would." Rose beamed at the fresh paint, a suburban riff on a Southwestern theme. The half walls were painted a sand color with wide stripes of turquoise and coral. The brick wall with the useless fireplace had been stuccoed over to look more "native," and it was guarded by Hopi kachina dolls. Wildly patterned Navajo blankets upholstered the rock-hard sofa and chairs. Individually, every piece was eye-catching. All together, they made her eyes ache.

"Oh, my." Lacey didn't know where to look. The clash of patterns was giving her a headache. "Takes my breath away, Mom. Hey, I feel a nap coming on. Maybe a light coma."

"That flight must have tired you out. You didn't drink enough water. You need to stay hydrated. You're in the guest room, your old room. It's not quite there yet, I'm afraid," Rose said. "I'm still working on it."

This could mean anything. "I can't wait, Mom." *No big surprises, please.*

On her way to viewing her mother's latest triumph, Lacey peeked into the room that had been Cherise's. It looked pristine as a shrine, still in the perky pinks that Cherise always preferred. Memorabilia from her high school cheerleading career were still tacked to a bulletin board. Even though Cherise had moved away from home, the room remained the way she left it for those occasions when she stayed overnight, like holidays and when her big sister came home.

"Still the same, I see," Lacey said.

"No, it's not." Cherise pointed out the new drapes, curtains, and rug. "It's completely different. I helped Mom pick out the paint."

"But it's still pink."

"There's pink and then there's *pink*. It's a totally different shade, more lavender pink, more sophisticated. Grown-up pink."

Rose stood before the guest room door and gestured. "Ta da!"

The guest room had once been Lacey's bedroom, a cozy retreat in shades of blue and violet. Rose had claimed the space as her own décor test site and redecorating laboratory the minute Lacey was off to college. Lacey's surplus possessions were all stored in the basement.

"It's—different." Lacey tried not to gasp, but failed. Each wall was a different color. One was deep brown, one banana yellow, one electric blue, one zebra-striped. The dresser was painted in leopard spots, and the sofa was upholstered in a tiger stripe fabric. Her head started to pound.

"I haven't quite decided which way to go," her mother said. "You like it?"

"It's really, um, wild."

"I think it's fun," Cherise said. "Every wall tells a story."

"A lot of plot." Lacey eased herself down on the angular sofa bed. It looked soft, but it was as hard as granite. *Home sweet home*. She smiled. "You've been busy."

Lacey reserved judgment on the butterfly chair with its eye-popping neon lime green canvas cover. Obviously, it was an *accent* piece. *The lime wedge in the crazy cocktail of this room. Ewww.* The preposterous iron and canvas beast glowed radioactively against the one brown wall. The wood floor was covered by a beige sisal rug. Lacey hated the way sisal felt under her bare feet, but she searched for a neutral statement.

"Sisal. Lots of, um, texture."

"It's a work in progress," Rose said. "I haven't decided on the accent color, but I am crazy about the zebra wall. That definitely stays."

You don't have to sleep in here.

It was impossible for Lacey not to compare the Smithsonian house with Vic's parents' traditional Northern Virginia home with its understated elegance. *Mostly* understated. Vic's mom, Nadine, was fond of pink and had used it liberally in her grand dining room. It somehow always made Lacey think of the court of Marie Antoinette, but tastefully, of course. *Who didn't like a little wretched excess?* And the Donovans' backyard was a lush landscape of winding stone paths through maples and oaks, dogwoods and holly trees.

Of course, plants and trees grew more easily in Virginia. Here in Colorado, the Smithsonians' grass was flat and yellow, like every other Denver lawn in wintertime. The evergreen bushes needed to be trimmed, but the pines and junipers stood tall against the winter storms. Heaven forbid that a leafy tree should intrude on the alpine splendor of it all.

"It's so good to have you home, Lacey. Now, take your time, relax, freshen up, but do hurry and get ready, dear. Your father is taking us all out to dinner," Rose announced. "And we'll hammer out this whole Cole Tucker business."

That's what I was afraid of. Lacey set her bag down in her old, yet not at all familiar, bedroom and fled to the living room. "Where's the newspaper?" She wanted to see how the local media were handling the story. Her mother pointed to *The Denver Post* on the blond coffee table.

"I bought an extra copy for you." Tucker's arrest was featured on the bottom of the front page, with a jump to the inside. WESTERN SLOPE RANCHER ARRESTED IN THREE MURDERS. "For your scrapbook."

Lacey perched delicately on one of the uncomfortable accent chairs. The story was long on background and short on relevant facts. *The Post* had clearly been caught by surprise and was padding the story with local color. A sidebar on the murders even pointed out that Sagebrush wasn't that far from Brown's Park, once a notorious outlaw haven in the Old West, and that some claimed the area was still a hangout for "criminal elements." *A century ago,* Lacey thought, *when Butch Cassidy and the Sundance Kid were hanging out there.*

"I've been thinking, Lacey," Rose said. "Cole must have a hidden life."

"It's impossible to have a hidden life in Sagebrush, Mom. Everybody is in your business all the time. Kind of like our family."

"Did you know he was a homicidal psychopath?" Cherise asked.

"Cole Tucker better be innocent. That's all I can say," Rose said. "My God, he was here with us for that one Thanksgiving dinner. I served him turkey at our table. He seemed so nice. Why, I never would have—"

"You never would have served a murderer your Thanksgiving turkey," Lacey said. "We know that, Mom."

"How's my girl?" Steven Smithsonian emerged from his workshop in the garage and gave Lacey a hug.

Steven was an even-tempered man who let his wife handle the family and the social calendar, which left him free to play golf. His golfing buddies had nicknamed him Even Steven. He and Rose were also fond of tennis. They played doubles with friends and were taking up birding. They had season tickets to the Colorado Rockies and Opera Colorado. He might have felt like the odd man out, outnumbered by the females in the house, but his daughters thought of Even Steven as the counterbalance to Rose's flamboyance.

Steven Smithsonian had always looked like the quintessential dad to Lacey, with his black Clark Kent glasses and combed-back brown hair. His daughters used to pretend he was more interesting than he appeared. They finally decided that he must be a CIA agent, rather than the manufacturer's senior sales rep he said he was. He sold plastic parts for some sort of machinery, but eyes glazed over whenever Steven went into detail.

"What's all this nonsense about that old boyfriend of yours?" he asked.

"That's what I'm trying to find out, Dad," Lacey said. "But what's going on with you?"

"Flying to Thailand on Monday." That was a relief to Lacey. He would be in transit for at least twenty-four hours, unable to aid and abet Rose in any of her schemes.

"Your mother tells me you have another young man on the hook."

"On the hook? Thanks, Mom."

"Isn't this new one from Sagebrush too? Something about that place, you know. There really should be a way to figure out whether these fellows of yours are going to turn out to be bad apples. Before you date them, I mean. Say, does he play golf? The new one, I mean. Not the killer."

chapter 5

"Try the buffalo burger," Rose suggested. "So much better for you than beef."

Lacey felt like she'd been buffaloed by her family all afternoon. Eating a buffalo might be poetic justice, but she never ate burgers of any kind.

"Skip the hairy beast, sis. Let's get the rattlesnake bites," Cherise suggested. "Yum."

The Smithsonian family was dining at the Best of the West Steakhouse in LoDo, the lower downtown area that had become Denver's nightlife hub. Rose had picked the place, but Lacey's dad liked it because it was close to Coors Field, home of his beloved Colorado Rockies baseball team. Like the rest of LoDo, it was hopping on Saturday night.

The steak house was decked out in high Western style, with copper, leather, and mounted trophies. The menu featured a dozen kinds of steak, including buffalo steaks, and novelties, like Rocky Mountain oysters and rattlesnake and gator bites. It was not cheap. Lacey was impressed. The Smithsonians' dining-out experiences had always been economical and family-friendly, heavy on chicken and burgers. Times had changed, but one thing had not: No matter what was cooking on the grill, grilling Lacey was at the very top of the menu.

"He really seemed like such a nice guy, that Cole Tucker," Steven said. "I let him carve the turkey. I hate to think of you going out with some murderer."

"Yeah, you didn't learn that at home," Cherise chimed in.

"It's a bad business," Steven said.

Rose patted his hand. "It just shows you never can tell."

"Imagine stabbing another human being," he said. "With no more concern than carving up a turkey. How's your buffalo steak, sweetie?"

"The victims weren't stabbed, Dad," Cherise said. "The paper said they were strangled. You're thinking of that other murder Lacey was involved in—"

"Can't we find something else to discuss over dinner?" Lacey asked.

"Don't worry, Cherise," Rose said. "We'll get to the bottom of this Cole Tucker business. And if you need us, sweetheart, we will be there."

Lacey opened her mouth to speak. Then shut it. The last thing Lacey wanted was the Smithsonians en masse, getting to the bottom of things. She managed to squeak out, "And how is the team this year?"

The Rockies saved the day, and her dinner. Sports talk led to an after-dinner stroll past Denver's Union Station and the Rockies' baseball stadium. Her dad was sorry that the season didn't start until April or they could have taken in a game. He was explaining something complicated about the team or the sport, but Lacey never could keep anything about baseball straight. Or football. Or basketball, hockey, soccer, lacrosse. It was all the same to her, whether it involved kicking a ball, hitting a ball with sticks, dribbling a ball, or running with a ball into a knot of gigantic padded men. He might as well have been speaking in Greek about the Peloponnesian War.

The only sporting event that Lacey was ever sorry she'd missed was the infamous state championship football game at Geronimo High School, the game when Cherise "Lethal Feet" Smithsonian had knocked out the quarterback with one high kick. But Lacey had been delighted to discover there was a video of the devastating blow, which had recently made its way to YouTube.

Cherise refused to discuss it, but it always brought a grin to Lacey's face.

Finally, Rose and Steven went home, and Lacey and Cherise headed for Larimer Square, one of the anchors of LoDo nightlife. Larimer Street had been redeveloped decades before, from the city's most notorious skid row into a chic shopping and dining area. It was filled with couples on dates, groups of friends, and at least two major bachelorette parties. One of the brides-to-be wore a rhinestone tiara and a Miss America sash. Her bridesmaids, ten or more of them, donned neon-colored wigs in lime, pink, orange, blue, and purple.

"Purple wigs? Hey, maybe Stella will have a rocking bachelorette party like that," Cherise said.

"Bite your tongue, Cherise. Stella would like nothing better than to stick me with a purple ponytail. And the rest of the pony outfit along with it."

They were drawn by the lights and milling crowd to Crybaby Ranch, a Western wear store that specialized in upscale cowgirl gear, jewelry, and boots.

"Something's happening at Crybaby," Lacey said. "The National Western Stock Show is over, right?"

"Oh, it's a boot show. I read about it," Cherise said. "Designer cowboy boots. They're open late tonight."

"A designer cowboy boot show? I had no idea."

"Wow, I know something about fashion that you don't!"

"I imagine you're also an expert in ski wear, bike wear, rock-climbing helmets, and running shoes. All of which I know nothing about."

"That sounded vaguely like an insult, sis."

"East is East and West is West, Cherise. We each have our own expertise. Trujillo is the expert on boots in my newsroom."

Cherise grinned. "You mean Tony Trujillo, that cute police reporter?"

"Tony the Terrible. An attractive nuisance. I like Tony, Cherise, but be warned, he's more in love with his boots than his ladies."

Trujillo was the closest thing *The Eye Street Observer*

had to a *GQ* kind of guy. He was a Westerner himself, from New Mexico, and he had a wardrobe of fancy cowboy boots in such leathers as ostrich, cowhide, alligator, python, and armadillo. Roadkill du jour, Lacey liked to call it.

Cherise pulled Lacey through the mob milling around on the sidewalk and opened the door at Crybaby Ranch. "Let's go to the boot show. Terrible Tony will be so jealous. And I really want a fabulous pair of boots."

They squeezed by the doorman into the throng inside the store, past colorful coffee table books and belt buckles and silver and turquoise jewelry. The place was filled with women in snug-fitting jean skirts and two-thousand-dollar boots. In D.C., Lacey thought, they would be the kind of gals who attended the Texas State Society's Boots and Black Tie inaugural balls, where cowboy boots and ball gowns were the dress code. Cherise disappeared into the mob and Lacey navigated past the finger foods and wine, finally arriving at the boot displays. She said a silent thank-you to her little sister. This was a Fashion Bite on the hoof. *Have I been asleep at the style beat?*

The boots on the shelf ranged from six hundred to six thousand dollars per pair. But tonight's event was for those daring frontier fashionistas who wanted to custom order their next pair of boots, with their personal choice of style, color, and material. This boot event was tame, Lacey was informed, compared to the one in January during the National Western Stock Show, when Crybaby Ranch became a boot-happy madhouse, with hundreds of serious boot shoppers clamoring for custom boots.

The good news is that some people have thousands of dollars to spend on one-of-a-kind boots, even in this economy, Lacey thought. *The bad news is it's not me.*

The boot designer himself was on hand to meet and greet his fans, and the occasional lost fashion reporter. He was long and lanky and went by the name of Ryder. His sandy red hair touched his shoulders, and he wore a million-dollar smile. Though he was surrounded by fans,

Lacey flashed her D.C. congressional press pass and wrangled a few words with him.

He picked up one of his display boots and stroked it lovingly. "All my boots have a stainless steel shank and are built by hand, using custom lasts. See this sole? Attached with lemonwood pegs. I don't use brass nails. Weather changes and they fall right out. Not the lemonwood. And I've got the best hides on the planet. The best workmanship. All handmade, hand pegged, hand lasted, hand stitched, every boot fitted to an individual foot."

"They're beautiful," Lacey said. "Cowboy boots are a frontier tradition, but do you think they also make a fashion statement?"

"Course they do." Ryder grinned like a shark. "They say, *Yee hah, baby! I'm livin' the Frontier and I'm kickin' it! Kickin' it hard!* Cowboy boots are high style, they're low style, they're yesteryear and next year, they're rockin' an ageless American renegade-rebel-on-the-road kinda thing. Real cowboys buy my boots, if they're rich enough. Movie stars and Nashville music stars buy my boots. Even Lady Gaga buys my cowboy boots," he said. Lacey wasn't taking notes, but she was engraving the good quotes in her reporter's memory.

"And Taylor Swift?"

"The country songbird? Goes without saying. How do you like these? Brand-new design." Ryder picked up a pair of knee-high black and red boots, hand-tooled cowhide with furious red-eyed bulls snorting clouds of rhinestones and silver filigree. The stacked heels were sky-high and so was the price. They would sell for five thousand dollars.

They were magnificent, but Lacey couldn't see a real cowboy wearing them. Those filigree bulls wouldn't impress the real bulls. They had a country music star vibe.

"Have you sold any of these yet?"

"Just delivered my first pair," Ryder said. "To a pretty lady who's already bought sixty-five pairs of my boots."

Sixty-five? Lacey did a quick calculation in her head. That might be a couple of hundred thousand dollars' worth of boots. "She'd need a special closet just for those boots."

He nodded with a grin. "I helped her design that closet. Custom built, like my boots."

"Does she ever wear anything else? I mean, on her feet?"

"I hope not." He laughed. Ryder was surrounded by fans begging for his attention and it was time for Lacey to move on.

Lacey gazed at the boots, mesmerized. She handled several pairs, admiring their construction—and their price tags. The variety of subject matter was impressive. There were no one-color, utility boots in this collection. There were calf-high and knee-high, with low heels and tall heels. They were works of art decorated in a multitude of moods and themes. There were boots intricately fashioned with skulls, bad kitties, cowgirls, and rattlesnakes wrapped around daggers and guitars. There were hand-tooled butterflies, flowers, and flaming hearts.

A woman around Lacey's age tried on boots in black leather with white and red cutouts in the shapes of spades and clubs, hearts and diamonds. Another shopper in her twenties wore a pair of yellow boots decorated with sterling silver roses. These women were confident, active, attractive, and obviously successful enough to feel no pain at price tags that ran into thousands of dollars for a pair of boots. Lacey knew she shouldn't be shocked, but she was.

Cherise was trying on a pair of baby-blue-and-bone-colored high-heeled boots and admiring them in the mirror.

"Aren't they beautiful?"

"Yes, but did you see how much these things are going for?"

"Oh, these are only nine hundred."

Only nine hundred! Have you lost your mind? Lacey held her tongue. She remembered how she'd once lost her own mind over that pair of Scarpabella designer heels. Of course, she'd been ganged up on by Stella and

Miguel and stoked with chocolate endorphins. And those shoes were on sale, $660 marked down from $1200. Lacey had surrendered to a moment of shoe madness. The beautiful shoes still sparkled in her closet. Who was she to cast the first sandal?

"Very pretty," Lacey said. "I suppose you'd have them forever."

"If my feet don't grow." Cherise looked worried. "I heard they keep growing when you get old. Is that true, big sis?"

"I guess it's your gamble. Of course you could always just display them on a shelf, like art."

Lacey wondered what Stella would think of these boots. Because cowboy boots weren't overdone in D.C., they would be that much more rare and exotic to Stella. Maybe Lacey should suggest a pair of cowboy boots for Stella's wedding. Did cowboy boots come in white tooled leather? No doubt Ryder would make them, for a price. And decorated with sterling silver roses, or at least rhinestones. And hearts and flowers.

Cherise paraded in front of the mirror, clearly in love with her boot choice.

"I want them. Everyone's wearing them. Besides, Lacey, you have cowboy boots."

"With a broken heel. And they only cost a couple of hundred. It seemed like a lot, at the time."

"I'll take them," Cherise said, handing the box and her shoes to the associate. "Can I just wear them? I wanna dance all night in these! By the way, Lacey, don't tell Mom how much these cost. Promise!"

chapter 6

"Really, when you think about it, they're a real bargain," Cherise said.

In her new baby blue and bone boots, Cherise pranced along with a new spring in her step. She smiled at random men on the street, ready to kick up her heels and flirt. She experienced none of the instant buyer's regret that would have had Lacey by the throat. Lacey envied her that.

Cherise was in the mood for a raucous dance club, but Lacey needed something quieter. She chose the Cruise Room. Because she was the big sister, she won. She always thought the Cruise Room at the Oxford Hotel was one of the most romantic places in Denver. Maybe a little less romantic if you were with your sister. Lacey realized she was missing Vic terribly. If only he were there with her! Not that she resented hanging with Cherise. Not exactly.

Dark and lit with a rosy glow, the Cruise Room famously had opened the day after Prohibition ended in 1933, and it was essentially unchanged. It was modeled after a bar in the Queen Mary. A dozen Art Deco bas-relief panels lined the walls above the cozy booths and featured Thirties-era toasts from around the world. Lacey and Cherise grabbed the booth beneath the Russian toast NA ZDOROVIE.

"You call this a bar? It doesn't even have a television," Cherise complained.

Lacey raised an imperious eyebrow. "Art Deco hates

television, and so do I. The Cruise is perfect just the way
it is. I need a dirty martini. Do you want to talk, or just
leave me here and go find yourself a sports bar somewhere?"

"When you put it that way." Cherise pouted a little
and settled into the booth. She gazed down at her new
boots. "I don't usually get down to this part of town."
She looked around. "Lacey, cute guy alert," Cherise
whispered. "At the bar."

Lacey glanced up. *Skiers heeding the late winter call to
the slopes.* They had the telltale ski-goggles tan. As if on
cue, two men with healthy white grins and neatly cropped
hair spun around on their barstools to admire Cherise's
new cowboy boots. The boots were working like a charm.
Cherise and the guys discussed the merits of skiing Tel-
luride versus Crested Butte, and they all swore allegiance
to the superiority of Colorado powder. Lacey had forced
herself down the slopes a few times, only to discover she
was *not* a skier. She smiled and nodded and thought of
Vic and Cole Tucker. Cherise collected the skiers' business cards as they left.

"You're right, Lacey. I'm not missing television now,"
Cherise said.

"But what about Tommy? You missing him?"

Cherise had been dating the high school quarterback she had once knocked out with her killer kick. She
shrugged.

"Not so much. We're just, you know, casual. Nothing
serious."

"Maybe he's afraid of you. The kick is mightier than
the sword."

"Very funny. That was ages ago. What about you?
You say you're here to find out about Cole Tucker, but
what about Vic?"

Lacey felt herself smiling at his very name. "I'm
pleading the Fifth Amendment."

Her sister had an irritatingly knowing air. "I thought
so. Will he be in Sagebrush?"

"He'll be there."

"Is his ex still after him? That cotton-candy blonde?"

Lacey tossed a straw at her. "I imagine so. Too bad I never mastered that cheerleader kick thing."

"Inborn ability. How long has it been since you've seen this cowboy?"

"Years and years." *An eternity ago.*

"You still care about him?"

"No. Not like that. But this whole thing is gnawing at me. He's not a killer. It can't be him. It's a mistake." She thought about Tucker's sudden arrest. *Who called the law on Tucker? Why? And what was the evidence that tipped the scales?*

"Cole Tucker seemed okay to me," Cherise said. "Cute too. But you read all the time about these seemingly normal guys. They have families, they lead the Boy Scouts, the whole nine yards. And they turn out to be mad-dog killers."

"Not this guy."

"Whatever. Anyway, I only met him that once and I can't get the headlines out of my mind."

"Me neither. And there will be people who'll swear they always knew something was wrong about Cole." Lacey pushed her hair away from her face.

"Why do you say that?"

"Because someone always says that. 'I could see it in his eyes. He had killer eyes.'"

Cherise nodded. "Monday morning quarterbacks."

"And then they'll say, 'He was always so quiet. It's the quiet ones who surprise you.'"

"I think you've been writing too much about murder. You're creeping me out, Lacey."

Cherise sipped her blue martini—to match her boots—as another man smiled at them. Denver wasn't like D.C., where most men seemed to be afraid of women, or too in love with themselves and their own self-importance to think of the opposite sex. Nope, here in the West, men weren't afraid to look at women. Especially women wearing boots.

I should have worn my cowboy boots. The ones Vic broke. Coincidence?

*   *   *

After a single blue martini Cherise was a relentless chatterer, even in the taxi on the way home. Even when Lacey leaned her head against the seat and closed her eyes and tried to ignore her talkative little sister.

"Show me that thing Tucker taught you," Cherise was saying.

"What thing?" Lacey opened one eye.

"You know. How to throw a lasso. I've always wanted to do that." She mimicked the motion of throwing a rope.

"Those cowboy boots are really going to your head." Lacey yawned. "And I don't remember how."

Lacey hadn't exactly forgotten, but it wasn't like she'd had much chance to practice lasso throwing in Washington, D.C. It was just one of those things, a memory of Tucker. Riding and roping were second nature to him. Not only was he a born cowpoke, he'd won his share of awards in local rodeos when he was a teenager.

"Come on, I'll show you," Tucker had said, on one of their first dates. It was definitely not dinner and a movie.

He had put his arms around Lacey to show her how to tie the honda, the loop at the end of the rope, and the stopper knot. He singed the end of the new rope to secure the knot. The rope looped through the honda, forming a kind of noose that was thrown with one arm high and circling. The warmth of his arms and the giddy feeling of an unexpected first love were a sharper memory than Lacey wanted to recall. She closed her eyes again to blot it out.

"I was never very good at it," Lacey said. She had captured a few tree stumps in her time with Tucker. That was about all. Tucker had turned her loose on roping a real live calf once, and it was that calf's lucky day.

"When we get home, show me," Cherise begged her. "Please."

"Sure," Lacey said. "Show you another lethal trick? Why not. Maybe you can rope Tommy What's-his-name, the quarterback." The cab pulled up to the house. Cherise jumped out, leaving Lacey to pay the driver.

"There are ropes in the garage," Cherise yelled, sprinting for the garage door.

Lacey trudged over the winter-yellowed lawn after her perky sibling. "It's got to have the right weight, you know."

"Lots of rope. Take your pick," Cherise said, hunting for her folks' house keys. "If Dad doesn't have it, it doesn't exist. Not at a hardware store, anyway."

"Do you know what time it is?" Lacey asked. It was only eleven p.m., but one o'clock in the morning in Washington. She had to get up early.

"It's not that late. And it's Saturday night!" Cherise lifted the garage door. A metal-on-metal screech cut through the silent night. Lacey held her hands over her ears.

The garage was Steven Smithsonian's man-cave. Tools and supplies were neatly organized on shelves and hung on hooks on the walls. There were ladders and drills, shovels and rakes and trimmers, and all manner of axes and hammers. There were wrenches and screwdrivers, buckets and old coffee cans full of nails and screws and metal hooks, all sorted by size and purpose. There were sheets of plywood and two-by-fours, everything a home handyman might require. And even though Steven rarely produced any particular *thing* with his hands—once there was a birdhouse, Lacey recalled—he liked to putter in the garage and listen to sports on the radio. His man-cave even contained a television, a green wooden Adirondack chair, a space heater, and a microwave oven to heat his coffee. And the Oldsmobile wagon.

Rose assured everyone the man-cave was essential to the health of her marriage. She didn't interfere with Steven's male habitat, and he didn't have a choice in her interior decorating.

"I feel like I'm trespassing," Lacey said.

"Don't be silly. Dad doesn't mind." Cherise pointed to her father's rope collection. At least a dozen different ropes were coiled and hung on a special Steven-made rack on the far wall.

"What on earth does he use all this for?" Lacey asked. Her dad had a mania for tools, the way some women had for shoes: collecting them, filling a closet with them, but never wearing them, simply admiring their sparkling high-heeled kingdom, or queendom.

Cherise thought for a moment. "He uses some of it to tie the Christmas tree to the roof of the wagon."

"Right." Lacey remembered their annual trip to fetch the Christmas tree . . . until Rose had found the perfect vintage aluminum tree with a rotating color wheel, to set on the floor near the unused fireplace. She thought it was the perfect holiday decoration for a midcentury modern home, hung with all silver ornaments. The effect was chilly, something the cartoon Jetson family might gather around. Her mother's idea of vintage and Lacey's were two very different things.

"What about this?" Cherise picked up one of the ropes and hefted it. "Ride 'em, cowgirl!"

"I give up. Here, this one is better." Lacey selected a rope that felt heavy enough to toss like a lariat, and she took it to the backyard. Cherise bounced along beside her. Lacey tied the knots and looped the loop. She showed Cherise how to tie the lariat knot, the honda.

"It's named after a Japanese car? Why?"

"Because Japanese cowboys use it to rope Honda Civics in Japanese rodeos." Cherise looked doubtful, but right on the verge of taking her big sister's word for it. Lacey couldn't help laughing. "Come on, Cherise! It's Spanish."

"Spanish for what?"

"Spanish for this knot you tie in a lariat! Now what do you want to throw it at?"

"Dad's lawn chair." Cherise dragged the Adirondack chair from the garage to the middle of the yard. Lacey turned on the back door light that stabbed into the dark like an aircraft landing light and illuminated almost the whole lawn. She demonstrated to Cherise how to twirl the lariat and throw the lasso. She had to try it several times before even hitting, but not lassoing, the chair.

"I blame the altitude," Lacey said. "Everything is lighter this high up."

"Cool! Let me try!" Cherise was dogged, if nothing else. Cherise hit, but did not lasso, one of her mother's potted geraniums, and she dissolved into giggles.

"Girls, what on earth are you doing out here?" Rose suddenly stood on the back porch, in her robe, giving Lacey a wave of déjà vu. She was a child again, playing kickball in the dusk. "Get to bed, it's late. You girls! I swear."

Giggling like a couple of naughty schoolgirls caught playing hooky, Cherise and Lacey came when they were called. But not before Lacey grabbed the rope one more time and held the coil in her left hand. She lifted her right arm high and started swinging the noose. She let it fly, keeping her wrist and hand straight on her target. Triumphantly, the rope caught. Lacey had lassoed the lawn chair.

Little Britches Rodeo, here I come.

"I miss you already." Lacey closed her eyes and listened to Vic's voice. It was like honey. Sweet and warm.

"Me too, darlin'. Every minute."

"Promise." Finally alone in that bizarre guest bedroom in her childhood home, sitting on the hard sofa bed, Lacey finally let go of the tension in her shoulders. Most of it. She closed her eyes, the better to conjure up a picture of him.

"I'll have to catch up with you Monday in the courtroom," Vic said.

"Monday? But I'm seeing you tomorrow in Sagebrush."

"Something came up."

"What?" *Better not be Montana.*

"I'm heading up to Wyoming with the deputy DA. You remember?"

"How could I forget Brad Owens?"

"There's a girl missing out of Baggs. Teenager."

"Oh, no." Lacey didn't want to hear any more bad news. "How old is she?"

"Seventeen."

How awful. "You don't think there's a connection to the Yampa County murders?"

"Brad thinks there might be. I'm going to tag along, see if there are any similarities to Rae Fowler and the others. We're meeting with the girl's family and the sheriff in Baggs tomorrow night."

"But if Tucker was in jail—" Lacey allowed herself to hope.

"She went missing a couple of days before they arrested him. Like I said, we're going to check it out. Best that can happen is she shows up. Maybe she's just a runaway. I'm sorry, darlin'. I'll be back in time for the arraignment. Have to be. Brad's due in court."

Lacey stretched her neck and back. "Have you seen your ex?" She tried to make that question elaborately casual, but she knew Vic could see right through her. Even over the phone.

Vic hesitated a moment too long. "I haven't seen Montana."

"Not *seen* her? But you've talked to her?" Lacey sat straight up at attention, wishing she could see his face. Instead of picturing him with his ex. Sometimes her mother was right. Lacey did have an overactive imagination.

"She called *me*," he clarified.

"And?"

"She wants to meet. A friendly dinner. That's all."

"Ha! I knew she'd try something." *Friendly dinner my eye! Men really can be dopes,* Lacey thought. *Why aren't they ever dopes for me? Okay, sometimes . . .*

"She's not trying anything." He started to chuckle. "Montana's concerned about the cabin. The one she bought from me. The roof is leaking."

"Come to my web, said the spider to the fly."

"You're cute when you're jealous."

"Should I mention Tucker and say the same thing about you?"

"Sweetheart, Montana and I are just trying to have a civilized divorce."

"That's what she's saying this week anyway." Lacey was glad he couldn't see the expression on her face. He wouldn't like her sneer. "And what did you say to dinner?"

"I said I'd love to. As long as you come with us."

She sank back against the pillows. "That's why I love you, Vic Donovan. Did you set a date?"

"Montana said she'll get back to me."

And with any luck that will never happen. "By the way, how did Montana know you were in town?" Lacey studied her daybook, tracing her schedule with her fingers. It was all written down in ink, along with the questions she wanted to ask Tucker. Her friends despaired of Lacey's Luddite tendencies, but she resisted the siren call of the BlackBerry and iPhone. Computers owned too much of her life already.

"Word travels fast. Apparently she's friends with Owens."

"How close a friend?" *The closer the better. Let her throw a lasso on anyone but Vic.*

"I'd say pretty close. He wouldn't talk about it."

"Owens won't talk about the time of day without a subpoena."

Vic chuckled. "You do remember him. I told him I was keeping company with you. He was a little surprised."

"He remembers me?"

"Hearing your name brought it all back. He recalled that you'd been Cole Tucker's girl."

"I can't believe Owens is still there. Same job too. Yampa County deputy DA. Doesn't he have any ambition at all?"

"Hey, he's a nice guy. He always helped out when I was in the PD."

"He didn't help out the reporters. And Bradley always looked like his mother dressed him. Even when he wasn't at work. Crew cut and ironed jeans. I think he's the only guy in town with starched underwear. That's just an educated guess, by the way, Vic."

"Well, darlin', this case has taken some of the starch out."

Lacey remembered Brad Owens as fresh faced and eternally boyish. He tried to disappear whenever she showed up: It was her job to hunt him down. It said so on her journalism diploma. Lacey figured Owens's antipathy to reporters most likely began with his dislike of the publisher of *The Sagebrush Daily Press,* Lacey's former boss, Dodd Muldoon. *What did Owens know about Muldoon? Did he suspect Muldoon too?* she wondered.

"Brad did allow that you were an attractive nuisance," Vic interrupted her thoughts.

"He's on my list." She paused. "Think he'll give me an interview?"

"Doubt it."

"Good thing he'll be in court. Then every word is on the record."

"That's my girl."

They sighed into their phones and signed off. Vic loved her and she was happy.

But as soon as she put her head on the pillow, jumbled thoughts assailed her. They veered from Montana to Tucker to the local officials—who no doubt would refuse to comment—to the few known former suspects in the killing: Dodd Muldoon, Zeke Yancey, and a mysteriously vanished miner. Worries bounced back and forth, in a game of insomniac ping-pong. She finally fell into an uneasy sleep, but her dreams were just a nightmare replay of her thoughts.

Be a Rhinestone Cowgirl—
Or Just Look Like One

Did you know that high-strutting, tooled leather, stacked-heel boots are not just for cowboys anymore? Sure, the cowboy boots of yore, with their worn leather, scuffed charm, and scars from hard work are still around, but there's a New Kid Leather in town.

Frontier footwear has always had an air of the dandy. And dandies love variety. How else to explain the dizzying variety of Western boots? Most common is the Western riding boot, which is the midcalf version with an angled heel, the boot we see most often in the movies. The Buckaroo boot, often two-toned, is a taller boot that can reach the knees. The Roper boot has a short, rounded heel and square or rounded toes. Traditional cowhide and horsehide sometimes yield to materials as exotic as ostrich, alligator, lizard, and snakeskin.

But the New Kid was never intended to ride the range and rope bulls. These beauties are made for strutting. Show off these boots with your favorite short jean skirt, and they can look devastatingly feminine paired with a dress. You can dance a Texas Two-Step or rock a Boot Scootin' Boogie in them.

Available in a rainbow of colors and styles, today's cowboy boots have it all. Bad kitties embossed on the shaft? Screaming skulls with pink bows in tooled leather? Attitude in alligator?

They're yours. You can fantasize, customize, and

personalize your boots just the way you want, by working with a boot designer.

Be warned: Today's Western-inspired designer boots aren't for the fainthearted. They can set the average woman back a month's salary or more, before taxes. But then, the average stylista wouldn't be interested in cowboy boots. Would she? These boots are for style mavericks. And while these boots aren't the norm in Washington, D.C., you will see them in full force in Western and Southern cities, and university towns like Charlottesville, Virginia.

Western women have traditionally embraced the boot, but now they embrace their favorite footwear in a reinvigorated way. With a closet full of expensive, colorful, one-of-a-kind Buckaroos, they live and work and dance in boots. They wear cowboy boots because the boots make them feel original, dangerous, and ready for anything.

How to decide? Some tips to keep in mind:

- Because fancy cowboy boots are an investment, be sure they fit well. Most boots are built for a medium-width foot, so women with a wider foot may find the perfect pair in men's or boys' sizes—or go custom-made. Traditionally, we think of cowboy boots with pointed toes, but your toes might prefer the round-toe or square-toe versions.
- Select a heel size depending on how you'll be wearing the boot. Boots made for walking come in a heel that is between three quarters of an inch and an inch and three quarters. Any higher, and you'll be doing more riding and strutting—or posing—than walking. The higher the heel, the sexier the strut—but don't wobble. Real cowgirls don't fall down. Except sometimes off their horses.
- When you try on a cowboy boot, experts say the upper or shaft should be comfortable and

loose, but slightly snug at the vamp, where the leg and foot come together. You should be able to move your toes. The foot bed should fit your arch. The heel will slip a bit at first, but a good pair of leather cowboy boots should soon conform to your foot and become more comfortable with continued wear.

So ladies, if the boot fits, wear it. Wear your boots with pants, shorts, skirts, and dresses. Wear them with a swagger and a glint in your eyes. Wear them with a purpose. Wear them with an attitude. Wear them walking toward your destiny.

But never wear them with *indifference*.

chapter 7

"You have nothing to worry about," Lacey assured her parents again before leaving Sunday morning. "There won't be any trouble. I'll be perfectly fine."

"Famous last words." Rose patted Lacey's shoulder and smoothed her hair. She sighed dramatically. "I don't know why you had to work in that terrible town in the first place. There are all kinds of adorable villages in the mountains. You could have worked in Glenwood Springs or Aspen. But no, you had to go to Sagebrush."

"It was the only reporting job I could find when I graduated from J school," Lacey reminded her.

"And you look tired. What on earth were you two doing on the lawn last night?"

"The trouble you all got into when your mother went to Washington last October was enough for a lifetime," Steven chimed in. "Promise your old dad you'll stay out of trouble. I'll be out of the country. I won't be able to help you."

Lacey fought to keep her eyes from rolling, while Cherise giggled.

"I'll keep your father up-to-date on you every day while he's in Taiwan," Rose threatened.

"Thailand," her husband corrected her evenly.

"Thailand sounds wonderful, Dad." Lacey changed the subject. "Have a great time. If you get a chance, pick me up some silk. Any color, any pattern, the older the better. But not shattered silk. That means—"

"I'll put it on my list," Steven said, reaching for a small notebook to jot down her request. "Silk."

Lacey seized the opportunity to run for her rental car. Her father put her suitcase in the trunk. Rose pushed a paper bag through the driver's side window. "It's a snack. Organic dried fruit and an organic power bar," Rose said. "Keep your energy up. And hydrate!"

"Call me," Cherise said. "Tell me everything! I want to hear about Cole!"

Lacey hit the gas.

Never say never.

Her vow never to return to Sagebrush mocked her as she headed west across Denver toward the Front Range, under an unforgiving blue sky, in an unfamiliar little rental car. She missed her vintage green BMW, Vic's Christmas present to her. And she had the switchbacks of Berthoud Pass to negotiate, cresting over eleven thousand feet above sea level at the Continental Divide.

The mountains in the East, pretty and green though they were, couldn't hold a candle to the Rockies, that beautiful, treacherous, and heartbreaking mountain range at the backbone of North America, still hiding the skeletons of ancient prospectors, gold seekers, and outlaws. More than bones, the Rockies held stories, and secrets.

Colorado's famous cannibal, Alferd Packer, killed and ate his companions during a disastrous prospecting expedition in the mountains in the winter of 1874. The beautiful and scandalous Baby Doe Tabor, who was married to a US senator at the Willard Hotel in Washington, D.C., later froze to death, penniless, at the Matchless Mine in Leadville, Colorado. And there was always Molly Brown, who everybody knew was unsinkable. Lacey told herself she was too.

Her luck was holding and the weather was bright and sunny, but she could feel the air temperature drop as the car climbed up the Front Range and over the Divide. The temperature was in the sixties when she left Denver. It must have been thirty degrees colder at Winter

Park, on the other side of the pass. She turned up the heat and kept her eyes on the road and the sky. March was the snowiest month along Colorado's Front Range. Despite the brilliant sunshine, she dreaded this trip more with every mile, her stomach knotting tighter and tighter.

The highway was relatively clear of snow, which was a blessing. But dirty snow remained piled high along the side of the road. Back in Alexandria, Virginia, the trees were already beginning to bud, but Lacey tried not to dwell on that. The slopes of Winter Park were full of skiers, no doubt marveling at the *balmy* weather.

What am I doing here? Really?

She told herself there was only one thing she could do: what she always did. Talk to people. Ask questions. Write the story. It wasn't going to be objective, of course. The article would have to be subjective, her own take on a story she'd played some small part in herself. As Mac said, that was what features were for.

First, Lacey needed to find out how Cole Tucker had gotten himself into such a stupid fix. But maybe, she admitted only to herself, she also wanted to make sure that any feelings she'd had long ago for that long, lean cowboy were long gone.

chapter 8

Vic said Sagebrush had changed, and he was right. It simply hadn't changed enough to suit Lacey Smithsonian. The buildings downtown were still one- and two-story brick cubes lacking any attempt at ornamentation, save for the old movie theatre with its tiled entrance and oversized marquee, and the town was still shabby around the edges.

She'd spent an hour in Steamboat Springs along the way, grabbing a latte and having her bootheel repaired. Steamboat was full of chic skiers and rich hippies, a very different world from Sagebrush. While waiting, she had wandered through F. M. Light & Sons, the famous Western wear store. Lacey half expected to run into Vic's ex at every turn, but Montana stayed out of sight, and Lacey's boots came back to her polished and good as new.

When she pulled into Sagebrush at twilight and cruised down Sundance Way, the main drag through town, everything seemed to be closed. There were limited options for dining even on a Saturday night, but her choices on the Lord's Day looked positively grim. There might be some cafés tucked into a corner here and there, places only the locals knew about, but Lacey didn't know those corners anymore. She stopped at a pancake restaurant across from the Wal-Mart. It didn't have to be very good and it wasn't, but the eggs were warm and the decaf was hot. Lacey picked up the weekend copy of *The Sagebrush Daily Press* that she found lying on a bench. The front-page story about Tucker told her nothing she didn't already know.

For a real blast from the past, Lacey toyed with the idea of staying in one of the old down-at-the-heels motels at the edge of town. But the idea's very thin amusement value (and thinner blankets) wasn't worth the low price. A newer chain motel offered modern amenities and a connecting room for Vic when he returned from Wyoming.

Lacey made it an early night, but not before calling Tucker's attorney. Her name was Karen Quilby and she sounded young and unusually helpful for a lawyer, especially considering that Lacey was calling her outside of business hours and she wasn't related to Tucker.

"I can try to get you a visit a few minutes before court, but no guarantees," Karen Quilby told Lacey. She sounded doubtful. "That is, of course, if Cole wants to see you."

"He'll want to see me." This was sheer reporter's bravado. *What if he doesn't want to see me?*

"Can you tell me anything that bears on this case, anything that might help with his defense?" Quilby asked.

"Nothing, other than I know he couldn't have done it," Lacey said. "I knew him pretty well."

"Pretty well, huh? I heard you were involved with him. Romantically."

"Years ago."

"I'll try to get you ten minutes, but I don't want to piss off the judge," Quilby said. It wasn't exactly the usual protocol, but Sagebrush wasn't a usual-protocol kind of place.

"Nobody wants to piss off a judge," Lacey said. "Especially not me."

On Monday morning the Colorado sun blasted through the cracks in the motel curtains, merciless as always. Again Lacey's sleep had been elusive, as the blue circles under her eyes testified. Looking her best, one of her prime defenses against the unknown, would be tricky this morning.

Who am I dressing to impress? she wondered. *Sage-*

brush? The judge? The world? The answer, as always, was herself.

She would be an object of curiosity no matter how she dressed. But clothing was a kind of armor for Lacey, a way of being—and projecting—her best self, so she chose her "new" vintage outfit, the moss green skirt and matching sweater, with the shot-through-velvet bolero jacket that shimmered green and gold. It was appropriate in the late 1930s, and it would darn well be appropriate now. She added her cupid pendant, Vic's Valentine's Day gift to her, stopping to appreciate both the imp and the impulse that made him give it to her.

Tights for warmth, her cowboy boots for bravado, and a large tote bag/purse with a shoulder strap for all the extras: sunscreen and Chapstick to protect her skin, lotion for her hands, makeup to hide the circles and her lack of sleep, hand sanitizer and towelettes, cell phone, notebook, wallet, and plenty of pens. The ensemble was a bit eccentric, she decided. Annie Oakley via Hollywood, but it would do. In D.C., Lacey would have worn heels or high-heeled boots. Not cowboy boots. But here? *What the heck. Ride 'em, cowgirl.* On her way out, she grabbed her leather jacket with the faux-fur lining. It was cold out there.

With more than an hour before her appointment to see Tucker, Lacey drove down Sundance Way. She parked her car and strolled past the courthouse and the newspaper office to Cassidy Avenue, where the three whole blocks of downtown Sagebrush resided.

It was nothing like Washington, where Lacey was used to the rhythm of the big city, the hum and the heartbeat. She even enjoyed the lunchtime crowds in D.C. She missed the great green grassy Mall and the endless marble monuments of long-gone war heroes. What Sagebrush did have in abundance: taxidermy shops. Dozens of them, all proudly displaying their stuffed and mounted elk, bears, mountain lions, deer, and pronghorns, all in dramatic poses. Even, *yes*, the damn, annoying, fictional, jumbled-together-out-of-spare-body-parts jackalope. Big-game taxidermy seemed to be a growth industry here in the Elk Hunting Capital of Northwest Colorado. But despite the cars and pickups parked along the streets, Sagebrush felt nearly abandoned.

Where are the people? In D.C., there would be crowds.

The town looked slightly better than she remembered. The trees downtown had grown tall and leafy since Lacey was a green reporter, and almost an entire city block of tumbling-down old buildings had been bulldozed and turned into a small park. A change in the town's leadership and a huge influx of money from energy companies, coal and natural gas, had apparently brought with it swimming pools, parks, a community college, and a new hospital. Improvements had been made, Lacey was willing to admit, but Sagebrush was still scruffy to its bones.

It was also plain to see that this energy boomtown was no longer booming. Bust times were back. The only people who seemed to be out on the streets were a few of her kind—reporters who had crossed the Continental Divide or driven up from Grand Junction to write about that local rancher Cole Tucker, notorious alleged murderer of three attractive young women. A broadcast news crew with a camera truck was setting up outside the courthouse for news updates. The judge, according to Karen Quilby, had banned cameras in the courtroom. "This ain't no reality show and we don't play to your big-city cameras," he had declared.

Lacey felt out of place. *The Daily Press* staff must have turned over at least twice, except for its notorious editor and publisher, Dodd Muldoon, and a few ancient holdovers. But then, Muldoon never could keep staff, unless they were related to him, or paroled to the newspaper from the state penitentiary. She paused at the thought of Muldoon as a suspect in Rae Fowler's murder. The man paid starvation wages and offered no benefits. The reporters used to joke that he was a sociopath, albeit a cheerful one. *But a killer?* She let the thought settle heavily on her shoulders.

The old café where Lacey used to buy her morning coffee had been razed to the ground. *So much for old times.* Ruby, the ancient, toothless, tubercular waitress who hated reporters, was gone as well. *Good times? Not really.* Ruby had perfected the art of flinging coffee cups across the table just *so*, spilling coffee all over the saucer and the table and leaving only a spoonful or so of java for the customer.

It was odd Lacey even remembered Ruby, or found it unsettling that the ancient germ shack was erased from the landscape. Missing that awful place was something she'd never expected to do.

Lacey spied a new coffee shop that had taken refuge in an old brick building. She strolled in past the HUNTERS WELCOME sign, left over from last fall's big-game season. The waitress was young and healthy-looking. Not remotely tubercular. Maybe she wouldn't hurtle the coffee at Lacey either. She wore a name tag that said "Jett." The woman had long red hair and freckles, a nice smile and not a trace of makeup. Her outfit was likewise casual, a navy sweatshirt over jeans.

Stop it, Lacey. You're not here to write about make-overs.

The shop was warm and featured a large glass bakery cabinet with muffins and sweet rolls. Mismatched wooden chairs and tables added to the cozy décor, as did a couple of women who gossiped in the corner. They stopped for a moment to check out the stranger in their midst. Lacey bought coffee and sat down at a table with a view of the street. She still had time before her meeting with Tucker. Her cell phone rang and brought a smile to her face.

"Hey, sweetheart, everything okay?" he asked.

Lacey exhaled. She hadn't realized how much she longed to hear Vic's voice, even if it was a poor substitute for him in the flesh.

"Why wouldn't it be? Here I am in gorgeous downtown Sagebrush, Colorado, last outpost of semi-civilization. The sun is shining and it's twenty-eight degrees. In March."

"That's the spirit. Beautiful day in the neighborhood. Bracing."

"Want to meet for coffee?"

"Love to, but I can't, even though you're a far sight

prettier than Brad," Vic said. "I'm at his office. Going over a few things. I'll see you at court."

"Wait a minute, what did you find out in Wyoming? The missing girl. Any word?"

"Tucker's cleared on this one. The girl showed up this morning about three a.m. Ran off with her boyfriend, but wouldn't you know, they broke up instead. She's in serious trouble with her parents."

"Finally some good news. The kid's in the doghouse, but not the morgue," Lacey said, more relieved than she had imagined. "By the way, I miss you. You're not going to pull another disappearing act, are you?"

"Me? Don't be silly." Vic chuckled. "Can't wait to see you. Where are you?"

"Having coffee at a new place. Then I'm going to see Tucker."

There was a brief moment of silence, heavy with disapproval. Vic's voice dropped a notch. "Lacey, I don't like it. And by the way, how'd you swing that one?"

"I asked nicely. His attorney might be a little new at this," Lacey said. "Don't worry. Tucker'll be cuffed or restrained, or something. And we're old friends, or we were last I checked. What's wrong with that?"

She could hear him sigh deeply. "You think he's going to talk to you? Give you an exclusive?"

"Why not? Tucker's not dangerous."

"I've heard that before."

"Buy me lunch after the arraignment?" *At least I'll see you later.* They signed off.

Her thoughts about Tucker and Vic tumbled together as she sipped her coffee. She slowly became aware of a large shadow darkening the coffee shop door. The shadow stopped to peer inside. It was looking at her.

You've got to be kidding. Lacey felt the hair on the back of her neck rise. She shuddered. The shadow opened the door and came in.

"Well, great day in the morning, look what the cat dragged in," said Dodd Muldoon, Lacey's old boss, the editor and publisher of *The Sagebrush Daily Press*. He sat down at her table without an invitation and waved at

Jett behind the counter for coffee. Though his longish hair was thinner and grayer and his jowls were even droopier, Muldoon looked much the same. *Like an over-fed walrus,* Lacey thought, *or a pig on a platter*. Lacey grinned at the old urge to shove an apple in his mouth.

Muldoon wore khaki slacks and a short-sleeve navy polo shirt, over which he wore a yellow cardigan sweater. It must have been what Muldoon considered his wise-old-editor attire, a variation of what he had always worn. As usual he shunned a coat. It could have been twenty below zero and Muldoon would have refused to wear a coat. It was his version of macho.

"Jett, her coffee's on me," Muldoon said, gesturing elaborately toward Lacey.

"Sure it is," Lacey said. "I already paid for it."

Muldoon chuckled his way into a coughing spell. "Then how about I split an omelet with you? No? Jett, gimme the omelet du jour. With everything. Lacey, Lacey. I was wondering when you'd come rolling back into Sagebrush. You want a job?"

"No." Lacey sighed. "Just visiting."

"You look good, Scoop. But then, you always did." Muldoon stirred multiple spoonfuls of sugar into his coffee. "Your old job's open, you know."

"Lost another reporter, huh? Maybe if you tried paying them. Just a thought."

"Aw, they come and go. Just say the word. I'll fire one of 'em and take you back."

"Take me back?!" Lacey stared at him. "You can't be serious."

"Serious as a crutch."

"Maybe you haven't heard, Muldoon, I have a reporting job. A real one, in a real city. Nation's Capital. Ever heard of it?"

"Don't try to hurt my feelings, Scoop. Better reporters than you have made the attempt. Heard you were doing some kind of 'lifestyle' beat back East." He made air quotes with his fingers. "Lifestyle. Ha. What happened to you? You were a hard news reporter when you left here. Trained you myself."

"I *am* a hard news reporter," Lacey spluttered into her coffee. "And since when did you ever train anyone to do anything but—"

"You're not writing serious stuff anymore. It's all hemlines and handbags, pigs' ears and silk purses. Fluff."

I'd like to turn you into a silk purse, you pig's— She took a deep breath. "I make my own beat. I write about fashion. And style. And murder."

"Murder, huh? Well, you always were different." He took in her outfit with a lascivious look. She didn't like him looking at her like that. He sipped his coffee-flavored sugar and smacked his lips. "Everyone knows fashion's not real news. Bet you don't wear those fancy boots back East. Where everyone is all fashion *this* and fashion *that*."

Washington, D.C., the City Fashion Forgot? "Score one for you, Muldoon."

"We got real news here. Solid gold news. Three murders, one killer. Your old boyfriend, Cole Tucker. Always knew there was something funny about that boy."

"There was nothing funny about 'that boy.' He didn't kill anybody. And I imagine there were other suspects." *Like you.* Lacey stared him down, then shook her head. It wasn't worth her time indulging her old boss in his head games. Not now. "What do you know about those murders, Muldoon?"

"This and that. You hear things."

"Anything specific?" She swallowed the last of her coffee.

"All in *The Daily Press*. Read it and weep, Scoop."

"Don't call me that," Lacey said. "Scoop" was Muldoon's pet name for whichever reporter he was trying to needle at the moment. *How many "Scoops" have there been since I left?* she wondered.

"I always called you Scoop. That's a badge of honor here. Till you got all snotty and went East. Our star reporter."

"It's not so hard to be a star when you only have three reporters."

Muldoon shook his jowls at her and his face turned

red. "You ought to be more grateful to *The Daily Press*. I gave you your start in journalism."

"My start? This town nearly finished me off. I'm lucky I made it out of here alive and onto a real paper."

"Yeah, yeah. Still a prima donna, aren't you, Scoop?" He looked even jowlier with his mouth turned down in disapproval. Jett arrived with Muldoon's omelet and a coffeepot. She refilled Lacey's cup. "Just because it gets a little cold in Sagebrush, you have to up and run off clear across the country? Gets hot here too, you know."

Laccy stood to go. "The day my plumbing froze solid, that was enough for me, Muldoon. I realized I could be just as broke someplace warm. And I'd rather be broke anywhere but Sagebrush."

Muldoon chortled into his omelet. "But now Scoop Smithsonian is back in town. Here to see your old boyfriend get charged with murder. Tucker's true love, come to town to write the real untold story. Ha. Hell of a story if you get him to confess." He stared at her over his coffee cup.

"Do you think Tucker is guilty?"

"Me?" He shrugged his big shoulders. "Got no opinion one way or the other. You know me, Scoop. I just print the news."

She crossed her arms. "But never *all* the news. Isn't that right, Muldoon? Like the advertisers' dirty secrets?"

"Hey, advertisers keep us in business," he protested. "There's always a little quid pro quo in the news biz. You know that. I just reserve judgment sometimes. A man's got to live with his neighbors."

"But it's okay to throw Tucker to the wolves? Like your front page story did? Didn't he buy enough ads?"

Muldoon put his hands up. "He'll have his day in court. Starting today. Now, an intimate jailhouse interview would sell some papers. You got as good a chance as anyone. What do you say? Front page, Scoop." He was tone-deaf to the mood of the conversation.

"I think I'm going to be sick."

He dug into his breakfast. "Cole Tucker never should have asked you to marry him. You never would have left. You'd still be my star reporter. My Scoop."

"You're insane, Muldoon. You paid me dirt wages, it was forty degrees below zero, and my toilet froze. I can't believe I stayed as long as I did." *It had to be brain damage.*

"Ancient history." He waved the thought away. "So what's on your *fashion* beat for the day? You writing a story for that D.C. rag? You talk to Tucker, you write that story for *The Daily Press,* I'll pay."

"No thanks, Muldoon. I work for *The Eye Street Observer.*"

"What kind of name is that for a newspaper? The *who* street *what*? It sure ain't *The Washington Post,* is it? Out here *The Daily Press* is the only game in town. And I'm sure no matter how much you smart-mouth Sagebrush, you still got a warm spot in your heart for this town and my paper."

More like acid reflux, she wanted to say. In the meantime, Muldoon was turning purple. Lacey could always tell when his blood pressure was rising. The other conversations in the café had stopped. She slipped on her jacket and grabbed her bag. "I don't think so."

"Someday you'll appreciate what we taught you here at *The Daily Press,*" Muldoon rattled on. "You piss me off, Scoop. You always did. But the offer's still open."

The door opened and two young men and a woman came in, looking freshly minted out of journalism school. They nodded to Muldoon and sat down at the table where Lacey had just stood up. Another older, tired-looking man walked in a moment later. Lacey recognized the paper's printer, still there after all these years. *Still on parole? Or did he drink Muldoon's Kool-Aid?*

True to form, Muldoon was holding his morning editorial meeting at a coffee shop. He was still too cheap to supply a coffeepot at the newsroom, or even buy the staff a doughnut.

"Muldoon, it's been real," Lacey said. "I'm out of here."

"Take a lesson, boys and girls," Muldoon said to his little staff, loud enough so Lacey would hear it on her way out the door. "That's what happens when you leave Sagebrush, Colorado, and *The Daily Press*. You get snooty as all hell and start to think you're too good to work on a *real* newspaper."

Lacey laughed as she stepped through the door. She had an appointment to see Cole Tucker, notorious accused serial killer. The man who used to love her.

chapter 9

"I'm going to leave you alone with him, Ms. Smithsonian. Ten minutes. If he tells you anything that could help his defense, you'll let me know, right?" Karen Quilby was nervous, as if this might be the stupidest decision she'd make all day. She'd apparently never defended an accused murderer before. The ink on her law degree was barely dry.

"Don't worry. I'll let everyone know." Lacey thought of her feature for *The Eye*.

Quilby nodded. Tucker's defense attorney looked just a few years younger than Lacey, but several years more serious. She even wore a black wool suit for the occasion, if a trifle ill-fitting. The skirt was a little short and the sleeves a little long, but Quilby was trying. Her luxuriant auburn hair was caught back in a large clip and she wore a bit of lipstick and blush. The attorney clutched a lawyerly leather briefcase and Lacey noticed that her nails were bitten to the quick.

"He hasn't been exactly forthcoming, if you know what I mean," Quilby said.

"Maybe he's still in shock," Lacey said.

"Cole said you were his girlfriend."

"A long time ago."

"And you're a reporter? First here in Sagebrush, and now in Washington, D.C.?"

"That's correct."

Doubt creased Quilby's forehead. "Oh, boy. He said

he'd like to see you. That's the only reason you're getting in. I hope I'm not making a mistake."

"You're not," Lacey said. "It'll be fine."

The women spoke outside the courthouse, near an oversized bronze statue of a cowboy, reflecting the area's ranching heritage. The attorney escorted Lacey up to the second floor, to the small waiting room outside the county courtroom. The building looked the same as Lacey remembered it, a midcentury concrete shell over the original blocky brick government building, constructed during the 1920s. The only thing new to her was the metal detector and gate they passed through at the top of the stairs, which guarded the entrance to the second-floor courtrooms.

Tucker wouldn't have far to travel to go to court. The Justice Center, which housed the police and sheriff's offices and detention facilities, was just a few blocks away.

The jail had once been housed below where Lacey stood, in the basement of the courthouse. The old cells were still there, left as they were the day the jail moved to the new Justice Center. Lacey wondered if they gave Halloween tours for charity. A Halloween "haunted jail" could conjure up the spirits of some of the most notorious outlaws of the Old West, all of whom had haunted the Northwest Colorado of yesteryear: the Wild Bunch, Butch Cassidy, the Sundance Kid, Kid Curry, Tom Horn, Etta Place, and Queen Ann Basset, among many others.

Feeling jumpy, Lacey paced around the table in the waiting room. Karen Quilby scanned court papers while waiting for her client to be delivered. The room was bare except for the wooden table and six padded chairs. There was nothing on the walls. The door was partially open. Through it, Lacey observed a few media types passing through the metal detector with their laptops. But no cameras. All cameras were being turned away at the gate.

Eventually a deputy stopped at the door. Surprisingly, it was someone Lacey recognized from her days of covering the Sagebrush Police Department and the Yampa County Sheriff's Office. Deputy Grady Rush had never been a ball of fire. He was still a deputy.

"Long time, Lacey." Deputy Rush smiled at her and inclined his head. He was big and baggy, with close-set eyes and thin lips, and he looked rather like a very large duck. When he smiled he looked a little crazy, but happy, his wide mouth barely closing over his crooked teeth. She supposed he couldn't help it if he had some duck in his gene pool, somewhere along the line. He smoothed his dark hair back with one hand.

"Hello, Grady. Nice to see a familiar face."

"Yeah, same here, and I guess I got someone here you want to see. I'll be right outside this door. Now, don't do anything I wouldn't do." Deputy Rush moved aside and Cole Tucker stepped into the room.

Tucker's attorney stepped close and murmured something in her client's ear that Lacey couldn't hear. She stepped back.

"Ten minutes, Cole. Then you and I need to talk again before we go see the judge. We don't have many minutes to spare this morning." Tucker nodded, and Karen Quilby left, closing the door behind her.

Lacey and Tucker both drew a long breath. She didn't want to make a fool of herself, if she could help it. She was the only reporter granted access to the prisoner. But he was more than just a prisoner. He was a part of her history.

She held her breath for a moment. The room felt very close. Lacey stared at him. It had been seven years since she fled Sagebrush with Tucker's marriage proposal still ringing in her ears. Her whole world had changed since then, but Tucker looked the same. Fit, tanned, trim, and muscular. His straight, light honey-brown hair fell across his forehead to his eyebrows. His face had a few more lines, but his eyes were the same deep brown eyes she remembered.

Lacey had expected to see him in typical jailhouse blaze orange, but he was wearing a brown jumpsuit, the color worn by delivery guys everywhere, except for the white lettering on the back: YAMPA COUNTY JAIL. His hands were cuffed to a chain around his waist. On his feet he wore a pair of brown slip-on sneakers.

He must hate wearing that, she thought. Still, he didn't look like a man defeated. His shoulders were straight, his gaze direct.

Tucker smiled at her, and memories rushed over her like Proust's madeleine on speed. His grin brought back the times they'd shared: their first date, their first dance, the first time he saddled his favorite palomino for her to ride. And lots of kisses, but not that first kiss.

"It's good to see you, Lacey. Why don't you take a seat?" He waited for her, ever the gentleman. She sat down and he took a chair opposite her. She had forgotten the mellow timbre of his voice.

Get ahold of yourself, Lacey. She shook her head to clear it. "You're not wearing orange." *Orange? I'm really asking him about his jumpsuit? Ten minutes, Lacey!*

"Seems orange is for small-time offenders. They tell me brown is for the big, bad boys. But brown goes with my eyes, right?"

"Oh, Tucker."

"Whatever are you doing here, Lacey? A special trip from Washington, D.C., just to see me? I'm honored, but I'm not at my best." He shifted in his seat, and his handcuffs and waist chain rattled. "Why are you here? To write a story about this disaster? About me?"

It must seem like such a violation of his privacy, she realized. Especially from her. "No. I mean, I am going to have to write some kind of story. But— I needed to see you. I need to know, Cole. I just need—" Lacey wanted to say more, but she couldn't seem to finish the sentence.

"Know what? If I'm a killer? You know me better than that," he said, with a flash of emotion. "Don't you?"

His brown eyes stared right through her, stirring feelings she thought she'd left behind years ago. "I'm one hundred percent sure you're not a killer," Lacey said. "But I want to be a hundred and fifty percent sure."

He smiled. "You haven't changed, have you?" He took a moment. "No, I didn't kill anybody, and you can be two hundred percent sure of that. Somebody's been working their tail off to set me up. They're railroading me, Chantilly Lace."

Chantilly Lace? Oh, my. She'd forgotten a few things about Cole Tucker after all. His pet name for her was one of them.

"Please don't call me that." It was the second time this morning she'd asked someone not to use an old nickname. Muldoon, because he was still an idiot and "Scoop" brought back only bad memories. Tucker, because he was still Tucker and "Chantilly Lace" brought back too many good memories. *"Your mama really named you Lacey? Like in the song?"* Tucker had said to her on one of their first dates, and he said it with a big smile and broke right into the old song, changing the words. *"Chantilly Lace ... I like it. Such a pretty face ..."*

"Cole, I want the truth. That's all."

"Okay. Lacey." He drew out her name, then settled back in his chair and gazed at her. His face was impassive, but his eyes were full of questions. "I guess this is not a reunion for us. It's just a story, and you just want to get your facts right. Okay. I'm all for that. Ask me anything."

"If you're innocent—and you are—then why did they arrest you?"

Cole shook his head. "I'm still trying to sort that out. Seems the sheriff found Rae's purse and things, buried down a hole out on my property. I thought they were saying it was some kind of fox hole or badger hole, but no, they say it was dug by hand. Said someone called in a tip about it. Somebody made that hole, and they went to a lot of trouble."

"Framing you?"

"Looks like it."

"Who?"

"I'll let you know when I figure it out. But Chant—Lacey, why do you want to write about this? I thought wild horses couldn't drag you back here. Don't you have enough to write about in Washington, D.C.?"

"You've heard about my stories?"

"Couldn't help hearing about them." Tucker smiled. "Google 'Lacey Smithsonian' and all hell breaks loose."

"I had to tell my editor something to get the time off to come here."

"I hope you get along better with that one than you did with Muldoon."

Lacey thought of Douglas MacArthur Jones. He was smarter than Muldoon, and Mac had a good heart, as opposed to Muldoon, who had no heart at all, but he could be just as stubborn. "A little."

"What kind of story you gonna write? Something personal?"

"Not too personal, Cole."

"No, I guess we wouldn't want that, would we, Chantilly?"

"It's Lacey. All I can do is ask questions and write about the answers. If there are answers."

"And all this effort to make sure I'm not a killer? You could write that without seeing me, couldn't you?" Tucker kept his gaze on her. Lacey tried not to break it, to show she could be just as tough.

"Maybe I can help somehow."

"How? There's me in here and three dead women out there and everything hanging in the balance," Tucker said.

"It's a horrible crime. And you were never horrible." He was gentle with people and gentle with his animals.

"Well, *someone's* planning to pin it on me like I'm some kind of dog that ought to be shot." Tucker's voice was low and slow. He seemed very sad, sadder than she had ever seen him. She had forgotten how deep his voice could be. Nearly as deep as Vic's. "Doesn't look like I'll get bail."

Yeah, bail is unlikely, to say the least, Lacey thought.

"I want to write about those women. Find out more about them, take a look at Western justice."

Tucker settled back in his chair and gazed at her. "Justice? Lacey, this is Sagebrush. Yampa County. Outlaw country. Always been outlaw country and still is. Justice goes to the man with the most money, the most ammunition, and the fastest horse."

She nodded. "How's jail?"

"Not exactly the wide-open spaces. The company's not so bad. I mean in the cell. Just some rowdy old boys in for drunk and disorderly. Then there's the deputies. The 'dope-uties,' we call 'em. But come on, why are we talking about all this nonsense when we could be talking about us?"

"Us? Tucker, there is no *us*. There hasn't been an *us* in years."

"That's what I thought, Chantilly. With you leaving Sagebrush in a huff the way you did. But I also thought you were never going to talk to me again, let alone come see me, let alone travel a couple thousand miles from back East to Sagebrush, just to see me. And here you are."

"I didn't leave in a huff." Lacey glared at him.

He laughed out loud. "A huff and a puff and a cloud of dust! If I'd known how asking you to marry me would set you off, I'd have kept my damn mouth shut. Anything to keep you near."

Lacey sat up straight. "You're as bad as Muldoon! He thinks I'd still be here covering the frontier for him! And Cole Tucker, you said you would never leave Sagebrush, and then you did!" *Old hurts die hard.*

"But I came right back. Missed the ranch. Missed my hometown. I was still missing you. Had to help out Kit anyway." That would be Kit Carson Tucker, his little brother. "And Starr." Belle Starr Tucker, his big sister.

"You married someone else! Six weeks after I left town! And on Valentine's Day! You told me there'd never be anyone but me, and then there *was*! You told me you'd never leave this damn place, not even for me, and then you *did*! What the hell was I supposed to think?" She had promised herself a hundred times she would not bring all that up, not let it get to her, not throw it in his face. Tucker, on the other hand, seemed bemused, not angry.

"You have been thinking about me, Chantilly. It was

all kind of a big mistake. Not you, but all the rest of it. Live and learn, you know?"

"Las Vegas marriages are always a mistake." *Like Vic's marriage*, she thought. She slumped back in her chair. She'd gotten some of the bitterness out. She felt drained.

"That's the truth. Mine sure didn't take." He paused. "You know, you're still the prettiest woman I've ever seen."

She didn't want to smile, but she did. "You ought to get out of Sagebrush more often." Tucker rattled his waist chain, and Lacey regretted her crack the moment she said it. But Tucker seemed to take no offense.

"You're even prettier now," Tucker said. "But more big city. I like those boots, by the way, but I'd sure love to see you in a pair of jeans again. You always looked pretty damn adorable in a pair of tight jeans, Chantilly."

"It's Lacey, not Chantilly. You're not going to tell me anything, are you, Tucker?"

"I can't tell you what I don't know. But hey, I'm real glad to see you. Thanks for coming. Circumstances be damned."

He leaned across the table toward her, but he couldn't lift his hands to touch her.

"Tucker, listen to me. We only have a couple of minutes left. We have to talk about these murders, to figure out who set you up, if that's what happened."

A bewildered expression flitted across Tucker's face. "What're you gonna do, call up the cavalry, ride the range like John Wayne, hunt down whoever really killed those women? Like something out of the movies?"

"We don't have to find out who killed those women, we only have to prove *you* didn't kill them. Two different things. And don't make fun of me."

The door opened and Deputy Rush ducked his head in. "Two minutes, Cole." He nodded. "Lacey. Court opens in a few."

"Hey, Grady, why don't you loosen these damn things for me." Tucker lifted his hands as far as his waist chain would permit. It wasn't very far. "Just for a minute."

The big deputy paused, thinking. "Now, Cole, rules is rules."

"Come on, Grady. You know me—you know I'm no killer. You know Lacey here, and you were always way more afraid of her than you were of me. With good reason too."

It was true, Lacey reflected. Deputy Grady Rush was always scared he'd be quoted saying something stupid, which he did more often than not. And in Sagebrush, saying stupid things was the sheriff's job, not the deputies'. Rush had once actually made undersheriff, for about a week, but that hadn't worked out. He was more muscles than brains, and more beer gut than muscles.

The deputy grimaced, his duck face concentrating. If *The Daily Press* had ever had a cartoonist (and Muldoon never would have paid one), Deputy Rush would have been a favorite target.

Lacey could see Rush struggling with the idea. He and Cole were old friends, or sort-of friends; at least, they'd grown up in the same little town and gone to school together. Everyone in Sagebrush knew one another and counted one another as sort-of friends or sort-of enemies, sometimes both.

"You don't want to get me in trouble now," Deputy Rush said.

"Aw, come on, who's ever gonna know?" Tucker asked. "Lacey came all this way just to see me and after all these years and I can't even give her a big hug to say thank you. Just loosen my wrists a little. What do you say?"

Lacey didn't say anything. She wasn't sure what Tucker was up to. She didn't want to ruin their last two minutes together. She held her breath.

The deputy rattled his keys. "If I was gonna do this, just this once, you'd owe me one, Cole, a big one, and no one could ever hear about it. It would have to be our little secret, you know?" He shut the door behind him.

"You'd just have to tell them I overpowered you, big guy, and got clean away," Cole said, with a grin on his face. Deputy Rush grinned back. Tucker was trim and well muscled, but the beefy deputy was nearly twice his bulk. He could block the entire door without even moving.

"You're a hoot, Tucker, that's what you are." Deputy Rush was still laughing as he pulled out his keys and began unlocking Tucker's handcuffs from his waist chain. "All right, you two take a minute for a big old hug and then I'll cinch you back up and we'll just march right on out of here into court. Mum's the word. You owe me one now, Cole."

Cole smiled and reached out his freed right hand for a brotherly handshake. The deputy took it, with that crazy duck-faced grin. It was a mistake.

Lacey wasn't quite sure what happened next, even though it happened right in front of her. Tucker was so quick. In a flash he pulled the deputy into a headlock and did something to his neck that Lacey couldn't see. The big man slid quietly to the floor. It was silent. Nobody came through the door, and Lacey was too startled to scream, or even speak. Instead she gasped.

"Little trick I learned out on the ranch," Tucker said. He swiftly unlocked the rest of his shackles and let them drop. He rubbed his wrists where the cuffs had been. "Works with cows too." He reached for her hand. "Let's go."

"No!" She flattened herself against the far wall. "Are you out of your mind? What were you thinking?" All she could think of were the three women who had been strangled, and now Tucker had done something mysterious to the deputy's *neck*. "You *killed* him!"

"Nah. Don't worry about Grady. He's just taking a little nap."

"Like hell he is! Get away from me, Tucker." Lacey leaned down to make sure the deputy still was breathing. He was.

Tucker tossed her bag to her. "I'm not arguing with you, Chantilly. I'm telling you. You're coming with me. My neck is in a noose and I need you."

"Not on your life!" She clutched her bag to her chest and backed away into the corner. "You are out of your freaking mind, Cole Tucker! This is just going to make things worse! They're gonna be in here and drag you back to jail in *one minute*!"

Tucker gave her the saddest smile she'd ever seen. But he didn't give Lacey any more time to protest. He picked her up, flung her over his shoulder like a sack full of Christmas presents, jerked open the door, and ran through it.

chapter 10

"Damn you, Cole Tucker! Put me down!"

"But Chantilly, you're light as a feather! Not even as heavy as a little calf." He held on to her legs, never slowing.

Lacey beat on his back, feeling as foolish as she ever had in her life. She was in the wrong position to try to disembark. It was hard to breathe and impossible to yell at him at the same time. She was mortified. From her viewpoint upside down over Tucker's shoulder, her tote bag swinging in her face, all she could see were legs running from offices and courtrooms.

The deputy who was supposed to be standing guard at the metal detector was not at his post. He was at the courtroom down the hall, opening the doors, surrounded by staff, spectators, and media. Tucker dashed for the unguarded exit as if this were the big game and the goalposts were in sight. He pushed unwary bystanders, who seemed frozen in place, out of his way with his free hand.

"You can't do this," Lacey managed to sputter.

"I'm doing it," Tucker said, not even breathing hard. "They don't care who leaves. They only check for weapons when you enter. I don't have a weapon. I only have you. Come to think of it, you're my secret weapon. Now hush. Duck your head, Chantilly."

Tucker had no trouble carrying Lacey through the metal detector gate and down the narrow stairway. She was aware of a ruckus behind them, people running and voices yelling, and among them she recognized Vic Donovan's commanding shout. But she had to keep her head down to avoid smacking it on the ceiling and the handrail. Tucker sailed down to the landing.

"Officer down," she heard someone yelling above them. "Prisoner's escaped!"

At the bottom of the stairs Lacey looked up. There was a bottleneck at the top, where the missing deputy, now back at his station, had closed the gate. He seemed to be trying to determine who was who in the clamorous mob threatening to trample him and plunge down the stairs in hot pursuit. Presumably he only wanted to keep the wrong folks from leaving the courtroom floor, unaware he was locking the barn door after the horses had bolted for freedom.

"I. Am. Going. To. Kill. You. Cole Tucker!" Lacey said, but her breath came in gasps, with her diaphragm bouncing against his shoulder.

"Get in line, sunshine."

They emerged from the back door of the courthouse, where a delivery vehicle for a local bakery had been left idling at the curb, door unlocked, key in the ignition. The old blue and white Jeep Cherokee had a sizable rack of elk antlers bolted to the grille. Hand painted on the doors it read: PETRUS BAKERY, WE BAKE IT, WE SHAKE IT. It was not a subtle vehicle, but one that could deliver the courthouse's daily doughnut run in the worst weather. Tucker headed straight for it. So far, no one was following them. *Where are they?* Lacey wondered.

"I will never forgive you, Cole Tucker. Never," Lacey yelled. She beat on his back again with her fists.

"A little down to the left, Lacey. That feels good."

Tucker opened the driver's side door and shoved her in, forcing her to bump her bottom on the console and catch one leg on the steering wheel. He pushed her leg over. Lacey struggled to right herself. She clutched her bag, digging for her cell phone, which was at the bottom of one of many interior pockets. She couldn't find it.

"Good old Tasso Petrus," Tucker was saying. "Not the best and the brightest, but he makes good doughnuts. I never could understand why people do that. Do you?

Run off and leave their car running?" He slid in behind her and slammed the Jeep into gear. "Just asking for a car thief to come along."

"You're not making me an accessory to your crimes. Let me out of here!" Lacey clawed her way toward the passenger side door. She had barely opened it as the car pulled out. Tucker leaned over and slammed the door before she could escape. He peeled out of the parking lot. She heard the door locks click.

A deputy she didn't recognize came running out the back door of the courthouse, a doughnut in his hand and a look of surprise on his face. Tasso Petrus the doughnut man was close behind, shaking both fists and yelling while running after his blue and white Jeep. The deputy dropped the doughnut and fumbled for his radio and his gun. Lacey ducked as they sped out of the lot and into the back alley. No gunshots came their way. She peeked behind them again.

"Looks like Petrus is trying to stop the deputy from shooting at us."

"Hell, yeah. Nobody wants his Jeep shot up," Tucker said. "Besides, he knows I'll take good care of it. It's a nice old Jeep, got the big 401 with the four-barrel and the Quadra-Trac. Man, they don't make 'em like this anymore—"

"Take good care of the *Jeep*? What about *us*? We could have been *killed*, Tucker! God, I've never seen you like this. You are out of your mind." She was dizzy and nauseated. Her mouth was dry and her pulse raced. She closed her eyes for a minute but that made it worse. The Jeep had a stiff ride and she was afraid she'd throw up.

"Never been this desperate before," Tucker said. "And you know what they say, desperate times require desperate measures." He kept his eyes on the road and his foot on the accelerator.

"Nice going, Cole. Now you're a fugitive from justice." Lacey felt bitter, not to mention stupid, for ever trying to see Tucker, for believing in him, and for going to Sagebrush in the first place. "And a car thief."

"That ought to break the bank, on top of three murder charges. Doesn't matter. I'm up the river already unless I can figure something out. Now, buckle up." He put the Jeep into reverse and floored it, spinning backward into the street, then back into drive. "Top speed ahead, Chantilly Lace." He pressed the accelerator to the floor and the Cherokee jumped ahead. "Man, you gotta love a big old V-8."

"Cole, slow down or you'll kill someone," Lacey barked at him. She was afraid to try to jump out until he slowed the car down.

"Add it to the list, Lace. I'm a wanted man."

"Let me get something straight for the article I will eventually write." *If I live.*

"Go ahead. On the record."

"You incapacitated one friend back there and stole another friend's car."

"Grady's sort of a friend, but not a great friend exactly, and like I said, I'm just *borrowing* Tasso's Jeep. But you got the gist of it."

"So Tasso Petrus won't mind?"

"Not as long as I don't get it all shot up. And I pay for the gas. Tasso knows what it's like in the Yampa County jail. He enjoys a good time, sometimes a little disorderly conduct. I was a little surprised he wasn't in that cell with me, but a good thing he wasn't, huh? As I said. He won't mind. Much."

The Jeep smelled wonderful, Lacey realized. Like a bakery. The backseat was half full of white bakery bags and flat doughnut boxes.

"It appears he was right in the middle of his deliveries this morning," Tucker said. "Lucky us. Hand me a doughnut, wouldja, Chantilly?"

"Does this make me an accessory?"

"Not if we eat the evidence."

Lacey fished out a doughnut for each of them. She realized she was starving. And there was chocolate on the premises.

"I thought the Petrus family were all sheep ranchers."

"Tasso doesn't like sheep. He's a city boy."

"Sagebrush is a city?"

"Passes for one hereabouts. Working at the bakery, he's still close to his family in town. And his wife Tina is one ferocious cook."

"So he's a pal of yours? I thought cowboys hated sheep ranchers, and vice versa."

"Not so much these days. You do what you gotta do to make a living up here. Hang on, Lacey."

The Jeep careened around a corner and headed west on Sundance Way like it was shot from a cannon. Lacey couldn't believe an old Cherokee could have that much speed. But Tucker said it was a hauler, and it hauled. She hugged her seat belt and prayed the air bag was in working condition. *Wait, does this thing even have air bags?*

She still didn't hear any sirens. She craned her neck to see if anyone was following them, but the Jeep was traveling at top speed and other cars on the road seemed to be in slow motion. Some just pulled to a stop on the side of the road and gave Tucker a wide berth.

Her tote bag was at her feet. She dug around in it again and finally pulled out her cell phone. She started to dial Vic.

"Oh, no, you don't." Tucker reached over and grabbed it away from her. He lowered the driver's window and pitched it out.

Her mouth fell open. For a moment, Laccy was speechless. It didn't last.

"Damn it, Tucker. What did you just do?" She stared at her empty hand.

"I threw your cell phone out the window. Don't worry about it. Signal's really spotty here anyway, you know, and there's no cell service at all where we're going."

"You jerk! You idiot! You—car thief!" She leaned as far away from him as possible and hugged the door. She pulled on the lever, but he had locked the doors from the driver's side. "Who are you? Do I know you at all?"

"You know me, Chantilly. I didn't do anything wrong. Get that through your head, Lacey. I didn't kill anyone."

Maybe not yet! Lacey kept her mouth shut. She didn't trust herself to talk, afraid a torrent of anger and indignation might spill out. It wasn't worth making a dreadful situation worse, and she didn't want Tucker to crash the Jeep. She was sick with apprehension. She tried to think of something to keep her mind off how frantic she felt and how worried she was. Like Vic.

Oh, my God, poor Vic! He must be out of his mind with worry. Not to mention pissed off.

Lacey covered her face with her hands. *Why did I come here at all?* She had wanted to reassure herself that Tucker was innocent, but she'd just witnessed the man commit who knows how many crimes, including assaulting an officer, fleeing the law, and stealing a car.

"It's not like I meant to kidnap you, Chantilly Lace," Tucker apologized. "But I saw daylight and I had to take my chance back there."

Oh, God. Kidnapping! Add that one to the list. Tucker had turned into a madman. Hadn't he? She looked over at him, spinning the Jeep's wheel like a race car. She worried he'd crash the getaway car, or that she would be shot at by a pursuing lawman. *Why didn't I stay in bed?*

Tucker steered the Jeep due west at top speed. There were still no visible pursuers, no cruisers, no sirens, no helicopters. Lacey assumed that meant someone was planning on putting up roadblocks, if they had a smart guess as to which way Tucker was heading. As Tucker seemed to be winging it, she wondered just how smart that guess could be.

Everyone would be after them: the police, the sheriff, and the Colorado Bureau of Investigation. She just prayed the law wouldn't shoot first and ask questions later.

"Oh, no!" Lacey sat up and clutched at her seat belt.

"What?" Tucker glanced her way.

"My mother! This is going to make her *insane.* Tucker, please, just let me out on the side of the road. I'll catch a ride, I'll go back, you'll get away, and then maybe my mother and my sister won't find out about this." She thanked God that at that moment, her father was on a plane to Thailand.

"Your sister. That would be the famous quarterback kicker?"

"That's the one."

"That's what families are for, aren't they, Chantilly? Anyway, looks like we're both in a heap of trouble. Can't let you go yet. Besides, I always liked your mom. And her Thanksgiving dinner that year was something else. I'll never forget it."

I'm sure she'll be thrilled to hear that. Lacey groaned. On top of everything else, the weather was bothering her. She snuggled into her coat. A snowstorm would really put the frosting on this particular cake. "It feels like snow."

"Yeah, there'll be snow. Feels great, like freedom."

"They're going to find us, you know."

"Maybe, maybe not." Tucker floored the Jeep to pass a semi. "They're thinking like cops. I'm thinking like a cowboy."

Great. All we need is a reenactment of the gunfight at the OK Corral, she thought, glaring at him. "So while you were planning your great escape, did you ever think of me?"

He glanced over at her, then checked the rearview mirror, his brown eyes serious.

"First of all, I didn't exactly *plan* it. The opportunity presented itself. I *carpe'd* the damn *diem*, you know?"

"You think Grady deserved what you did to him?"

"Don't know. Been thinking about Grady. Could be someone's using him."

"Using him?"

"Didn't I tell you? Grady's the deputy who took that so-called anonymous tip about that so-called evidence on our ranch. But Karen, my lawyer, found out there's no paper trail on that tip, no phone call, no recording, no notes on paper, no nothing. Grady says he got a call, but all they've really got is what he told the sheriff himself. Someone planted that tip. Maybe Grady himself. Did he plant the evidence too?"

"You don't think Grady Rush is the mastermind behind this?" she said.

"Grady, a mastermind? No way. You see how easy he

is to fool. Maybe he didn't create this fancy frame some-one's trying to hang on me, but he could be someone's tool."

"Whose tool?"

Tucker took a deep breath. "That would be the big question. I don't know."

She stared out the window, her thoughts in a jumble. "Did Grady know the dead women?"

"Everyone knew Ally—she bartended all over town. Lots of people knew Corazon. I couldn't say about Rae Fowler. Who knows? I heard she wasn't in town for long. She was just a kid. He probably saw them around, like anybody else here would. But he's no ladies' man."

"I guess not." *Even a girl duck would think twice about kissing Old Duckface.*

They were well beyond the Sagebrush city limits by now, out in the country. The sky had turned steel gray and it was full of the snow it hadn't dropped yet.

"Boy, is Grady's butt in trouble now." Tucker swerved to avoid a rock in the road. Lacey noticed another county road sign riddled with bullet holes. Only the signs in town were safe from bored teenagers with nothing on their hands but time and ammunition. Out in the county they were fair game.

"You've gotten all of us in trouble."

"Chantilly Lace, Grady didn't have to take the shack-les off me. He let me talk him into it. That was stupid. Welcome, but stupid."

"Maybe he did it for a friend," Lacey said.

"Maybe. In which case, he's going to be very unhappy. You, my dear, were a victim of my circumstances."

There were no cars on the road, and Lacey prayed that no wildlife would cross the highway while Tucker was at the wheel. Hitting an elk or a pronghorn at high speed could be fatal for all of them. Lacey had no desire to be intimately associated with venison smeared all over the highway.

"Why did you drag me along, Cole?"

"You came all this way just to see me, Chantilly.

Would have been rude to run out on our date and leave you all alone."

"You're so not funny. And stop calling me that."

"You've been worried that I've always secretly been some kind of crazy homicidal maniac and you didn't know about it."

She gave him the evil eye. "I'm still worried. And Vic is going to freak out." Lacey closed her eyes. She wished she could close off her thoughts as well.

"That's another thing. You're going with Vic Donovan, the cop? I heard a rumor. Couldn't believe it. What happened to you?"

"None of your business."

"You can't be serious. I know he was sweet on you all those years ago. But he was married, to that blond man-eater. What's her name? Montana?"

"Vic is divorced now. Montana's in Steamboat. And he moved back to Virginia."

"So he's a stalker. He moved back after *you*. You should worry about him, not me."

The car radio crackled. The Sagebrush country station covered the entire county, but the signal came and went depending on the landscape. *No satellite radio for this old Jeep.* Tucker twiddled the knobs and brought in the station. There was a special news bulletin on the escape of murder suspect Cole Tucker. ". . . *Last seen in a Petrus Bakery delivery Jeep, described by witnesses as blue and white with a rack of elk antlers on the grille.*"

"You had to steal a car with antlers?"

"Maybe I can find us a herd of blue and white elk. We'll blend right in." Tucker switched the radio off. "And I *borrowed* it."

In the silence the landscape was bleak, the snow blending into the sky, the gray green sagebrush poking out of the crusted snow as far as the eye could see. The Jeep raced past the small town of Cowbell, the cross-roads to the west of Sagebrush, with not another vehicle in sight. Then a sign on the side of the road, full of bullet holes: NO SERVICES NEXT 50 MILES.

This day is just not getting any better.

Lacey wondered how on earth she could ever explain this to anyone, let alone live it down. She switched the radio back on, but Tucker turned down the sound.

"Just ignore it. We'll be out of this Jeep soon enough." Tucker spun the Cherokee off the highway and headed down a side road in the general direction of Utah. "I just don't see it, Chantilly. You and Donovan, I mean. He's just not your type."

"Oh, yeah? And how would you know that?" Lacey stared out the window. Cole Tucker might not have killed those women, but he was a desperate man in a stolen bakery Jeep. *No cell phone, no radio, nothing to eat but doughnuts. What next?* "He's going to kick your ass, you know."

Tucker grinned at her. "He's got to find me first. How about another one of those doughnuts?"

"Oh, all right." She reached in back for one of the boxes. She handed him a raised glazed.

"Mmmm. You know what I like."

Yeah, Chantilly Lace and a pretty face. She helped herself to a chocolate glazed. It was delicious. She decided the Petruses knew what they were doing.

Lacey gazed at Tucker's profile against the snowy landscape racing past the window. Cole Younger Tucker was turning into an outlaw, she decided, just like his namesake. His rancher parents had found it amusing to name their kids after notorious figures in Western history: Cole Younger Tucker, his brother, Kit Carson Tucker, and his sister, Belle Starr Tucker.

"This doughnut box is marked for the police department. Cops take it amiss when you mess with their property," Lacey said to fill the silence. "A kid in my high school stole a police helmet off the back of a cop's motorcycle one night. Just a helmet. When the cops finally caught him—"

"No doubt using their crack police intelligence—"

"They made him wash police cars every Saturday for a month."

He whistled. "So you're telling me I could end up

washing cop cars if I don't go straight? Damn, Lacey. Now you're scaring me."

"Oh, shut up." Lacey sighed and covered her face with her hands.

"Hey, Chantilly Lace, what's wrong?"

Her eyes nearly popped out of her head. "What's wrong? Besides this absurd predicament we're in? Isn't that enough? Vic didn't want me to come to Sagebrush. He asked me not to see you. He said it would be a mess. And it's a disaster."

Tucker pressed his lips together for a moment. "Well, I can't say he was wrong. But I'm real glad you did come," he said. "Else I'd be back in jail by now, waiting for a court date six months or more down the road. And whoever killed those girls would be home free."

"Looks to me like he's still home free, Cole."

He swung the wheel without slowing down and pointed the Jeep down another gravel side road. "I heard you solved some murders back in D.C."

"I got in the middle of a few." She thought about those cases, and the clues that had sometimes led her to the right answers. Fashion clues, she usually called them, when she was needling Vic. "Sometimes I saw things other people didn't. By 'other people' I mean mostly men. Like cops."

"I heard. Seems you have fans all over the weird worldwide Web. Tell me about these killings you investigated, star reporter Lacey Smithsonian. These things you saw that other people didn't see, so you could help nail the ones who did it. How would you go about proving someone *didn't* do it? How would you prove *I* didn't do it?"

chapter 11

"How would I prove that?" Lacey repeated.

"You seem to be the expert." Tucker looked vulnerable at that moment, despite the jail jumpsuit and the bad-ass elk-antlered Jeep Cherokee he was driving like an off-road racer.

"I'm no expert. Sometimes the obvious answer is the right one. That's what the cops say. But—"

"But what?"

"There are different ways to look at a crime. Sometimes, especially in a cold case, the answers aren't obvious." *Clues are made of multiple threads,* Lacey thought. *Threads that weave together to make a picture of the victim and the killer. You pull a thread, you cause a ripple in the fabric.*

"They think they've got me, Lacey. They got their fall guy."

"Maybe not." She pulled her collar up around her neck to ward off a draft of cool air from somewhere in the Jeep. "All I do is try to put together a picture, Cole. Reporters ask questions."

"I know that."

"I try to see where the picture doesn't fit the way the killer wants it to. And don't laugh. With me, it usually involves clothes. Something about what they wear reveals who they really are or what they're trying to hide."

"I read some of your stories on the Internet."

"Really?"

"There's this Web site. Did you ever hear of it? Conspiracy Clearinghouse."

She growled. "I've heard of it." Brooke's boyfriend, Damon, and his accursed Web site were a thorn in her side, even here, in the back of beyond.

"Well, that's what this has to be. A conspiracy to set me up."

"Whether it's one person alone or a whole town full of people, you still have to ask the same basic questions. Means and opportunity. And motive. But motive is murkier. Lots of people have motives but never act on them. Motive alone can point you in the wrong direction. After everything else, you go with your gut."

"Go, then," Tucker said. "Ask your questions. Ask me anything. Walk me through this."

Tucker didn't know he'd said just the right thing. He recognized that Lacey had a certain expertise. And a track record. It was different with Vic—Vic was born skeptical. He didn't trust feelings and intuitions. And Lacey's PI boyfriend had far more expertise with crime than she did. But Tucker trusted her with his freedom. She felt the compliment. Still, it didn't make up for the rest of the morning.

"First tell me about your attorney, Karen Quilby. Is she any good?"

He shrugged and gave her an I-don't-know look. "The guy who handles legal stuff for the ranch is the same old goat my dad used, and all he's ever done is deeds and titles. So I got handed a public defender. Just out of law school. Needs a wet nurse."

"She's young," Lacey agreed. "She seemed nice enough. But untried."

Tucker smiled slightly. "Karen did arrange for me to see you. I'll give her that."

"Yeah. Thanks, Karen." If Lacey didn't watch it, sarcasm might creep in. "I guess it wasn't her fault. I asked to see you, didn't I?"

She gave herself a mental slap. Lacey wished fervently that none of this had happened. She wished she had waited until after the arraignment to see Cole. She was way too far inside this story. Inside the story, and the getaway vehicle, and heading for parts unknown.

"Don't frown like that, Chantilly Lace. Your pretty face will freeze."

She glared at him. "I'm betting Karen Quilby won't be in any mood to keep up your lawyer-client relationship after this little stunt of yours."

"She wouldn't anyway. They want to bleed me. Make me put up the ranch to pay a fancy attorney. And the ranch doesn't just belong to me. It also belongs to Kit, and Starr and her husband. And bail would be too high to pay anyway."

"There's no chance of bail now," Lacey pointed out.

Tucker shook his head. "There never was any chance of the judge letting me go. Three murders? If I had a million bucks in my hip pocket to make bail, they'd have set it at ten million. If I had ten, they'd have made it a hundred."

For all his bravado, there was an air of wild despair about Tucker.

But what about the victims' despair? Did they have the same air about them, the same hopelessness and fear when they knew they were trapped and they were never going to get out alive? Lacey wondered what it was that made Ally, Rae, and Corazon vulnerable to the killer. And what made Tucker vulnerable to being framed. Lacey's head hurt.

Tucker suddenly drove off the side road onto a deeply rutted dirt path, the Jeep bouncing from side to side in the ruts. Lacey held tight to her shoulder belt. After the first curve, he pulled off the path and parked the Cherokee behind a bluff where it couldn't easily be seen from any road.

"Time to get out," Tucker commanded.

Lacey glared at him and folded her arms. She made no move to leave. "Where the hell are we?"

He jumped out the driver's side, taking the keys, and walked around to her door. She locked it and he unlocked it with the remote. "Please get out of the car, Lacey. We have to hike in some. Not very far."

"Fine. You take a hike. I can just walk out to the highway and hitch a ride." It couldn't be that far, she thought.

"With who? Prince Charming? You have no idea when the big rescue squad will get here. They don't even know where *here* is. You could die of hypothermia. No joke, Chantilly Lace, that No SERVICES sign wasn't kidding. And we're a good twenty-five or thirty miles from Sagebrush." He yanked open her side door.

Reluctantly leaving the warm Cherokee, Lacey zipped her coat, put the hood up, and retrieved her gloves from the bottom of her bag. Tucker rummaged around in the back of the Jeep and pulled out a fleece jacket that must have belonged to Tasso Petrus.

The early spring weather was unpredictable in Yampa County. In a flash it could turn deadly cold and dump three feet of snow. People in this part of Colorado carried blankets and an extra jacket or two in the car. Tucker also fished out a couple of bottles of water and tossed one to her. Lacey opened it and drank greedily. Her throat was parched from the dry air. She had forgotten how dry it could get. She'd lost her tolerance for high altitude and low humidity.

"Slow down, you're going to have to make that last," Tucker said.

Lacey reluctantly capped the water and put it in her purse. "Where are you taking us?" She wished she had her cell phone. The landscape was lonely and she didn't relish being outside in the wind.

"Not far. Kit's pickup is probably no more than a hundred yards from here."

"Your brother?" Lacey looked around, but she didn't see any pickup. Nothing but sagebrush as far as the eye could see. She remembered Kit Carson Tucker as younger, skinnier, and not quite as handsome as his big brother, Cole. "Did you plan this whole escape? Has he been waiting for us all along?"

"Hell, no. Kit's out here rounding up cattle for old Truman," Tucker said. "Next ranch over from ours. He told me yesterday he'd be working strays out this end of the draw. I know where he leaves his truck."

"Wasn't he at the courthouse?"

"What could he do there? We got a ranch to run, and Kit— Well, he said it was too damn depressing anyhow. Can't blame him. It depresses me too. Said he wanted to think about things. And you know Kit, he thinks better on a horse."

"So do you. What's he thinking about?"

"Same thing I'm thinking about, and what Starr is thinking about." Tucker's face looked grave. "Getting my neck out of this tangled rope."

"So now you're going to steal Kit's truck? And leave him stuck out here?"

"*Borrow,* Lacey. He's my brother. He'll put two and two together when he gets back and sees the truck gone. And Tasso's Jeep. Probably just ride on back to the neighbors' place, get a lift home. Hey, I'm just winging it here, Chantilly."

Tucker trudged around the other side of the little bluff while Lacey stomped behind him, angrier with each step. At one point she threw a snowball, glancing it off his shoulder.

"It's all fun and games till you put somebody's eye out, Chantilly. We got to move." He grabbed her hand and pulled her along.

It wasn't easy to walk in the deep snow over uneven ground, dodging the scruffy sagebrush poking through the icy crust. The wind kicked up and chapped her cheeks. But in a few minutes, she saw Kit's dirty white pickup truck waiting for them behind the bluff among the sagebrush, where it blended with the snow. Tucker opened the cab door for Lacey.

"Get in and stay warm," he said. It wasn't any warmer inside the truck, but at least she was out of the wind. She turned the rearview mirror so she could watch him.

In the bed of the pickup, Tucker found a steel box. He popped it open and retrieved a fleece-lined jean jacket and some faded jeans, which he pulled on over the pants of the jail's brown jumpsuit, and an old pair of cowboy boots. He threw the jail shoes in the back. In boots and denim, he looked much more like the Cole Tucker Lacey remembered so well. A beat-up, sweat-stained cowboy hat completed the look.

"That's better," he said, getting into the cab and moving the mirror for a glance at his reflection.

He pulled a spare ignition key from a small magnetic case under the dashboard.

"Call me suspicious, but it appears this was preplanned," Lacey said.

"Just taking the breaks as they come. We always carry extra boots, gloves, blankets, water. Shovels. You know that. Weather can turn on a dime here. You don't want to be caught on the open range without some survival gear. Besides, what are you dragging around in that big old tote bag of yours, an IBM Selectric?"

She clutched her tote tightly to her chest. She had spent a long time looking for just the right bag to travel with on assignment, and the soft brown leather tote met all her requirements. It had a cross-body strap so she could wear it hands free. It was deep, it had lots of pockets, including a big one on the outside, and it zipped across the top so things wouldn't fall out. It was clean and classic, so it went anywhere, with almost anything, short of black tie and evening gowns.

Tucker was right. Lacey had her own version of a survival kit, and she took a mental inventory of it. The ancient tools of her trade, a notebook and pens. Digital camera. Her address book. Her motel key. She'd left her laptop and tape recorder back at the motel. Karen had told her she wouldn't be allowed to record her meeting with Tucker. Of course the most important survival tool, her cell phone, was missing, thanks to Tucker, and no doubt flattened like roadkill on the side of the highway.

She also had an essential supply of war paint: some touch-up, a mirror, mascara, lipstick, eyeliner. Tissues and hand sanitizer, lip balm, extra thick moisturizing lotion for her hands and face. A comb and hairpins, as well as elastic bands, in the event her hair wouldn't behave and she had to put it up or pull it back. And rolled up in the corner of her tote was a dark green wool shawl that coordinated with her outfit. The one she'd thought would be such a knockout in court. *Vanity goeth before the fall.*

"None of your business," she said.

He laughed. "I thought so."

"I'm glad you were able to change clothes, Cole. You look more like yourself again."

"Thought you didn't care."

Tucker fired up the pickup and circled back past the bakery Jeep. He tossed Tasso's jacket and the keys into the driver's seat and grabbed one of the white bakery bags. The pickup roared back down the dirt road and headed for the highway.

The AM radio crackled to life and a country DJ's voice drawled over the speakers. "—late great Marty Robbins, singing his classic cowboy lament and love song, 'El Paso.'" The familiar Spanish guitar intro surged through the AM static with a Mexican flourish. Normally, Lacey would have been thrilled to stumble upon this innocently nostalgic tune about a cowboy outlaw gunned down for a crime of passion. She hadn't heard it in years, but at the moment, it was a little too close for comfort.

Lacey spun around in the pickup and scanned the barren, snowy sagebrush flats of Yampa County, half expecting to see the law riding after them in flaming pursuit.

Fashion Bites

Pack Up Your Troubles in Your Bag, Tote, or Purse

Aside from a dog, and diamonds, a great purse may be a girl's best friend. There are so many great bags out there, you needn't settle for second best. As with men, it pays to search for the right one. And it doesn't have to be at a high-end department store. In fact, as with men, the best surprises often arrive when you're not expecting anything.

The pursuit of the perfect purse is exciting, but, trust me, the girl with the most bags does not win. First of all, take a breath. This isn't a race. Have patience. If you don't see what you want today, don't buy just anything. The stores will be there tomorrow. The stock will be replenished. You will live to shop another day.

We all want a purse with top-quality materials, but you shouldn't be a sucker for the big-name designer label. Some designer bags are like flashy gigolos: overpriced, gaudy, and not suitable for everyday use. A bag that doesn't shout its name often has more class and can go more places.

If your funds are limited, just two or three well-constructed and well-chosen bags can take you nearly anywhere you need to go. Whether you want canvas, fabric, leather, or some man-made petroleum byproduct, there is a purse for everything. A minimum wardrobe for the working woman includes a subtle evening bag, a tailored purse for work, and a casual tote for weekends.

You should know what you really need most in a bag. Do you need a tote bag for shoes and papers, along with a smaller pocketbook? Or do you want one immense superbag that does it all? Do you love having twenty tiny compartments to organize everything, or do they drive you crazy because you can't remember which pocket you tucked your keys in?

Perhaps you need a briefcase as well as a small bag. In that case, the purse should be compact and tailored, sending a professional vibe. While it does not have to match the briefcase, it should be compatible.

For the city or work purse, look for a shoulder or cross-body strap that leaves your hands free to fumble with your Metro card.

Think about what your purse says about you. Black or brown leather is traditional and conservative, but also versatile. A red patent leather has extra zing and works with a variety of looks, perfectly acceptable in the working universe. In a place like Washington, D.C., where certain professions, such as lawyers, lobbyists, and bankers, require a sober style statement, women show off their personality with their choice of bags. Even if it's a plaid Burberry tote. *Sigh.* The mild-mannered D.C. rebel might choose a gold, purple, or turquoise tote. Go crazy, ladies!

Don't become so attached to a bag you fail to see its flaws as it grows old and becomes a candidate for retirement. Scarred and scuffed might be okay for a laid-back weekend, dashing to the hardware store for a gallon of paint. After all, that shabby old bag may feel like an old friend. But it's not appropriate for that important meeting or interview. So here are a few tips:

- Proportion is key. You're looking for the Goldilocks of bags. Not Papa Bag or Baby Bag, but the bag that fits *you*. A petite woman should not be overwhelmed by the size of her bag. Likewise, larger ladies should avoid the visual irony of a tiny clutch. Unsure? Look in the mirror, or shop with a friend.

- Don't buy a faux Louis Vuitton or anything else from that T-shirt and sunglasses vendor on the street corner. Besides the moral implications of buying a fake, they always look phony too.
- Beware of the clutch. Without a strap, it requires you to either jam it under your arm and hold on for dear life, or keep it in your hand at all times. A strap simply makes life easier.
- Showing up at that congressional budget hearing looking like Little Orphan Annie toting all her possessions in a recyclable grocery sack will *not* win points.
- Magnets may seem like a good idea, but they can deactivate your subway cards and hotel keys. Buckles, on the other hand, rarely let you down.
- It's a tote, not a suitcase. The point is not to look like you're fleeing a burning building with everything you could grab on the way out. However, with a good tote and some editing, you can pack all the essentials to see you through a busy day on the run.

Details matter. Maybe they shouldn't, but someone will always judge you by your bag and shoes. Make sure yours are presentable to the judges. Then you'll never have to worry about your style. *It's in the bag.*

chapter 12

"What kind of evidence do they have?" Lacey shouted, while hanging on to both her shoulder strap and the handle over the pickup's passenger door.

The old truck was even louder and rougher riding than Tasso Petrus's Jeep. Kit obviously needed to have some work done on the shocks. She'd given up on the idea of jumping out of the car whenever the speedometer dipped lower. They were in the middle of snowy nowhere, and besides, Tucker showed no signs of ever slowing down. And if Lacey were to be completely honest with herself, she was curious to see where this story was going to land. Her reporter's curse: the desire to follow a story to the bitter end.

"Not sure. Karen Quilby said we'd find out more at what she called 'discovery.' Some of the victims' personal things they found at the ranch. I heard they found Rae Fowler's backpack. One of Corazon's too, and some other things. According to Sheriff T-Rex, it was Corazon's necklace."

"Do you remember the necklace?" Lacey grabbed hold of the cupid pendant around her neck, rubbed it, as if for luck, and made a wish to see Vic.

"Course I do. She wore it all the time. It was a turquoise heart on a silver disc. Her name engraved on the back. It was a present from her parents for her *quinceañera*."

That made sense, Lacey thought. The name Corazon meant *heart* in Spanish. "And the evidence they found from Ally?"

"Not sure. They may have told me, but I was kind of

stunned, like I'd been stomped by a bad bull." He shook his head. "Sheriff said I should know. I'm guessing it's jewelry."

"Why was it all found on your property?"

"No idea." Tucker kept his eyes on the road, scanning for police vehicles. "Their bodies weren't found anywhere near our land. I got no idea how these things got to where they were dug up. If they really were dug up. But sure enough, all this stuff showed up after Grady got his anonymous tip."

"Vic said you were dating Corazon Reyes."

"He would, wouldn't he?" Tucker made a face. "We went out a few times. That's all."

"Corazon was very pretty." Lacey thought about the picture of Corazon with her wide smile, dark eyes, and luxuriant hair.

"That she was, but not really my type. A sweet girl. Turned out we really didn't have anything to talk about."

"I'm sure you had better things to do than talk." Lacey couldn't believe she made that crack. She couldn't be jealous of anyone who was with Tucker. Not at this late date. Could she? Besides, there was Vic. The thought of Vic made her suck in her breath. *What's Vic doing right now? And more important, what's he thinking?*

"Corazon was a nice lady and I liked her. We just didn't click. The way it happens. I've dated a few women since. Even so, when they found Corazon's body, I felt pretty torn up."

"Did she date anyone after you?"

"Sure. She liked a good time, she was fun, she liked to salsa. We didn't stay in touch. I'm real sorry she died, especially like that."

"I'm sorry too," Lacey said. "How did you meet her?"

"She was a cook over at Henderson's cow camp last spring and summer." Tucker smothered a laugh. "I don't know how she got that job. She couldn't cook worth beans, she couldn't *even* cook beans, and what she did to a pie was a crime. Even hungry cowpokes found her food hard to handle. And swallow. She hated it, but it was work."

"How many people did she cook for?"

"Maybe six, maybe eight, depending on how many hands were helping out with the herd. Anyway, she'd get weekends off and head into town. Then she didn't show up to cook one day. Folks figured she just gave it up, left town. But they found her body the next week. Way up north of town."

"What was Corazon like? What did she want to do, if she didn't want to cook? And what kind of clothes did she wear?"

"Oh, Chantilly Lace, you always did go on about clothes."

"Hey, I just want to get a picture of her. Clothes are important. Especially for a woman." *Even way out here.*

"But what's that got to do—"

"Cole Tucker, if I'd never seen you before, I'd still know you were a cowboy. Maybe not in that brown jail outfit. Uniforms take away your identity, or give you a new one. But in your jeans and jacket and hat and boots, I'd know exactly what you are, and I'd know you're the real thing. Everything you wear is worn just *so,* because your clothes work for a living on a real ranch, on a real horse, or bouncing around in this junker of a pickup truck. Not because they were stonewashed or acid-washed or distressed to look *faux* real."

"You got me there. You've thought about this some."

"And it's not just your clothes and how they're worn, it's how you wear them. You've got a cowboy swagger when you walk." She would never tell him he was ever so slightly bowlegged.

"Cowboy swagger, huh?" He glanced sideways at her and grinned. She ignored the look. "Sexy, huh?"

"Even that ballad, 'The Streets of Laredo,' says, 'I see by your outfit that you are a cowboy.'" *Of course that song was about a cowboy's funeral.* Lacey didn't want to think about that. "Clothes give people a particular attitude and history and they tell stories about them. All you have to do is look at them the right way."

"I'm sure it comes in handy in your line of work now," he said. "Fashion articles and murder stories.

There are more parts to you, Chantilly Lace, than ever I thought."

She shifted in her seat. "Back to Corazon Reyes. Unfortunately, dressing well is tricky for a woman in a place like Sagebrush. Her stylistic range of expression is limited, because her shopping choices are limited. It's not so bad if you're a cowboy or a miner or a construction worker."

"Are you slamming Sagebrush again?"

"I'm thinking here. Don't interrupt. There's a new Wal-Mart and a couple of discount outlets. A second-hand store. Everyone dresses out of the same bins. Some people here will go shopping in the city, once or twice a year, in Steamboat, or Grand Junction, or even Denver. Yet a woman with an imagination or sense of style can make any outfit her own."

Accessories could make a difference, and the way a woman put things together, she thought. And in Sagebrush, Colorado, the men really *looked* at women, and women liked to be noticed. It wasn't Washington, D.C., where the female of the species could wear a fabulous dress to a glittery party and still feel like wallpaper.

Again the question: What was it about Corazon Reyes that had attracted her killer? What was different about her? And what about the other women? Lacey had only seen their snapshots in the news stories. How did they see themselves? *If a picture is worth a thousand words, then so is a woman's wardrobe.*

"Okay. I get it. This stuff matters." Tucker's voice softened. "There's no one here like you, Chantilly. They don't have your sense of style."

"They don't have Aunt Mimi's trunk." Lacey stroked her velvet skirt, the deep nap, the comfort of a garment well designed and well made. A legacy from Aunt Mimi. "The locals always thought I was crazy, didn't they?"

"But crazy in a good way." He grinned at her. "You always were like a star out of an old movie. A film noir femme fatale."

It was Lacey's turn to laugh. "Thank you, I think. But tell me about Corazon. What did she wear?"

"What I remember most is that Corazon liked to dance. We only went out a half dozen times. Not even that. Maybe half those times we went dancing. Why on earth would I want to hurt her? Why even set me up to look like I did? Makes no damn sense. But her duds? She usually wore a tight little shirt, the kind with the pearl snaps, maybe a jean skirt, cowboy boots. Silver and turquoise jewelry. Stuff like that."

"Denim skirts and cowboy boots." Like the women who shopped at Crybaby Ranch. "But you said something about boots. Like mine?"

She propped one green and brown boot on the dash, and Tucker spared a quick glance away from the road. "I helped you pick those out, didn't I? That was quite a day."

"Yes, it was." Lacey didn't want to think about that day. A day when she was in love with Tucker. They'd made a special shopping trip to Steamboat Springs, to F. M. Light & Sons. "Back to Corazon's boots."

"Hers were fancier than those. I guess I'd call them Texican. Flashy. Hand-tooled sombreros and cactuses all over them, all different colors. She said she could wear them with anything."

"Everything except death," Lacey said. "She was found barefoot. Do you know whether they ever found her boots?"

"No idea."

"New question. Who has a reason to frame you?"

"Nobody, but—" Tucker slapped the steering wheel. "Hell, I got my suspicions." He swallowed hard. "Listen, the ranch has got to survive, no matter what happens to me. It's always been touch and go, but if I'm not there to keep it going, I'm worried the vultures will swoop down and take it."

Maybe it's time to stop thinking about the ranch. And start thinking about yourself, Lacey thought. But she knew that wouldn't go over well. "It's like you to put the ranch above everything else."

There were always cattle to feed and herd, horses to tend and water and run. He told her once that as long as grass grew and the Yampa River ran, there would be Tuckers to ranch that land.

"It's more than a job. You know that, Chantilly Lace. I'm just afraid—"

"You think someone's after the Tuckered Out Ranch?" She always thought *Tuckered Out* was a silly name for a ranch, but several generations of the ranching Tucker family thought it was downright hilarious. And appropriate.

"Not the ranch. The land. And what's under it."

"Who? Certainly not housing developers."

"No, I don't see a bunch of yuppie town houses filling the horizon out there. Some kind of energy development. The whole history of this area is boom and bust. And it's been bust for too long now."

"And the energy companies are banking it will boom again?"

"It's all a matter of the price of things. Coal or oil or natural gas, even water. Price goes up enough to make a profit and they'll tear this county apart and suck the land dry. They're ready to do it. I know you don't like this landscape, Lacey, though I never understood why. You can see forever out here. Nothing between you and the sky."

Almost like living on the moon. She gazed out at the desolate landscape passing them by at top speed. Not many trees, but plenty of rocky bluffs and cliffs, in shades of tan and sandy brown and pale pink and dusty rose. There was an occasional shed or stable, and here and there a playful pack of pronghorn antelopes bounding through the sagebrush.

"I like it green." Lacey already missed the green of the East Coast, the woods that wrapped her in an emerald green blanket. She especially missed the bright spring green of Virginia and D.C. Soon the trees there would be budding in their annual ritual of spring, bursting into pink and yellow blossoms. Lawns in the Mid-Atlantic stayed alive and green over the winter, unlike this wild and rocky place. And the mountains were less spectacular in this corner of the state. It was a high arid plateau, and from Sagebrush the mountains ringing it looked more like foothills, though some were eleven thousand feet tall.

"This land is valuable. Mineral rights and water rights are like gold," Tucker said. His voice turned harsh. "Out-of-state carpetbaggers swooped in a while ago and bought up a lot of land from ranchers, the ones who were sick and tired, sick of breaking their backs, tired of breaking their hearts. The buyers spun a big fantasy about what they were going to do to keep the range and preserve the land. They turned around and sold the water rights for golf courses in Nevada, swimming pools in California. Robbed this land. This state is nothing without water."

She nodded. "That can't be legal."

"It's not anymore. County commissioners finally did something, but not until a lot of damage was done. Colorado water was already flowing out of state. Right now the remaining water rights have got to stay with the land. But there are still minerals and natural gas to plunder. The energy companies have their sights on all of us, the Tuckered Out Ranch too. I'll never sell as long as I'm a free man. But if Kit and Starr end up having to sell the land or the mineral or water rights to defend these damn phony charges against me, well, it's all over."

chapter 13

"Why did you stop? Where are we?"

Tucker took a sharp right off the county highway and plunged down a dirt side road. He pulled the pickup off into the sagebrush where it couldn't be easily spotted. Lacey looked for signs of life up and down the lonely road. Nothing. A barbed wire fence broke the line of the horizon.

"We're getting out," Tucker said. "Come on."

"How about I just stay here until the police come?"

He sighed loudly. "We've gone through this before. I'm not leaving you out here all alone."

Lacey opened her side door and stepped down, grateful for her leather jacket that kept the wind out. "And if I just start walking back?" She figured a car had to come by sooner or later.

He shook his head. "It's a mighty long walk back to Sagebrush, Chantilly. And a little lonely out here all alone, what with the coyotes and the rattlesnakes. This is rattlesnake country, you remember that?"

"Rattlesnakes sleep in the winter. Don't they?"

"That's what they say. Unless you step on one."

"But you'll be on foot too," Lacey protested.

"Not for long. We have horses sheltered right off the road here, in a little shed out of the wind."

"I don't see any shed. And just how do you know that?"

"That's where I put 'em. Before they arrested me. Kit was supposed to be out here to feed and water 'em."

"We're close to your ranch? I'm all turned around, Cole."

"You probably never saw this end of the spread. Let's go."

Tucker started walking into the bitter cold wind. Lacey reluctantly followed him. She slung her bag over her shoulder and pulled her hood up, her scarf wrapped around her face.

"You look like an Eskimo," Tucker said, looping one arm through hers. "It's not that cold."

She pulled her arm free. "Speak for yourself."

They trudged through the sagebrush in silence for several minutes before Lacey saw something that looked like a low shed in a little draw. Inside were two horses.

"Why are they all the way out here?" she asked.

"Change of scenery for them, what with the nice weather and all."

"Nice weather, my eye." She shivered.

"We're having a heat wave. It got to thirty below this winter. Must be thirty above now. Course, March can be unpredictable, you might recall."

Tucker stroked the horses, which seemed happy to see him, and hefted a saddle off the back wall onto a pretty palomino. He nuzzled her neck and the horse whinnied to him. "Hey, Buttercup, this here is Lacey. You remember Chantilly Lace, don't you? She used to ride you way back when."

The horse neighed softly. Tucker pulled a couple of dried apples from a bag hanging on the wall and gave one to Buttercup. She gazed at him adoringly.

"You want me to ride a horse?" Lacey asked, eyeing him suspiciously. *No. Impossible.* "Buttercup?" She hung back at the entrance to the shed.

"You remember how, right?"

"They say it's like riding a bike, but I hadn't exactly planned on riding a bike either. Especially not in a skirt. In vintage velvet." Tucker had taught her to ride. But that was in the warm golden days of autumn. *Long ago and far away.*

Tucker seemed a little exasperated. He grabbed Lacey's hand and trotted her over to Buttercup. He cinched up the saddle on the palomino mare. "Buttercup's gentle as a kitten. Just hang on and ride astride. Don't be worrying about your skirt."

"I'm not. I'm worried about my neck."

She patted the horse's nose and whispered to her not to throw her off. The horse snuffled and nodded, fluttering long lashes over her big brown eyes as if she were amused. She nuzzled Lacey.

"She likes you, Chantilly Lace." Tucker saddled Buttercup's companion, a big black horse with a white star on his forehead. "Now, this is Ricochet. He can be a handful." The black horse danced back and forth in a show of impatience. He reared and came down with a snort. Tucker patted his neck. "Chill out, little Ricky. I know you been bored out here. We'll run later, buddy." Buttercup didn't bat an eye. She was used to Ricochet showing off.

Tucker led the two horses out of their stalls and turned to Lacey. "Here, let me help you." Lacey found it hard to focus when Tucker was standing so close to her.

"Where are we going?"

"Where there aren't a lot of roads. If we're lucky, we still have a decent head start."

Lacey's stomach growled. "I'm starving, Tucker."

"Running from the law sure gives you an appetite," he cracked.

"I'm not running from the law. You are," she corrected him. "Couldn't I just go to the ranch? I mean the house, your house, wherever it is from here." She imagined a warm fire on the stone hearth.

"It's miles from here, and I imagine Sheriff Rexford and his boys might be there waiting for us."

"Great. I can't believe T-Rex is still the sheriff."

Lacey had had her share of run-ins with Sheriff Theodore Rexford, widely known around Yampa County as T-Rex. Folks in and around Sagebrush thought he somewhat resembled that ferocious dinosaur found in fossilized form in Northwestern Colorado. Like the tyrannosaurus, Sheriff T-Rex had a forward-thrusting jaw and a big nose, and rather jagged teeth. And he could be fierce when crossed.

"Yep, still sheriff."

"Fine. He could take me back to Sagebrush. You could go some other way." Lacey's shoulders slumped and she felt defeated. For a moment. Just one. "What the hell do you think you're doing, Cole Tucker? Playing Lone Ranger?"

"Long as I got Tonto along for the ride." He grinned at her, his teeth showing white and even. "Those are the breaks, Chantilly. I know you think justice will just naturally win out, and the law will do the right thing. But why would that happen when they've got a perfect fall guy?"

"You have a point," she admitted. Reluctantly.

"I'm afraid we're gonna have to figure this out, whoever killed those girls."

"Grady Rush took that anonymous tip—" Lacey started.

"This is Yampa County, Chantilly Lace. Think about it. We don't have 'anonymous tipsters.' Everybody knows everybody else."

Tucker was right. There were damn few secrets anyone could keep in Sagebrush. Except for who killed those three women. She looked at her watch. It was barely noon.

"You think Grady's involved?"

"Don't know about *involved*. He knows something, even if he doesn't know he knows it."

He looped her tote bag onto the saddle and gave her a boost onto Buttercup. Lacey was glad her skirt flared out at the bottom so she could ride without hiking it up to her hips. Trying to ride in a short tight skirt would be a nightmare. She flinched when she sat down. "Yeow! This thing is cold as ice."

"You stay fresher longer." He laughed. "It'll warm up."

"Thanks a bunch, Tucker." Her tights weren't enough to keep the cold out. Buttercup neighed, and Lacey held tight to the reins.

Buttercup was blasé about getting saddled up, but Ricochet was so excited he was dancing a jig. Tucker slid one boot into a stirrup and swung himself up and onto the saddle with a cowboy's grace. Ricochet settled down immediately—the horse knew the boss was here, and he was eager to get to work.

"Let's ride, Lacey." She hugged Buttercup gently with her stirrups and they were off.

Lacey and Tucker argued through the afternoon as they rode over the rugged terrain of snowy sagebrush flats, sandstone hogbacks, and looming red orange bluffs. Tucker led them at a walking pace through tangled draws full of willows and cottonwoods, but wherever the country opened up and left them exposed he let Ricochet break into a run. Lacey kept Buttercup glued to Ricochet's flank, the wind stinging her face. She knew she would be saddle sore later.

She had no idea where they were. At times Lacey swore they were riding in circles, the same bluffs and draws recycling again and again. She relied on Tucker to know where he was going: down horse trails, across dirt roads and jeep tracks, and through creek beds. Her heart in her throat, Lacey held on and prayed.

It seemed like hours before they rode up over a rise and found an old cabin nestled in a draw at the edge of a small winding creek. There was even a stand of a few scraggly trees, bent low from the winds. A barbed wire fence barred their path to the cabin.

Hung on the wire gate, as if a warning to strangers, was the carcass of a long-dead animal, the size of a large dog. The long, narrow skull was smooth, bare bone, with jaws full of gleaming white teeth and an impressive set of canines. Stripped vertebrae protruded like white piano keys from the shreds of fur and skin that still clung to the body. One paw was raised as if to ask a last question.

Lacey pulled Buttercup up short and stared. "Ewww! What on earth is that?"

"Coyote." Tucker dismounted and swung the gate open. A dead coyote was mere landscape to him. "Pretty, huh?"

"And why is a skeletal coyote hanging on the fence?"

"It's a caution to other coyotes to stay away."

"Does it work?"

He shrugged. "You see any other coyotes?" Lacey wasn't sure whether he was joking. Buttercup sniffed delicately and edged, her tail swishing, past the dead coyote and its empty eye sockets. Lacey shuddered. This sure as hell wasn't Washington, D.C. There, of course, the coyotes had a free rein, and they wore business suits.

As good-natured as Buttercup was, Lacey just wanted to get off her mount and feel the ground under her boots again. Tucker reached for Lacey as she slid off the horse on rubber legs and almost hit the ground, but he caught her and held her. Perhaps a moment too long.

"You look all done in, sunshine."

"Me? I'm fresh as a daisy." She yawned. "What are we doing here?"

"We're here for the night."

"What! The night? But we can't stay—I mean I thought—" *What about food? And the law? And Vic? I don't even want him to have* dinner *with his ex! I can't stay with Tucker. Overnight?!*

Tucker paid no attention to her. "We need to think. Make a plan. This is a good place." He led the horses to shelter among the trees, where they were hidden from view. Tucker tied up Buttercup and Ricochet and filled their feedbags from Ricochet's saddlebag.

"It looks deserted." She didn't know whether to be relieved or not.

"Most likely. No one uses this cabin this time of year. Not much," Tucker said. "But we can take cover here. Owner was a friend of mine. Died a few years ago. We can stay warm, figure out what to do next. Why don't you go on in and start a fire?"

"Start a fire?" She must have had a stupid look on her face.

Tucker fiddled with the cabin door and it opened. "Go on inside out of the wind and I'll finish taking care of the horses. I need to haul up some water from the creek for them."

She stood there, staring at him. "Who lives here?"

"Nobody."

"Great," she muttered, looking at the listing structure. "Now you're taking me to a haunted cabin. Where are we anyway?"

"Somewhere in Yampa County. You know it's a big crazy quilt. We've been crossing public land, part of it owned by the state, part of it Bureau of Land Management, right up to that fence with the coyote on it. At the moment, we're on no-man's-land. Move along, Chantilly."

"My name is Lacey." She stood stock-still. "And if you didn't notice, it's the middle of winter, it's freezing, it's the middle of nowhere!" Lacey was just warming up. "I'm starving, I've been on a horse half the day, I've been abducted, and you're an outlaw! What happened to *you*, Tucker?"

"Stuff happens." He shrugged again. "And, *Lacey*, sunshine, you used to be tougher."

"I am tough! I mean—you know what I mean. Meanie." She glared at him. She untied her tote bag, slung it over her shoulder, and stalked past him. Tucker picked up a few logs from a woodshed on the side of the cabin. She noticed there was an outhouse too, a dozen yards or so past the cabin. The thought of having to use a freezing old outhouse, or *any* kind of outhouse, made her groan.

He stacked the wood in her arms, topped the stack with some smaller twigs for kindling, and gave her a gentle push toward the door. "These ought to burn."

She stepped into a dark space with still air. A musty chill hung over the place. The owner may have been dead for a few years, but the cabin showed signs of other visitors. *How many people know about this cabin? And where the hell are we?*

The dwelling was in pretty good shape and the unbroken glass in all its windows was a sure sign, Vic had taught her, of recent habitation. A scarred wooden table and two chairs centered the main room, and a brown bachelor-plaid sofa anchored one wall. How on earth anyone had managed to get that hideous thing out here was a mystery to Lacey, but ugly plaid sofas never died.

A water-stained "Colorful Colorado" calendar, ten years
out of date, hung crookedly on the wall over the sofa.
The cabin was all of two rooms, the larger one a com-
bined living room, dining room, and kitchen. The second
room featured a large bed with a stained bare mattress
and a blanket, and a set of bunk beds. Tattered brown
insulated curtains hung on thin rods at the windows.

No one could live here, she thought.

Lacey dumped her armload of wood by the stove and
searched in vain for a light switch, realizing with a start
that there were none. There was no electricity at all. Not
that it would be turned on if there was. She found a couple of hurricane lamps and candles, and fresh-looking
matches from the Red Rose Bar in Sagebrush.

An impressive and ornate cast-iron woodstove fitted
into the fireplace box for both cooking and heat. It had
four flat burners with an oven below, set next to the wood
box, and a food warmer up above. On top of the stove sat
a teakettle, and there was a reservoir on the side for heating water. Lacey checked to make sure the flue was open
and prayed she wouldn't burn down the place. There was
no telling when this thing had last been cleaned, if it ever
had. *Who's the patron saint of woodstoves?* she wondered,
offering up a silent prayer to whoever might be listening.
Lacey also called on her long-ago, half-remembered Girl
Scout training to help her build a fire. She'd never scored
a merit badge in that particular skill.

A stack of musty newspapers, some dating back five
and six years, was stored in a tin wastebasket by the
woodstove. The papers were, of course, *The Sagebrush
Daily Press.* As she crumpled them into the firebox for
tinder, she couldn't resist reading a couple of headlines,
curious about the stories, and the reporters who wrote
them after she left town. Any stranger reading this newspaper would believe the high school football team was
the single most important activity in the state. Lacey put
the sports sections in the pile to burn, and set aside a few
front sections to read later. One headline caught her
eye: BARTENDER SHAKES THEM AND STIRS THEM.

Written five years earlier, the story was about one of

the victims, Ally Newport, who had been voted "Favorite Bartender" in some kind of readers' survey *The Daily Press* had concocted.

Good grief, Lacey thought. *Muldoon ought to have a sign on his desk: The Hucksterism Starts Here!*

She scanned the story for quotes and ignored Muldoon's blather.

"I love my customers," says Ally Newport, our readers' favorite bartender, behind the bar at the Little Snake Saloon. "I remember their favorite drinks. I listen to their hunting stories. I love my job!"

The story was a fluff piece, a picture of a professionally perky good-time gal. The photograph showed Ally standing in front of the Little Snake, wearing a white shirt, blue jeans, and a white apron wrapped around her waist. She had a wide smile and held a beer in her hand as if serving it up.

Lacey folded the page and tossed it in her tote bag so she wouldn't inadvertently pitch it into the fire. She lit a rolled-up page of high school football to warm the flue and made sure the draft was going up and out and not coming in. She stripped some of the bark off the logs to add to the kindling and stuffed crumpled paper in between the logs.

It was so not Lacey's thing, Girl Scout training notwithstanding. She lit a match to the crumpled newspaper, but the fire proved balky. She poked at it and added pine needles, pine cones, and more football and basketball games and swim team scores. Finally, the fire caught and started to crackle, the dry logs leaping into flame. She leaned back on her heels to admire her work.

"I see you got it going," Tucker said. She hadn't heard him come in behind her. He had an armload of firewood. "We'll be warm in no time." He dropped the wood and pulled a red bandana from his jeans and wiped a smudge from her nose. "You got a little bit of soot. Or maybe newsprint. There, I got it."

There was a pause. *If he were Vic . . . But he's not.*

"Thanks." Lacey pulled out a hand wipe from a little packet in her tote bag and wiped her hands clean. "You seem to know your way around this place."

"I do. I put some of the glass in myself. I used to visit old man Thompson up here. He's buried up on the hill. Place may not look like much, but he loved it. He wouldn't mind us taking shelter here."

"Good to know. But someone must own it."

"His granddaughter. Out of town. She paid the taxes, but I guess she hasn't found time to visit, or decide what she's going to do with it."

"Someone's been here," Lacey said. "The matches look new."

"Kit and I've been around some to make sure it didn't fall down," Tucker said, inspecting the stove. "And there are the horny teenagers with no place else to go. Caught a few of them last summer. Ran 'em off, but I knew they'd be back."

"The cabin doesn't look vandalized. Nothing's wrecked." Lacey looked at a broken chair. "Not very wrecked anyway." She trailed her finger through the dust on the table.

"Cheaper than Motel 6."

"It's filthy." Her nose tickled at the dust. "And you think it's turned into a no-tell motel?"

"Too risky for kids to go to a motel in Sagebrush. Somebody'd see your car, your parents would find out, and the backseat of the station wagon is a little cold this time of year. A cabin out of the way up here? Pretty romantic. Particularly if you're seventeen." Cole Tucker sounded suspiciously like the voice of experience.

"Not my idea of romance." Lacey sneezed. "I hope they bring fresh sheets and pillowcases."

"You are such a girly girl, Chantilly Lace." Tucker laughed. "My guess is they bring in sleeping bags. Maybe a blanket. And lots of beer. You got to admit, it's cozy."

"I can still see my breath." Her limbs were stiff from the saddle and her clothes smelled like Buttercup. She stretched her legs. "I need to wash." She turned on the tap in the sink. Nothing.

"Oh, yeah. Meant to tell you. Used to be well water. But it's hard work to keep up a well," Tucker said. "I'll get some more water for us from the creek." He picked up a large bucket by the stove and inspected it for holes.

"Great. Just great. I need to use the outhouse too."

"Let me check it first," Tucker said.

"Check for what? It's not like I'm going anywhere else."

"Varmints," he said. "Badgers, skunks, bears. That kind of thing."

"Bears in the outhouse? Is there a Motel 6 handy?" He laughed and opened the door for her, and she reluctantly trudged outside. "I hope they find us soon."

Tucker gallantly made sure the outhouse was clear of bears. While she acquainted herself with the primitive facilities, he collected water from the creek for washing and drinking.

"I rinsed out the bucket." She gave Tucker The Look. "Why, Chantilly, this is Rocky Mountain springwater." He poured it into the reservoir on the side of the stove and went for another bucketful.

"We'll have to boil it," she said when he came back, eyeing the old teakettle on the stove. She blew the dust out of it. "What if there's a dead coyote floating in your Rocky Mountain spring?"

Tucker shook his head. "I hate to say this, Chantilly, darling, but I don't think you'll be winning any Frontierswoman of the Year Award."

Lacey Smithsonian was beginning to hate Cole Younger Tucker. The gray sky darkened ominously. It was later than she thought. She'd had fond hopes of their being found by now. And laughing about all this with Vic, over martinis and a steak. *Where the hell are the police? Where is Vic? Where am I?*

"Where are we? And how old is this place?"

"Edge of the Sand Wash. This place was built in the Twenties or Thirties. Lot of homesteading going on back then. You'll feel better after we eat. I promise."

Inside a yellow-painted cupboard over the sink were several old cans of chili, soups, and stew. Lipton's tea bags filled a Mason jar, and a rusty can opener hung on a nail on the wall. A few chipped dishes and a beat-up old frying pan were left on an open shelf, an empty coffee can held some forks, knives, and spoons, and a vintage coffeepot rested on one of the burners. Unfortunately, there seemed to be no coffee. Or soap. Or running water. She wiped out the pans with another moist towelette.

Tucker dusted the dirt off the canned goods with a finger. "We won't starve."

"We don't know how old those cans are."

"They won't go bad as long as they're sealed."

"Says you." Lacey resisted the idea of eating anything out of those cans, but her stomach growled, betraying her.

"Why don't we eat the bagels and decide later on the stew or the chili." Tucker produced from his saddlebag the last bakery sack from Tasso Petrus's Jeep. "We got poppy, sesame, and a couple of plain. Hard as rocks, but we can fix that. And look what I got!"

He tossed her a big tub of cream cheese and Lacey yelped with relief. They each picked a bagel and Tucker put the remaining two away for later. He split them with one of the dull knives and toasted them in the frying pan. He slathered them with cream cheese and handed her one.

"You spoil me, Cole."

"Eat your bagel, smart-ass."

The sesame seed bagel and hot tea from boiled springwater tasted better than it had any right to. As Tucker predicted, Lacey started to feel better and less like snarling at him. The lovely carbohydrates were calming her down, but chocolate would be better, she thought. She promised to have something sinfully chocolate when she made it back to civilization. If she made it back.

The room was getting warm enough for her to take off her coat. She hung it on the back of the chair, but kept her scarf and the bolero jacket. She began the process of unkinking and stretching her limbs. Tucker eyed her, as if he wanted to offer her a back rub but didn't quite dare. She handed him a fragrant moist towelette from her tote bag.

"You are a wonder, Chantilly Lace. Is that satchel of yours bottomless? You got any top sirloin in there?" He chuckled and cleaned his face and hands with the towelette. "I almost feel civilized."

She checked her small mirror and shuddered. Her cheeks were chapped and so were her lips. Her makeup had caked. Dark circles had moved in under her eyes. Her hair was a fright. "I look terrible," she mumbled.

"No. Beautiful. Best thing I've seen in years."

She shot a dirty look his way and squeezed some cold hand lotion into her hands to smooth her wind-burned face. She combed the tangles out of her hair and felt slightly better. At least, better under the circumstances: on the run with Cole Tucker, her former boyfriend and current least-favorite fugitive from justice. She put a dab of makeup on her chapped nose and almost felt human again.

"That's not necessary, you know," Tucker said. "You look great without that stuff."

"I'm doing this for me. Not you. And I bet you'd like to see my skin if I wasn't using sunscreen and lotion in this climate. I'd look like an old saddlebag."

"Why don't you sit on the sofa, Chantilly. It's way more comfortable than the chair."

She cast a glance toward the plaid eyesore of a sofa. "I don't know what kind of wildlife might be living in it."

"Bugs? Gets too cold up here for that kind of wildlife. Unless you mean raccoons. It's just a little dirty. Don't be afraid." Tucker smacked the arm and a cloud of dust rose for emphasis. He sat down. More dust rose around him like a halo. "See, it's fine. Cozy."

"That's okay." Lacey didn't want to get too close to him.

"Suit yourself."

Why haven't they found us yet? By now, her mother and sister would know about the incident at the courthouse. They would be springing into—into what? Some kind of action. Some inappropriate and mortally embarrassing kind of action. At the moment, Lacey didn't know what she was more afraid of: Vic's reaction, or her mother's.

Then there would be the media. Camera crews had been staking out the entire courthouse. Did they get footage of their escape, with Lacey slung over Tucker's shoulder, like a caveman abducting his prehistoric bride? Surely she and Tucker would be filling the local news at six and ten p.m. Lacey almost cried.

She knew if she'd been handed a juicy story like this when she was writing for *The Sagebrush Daily Press*, she'd have sunk her teeth into it and never let go. But now this story had sunk its teeth into her. And those teeth felt a little different from this angle.

chapter 14

"What are you doing?" Tucker asked.

"What do you think I'm doing?"

She pawed through her bag for her notebook and pen. After years of being a reporter, Lacey always thought more clearly when she could jot down notes, even if she never looked at them again. The act of putting words on paper helped sort things out in her head. It was getting dark outside, but the soft light from the stove and the candle lanterns kept the gloom at bay in the cabin. She could see just enough to write.

"Writing a searing exposé? The private life of the notorious outlaw, Cole Younger Tucker?"

"Yeah, right. I'm jotting down notes on who you think might have set you up."

"Oh." He settled deeper into the dusty plaid sofa. "But what about my exposé?"

"I still have to write an article for my paper." What was it supposed to be about? Justice in the West? Cowboy hats? THE LIFE AND TIMES OF COLE YOUNGER TUCKER? It all felt so far away from her now. She put her head in her hands.

"What's the matter, Chantilly Lace?"

"This is another story where I wind up looking like a fool." *What kind of reporter gets herself kidnapped by her ex-boyfriend, the murder suspect?* No reporter Lacey Smithsonian knew. Except her.

"Chantilly, if anyone looks like a fool, I do. How do you get yourself arrested for murder when you didn't do anything? It's the height of ridiculousness. I'm the idiot here. You're just a—a victim of circumstances."

"Yeah, circumstances. Like you carrying me out of that courthouse thrown over your shoulder like—like an old carpet."

"Seemed like a good idea at the time." Tucker looked exhausted.

"I suppose that's a quote. Maybe I can finesse it later for my editor." Tucker groaned. Lacey sat up and ran her hands through her hair. "Back to business. When Rae Fowler went missing, Vic was still top cop here. It was one of his unsolved cases. It still bothers him. One of the key suspects was a man named Yancey."

"Zeke Yancey. He's part of the furniture at the Little Snake Saloon. Other bars too, I hear."

"I didn't think you ever hung out at the Snake."

"Everybody's been to the Snake once or twice. Even you've been to the Snake, Chantilly."

"Long time ago. I was on some kind of story. All of a sudden, chairs started flying around the room and a couple of guys were duking it out." Lacey fiddled with her pen. "Anyway, Vic said Yancey was at the top of his short suspect list. But there was no evidence, no arrests, and Vic had left town by the time Ally and Corazon disappeared. So Zeke Yancey fell off the radar. What do you think of him?"

"Bad news. Never had much to do with Yancey. He always had a reputation as a bully. Loser with women. I can see him pushing around a small woman. But I can't see *these* women getting within fifty yards of him. Out of his league."

"What if he didn't know that? You didn't know he was a suspect?"

"Working on the ranch doesn't leave a lot of time to peruse *The Sagebrush Daily Mess*. Since you left Sagebrush, I don't consider it a daily necessity. And I don't listen to gossip unless it's about the price of cattle." Tucker paused for a moment. "Honestly, Chantilly, I can't get the ranch out of my mind, how those girls' things showed up there. I don't think Zeke's after the Tuckered Out Ranch."

"And the two things go together?"

"I think they have to," Tucker said.

They were back to the land issue. She sipped some tea. She wondered if the tea bags still had any caffeine left in them, and she wished it was something more energizing, like black coffee.

Someone had gone to a lot of trouble to set up Cole Tucker. Someone who had possession of the victims' personal effects. *A killer, or just a thief?* Who had reached out to Grady Rush? Why the "dope-uty," not the sheriff or the chief of police? Was it really an anonymous call and Deputy Rush just happened to answer the phone? Or did he, or she, decide the deputy would be their dupe? Why wasn't there any record of the call? Was Sheriff Rexford in on the frame?

"What do you think of Grady Rush?" she asked.

Tucker raised his face to her. "Good old Grady. Not quite as dumb as a stump. But close."

"Do you think he set you up?"

"Maybe without knowing it? Of course, maybe I'm underestimating him."

"Do you think he could have killed those women?"

"Physically, sure. They were little, all of them. You saw how big he is." Tucker placed his hands on the table.

Lacey searched her bag for Advil. It was the only thing she'd forgotten. "Tell me about the people who want the Tuckered Out Ranch."

"Dodd Muldoon's one of them. His offers always come through the Avery brothers. Biggest real estate agents in town."

"Muldoon?" Muldoon's name kept popping into the discussion. First Vic and now Tucker. She didn't like it. "Muldoon has no interest in ranching."

"That's what I thought. But he's got connections. He knows things, and he made an offer."

Lacey knew Muldoon had bought and sold property around Sagebrush for years. But he was more of a slum-lord than a gentleman rancher. He had flipped his share of shabby houses in the heyday of local real estate, when Sagebrush was booming and there wasn't enough housing for all the energy and mine workers flooding the town. Muldoon had even tried to get Lacey to rent one of his slum properties, which came without appliances.

"How recently?"

"'Bout a year, year and a half ago."

What did Muldoon know about energy development? Did he know the victims' property was buried at Tuckered Out Ranch?

"That doesn't make sense, unless he had some inside information, a way to turn a quick buck," Lacey said.

"Maybe he did. And since then, Virgil Avery's made other offers, including his own, for the ranch. And he's no rancher, even if he does wear a cowboy hat."

"Avery? Why do I know that name?" An image of little green and white real estate signs featuring a covered wagon popped into her head.

"They're from Sagebrush," Tucker said. "Virgil and Homer Avery. Virgil's the front man, the smart one. Homer is his brother. He's a strange one. Makes people uncomfortable."

"Uncomfortable how?"

"He's real big, about six-four, weighs two-fifty or more. Doesn't know his own strength." Tucker drained his tea and added some more hot water to the cracked cup. "I don't know whether you'd call Homer slow or special or mentally differently-abled or what, now that you can't say *retarded* anymore. But then, Homer was never stupid, just very odd. Growing up, he'd just sit and rock back and forth in class. That's what Belle always said. She was in the same class."

"Autistic?"

"Something like it."

"So he was picked on." Lacey added the last of the hot water to her own tea.

"Yes, he was." Tucker smiled at some memory. "Until one day Dustin Green, class bully, did something or said something and Homer just hauled off, one fist flying, then the other, awkward as all get-out, and he just flattened the little bully. Knocked him out cold. Homer didn't even look back. He kept on walking home. Nobody ever bothered Homer Avery again, that I know of."

Lacey could picture the scene. The large awkward kid people tormented finally had enough. "Was he punished for it?"

"Nope. Dustin had it coming. Jackass. Got killed in a bar fight when he was eighteen."

"What happened to Homer?"

"I hear he does all the bookkeeping and accounting for his brother. He always was good with numbers. Not so much with people though. And he makes these mobiles, things hanging from antlers? Strange-looking stuff. Sells them in town at the crafts shop."

"And Virgil Avery?"

"The capable brother. Older. Always trying to make a buck, mostly in real estate. Thinks he's slick with the ladies."

"Sounds a lot like Muldoon." Lacey stretched out her legs. She was beginning to feel drowsy. It must have been the bagels and all those carbs and the fire finally warming the place. "Is Virgil married?"

"Nope. Came close once, I think. Don't know what happened."

"Two bachelor brothers," Lacey mused. "What would they want with the Tuckered Out?"

"My guess is they're after the mineral rights. And the water rights. They don't care about the land on top."

"And once they've got their hands on these rights?"

"Sell them to Mitchell Stanford, for one. Oil and gas man for some of the energy companies. Stanford's been haunting the Clerk and Recorder's Office in Sagebrush for months, looking for mineral owners. One particular geologic formation runs right through Yampa County, just brimming with natural gas. The Tuckered Out Ranch sits on part of it."

"There's always been drilling in Yampa County."

"Sure, but they couldn't reach much of the oil or gas

before. Now they've got some kind of new technology and drilling methods where they can reach it. They drill sideways, fracture the rock, all kinds of new stuff. Finally this whole Niobrara Formation is drillable. And Stanford is buying up mineral rights like a drunken sailor on shore leave. He's leasing hundreds of thousand of acres. But not my land. My great-grandfather homesteaded our land."

Lacey knew that. For reasons unknown, Tucker's great-grandfather thought this remote, godforsaken corner of the state was a good place to homestead. And for the same unknown reasons, Tuckers ever since felt their land was some kind of sacred trust. It was in their blood.

But why hadn't Old Man Tucker gone for something more scenic? Lacey had seen the tiny dugout house Great-grandpa Tucker had carved into the side of a hill overlooking the Yampa River, where he and his wife had raised six children. The family was pretty proud of that collection of logs and stones, impossibly small for a home with all those kids.

"Your great-grandfather was probably an outlaw too, you know that, Cole."

"Not so you could prove it." Tucker grinned at her take on his family history. "He liked running his cattle and his horses, and catching the wild ones up here in the Sand Wash. He wasn't thinking oil rigs and natural gas pipelines."

"You could still ranch the land, couldn't you?" Lacey knew that's what other people were doing. "Keep the surface and water rights?"

"That's what Stanford says, but you sell the water rights and you end up with no water. You sell the mineral rights and the drilling screws up the land. Companies say it's safe, but there's evidence the drilling contaminates the water. Then the fracking makes it worse."

"Another fine mess."

"Besides, I always thought if you owned land, you ought to own it all the way up and down. Right down to the center of the Earth. Right up to Heaven."

"Where does the rest of the family stand?"

"They're with me. For now. But they'd do anything to save my hide from a phony murder rap."

Lacey's notes were a mess. She was too tired to think straight or write legibly. "Tell me about the oil and gas man."

"Mitch Stanford came to us directly. Without the Averys. Offered us the same deal. We gave him the same answer. No lease, no sale, no way, José."

Lacey leaned back in her hard-bottomed chair. The sofa was looking more inviting.

"But Tucker, what does any of this have to do with the murder of three women?" She tried to clear her head. She swallowed the last of her lukewarm tea. "If any of these guys set you up, then *they* would have to have Corazon's things. One of them would have to be the killer, or know who the killer is, or make a deal with the killer. What are the odds against that? Or maybe—"

"What?" Tucker leaned forward.

"Who's to say they didn't somehow steal Corazon's things, and manage to get their hands on the other women's property? Maybe these guys have nothing to do with the murders. They're just taking advantage of them to put you in a bind. And in jail."

"That sounds just as far-fetched as anything else, Chantilly. All I know is the Averys have been after my land, Muldoon's been after my land, and Stanford wants it any way he can have it, leasing or buying. If those guys want it, other people want it too. And Grady Rush is a tool."

"Did any of these guys know the victims?"

He shrugged. "Probably. You know how it is in a small town. Your old boss was seeing Ally for a while."

"Muldoon? He's married! And ugly!" Lacey sat up straight, her eyes open wide.

"I think he finally got a divorce. And when did ugly ever stop him?"

True, Lacey thought. Muldoon and morals performed a complicated dance. Dodd was acquainted with the concept, but he rarely let that stop him if he was after a goal, whether monetary or otherwise pleasurable. He thought having affairs made him a big man. He always liked to hit on younger women, occasionally even his own reporters. But how much was talk and how much was action? Lacey was never sure.

"He really dated Ally Newport? Miss Sagebrush's Favorite Bartender?"

"I'm just saying he knew Ally. Biblical sense and all that."

"And he tried to get your land."

"You gotta keep taking notes, sunshine." Tucker yawned. "He's just one on the list."

After her years of hard labor at *The Sagebrush Daily Press*, Lacey was willing to believe just about anything bad about Muldoon. Starvation wages, seventy-hour workweeks, no benefits, no respect, and one measly week of vacation a year added up to very little sympathy for the man. Muldoon's only saving grace was that he loved his newspaper and loved being a newspaperman, even if he treated the newsroom like his personal fiefdom.

"I always thought he'd rather assassinate people in print than in person." Her head was whirling. "Still, we have to consider everything."

"Everything?" He leaned in to her. "Does that include us?"

"Everything about the murders. Not us." She looked away. "And we've been over for a long time."

It was time for Tucker to stand and stretch. "That was almost a nice moment. But okay, Chantilly Lace, what else is on your mind?" Tucker put another log on the fire in the woodstove and stirred up the flames.

"There's another possibility, Cole. What if the murderer is what they call a highway killer? He comes to town, stalks, abducts, and kills a woman, and leaves. No connection to any of them. There are three murders, so maybe it's someone with a schedule of visits to Sagebrush or the area. Like a sales rep or a delivery driver. This guy's not on anybody's suspect list because he's not local, he's just a predator with a regular route. There might be other disappearances or murders like these in other towns and no one has connected the dots yet. Maybe he dropped his cache of trophies somewhere, and someone else found them and figured out it belonged to the victims. Now that someone else is using the victim's property to frame *you*."

"You have a very dark turn of mind, Lacey Smithsonian. Is this what happens when a reporter covers the seamy world of fashion?"

She ignored the crack. "You already pointed out that in a county this big, there are places to lie low. We're lying low in one of them right now. Maybe this predator has hideouts somewhere. Like this place. I hate to think those women died in such a lonely place. Barefoot. With nothing but the ghosts of Butch Cassidy and the Sundance Kid haunting the hills."

Lacey stopped talking. She was in just such a lonely place herself. Off the beaten path, whereabouts unknown, in the company of a murder suspect. She was grateful to be indoors and warm, but in the quiet of the flickering firelight, there was something chilling about this remote cabin, a hermit's lonely home on the range. Some bad vibration in the walls, a melancholy in the air. Or perhaps it was all those illicit teenage trysts. Her imagination was slipping into overdrive.

Taking the hurricane lamp, she surveyed the cabin's tiny bedroom. A thin blanket covered a stained and sagging mattress on the old bed. The bunks had no mattresses, just rusty springs. She lifted the lamp to the walls. Old-fashioned wallpaper, torn and faded, green with pink roses: a forlorn stab at homespun comfort. Without a homeowner to give it life, the little cabin was a sad place indeed.

"There's a bed," Tucker said, behind her. "Why don't you take it? I'll take the couch. I won't bother you, Scout's honor. Unless you say so."

"That bed gives me the creeps. You can have it."

"Lie down, Lacey. You look about ready to fall off your horse."

She eased herself down gingerly on the hideous plaid sofa, too tired to say another word. No exotic animal life emerged from the cushions. With her last crumbs of energy, she made a pillow of her shawl.

"Just for a minute." She closed her eyes and she was out like a light.

chapter 15

When she awoke, Lacey's head felt heavy and her limbs were stiff.

She hoped for a moment it was all a bad dream, Tucker's great escape from the courthouse and their subsequent flight from the law, but no luck. It all came back to her in a rush. She was lying on the sofa with her coat tossed over her and a threadbare blanket over her legs. She sneezed.

"You're up," Tucker said.

"No, I'm not." She yawned and sniffed the air. She raised herself on one arm. "Something smells good. How long did I sleep?"

"Couple of hours. I'm heating up that can of stew. Tastes okay to me, but you don't have to eat it if you're afraid of being poisoned. Me, I'm an outlaw, can't poison me."

"I take back what I said." A doughnut and a bagel a day weren't enough to keep Lacey's hunger away. "Prehistoric canned stew, yum. Probably woolly mammoth stew. Let me know when it's ready." She let her head fall back.

"Are you gonna go back to sleep again?"

"No. I'm wide-awake. I'm just resting my eyes." She shifted her position, adjusted the coat, and wiggled her toes. Tucker had taken her boots off. Lacey opened her eyes and saw them on the floor.

How on earth could I sack out? Some part of her must have trusted Tucker or she never would have been able to fall asleep.

She was still out in the middle of nowhere where they would be hunted down. And somewhere out there was a killer who believed the heat was off him. She was still angry and frightened, but there was a measure of trust growing in her heart. She hoped she wasn't wrong. At the moment, however, her instincts were the last thing she'd trust.

Lacey gazed at Tucker's back. He was busy at the stove, stirring the stew. He wasn't Vic Donovan. And in spite of the incident at the courthouse, he wasn't a monster either. Lacey felt a pang somewhere in the region of her heart and told it to go away.

It's just hunger, Lacey. Nice predicament, Smithsonian. At the moment she couldn't remember a worse one, and she didn't try. Her limbs felt like lead. She told herself she'd get up in a minute. Really she would. Still lying down, she put an arm out for her boots. They were just out of reach. Her eyes were adjusting to the dim lantern light.

"What time is it?"

"About eight. It snowed some. Sky's clearing up. It's real pretty. You can see the stars."

Lacey was almost upside down, one boot nearly in her grasp, when something caught her eye under the sofa, toward the back. Firelight glinted off it. Lacey rolled onto the floor and stretched one arm under the sofa, but she couldn't reach it.

"What on earth are you doing?" Tucker removed the pan from the stove.

"Something's under the sofa."

"Probably a mouse."

"Yuck!" She pulled back her arm and sat cross-legged on the floor, peering into the darkness beneath the sofa.

"You face down killers and you're afraid of a mouse?" He looked bemused.

"Well, I'm just not fond of disease-carrying four-legged vermin."

With Lacey still crouched on the floor, Tucker pushed the sofa away from the wall and lifted the flickering hurricane lamp over the gap. The cabin had settled over the years, leaving the floor uneven. Something was wedged between the wall and a floorboard. Tucker crouched down and extracted the thing that had caught Lacey's eye. It gleamed in his hands.

"What is it?" Lacey asked. "Let me see."

"Looks like a heel. Heel of a boot, maybe."

"Please. Give it." She put out her hand.

He tossed it to her. She caught the thing and turned it over. A bootheel. She compared it to her own. It was almost the same size, about two inches tall. A thin strip of slightly tarnished filigreed silver wrapped around the outside of it. The bottom of the heel was badly scuffed and part of the silver filigree was dented.

"This is from a woman's boot." Lacey turned it over and over.

Tucker shrugged. "Could be from a small man's boot. Or a big kid's."

"With silver decoration? Pretty fancy for a kid." Lacey held it up to the light of the lamp.

"You see some fancy boots at the stock show. Rodeos too."

"If this is any indication of the rest of the boot, it must have cost a lot."

"No argument there. You ready for some woolly mammoth stew?" He indicated the table, but she stayed put, staring at the heel.

"Does this look like the kind of thing your old friend what's-his-name would have worn?"

"Thompson? Hell no, he was a big guy, and a simpler man you've never met."

"It's a woman's heel anyway." Lacey was convinced. "Was a woman living here?"

"No. Thompson was near eighty years old and damn near a hermit. Hadn't anything to do with women in forty years or so, I'd guess. His wife died, his daughter left. He just had this one granddaughter back in Grand Island, Nebraska. She never visited." He paused. "Hey, if that thing was really old, the silver would be tarnished black."

Lacey turned the heel so the silver glinted in the lamplight. "When a heel comes off, especially one this expensive, you'd take it to a boot maker. There's one in Steamboat."

"Or else it rolls under the sofa and gets lost," Tucker said. "You getting at something? Is this where the magic happens? That fashion clue thing you do?"

"Sarcasm will get you nowhere, Cole." She made a face at him. "For argument's sake, this is a lady's bootheel that belongs to a pretty fancy pair of cowboy boots." The cowboy boots decorated with silver rosettes that she saw at Crybaby Ranch flashed in her mind. *What is it doing way out here?*

"I've seen some fancy ones," Tucker said. "Silver-tipped toes, silver heels, with Mexican coins stitched in them, but you don't see much of that around on a ranch."

"These are custom designed, Cole. You wouldn't be able to replace them off the shelf. If you lose that heel, you're going to look for it, long and hard." Lacey wondered if this heel could be traced.

"We can agree this one got lost. Now let's agree on that stew. I'm hungry."

"How did the heel come off? Perhaps in a struggle? Or was it dragged along the floor?"

"Or pulled along the ground by a bull," Tucker suggested.

"And if it belongs to a dead woman?" Lacey stared at him and held out the heel.

"I wouldn't know about that."

"You said Corazon had a pair of fancy boots."

He took the heel from her. "I don't know whose this is, but it didn't belong to Corazon. Her boots were pretty nice, but there was no silver. I would have remembered that."

A piercing howl from outside the cabin startled them. It seemed to go all the way down Lacey's spine. She jumped off the sofa. "What was that?"

"Coyote call. Moon's out." Tucker grinned at her. "They don't just howl at the moon. They howl because they feel like it. Or they got something to say."

"That's a pretty hair-raising sound." Her heart was beating fast. Tucker laughed.

"Only to you! Probably just an old coyote looking for his mate."

The coyote howled again. More chills tickled the back of Lacey's neck. She breathed deeply and went to the window, pulling the ancient curtains aside. She couldn't see anything but her reflection in the black glass. She turned back to Tucker.

"Maybe the heel isn't Corazon's. But what about the other women? Ally and Rae?"

"That's a mighty big stretch, Chantilly Lace. They weren't found anywhere near here. We're hell and gone on the other side of the county." He scratched his head. "So this is what you'd call a fashion clue?"

"Maybe." Lacey sat down at the table and Tucker set the heel down in front of her. She fished out her camera and started taking photos of the heel from every angle. She even took off one of her boots to compare it with the silver and black heel, and snapped some more pictures, using her own boot for scale.

"I'm going to see about the stew."

"Think about it, Cole. This cabin is out in the wild. Far from the road. The owner's been dead for a couple years and teenagers are using it for a party palace, if what you say is true. Rae Fowler was a teenager when she disappeared. A girl like Rae could have been brought here against her will." Lacey glared at him. "Like you brought me."

Tucker dropped his head. "Chantilly Lace, I'm real sorry about today at the courthouse. But what can a man do when he's trapped? I'm a cowboy, not a killer. I saw daylight and I cowboyed it, without considering your feelings. I regret it, but there's no one I'd rather have along for the ride."

She ignored his remorse. "All the victims were found barefoot. Someone took their shoes. Or their cowboy boots. And we've got a bootheel."

Tucker retrieved the pan of hot stew from the stove and set it down in the middle of the table. He tossed Lacey a fork. "We'll share. And we'll save the last two bagels for the morning. Good by you?"

"Good by me." She poised the fork in the air, sniffed the stew and decided it was edible. She took a bite. Beef, not mammoth. It was remarkably tasty, but then she was remarkably hungry. "Do you think one of them was killed here?"

"Damned if I know. I never thought about it until you started waving that silver heel around. But this cabin is kind of a high traffic place, for being so out of the way. What with kids coming up here and all. Please, eat up while it's hot."

"Why aren't they here tonight, then?" Lacey was in a mood to argue.

"Monday's a school night. I figure the partiers come on the weekends. If they see it's already occupied, they'll move on to some other lover's lane. And they won't alert the sheriff either."

"So you don't think those women were killed here."

"Beats me. If that heel belongs to one of them, it sure changes things. But there are other places, old cow camps, line camps, that would be a better place to hide what you're doing."

"Line camp? Explain, please."

"Cowboys used to bunk overnight at line camps when they were running cows on the trail, herding them out to different pastures for grazing. Most haven't been used in years. Not since we started using trucks and Jeeps and ATVs to get to the herd. Hardly anybody overnights it out on the range anymore. Sheepherders maybe. But a couple of old camps have been kept up. Some are not too far from here, but nestled by the rocks and hard to spot unless you know where they are. If you're right, Chantilly Lace, there are a few places around here those girls could have been taken."

During her reporting days in Sagebrush, Lacey had seen plenty of abandoned cabins out in the county. There was even one that she remembered the cops and sheriff's department used for training. The walls were so riddled with bullet holes it looked like a feast for giant termites. It made the shot-up highway signs look like the work of amateurs.

Dear God, if they come here, I hope they don't shoot first and ask questions later.

"And there are other places that are even more remote," Tucker said.

"And you know about them because—?" Lacey asked.

"I run a ranch, remember? Takes a lot of landscape to feed a single head of cattle in the West. We graze our herds all across this county, on our own land, on land that we have cooperative grazing deals with, on state land, on BLM land. I've seen a lot of this county from horseback, from truck windshields, from the air. Not many corners of it I haven't set foot on."

"And the Averys would know these places too, because they're in real estate dealings?"

"Virgil would. He gets around. Homer, the other one, he sticks closer to the office."

"You said Mitch Stanford's been haunting the county clerk and recorder's office in search of mineral leases?"

"Him and a bunch of other people. Anybody in the energy business up here would have come across places like this. Hunters too."

"But why wouldn't a killer just use his own place, where he's less likely to be caught?"

"Why foul your own nest with something as ugly and messy as murder?" Tucker said. "Maybe the killer figures it's better to have no direct ties to a killing place." He took a thoughtful bite of stew. "Whew, you fashion reporters sure can make a fella glimpse the dark side of human nature."

A new sound shattered the quiet of the cabin. This time it wasn't an animal. Lacey jumped and Tucker put a finger across his lips to silence her.

chapter 16

"It's a car," she whispered.

"No, it's a snowmobile." The noise came closer to the cabin. "Shhh."

Was it Vic? Or the sheriff? Or someone more dangerous? Lacey didn't know if help or danger was near, but her heart beat wildly. She was anxious to leave the cold little cabin and her fear behind. She pushed the chair back and stood.

"Careful, Chantilly. Might be some trigger-happy fool," Tucker said, echoing her thoughts. "Might not care if he hit a hostage. Not that you're a hostage, you're more like a dinner date, but, well, you know. They don't know that."

Lacey retreated into the shadows. She wasn't interested in being collateral damage. Tucker darted in front of her, gamely putting himself in front of any stray bullet. Someone cut the engine of the snowmobile. There were footsteps outside the cabin, then a whistle, like a birdcall. The call was repeated twice.

The tension left Tucker's shoulders. He whistled back and went to the door. He opened it slowly and peeked out. Lacey held her breath.

"It's Kit," he said over his shoulder.

"Your brother? But how—"

Tucker opened the door. "Hey, Kit! Come on in."

Kit stomped the snow and mud off his boots on the stoop outside before entering. Instead of his usual cowboy hat, he wore a fleece stocking cap. He pulled it off, leaving his hair sticking up around his head. He gave Lacey one dark look, then focused on his brother.

"What in purple hell do you think you're doing, Cole?"

"How did you know I'd be here?" Tucker asked.

"Wild guess. After you borrowed my pickup and left it out on the range and took the horses? Wasn't hard to figure where you were heading." Kit walloped Tucker in the arm, and Tucker smacked him back in a show of brotherly bonding. "And you had to bring her?" He pointed to Lacey. "Aren't you in enough trouble without grabbing your old girlfriend? Unless it was her idea."

"My idea?" Lacey inhaled sharply. "Are you crazy?"

"If I am, I'm not the only one," Kit snapped back. "I'd reckon there are three crazy people here."

"Give her a break, Kit. It's not Lacey's fault. It might not have been too smart of me, but done is done. Won't be the first stupid thing I've done, or the last. Now, you hear anything in town?"

"I had the pleasure of a chat with Sheriff T-Rex. Luckily, it was after I found my pickup. He seems to think you're still in Petrus's old Jeep that you stole."

"Borrowed. He doesn't think you helped me, does he?"

"Couldn't rightly tell," Kit said. "But I can tell you this. Our tyrannosaurus sheriff is in a rattlesnake-spitting rage."

"He'll get over it. Anything else?"

"T-Rex didn't believe a word I said." Kit stomped his feet to knock more snow off his boots. "Cole, what are you doing out here with her? Aren't things bad enough?"

"We're just talking over old times." Tucker took a seat. "Lacey came all the way from D.C. to see me."

"To write some trash about you. She's with Vic Donovan now, she tell you that? He's looking for her and the sheriff's looking for both of you, and the state patrol and the CBI and the posse and the whole damn county. I'd say you're in worse trouble today than you were yesterday, and that's going some. Why don't you let me take her with me? Get her off your back, so you can travel lighter."

Lacey stood up. She was ready, even if she had to go with Kit, who still seemed to be holding a grudge against her. *Why, because I didn't marry his brother? Or because his brother ever wanted to marry me?*

"Can't do it, Kit. You have to go back alone," Tucker said. "If you take Lacey, you're going to look like my accomplice and they'll throw you in jail too. And you can't tell Belle Starr where you found us. I don't want her to get some wild hare and come out here looking to help me. You two have a ranch to run."

"Maybe you should have thought about that before you skipped out of the courthouse. I know you couldn't kill those women, Cole. But running away makes you look pretty damn guilty after all."

"I wasn't going to get bail. I was going to sit in jail for months while they dragged their heels on a trial. The trial would take weeks and weeks and then they were going to railroad me into prison on the first train to Supermax. I'd never see daylight again. So I reshuffled the deck a little, gave myself a fresh hand, see if the cards might get a little better. Luck of the draw, little brother. Do they have any idea where we are?"

"They think you've gone to Brown's Park, far as I can tell."

Tucker laughed. "That's where outlaws go, ain't it?"

"What did you say?" Lacey asked.

"I agreed." Kit grinned and ran his hands through his hair to smooth it down. "Said maybe it was Brown's Park. Good place to hide out, just ask Butch and Sundance. I added that you have friends way out in the backcountry in Utah, Wyoming too, and I mentioned he'd never find you if you made it down into the Canyonlands area. It's all true. I didn't tell T-Rex any lies. I just opened his mind a little. Hopefully in the wrong direction."

"Good thinking," Tucker said.

Kit turned his back to warm his hands by the fire. He put his gloves on the stove top, along with the hat. He loosened his jacket. "T-Rex and his deputies alerted the other ranchers, asked for their help. It's posse time."

"Posse time?" Lacey asked.

"Everyone has horses, trucks, and guns," Tucker said. "Sheriff can call up the whole county in an emergency. Ranchers know their own land like nobody else, and everybody likes to help round up bad guys."

"Yeah, but they're all friends of ours." Kit finally smiled. It lit up his whole face and he looked like a younger Cole. "Old Truman told me he swore to old T-Rex he'd do anything he could to help catch you."

"Oh, Lord," Lacey said.

"Relax, Lacey. He was laughing when he said it. Everybody here knows Cole's no killer. The ranchers in Yampa County have known Cole and me and the rest of us all our lives. "

"We can't say the same for the feds," Tucker said. "Fish and Wildlife, BLM."

"What on earth does the Bureau of Land Management have to do with a county fugitive?" Lacey slumped in her chair.

"T-Rex and the CBI probably alerted the various agencies. God knows there's a slew of them," Cole explained. "They know the lay of their own land, the county roads, back roads, horse trails, ATV trails."

"But they're not authorized to hunt for you. They're not cops."

"They have their own law enforcement people. They work together when they feel like it. The agencies, they're sort of another unofficial posse. They'll be on the lookout for me. And they've got no love for cowboys."

"You have any idea how to get out of this ridiculous fix?" Kit asked.

"No, but Lacey might. We're discussing it. She's had some experience."

"Lacey?" Kit turned his gaze on her, clearly unimpressed. She didn't rise to the bait. "Whatever. You two better work fast."

"I'm going to send her back soon as I can. Maybe tomorrow," Tucker said. Lacey looked at him and cocked her head.

Kit pressed his lips together and nodded. "I've got to

get back tonight before I get another visit from T-Rex. Don't want him wondering where I've been."

"Okay, then," Tucker said. "You didn't bring a hamburger with you, did you?"

"No. But I have something else you might be able to use." Kit reached inside his jacket and pulled out a white envelope. "Five hundred. All I had in the kitty. I can get you more later, but I don't want to use the bank in town. T-Rex'll hear about it."

Aiding and abetting. What are brothers for?

Cole Tucker took the envelope and stuffed it in his jeans. "Thanks, Kit. I won't forget it."

"It's on your tab, Cole." Kit punched his big brother's shoulder again. He picked up his warmed hat and gloves and jingled his keys out of his pocket. He and Tucker shared an embrace, and a few private words Lacey couldn't hear. Then Kit was out the door, into the starry night.

After Tucker bolted the door against the cold, he and Lacey returned to the stew. They finished it in silence. It was probably wrong, but Lacey was glad that Tucker had a little money in his pockets. She was probably guilty of mentally aiding and abetting. It might be enough to give him a shot at escaping, perhaps enough to hide out in the backcountry until things cooled off. But not enough to even start getting at the truth.

Lacey was thinking about how distant from civilization she was. She also considered the dead women and how they died in such a far and lonely place. Perhaps like this one. She put down her fork and got up to stretch her legs.

"Cole, help me think this through. Rae and Ally and Corazon were found barefoot on country roads. Do you know what roads they were on? Was it the same road?"

"No, not the same road. Not that I recall."

Lacey picked up her bag. "Can you draw me a map? Give me an idea where they were found in relation to each other? And to these places you're thinking about?"

"You got some more paper?"

"I'm a reporter. They'd take my press pass away if I didn't have paper and a pen."

"What good is all this talk going to do, if I get caught?" Tucker lifted his head and looked at her.

"For one thing, when the cops don't believe you, you could hire a private investigator. Like Vic."

"Your new boyfriend."

"He's good at what he does. PIs have tools, expertise, and they have something the police often don't have."

"What's that?" Tucker stabbed unhappily at the stew.

"Time."

"T-Rex has got nothing but time to hang me out to dry. And I bet he's already got the CBI doing the heavy lifting on this thing."

Lacey had dealt with agents from the Colorado Bureau of Investigation on a few stories. Rural counties and municipalities routinely called on the CBI for investigative help and forensics services. They were no doubt working right now to find Tucker, and her.

"When they catch you—and Tucker, they *will* catch you—when they do, you've got to have some kind of theory for your defense. So I need to know where those places are—line camps, cabins, whatever—where Ally, Rae, and Corazon might have been murdered."

"Did you just jump to a big old conclusion, Lacey? What if they were all killed in different places?"

"Best guess, Tucker. You just told me you know every inch of this county."

He shook his head. "Okay. What kind of place are we looking for, Lacey?"

"Someplace like this." They looked around the candlelit cabin in silence for a moment. "Someplace where someone would feel safe taking an abducted woman. Where she couldn't easily escape. Where he wouldn't be disturbed, and maybe where the bodies could be dumped nearby afterward." She stopped for a moment. "But the bodies would be dumped far enough away so the cabin wouldn't come into the picture. I guess it depends on how far a killer wants to travel with a dead body in the car. Or on horseback."

"Nobody's going to do that on horseback."

Tucker put his fork down and took her pen and notebook. He drew a rough map extending north and west of Sagebrush. He filled it with five county roads and the two main highways, the one that headed west to Utah and east toward Denver, and the other that went north to Wyoming.

"Corazon was found along Firebrush Road. That's what the paper said. I can't say for sure where the others were, but from what I heard I think they may have been found on Elkhorn, and Old Gunslinger's. Maybe five miles from each other. This is where we are now." Tucker marked a tiny square for the cabin they were in, and a square each for two line camps he had described. "You need a horse or a four-wheel-drive to get to those cabins. In the winter, a snowmobile." He put down the pen.

She took up the map and held it to the lamp. "So this is where we are now, and that's Sagebrush."

They weren't as far away from town as she thought. They'd made a wide loop out west toward Brown's Park and then back northeast. Lacey felt as if she could have gone to the moon and back in the time she'd spent with Tucker. Maybe this *was* the moon: The moon *might* be covered with snow and sagebrush, so far as she knew. And she was still furious with him for abducting her. Yet they had fallen into the rhythm of each other's company. They were almost friends again. If Lacey wasn't exactly comfortable, she wasn't afraid.

"I'm taking the heel with me," she said.

Tucker dug into the stew again. "All yours. What do you plan to do with it?"

"I have to show this to the cops."

"How are you going to do that?"

"You have to let me go back, Tucker. You know that, don't you?"

"I guess this isn't really your idea of a good time."

Someday this might be quite the story, Lacey knew, suitable for amusing audiences at cocktail parties. *If I live through the experience.* Right now, though, it wasn't a charming story yet. It was painful and ridiculous and humiliating. She laughed at the thought it could be a good time. She laughed again and laughed longer, until tears came to her eyes.

"A good time? Oh, Tucker." She wiped the tears away. The laughs finally subsided in a lamentable sigh. "No, it's not my idea of a good time. I really prefer my cabins with plumbing and heat, and not being chased by the law." She was laughed out, and drained. Close to tears.

He smiled sadly, and pushed the hair from her face. He let his hand linger. "I'm real sorry, Chantilly Lace. I know it's been hard, but I've been thinking about the old days, when we were a couple, and I have not been hating this day. Not at all. Even with you mad as a hornet."

"So help me, if you tell me I'm cute when I'm mad I will kick you where it counts."

"I won't say it, then. Cowboy's life can be solitary, but I didn't feel lonely today."

They fell quiet and the howl of the coyote sounded again. This time not as close as before, but it echoed like a heartbroken lament in the night.

"Listen, Chantilly Lace," Tucker said at last. "If you really think this silver heel will help T-Rex look at this business in a new way, then I'll help get you back to town. First thing in the morning."

"The bootheel, and your map, and what you've told me, it could change everything—"

"Let's see how the heel goes over first. There's no sense in giving them everything all at once." He gave her half a smile.

"There's a chance the sheriff won't listen to me, and who knows about the cops and the CBI. But Vic will listen to me, Tucker. He'll believe me." *I hope.*

God, how she wanted to see Vic, talk over the day's events with him, feel his arms around her. *And maybe a steak and some sautéed mushrooms and a glass of wine, some hot bread with butter, maybe a Caesar salad—*

"I do wish you hadn't brought his name up, Chantilly. I really do." Tucker scowled at her and brought her back to reality.

"Vic thinks just as highly of you too. But Tucker, you have to accept it. Vic Donovan is my guy now."

"Well, I don't have to like it. Tell me, Chantilly, what's he done for you?"

Where do I begin? "For one thing, he taught me how to shoot a gun."

Tucker chuckled. "He's probably wishing you had a gun with you right now."

"I imagine so." She didn't want to have to use a gun. Ever again.

"Well, sunshine, I'm glad you don't have a gun. You don't need one. You can slay me with a look. And I taught you how to ride and rope, so there."

Lacey thought about roping the lawn chair with her sister two nights before. *That went well.* "I'm a little out of practice, Cole. I could barely hang on to Buttercup. As for me and a lasso—"

He took her hand and stroked it. "It's all in the wrist, and the hands, and the rope and knot. You gotta concentrate. Anyway, as I recollect, you were getting pretty good at roping a fence post."

"Yeah, fence posts just quiver in fear when they see Lacey Smithsonian coming."

"It'll come back to you. Like Buttercup. Stick around— we'll get in some practice."

Lacey had spent most of two years keeping company with Cole Tucker. She hoped she wouldn't have to spend an equal amount of time talking about Tucker to the authorities. She did not relish the idea of chatting with Sheriff Theodore Rexford about her unwilling part in Tucker's escape from the courthouse. Sheriff T-Rex never cared for any media of any description, be it print or radio or television, or Lacey Smithsonian. He liked Dodd Muldoon and *The Sagebrush Daily Press* even less. She wondered if T-Rex had mellowed. That seemed doubtful.

"Tucker, you have to take me back to Sagebrush."

"I said I'd help get you back to town, Chantilly. I didn't say I'd personally deliver you into the lion's den. Or Vic Donovan's arms."

Lacey squinted at Tucker. "You know, I never liked

that woman you married either. I thought she was a trailer-trash gold digger. She couldn't wait to take you away from me. She had bad hair. And a big butt." *Oh, Tucker, how could you!*

He put up his hands in surrender. "Okay, truce."

"If I could get to a highway, one with some actual traffic," Lacey said, "I could hitch a ride."

"Here you're talking about highway killers and you want to catch a ride with a stranger? Why don't you let me worry about all this in the morning?"

"No, I'm worrying about it now. I need a plan. For crying out loud, Cole, aren't you worried? They're out there hunting us like rabid dogs! And there's a killer out there too, and whoever it is has got just as much reason to want you back behind bars!"

"I'm worried plenty. Worried sick. But no one's going anywhere tonight. It's cold outside and it'll snow again. I know how much you love that. No, tonight the search party and the posse will all be at the bar somewhere, swapping war stories about how brave they are and what happened back in '98 or some such bull. I reckon they'll regroup in the morning, when they call out the dogs and refuel the copter. Maybe call out snowmobiles to search up in the high country, where the snow is still too deep for the sagebrush to poke through."

"Oh, God, you think—"

"If it was me out searching for *you*, that's what I'd do. Of course, there is Sheriff T-Rex. We know he's not all that fond of you reporter types. So maybe he didn't pull out all the big guns. You should never embarrass a man in print. Especially when it goes on the Internet."

"It's not my fault he fell asleep at every county commission meeting," Lacey said. She scooped stew out of the pan.

"T-Rex didn't take kindly to that picture you took of him, snoozing with his mouth open. Drooling too."

Lacey grinned. "It was a public meeting. Fair game."

"That picture sure would look great on a campaign poster. 'Theodore Rexford for Sheriff! Asleep at the Switch! Your Tax Dollars at Work!'"

"Stop teasing me."

"Chantilly Lace, it's so easy."

"The sheriff may not care about finding *me*. But *you're* a fugitive on the run."

Tucker leaned back in his chair. "T-Rex knows I didn't do it."

"Oh, yeah? How do you know he knows that?"

"He was there when I was arrested. He told me he didn't see how I could have done it, but evidence was evidence. Something about the way he said it makes me think he's got doubts. He knows, Lacey."

"You think he's part of the conspiracy?"

Tucker shook his head and speared a piece of potato with his fork. "Nope, I don't. T-Rex is an honest man. He's a cranky old coot and hard to take, and maybe not the sharpest knife in the drawer, but he's honest. He kept staring at Grady when they put the cuffs on me. T-Rex didn't like it—he just doesn't know what to do about it."

They finished the pot of stew in silence. "How am I going to get back to Sagebrush?" she asked.

"Same way you got here."

Lacey looked up in surprise. "Steal a car?"

"I *borrowed* those cars. Tasso Petrus probably got his Jeep back by now. All he's out is some bagels and a little gas, and he's a celebrity for a day. No, my Chantilly Lace. You're going back on Buttercup. Just the two of you."

Ride a horse back to Sagebrush? It was one thing to ride along with Tucker, who was born to the saddle, a cowboy who could help out if she got into trouble.

"Alone! You're kidding, right? What if I get lost?"

"Ride next to the road, on the soft ground. Ride gentle and follow the signs."

"The ones riddled with bullet holes?" This wasn't making her feel any better.

"You got it."

"It could take hours."

"Yeah, but you get to take some shortcuts. And you'll have Buttercup. It'll be a gentle ride. Just let her stop whenever she needs to. Maybe three, four hours. Now get your coat on." Tucker held out her leather jacket.

"Now? In the middle of the night? I thought we weren't going anywhere till morning."

"I have to check on the horses. And you probably want to visit the outhouse before turning in. Course, we might be able to scare up a chamber pot for you, milady. Or a bucket."

"This adventure just gets better and better," Lacey growled at him. All she wanted in life, she decided, was modern plumbing and a hot bath. And a clean bed. *Oh, and justice for the innocent and retribution for the wicked. That's all.* She grabbed her coat.

It was bitter cold outside, and stars were twinkling like ice crystals scattered on black velvet. When they got back inside, Tucker dragged the mattress from the bedroom to a spot in front of the stove. "I'll stay here, so I can stoke the fire. You can join me if you like. Stay warmer that way."

"No, thanks. I'll take the sofa."

"Last chance. You gonna be warm enough?" he asked.

"Sure. Got my coat and my shawl, and this shabby blanket, and it feels a lot better in here. But I'm keeping my boots on too. But what about you?"

"I got my fleece jacket. And a couple of these old spreads." He shook them out in the bedroom, raising clouds of dust. "I'll be toasty. Don't you worry about me. Sleep tight."

Despite her exhaustion, Lacey did not sleep well the second time. Her head was full of a thousand contradictory ideas and emotions. Whenever she dozed off, it seemed she was awakened by the lonesome cry of a coyote. And one time, deep in the night—she couldn't be sure; she might have been dreaming—but she thought she heard Tucker whisper softly, "I love you, Chantilly Lace."

chapter 17

"Time to ride, sunshine," Tucker said. "You ready?"

"Ready as I'll ever be." Lacey squinted into the early-morning sun as she rummaged through her tote bag for her sunglasses. She would be angling east into the sun all morning. The day was bright and cold, with fresh snow on the ground, but it held the promise of warmer weather. She double-checked to make sure the silver bootheel was tucked inside her bag, at the very bottom, next to her little camera and the article about Ally Newport. Tucker's map was slipped into a slit in the tote bag's lining.

Tucker was gentle with the horses. He simply had a way with them. Ricochet was impatient and ready to run, while Buttercup was placid and a little curious.

Lacey tried not to think about how filthy she felt wearing the same clothes as the day, and night, before. By now, she was thoroughly rumpled. She made do with some towelettes and a dab of makeup on the circles under her eyes, some eye shadow and mascara, and she'd combed her hair, pulling it back into a ponytail. Not her favorite look.

"You sure do look pretty this morning, Chantilly."

"I feel like I've been dragged through the mud."

"Impossible. Ground's frozen hard."

"Could you give me a lift onto Buttercup?" The horse neighed at her name and nuzzled Lacey's neck.

"Sure. In a minute." Cole stepped closer to her, pinning her against the horse's warm flank.

"Hey, what are you doing?" Lacey didn't care for the look in Tucker's eyes.

He took her in his arms, leaned down and kissed her, sending shock waves and unwanted memories through her. She tried to move away from him, but he held her for a long time.

"Now you can go back to your Vic Donovan," Tucker said. "But you'll remember me."

He had her there. Lacey might not be able to recall their first kiss, but she would never forget this one.

"Are you mad at me, Lacey?"

She gulped to catch her breath. She didn't know what to say. "Yes! No. No madder than I was before."

He laughed and kissed her forehead and helped her onto the horse.

Tucker rode with Lacey for a few miles to put her on the right trail to Sagebrush. Among the bare cottonwoods near a small creek, he and Ricochet stopped.

"Here's where we part company, Lacey. It's breaking my heart, love."

"Tucker, please be careful." She felt a pain in her heart too, for him, for old times. "This can't be like a Marty Robbins song, where the outlaw gets gunned down in the last verse."

"I won't sing that song, then. Happy trails, Chantilly Lace."

Tucker tipped his hat and tapped Ricochet's flanks. The black horse spun around and they galloped off in the opposite direction. Lacey watched him go until he was just a dot on the western horizon.

Buttercup knew the way, as Tucker promised. The shortest trail to the Tuckered Out Ranch (and Buttercup's stable) would take them first to Sagebrush, where Lacey planned to call Kit. The palomino stopped every so often to sniff the air, or swish her tail and look around, or munch some snow. Lacey wasn't about to urge her into a spine-shaking gallop, so Buttercup took her time and enjoyed the scenery. After a few hours of walking and trotting, the horse seemed to grow a little more ea-

ger to see her barn again and quickened her pace. It was
nearly noon when Lacey finally crested the bluffs north
of town and caught sight of the outskirts of Sagebrush.
She was stiff and starving.

She was surprised by the sight of Kit Carson Tucker
already waiting on the side of the highway, with his dirty
white pickup, the same one she and Tucker had borrowed, and a horse trailer. Had Tucker somehow been in
contact with Kit this morning? Or had they made this
plan last night without telling her? How else would Tucker's brother know to meet her at the right place at the
right time? Whatever the reason, Lacey was grateful Kit
was there to take charge of the horse.

Kit waved to her, and Lacey waved back. She rode up
to the trailer and was about to dismount when she saw
Kit Carson Tucker wasn't the only one waiting to welcome her back to town.

Welcome might not be the exact word, she thought.

Sirens screaming, the sheriff's SUV careened up the
road toward the horse trailer. Buttercup reared in a
panic. Lacey yelped and hung on tight. Kit managed to
grab the horse's bridle to calm Buttercup, and he helped
Lacey off the horse. She felt wobbly and her legs were
like rubber, but she did not fall. It took her a few moments to realize she was shaking.

Sheriff T-Rex Rexford screeched to a stop, jumped
out with the engine still running, and slammed the door.
Another man exited the passenger side.

Lacey was cold, tired, and hungry. She was worried
about Vic and her family. She knew she was a wrinkly,
dusty, saddle-sore mess that smelled more like a horse
than a woman, and Buttercup wasn't her favorite perfume. Buttercup neighed and nuzzled Lacey with her
nose, back to her placid self and apparently eager to remind Lacey to show some appreciation for a pleasant
morning's ride. Lacey patted the horse's neck and leaned
against the big animal for support. Kit took the reins
and fed Buttercup an apple from one of his pockets.

Sheriff Rexford was right in her face. "Where's Cole
Tucker?"

"How should I know?" Lacey backed away from T-Rex. "He just put me on the horse and sent me here. Hours ago. He let me come back and he didn't hurt me. He didn't kill anyone, you know."

"Don't tell me what I know, missy."

"All right, I'll tell you what *I* know. Cole Tucker didn't murder those women."

The sheriff had a mighty big voice for a moderately sized man. He was no more than five-foot-seven, but his ten-gallon hat pulled down tight on his bulky head, and his stacked-heel boots, gave him the illusion of height. He wore a dark brown uniform jacket over khaki slacks. He was as lean and weathered as if he'd been baked in the sun, the same shade as his mud brown hair. *Or maybe he's just red faced with the excitement of seeing me.* Lacey couldn't tell, but the flush of his face made his angry eyes look bluer by contrast. His face was a barometer of rage, just like Muldoon's. He reminded her of an agitated banty rooster ready to fly up and fight. A rooster wearing a cowboy hat. *Or a tiny angry dinosaur.*

Behind him, the other man, larger and quieter, but with the same air of authority, stepped closer to the sheriff. T-Rex took a deep breath and calmed down a little.

"Rico Firestone? Is that you?" Lacey asked.

He put out his hand. "Long time, Lacey."

CBI agent Rico Firestone was about the same age as the sheriff, but taller and broader. His black hair was streaked with gray. Deep wrinkles spread out from his dark eyes. He seemed less likely to shoot her than T-Rex. She remembered him as a calming influence. He'd been a friend of Vic's, back when Vic was the chief of police.

"Are you all right, Lacey?"

She nodded. "If the CBI is involved, where's the FBI?"

"Standing by," Firestone said. "We're in touch."

Lacey swayed back and forth, but she had never fainted in her life, and she was not about to start now. Firestone had relaxed his grip on her hand, but he tightened it to keep her upright.

"Kit?" She turned around and shook off Firestone's hand.

"Yeah, Lacey?" Kit was leading Buttercup to the horse trailer. Lacey watched as he expertly handled the palomino. The horse had already shifted her allegiance and left Lacey behind without a second thought. She was happily neighing and nuzzling Cole's younger brother, who had pockets full of treats for her.

"How did you know I was coming this way?"

"Got a call from Truman up the road. Said he saw someone on Buttercup, riding this way. I figured Buttercup would be tired out by now and could use a lift home. She's hungry too. Looks like she got her exercise for the day. Good girl, Buttercup, we'll be home soon." The horse was family to Kit. Lacey obviously was not. Kit tipped his hat. He was ready to go.

"Tucker call you?" Firestone called to him.

Kit's eyes skipped lightly over the sheriff and the CBI agent and revealed nothing. "I imagine he has other things on his mind. I heard about my horse from a neighbor to our north. Call him, he'll tell you."

"You can go, Kit," T-Rex said. "But stay available, you hear?"

Kit shrugged and returned to Buttercup, leading her onto the trailer.

T-Rex advanced on Lacey. "You got a lot of questions to answer, missy."

"My name's not Missy, and you know it, T-Rex. I've had one hell of a night and a bumpy morning, and I suggest you back off."

"And my name's not T-Rex! It is Sheriff Rexford to you, Miss Smithsonian."

Agent Firestone stepped between them, playing good cop to T-Rex's Neanderthal cop. "No problems here, Sheriff. I'm sure Lacey has had quite a difficult time of it and she'll tell us all about it."

"Each and every detail," T-Rex said, but he backed off. "Well, Lacey? Did Tucker hurt you?"

"Only my pride," she said, remembering her humiliating exit from the courthouse. She eyed the barren landscape at the edge of town and turned around, searching in vain. The face she wanted to see wasn't here. She was unprepared for the disappointment she felt. Lacey rationalized that Vic couldn't know Tucker had released her. It wasn't like he was psychic. *The way a woman would be under the same circumstances,* she told herself.

"Where's Vic?" Lacey asked Firestone.

"That would be former Police Chief Donovan?" T-Rex butted in. "No idea. I understand he's your *boyfriend* now?"

She exhaled before speaking. "I asked *you,* Agent Firestone."

Firestone gestured gallantly to the Yampa County SUV and she followed him. "Vic is out with the posse. Looking for you and Cole Tucker."

"The posse?" *So they really called out the posse?*

"That's right," the sheriff said. "I called up the posse. I can do that, and I did."

"Good idea. It is 1893, isn't it? The Wild Bunch will be shooting up the saloon any minute now."

Firestone opened the front door for her. At least he didn't make her sit in the back like a prisoner. He took the backseat himself. T-Rex hopped into the driver's seat, slammed the door, and put the monster SUV into gear.

"Every county sheriff is legally empowered to convene a posse to assist law enforcement with voluntary manpower, if necessary," Firestone said.

"That's right," the sheriff growled. "We got us an escaped fugitive. Hell, Tucker abducted you right out of the courthouse, in front of witnesses. I never thought he was capable of doing such a crazy-ass thing. Of course we need the damn posse!" The sheriff clicked his safety belt and gunned the engine. "The other agencies are also on the lookout. Time those Fish and Wildlife and BLM folks did something for us."

"So you unleashed—what? Fifty or sixty overage Boy Scouts, with pickups and guns and itchy trigger fingers?" Lacey pictured the chaos a posse like that could wreak.

"More or less," T-Rex said with a smirk. "It's a mighty big county."

"What about Deputy Rush? Is he all right?"

"Is he all right? If you call getting your ass reamed out by me for dereliction of duty and allowing a dangerous murder suspect to escape and embarrass the Yampa County Sheriff's Department, okay then, yeah, I guess he's okay. Grady's lucky to have a damn job after pulling that idiot stunt. And I'm not too sure how long he's gonna keep it. But I reckon you'll be helping me corroborate his statement about the escape and the kidnapping."

Depends on his statement, Lacey thought. "How did Grady catch that tip about evidence at Cole Tucker's ranch?"

"And how'd you know that?" T-Rex said.

"I'm a reporter. Remember?" Lacey said. "And it's a small town."

"It is that." T-Rex's expression was dark under the shadow of his hat. He pulled the truck onto the road. "No comment."

"Where are we going?"

"My office. For questioning."

"Wait a minute. I'm starving. I need a shower. I have to change my clothes. And make some phone calls."

"And people in Hell want ice water," T-Rex said with a smirk.

"So you're taking me to Hell, or to Sagebrush?" Lacey inquired. "But wait, I repeat myself."

"Don't get smart with me! You're going to answer our questions," the sheriff said.

"Why? Am I under arrest?"

"Not yet," he snarled, "but it can be arranged."

In the backseat, Firestone cleared his throat.

"You're treating me like some kind of criminal?" Lacey was so angry she could spit. "I'm a member of the press. I'm not saying a word to anybody until I get some coffee and some food and I make a few phone calls. And I'm not eating your lousy jail food."

The sheriff stopped the SUV in the middle of the road. "We can do this one of two ways."

"Want to try it the stupid way? Arrest me! Go ahead. Arrest a reporter who didn't commit a crime. You'll have to drag me out of this truck in front of the media and I guarantee you it will not be a pretty picture. You could add it to your collection. And I will promptly lawyer up and you won't get a word out of me. But I *will* write my exclusive, and I *will* have words to say about you and your department. Now, what was the other way?"

T-Rex pressed his lips together and his face turned bright red. Firestone stepped in like a man defusing a live bomb.

"Sheriff, the town is full of reporters. Major media from all over the state. Maybe even out of state. Lots of TV cameras. You really want that kind of headache?"

More of her reporting tribe must have come to town since news of Tucker's escape and her abduction got out. At the moment, Lacey was grateful for the competition.

"It won't hurt to go to a restaurant, and sort this out like adults," Firestone continued smoothly. "The posse's still out there. We got our people out there. They know Cole Tucker is probably on horseback. If Lacey's been riding for, say, three, four, five hours, he's had that much time to get away, most likely in the opposite direction. Gives us a better radius to work with. We got time."

"Guess you got a point there." The sheriff knew when he was stalemated. T-Rex put the truck in drive again and turned toward her, a slightly paler shade of red. "Okay. We'll do it your way. We'll all go get something to eat. Together. But you tell me something here and now, Miss Smithsonian. How did Cole Tucker force my deputy to take off the cuffs and the waist chain? I want the truth, the unvarnished truth."

Like I'd varnish it for you. Lacey smoothed her hair back. "He didn't force him. Tucker asked Grady nicely to unlock the cuffs and chains, and Grady did."

"He did what? You're lying to me, Smithsonian. Tucker overpowered Grady. Somehow."

"You've already reamed out Grady, so why ask me? You don't think your deputy is telling the truth?" They stared at each other for a moment. "Tucker *fooled* Grady, and it wasn't hard, because your deputy is a fool. Tucker told him it was a shame he couldn't even hug me after all the trouble I went to, to come see him. Grady thought about it. Then he told Tucker it would be on him and Tucker would owe him one. They laughed, the way all you good old boys do. Grady unlocked the cuffs, and Tucker shook off the chains, grabbed him and did something to his neck. Grady slipped to the floor like a sack of flour. That's when Tucker, um, threw me over his shoulder and— You know the rest."

A sort of strangling sound came from the sheriff's throat. In the rearview mirror, Firestone's eyes were unreadable, but he shook as if he were trying not to laugh.

A vehicle parked on a side road caught Lacey's eye. Something that looked suspiciously like an old turquoise station wagon. It wasn't the original paint. Lacey knew that wagon.

"Oh, no!"

"Something bothering you, Lacey?" Firestone asked.

"My mother is in town, isn't she?" And if her mother was in town, then her sister would be in town too. The only lucky break she'd caught was that her father might still be on that plane to Thailand, or maybe he just landed. Lacey groaned. *Things just aren't bad enough, are they?*

"Indeed she is. I met her this morning. She's extremely concerned about your safety." The sheriff had a pleased smirk on his face.

"This is terrific."

"Aren't moms something." Rico Firestone smiled for the first time. "Wouldn't want my mother coming up here to check on me."

Lacey was going to offer a clever retort, but she couldn't think of one.

"Why'd you even come to Sagebrush?" T-Rex demanded.

"To see Tucker."

"A man you hadn't talked to in what, seven, eight years? A man you ran out on?"

"I did *what*? Everybody thinks they know everything

about everyone in this town, don't they?" Lacey snarled. "I came to see Tucker because he didn't kill those women. No way."

"Is that all?" Firestone broke in.

"Well, I thought maybe I could see him, and there might be a story in it."

"That sounds a little bit more like the Lacey Smithsonian I know," T-Rex cracked. "You plan to exploit his misery for a newspaper story. That's real sentimental."

"I'm a journalist, and I write the facts. I don't exploit misery, if I can help it. But just maybe, Sheriff T-Rex, I'll be exploiting *your* misery, not to mention shedding light on your idiot deputy and your whole dim-witted department. Don't you have an election coming up soon?" The sheriff shut up. His face was getting redder again.

"How'd you find out about Cole's arrest?" Firestone asked.

"I read it on the Web. Believe it or not, Tucker's arrest wasn't just a local story. The whole country is watching Yampa County screw this up." Lacey ran her fingers through her tangled hair. She was too tired to hunt for her comb. She had grit in every pore. Her dishabille was making her cranky. "Vic saw it too. We discussed it."

"Let me get this straight," Sheriff T-Rex sneered. "Your new boyfriend discusses your old boyfriend with you and you immediately decide to grace the old boyfriend with a visit, thinking of the possibilities for a damn newspaper story. And what's wrong with Donovan to let you do this? Thought he was smarter than that."

"Let me? He *let* me do this? What century are you living in, Sheriff? Wait, I remember, it's that century where the sheriff calls out the posse while a bunch of good old boys frame an innocent man for murder."

"You're a piece of work, lady."

Lacey turned to Firestone in the back. "Hey, Rico, isn't it time for you to referee this fight? You can be the *good* cop."

He might have chuckled, but he quickly cleared his throat to cover it. "Why did you come back to Sagebrush, Lacey?"

*How many times am I going to have to answer that
one?* She leaned her head back and closed her eyes.

"Because . . . because there was no way I could believe Cole Tucker was a killer. If Tucker is a killer, what
does that make me? What does that say about what I
believe and who I trust? I couldn't live with that."

There was silence while the two lawmen considered
her words. Sheriff T-Rex chewed his lip and headed the
big SUV into Sagebrush.

chapter 18

"Make it quick," T-Rex said. "We got work to do." He squirmed in his seat, clearly thinking this was a terrible idea.

"It will take as long as it takes," Lacey said.

She was seated between Sheriff Rexford and Agent Firestone at the Amarillo Café on Sundance Way in Sagebrush. The café was still painted the same dirty seafoam green that she remembered. From inside, the word *Amarillo* was crookedly spelled backward on the window in a crescent shape.

A few faded pictures of mountain ranges hung on the walls. Pale gray linoleum-topped tables and wooden chairs were scattered around the room. The fluorescent lighting did no one any favors. A few coffeepots were set on burners on a table where the patrons could grab them if the waitress was busy, but the waitress really hated that. The Amarillo Café hadn't changed a bit.

It was the kind of place Lacey once found hard to appreciate, until now, when she straggled in, hungry and dirty and worried. Today the Amarillo provided an oddly familiar comfort. She tried to keep her mind on her theory that the silver bootheel resting at the bottom of her tote bag might have something to do with at least one of the dead women. It seemed more and more farfetched the longer she thought about it, but it was her number one exhibit for today's show-and-tell.

In front of her was a steaming mug of coffee, aromatic and freshly brewed. She closed her eyes and inhaled the fragrance before sipping. Rico Firestone and T-Rex also had mugs of coffee, but they were not as enchanted as she was.

When a large bowl of homemade vegetable-beef-and-barley soup and fresh bread were served, Lacey almost wept with joy.

T-Rex grabbed a copy of *The Sagebrush Daily Press* from another table. He shoved the paper at her. "I'm sure you'll want a souvenir."

A years-old picture of her was on the front page, under a blaring two-line headline: DAILY PRESS REPORTER ABDUCTED AT YAMPA COUNTY COURTHOUSE!

Dodd Muldoon strikes again. Lacey felt the blood drain from her face. "What did that maniac write about me?" She read through a few paragraphs, wincing with horror. Muldoon had made her sound like a combination of Joan of Arc and Brenda Starr. Worse, he personally took credit for her entire reporting career, by virtue of his "having initiated" her into the world of journalism. *Ewww.*

Never one to let an opportunity pass by, Muldoon also dug up a story about the time Lacey had crawled through a "massage parlor" window to interview the "masseuses" inside. The massage parlor, to which no one working there seemed to have a front door key, turned out to be a front for a prostitution ring out of Denver. It had proven to be a hot news story back in the day, for *The Daily Press* and a young reporter named Lacey Smithsonian. Muldoon's recollection of her role in the episode managed to be simultaneously flattering and embarrassing, a patented Muldoon combination.

"This is horrible," she gasped and felt herself color. People in Sagebrush read this paper cover to cover. Nobody believed every word, necessarily, but they read it.

"See how it feels," T-Rex said. Firestone lifted his coffee cup and chuckled.

"I'm familiar with Dodd Muldoon's brand of journalism. One reason I left."

Lacey returned to the article, which ended with this

boast: "... If Lacey 'Scoop' Smithsonian survives this shocking abduction, *The Daily Press* guarantees you'll read her exclusive report here first."

She muttered under her breath, "I'll kill him."

"Good. That would rid me of two of my problems," T-Rex said. "I got a cell all picked out special for you. Right next to Cole Tucker's."

"Very funny, Sheriff. I expect your ace deputy will have the third cell."

The restaurant was empty when the trio strolled in, but not for long. Word quickly spread of Lacey's return to Sagebrush on horseback. The place filled up. People crowded around, trying to listen in on the table where Lacey sat between the two lawmen. She focused on her soup and paid them no attention. T-Rex barked and they backed up.

"Can't you eat any faster?" he asked Lacey.

"I'm not you." She ignored them all and ate slowly and with great satisfaction.

The noise level rose until a group of newcomers showed up. A tall man with a sandy mustache and a cowboy hat entered first, followed by a couple of men in billed caps. She recognized one of them: Deputy Grady Rush out of uniform, in jeans and a denim jacket.

With the tall man's arrival the atmosphere changed subtly. The chatter stopped and tables of locals started listening again.

"So you made it back," the tall man said to Lacey. He seemed familiar, but she couldn't place him or his toothy smile. "Safe and sound, I see."

"Doesn't matter," Sheriff T-Rex said. "Cole Tucker is still out there."

"I'm sorry. You are?" Lacey said.

"Virgil. Virgil Avery." He offered her his hand. She ignored it. "You remember me, Lacey. You wrote a nice little news story about me way back when. About my real estate company. I'm mighty glad to see you safe and sound."

"Virgil here is one of our key posse members," T-Rex put in. "He's been hunting you since yesterday."

Lacey felt a curious sort of calm, watching the man who had made offer after offer on Tucker's land. All of a sudden she couldn't eat another bite. She pushed the soup away.

"And your friend is?" She indicated the shorter, stouter man standing behind him, wearing a cap that advertised natural gas. His stubby fingers were covered with chunky turquoise rings, his nails dirty.

"Where are my manners? Let me present my friend Mitchell Stanford."

Stanford stretched out his right hand. Lacey kept both hands on her coffee cup. Stanford dropped his hand without dropping his big smile. She tried to look like she had heard nothing about either of them, as if Tucker hadn't painted them with a specific brush of villainy. They were after the Tuckered Out Ranch.

"Grady, what the hell are you doing here?" T-Rex shouted at the big man who was trying to shrink into the crowd.

"I'm, um, off duty, Sheriff. I just thought I'd help out the posse," Grady said. His head was bowed. He ignored Lacey. "Maybe I could help catch the, uh, fugitive, you know?"

"You mean help chase the runaway horse after *you* opened the barn door? Do you have a brain in your head, Grady? You are on administrative leave, pending the completion of my investigation into the events at the courthouse yesterday." T-Rex's face was beyond red; it was turning an outraged shade of magenta. "And you are not welcome on this posse, or anywhere else in my county. The very sight of you gives me a pain in my gut. And lower. Now get your sorry prisoner-losing ass out of here!"

Lacey was mentally writing down that "sorry prisoner-losing ass" quote. She was sure it would come in handy. Other customers watched, happy to witness the sheriff ream out his deputy. In public. At the Amarillo. They would have a story to tell at the Little Snake Saloon that evening.

Grady exchanged a look with Virgil Avery and the

others before he shuffled out the door. Mitch Stanford watched Grady go, but Avery kept his attention on Lacey and the lawmen.

"Did he hurt you?" Avery asked Lacey. "Abducting you against your will like that? Terrible thing, a thing like that."

"Man like that's capable of God knows what kind of ugly behavior," Stanford said. "When I think of those poor pretty young women, I think that Cole Tucker must be a real animal."

Lacey's stomach turned. She wished she could send death rays from her eyes, but she settled for giving them The Look. "Tucker never hurt me."

"Yeah, it's a real good thing that Miss Smithsonian's safe and all, so she can write some new damn exposé about this town, but our work's not over," T-Rex said. "We still got to find Cole Tucker."

Virgil Avery never took his unblinking eyes off Lacey. "I imagine Miss Smithsonian could point us in the right direction. Where did he go, Lacey?" He leaned in to the table, and she leaned away from him.

"Let the poor girl rest a minute, Virgil, for crying out loud," Stanford said. He seemed a more jovial sort, with his red round face and ever-present smile. He turned to Lacey. "We're all mighty glad you're safe. This town doesn't need any more victims of this guy."

Stanford had an oily kind of salesman manner. Probably came in handy when he was peddling future riches for mineral leases today.

"Back off, boys, we'll be doing the interviewing," Firestone said. "Let the woman breathe."

Stanford and Avery smiled and backed away from the table. Avery leaned over to the coffeepot station, grabbed himself a cup, and poured from the pot. He earned a glare from the waitress, but he smiled at her. "Come on, Sally, I'm saving you a trip." He turned back to Lacey. "Maybe Tucker didn't get around to victimizing you yet. But I guess you and him have quite a history, so maybe you two—"

"Agent Firestone," Lacey said, "can you shut him up?"

Firestone stood up. Sheriff T-Rex stood up too, not to be left out.

"That's enough, Avery. The lady's had a rough night," Firestone said.

"Let's remember we still got a fugitive out there," T-Rex added. "Why don't you boys brief my undersheriff and we'll talk later."

Lacey reached down to reassure herself that her bag was still there. The silver bootheel nagged at her. She glanced down at the men's feet. Avery and Stanford both wore cowboy boots. Like several of the other posse members. Like the sheriff and Firestone.

When she straightened up, Mitch Stanford met her eyes. "That's a mighty nice pair of boots you got there, Miss Smithsonian." Lacey felt like she'd been living in her boots for ages, though it had only been two days and a night. "F. M. Light, I bet," Stanford continued. "I bet they don't wear pretty boots like that back East." There was a bit of "back East" in his accent.

A phone jingled. It sounded like Lacey's cell phone, the one Tucker threw out the window. She turned her head in the direction of the sound, puzzled. Rico Firestone took a battered phone from his inside jacket pocket and handed it to her.

"For you, I think."

"How'd you get my phone?"

"Someone turned it in. Do you want to answer?" Firestone was waiting to listen in.

Her phone was scratched and dented, but still jingling. Scowling, she answered. "Hello?"

"Smithsonian, where are you? Are you safe? Can you talk? Are you with the fugitive?"

"Mac?" Why was Douglas MacArthur Jones calling her from Washington? Did he want her to file a story *already*?

"What's the story, Lacey? Are you with him? Are you being held captive? Are you all right?"

"If you heard I was kidnapped, why did you call me?"

"To see if you'd answer. I thought you might have your phone with you. People in car trunks have cell phones."

"I wasn't in a car trunk! Tucker was . . . a gentleman." *Well, pretty much. Except for that kiss.* "He sent me back this morning. I'm in Sagebrush right now. Trying to eat lunch."

"What about your killer?"

"He's not a killer! And he's still out there." There were odd noises in the background. It didn't sound like the newsroom at *The Eye Street Observer.* "Where are you, Mac?"

"Denver. At the airport. Tony's seeing about getting a flight to where you are."

"You're at DIA? You've got Trujillo with you? Why?" Her face was burning. Lacey had had too many shocks today. Her throat constricted.

T-Rex and Rico Firestone were staring at her. Lacey turned away, but she saw the sheriff smirk. "Payback is a bitch," he said to Rico. He waved to the waitress to top off his coffee.

"Listen, Smithsonian," Mac said. "We can't have an *Eye Street* reporter grabbed from a courthouse by a suspected murderer and not follow up. What kind of paper would we be if we didn't respond? Someone's got to keep an eye on you, all the trouble you get into." Funny thing was, Mac didn't sound unhappy about anything. He sounded like a former reporter who was getting bored as an editor. Mac Jones was champing at the bit to get back in the saddle. So to speak. "When did you get back?"

"Not quite an hour ago."

"We're going to cover this story like a blanket. The works."

"The works? You and Tony are the whole works?"

"The *works*," Mac said without any apparent irony. "That's why I'm bringing in our police beat reporter." The thought crossed Lacey's mind that Mac had always had a hankering to see the Rocky Mountain West, what with all his talk of cowboy hats. And he was a Californian by birth, after all. Practically next door, from a Washington, D.C., perspective. "What are they doing to find Cole Tucker?"

"The posse is after him," Lacey said. T-Rex and Firestone studied her, along with the rest of the restaurant. She turned her back on them.

"Did you say posse? A real posse?" Mac half covered his phone and Lacey heard snippets of urgent conversation with someone, presumably Tony Trujillo. When Mac came back on he informed her there were no planes heading her way anytime soon. "We're renting a car and driving."

"You're driving? You hate to drive."

"Trujillo will drive, says he knows the territory. Call you later!"

Mac hung up, leaving Lacey to stare at her cell phone. She noticed she had more than twenty-five voice-mail messages waiting. *Oh, no. Stella and Brooke and Cherise and my mother and Mac. But where's Vic?*

"Who was that?" Firestone asked.

"My boss." Lacey was still staring at the phone. "Not Dodd Muldoon. My *real* editor, Douglas MacArthur Jones of *The Eye Street Observer*. He's coming to town and bringing reinforcements."

It was beginning to feel to Lacey like a scene in a surrealist play. People who didn't belong anywhere near Sagebrush were threatening to make dramatic entrances.

A loud commotion at the front door of the Amarillo made every head in the café swivel. "That's my daughter! You have to let me in." The Smithsonian family cavalry, minus dad, had arrived. "I'm not going anywhere until I'm sure she's safe," Rose Smithsonian told the big deputy at the entrance. If Lacey could have sunk through the floor she would have.

"I told you, Firestone, we should have taken Smithsonian back to the Justice Center, where we'd have some control," T-Rex said. "But no, you insist on *feeding* her."

T-Rex knew when to give up. He could withstand a lot, but he couldn't fight an angry mother. He nodded tiredly to the deputy and Rose came charging in.

Lacey found herself engulfed in her mother's hug, followed by Cherise's. Rose broke away and held Lacey at arm's length, her nose wrinkling. "Honey, you need a shower. You smell like a horse."

"No kidding," Lacey said. *Eau de Buttercup.*

"I knew you'd make it out all right, sis." Cherise looked bone weary, but relieved. "Mom, on the other hand, is driving me crazy."

There was another commotion at the door. "Where is she?" It was the deep baritone voice Lacey had been longing to hear.

"Vic, over here!" She raised both arms and broke free of her ferocious family hug.

Their eyes met. Vic was wild-eyed and unshaven. His rebellious curl dangled over his forehead. He parted the crowd with one arm. Even her mother stood aside for Vic. He grabbed Lacey and held her close.

"I smell like a horse," she managed to say.

"You smell wonderful," he said.

Lacey realized tears were leaking from her eyes. She rested her head against Vic, not caring about the spectacle they were making. She ignored Avery and Stanford and the posse, the deputies and the sheriff, the CBI agent and the crowd. And her mother. She kissed Vic long and hard.

"Vic, I have to tell you," Lacey started. "So much."

"That's it." T-Rex had had enough. He stood up, his thumbs tucked into his gun belt. "Show's over. We're going to the Justice Center. Now."

"Wait a minute, Sheriff," Vic said. "I just got here."

"Later, honey. I promise." Lacey grabbed her tote bag and held it close to her chest. Vic followed her and the sheriff to the door, holding on to her.

"You're not the top cop here anymore, Donovan. And it's Smithsonian's turn to answer some questions." T-Rex took her arm and wrestled her away from Vic. "Firestone. Pay the bill. Get a receipt. This is on the county."

chapter 19

"It's a fancy bootheel. So what? You got a point?" Sheriff T-Rex sat back and scowled at the ceiling, arms crossed over his chest.

The bootheel, with its delicate silver filigree decoration, looked smaller sitting in the middle of the table in the sheriff's interview room. It was oddly elegant, yet stubbornly silent.

"I already told you," Lacey said.

"You expect me to believe this heel's got something to do with those women? You been smoking dope or something? Can I add that to your aiding and abetting a fugitive?"

Lacey was trying to hold on to the last of her cool. The interview room was small and tight. She felt penned in by Rico Firestone and T-Rex Rexford.

"I'm saying this bootheel was found in a remote cabin," Lacey repeated. "The kind of place where a killer could take a victim. Victims who were found barefoot. Just saying."

"The cabin where Tucker took you?" Firestone said.

"Yes."

"And where is this cabin?"

Lacey sighed, long and eloquently. "It's not like I have the address. West of here. Tucker said the owner was an old guy, Thompson, who died a couple of years ago. Local kids have been going up there and using it as a no-tell motel."

"Sound familiar?" Firestone asked T-Rex.

"Maybe. More than one cabin in this county fits that description. Anything else you can think of might help us pinpoint this cabin you allegedly stayed at?"

"There was a dead coyote stuck on a fence. Not that I could tell. It was mostly bones and teeth, but Tucker said it was a coyote."

"Dead coyote." T-Rex nodded. "That's more like it. If it's the one I'm thinking of, it's a high school hangout." He pointed at the heel. "How do you know this doesn't belong to one of them kids?"

"I don't know," Lacey said. "But if I'd lost an expensive custom-made bootheel, you can bet I'd look for it, particularly if I was a seventeen-year-old girl living at home. And my parents paid for those boots. I'd sure as shooting get down on my hands and knees and move the furniture. But no one found this heel. Until I did. Why not? And I don't know that it belongs to any of the dead women, because they were found barefoot. But if it came off one of their boots, they weren't in a position to look for it. Did any of them wear cowboy boots?"

"We'll ask the questions," T-Rex said. "If you don't mind, Miss Fashion Reporter."

"Maybe the killer took them as trophies," Lacey added. "Maybe I have part of a killer's trophy right here."

"Trophies. Believe it or not, we've considered that possibility." Agent Firestone put his hands on the table. "We do know what we're doing out here, Lacey. The fact they were missing their shoes has been taken into consideration."

"Then you don't know what *kind* of shoes they wore? High heels, tennis shoes, loafers, fuzzy bunny slippers?"

"I should have guessed a female would get all het up over something like shoes," T-Rex said, disgusted. "Maybe the killer just took their shoes to keep them from running away. Didja think about that? Maybe he threw them all away, put them in a Goodwill box, or burned them in the dump. Might have nothing whatsoever to do with trophies or this bootheel you found, wherever you say you found it."

Lacey slapped her forehead. *Why is this so hard?*

"All right. You don't know what kind of shoes your barefoot victims wore. And you haven't found any of their shoes. Did you *ask* anyone who knew them?" They didn't answer, so she knew she was right. "Are you going to just sit there and do nothing with this clue, and let me write it up the way I see it?"

The sheriff of Yampa County was not used to being talked to this way by a reporter. He started turning beet red again. Agent Firestone cleared his throat. Lacey turned to him in disgust.

"Help the class out here, Rico. Were the dead women missing more than their shoes? Something that wasn't in the papers?"

"You know we wouldn't release all the information pertinent to the case," Firestone said. "Of course, we held back some key elements of the killer's signature."

"His signature? Like what? Besides taking their shoes?"

"You've got nothing, Miss Smithsonian, except a fancy bootheel and an even fancier imagination," T-Rex said, after catching his breath. "That sort of thing might go over big in Washington, D.C., but not here in Sagebrush. My God, what's next? Am I going to have some lunatic psychic walk through the door and tell me my business?" He slammed his hands down on the table and glared at her.

Their skeptical reaction to the bootheel made up her mind. There was no way Lacey was going to tell them Tucker's theory about the line camps that might have sheltered the killer. The map Tucker drew for her was safe and sound in the lining of her tote bag. Lacey told herself that she wasn't withholding evidence. *They didn't ask me about any maps. I'm no psychic.*

She wanted to talk to Vic. She longed to wash off this day and its bad memories in a long, luxurious, hot shower. She wanted to change her clothes and go to sleep. T-Rex raised his voice another octave.

"Is someone else going to walk in here and tell me something else I don't need to know? I am beset by morons! I got a murder suspect on the run, I got a prisoner-losing dumb-ass of a deputy, and I got a fashion reporter who thinks she's a detective!"

The room was warm and stuffy. Lacey yawned and covered her mouth. Her only comfort was that these buckaroos were beginning to look as tired as she felt.

"Are we boring you, Miss Smithsonian?"

"Heavens no, T-Rex. It's just hard to get any rest with coyotes howling all night."

"Did Tucker tell you what he did to those women?" It was Firestone's turn again.

"Yeah. He did." Lacey stared him down. "He did *nothing* to those women. Cole didn't have anything to do with them. Except Corazon Reyes, whom he was seeing for a few weeks. But you already know that. You've asked me that question ten times, five different ways, and my answer is not going to change."

"What did he tell you about Corazon, then?"

"She was pretty. She was a cook who couldn't cook. They went out dancing a few times. Corazon wore cowboy boots when they went dancing. Short skirts and cowboy boots. Her signature style."

"Did her boots have silver heels like these?" Firestone pressed.

Lacey shook her head. "Her favorite boots were tooled leather with multicolored sombreros."

T-Rex leaned on the table. "We're going to go over it one more time."

"I've been through it over and over, and I'm done." Lacey glared at the two of them and stood up. "I'm leaving."

"No, you're not!" The sheriff was taken aback. "Material witness, probable conspiracy, suspicion of aiding and abetting a fugitive, other charges pending. Law says I can hold you for twenty-four hours."

Lacey looked from him to Firestone, who simply shrugged. "He can do that."

"I want a lawyer. Now." Lacey realized those words were the first ones that should have come out of her mouth, as Brooke Barton, no doubt, would have lectured her. *And no doubt will.* "You can keep me for twenty-four hours, but you can't make me talk." *Any more than I already have.*

There was a knock at the door. A deputy she didn't recognize opened it and waved to the sheriff. T-Rex slipped out of the room, leaving her with Agent Firestone. He leaned forward, his elbows on the table.

"This is the problem we're having with your little boot story, Lacey," he said. "Why should we waste our time going out to that cabin on this wild goose chase, when Tucker has already skedaddled out of there? Are you playing games with us?"

Lacey tried to speak slowly and patiently. "If one of those victims was in that cabin, you might find more evidence. Wouldn't more evidence be a *good* thing?"

"I appreciate your loyalty to Cole. You might have a low opinion of our good sheriff here, and off the record, I just might have an opinion of my own, but the law doesn't arrest people for murder without cause."

"Says you." She sat down again. "Rico, do you have any idea what kind of shoes those women were wearing when they disappeared?"

"No, we don't know. We don't really care. If they turn up, fine. If not, that's fine too. Tucker—the *killer* probably destroyed them. Taking them probably was just a control measure to make them even more helpless. And anyway, you women, you change your shoes a lot, don't you?"

I tried. "You going to tell the media what I've told you? About the heel and the cabin?" She hoped not. She still had a story to write. *I want to tell it my way.*

"Why would we?" Rico Firestone fiddled with his coffee cup. "Hey, I know the sheriff here can be a little hard to talk to. But if there's anything else you want to tell *me*, this would be a good time. Are you sure you've told us everything?"

Aha, Lacey wondered, *is this good cop–bad cop? Did the sheriff stomp out of the room just so Rico could take his shot at making me betray Tucker?*

"What do I know? I'm just a fashion reporter." She shrugged elaborately.

The door opened and T-Rex popped his head in. "Get out," he snarled to Lacey. "Your lawyer is here."

My lawyer? Maybe he means Tucker's lawyer, Karen Quilby? "You're giving me a lawyer?"

"Hell no. This one just showed up out of the blue, and I'm not interested in any more headaches today. You are headache enough without a fancy-ass lawyer to piss me off."

Lacey stood. She gazed at the silver-trimmed bootheel sitting alone and unloved on the table. No one seemed interested in it but her. She reached for it.

"Leave it," T-Rex commanded. "If it is evidence, and I'm not saying it is— Well then, it's *evidence*."

chapter 20

The first thing Lacey saw as she left the interview room was a pair of perfectly polished black wing tips. Then a perfectly tailored, charcoal gray, three-piece suit. A perfectly crisp pale blue shirt and a perfectly tied blue-and-gray-striped tie. She blinked and gazed at the man's face. He smiled.

"Ben? Benjamin Barton? Oh. My. God. What on earth are you doing here?"

Lacey was stunned to see her friend Brooke's younger brother, attorney Benjamin Barton of the fine old D.C. law firm of Barton, Barton & Barton, standing before her in the Yampa County Justice Center. Ben was a perfect example of his type: tall, blond, fit, good-looking, and very *Gentleman's Quarterly*. He looked like an elegant alien from a sartorially superior planet, with no rough edges to give him character. *Yet.*

T-Rex appeared right behind her. "Your *lawyer*. I understand he's imported from back East." Now free of the burden of Lacey Smithsonian, the sheriff practically skipped down the hallway. He spun around, happy as a wild horse. "We're done, Ms. Smithsonian. But if I have questions, I want answers. Pronto. Understand?"

Lacey turned to her attorney.

"Naturally, Sheriff," Ben Barton said, "my client and I look forward to assisting your investigation in any way we can. Within the letter and spirit of the law." He smiled broadly at the sheriff and squeezed Lacey's arm meaningfully.

"Like he said," Lacey said.

"Adios, Miss Fashion Reporter." T-Rex disappeared into his office. "Don't quote me."

Lacey whistled under her breath. "Ben? What just happened?"

"Without me and the services of Barton, Barton and Barton, you'd probably be enjoying the dubious hospitality of the county for the next twenty-four hours. Until sometime tomorrow, about cocktail hour."

"I'm grateful." She'd heard Brooke talk about her whip-smart little brother Benjamin, and she'd met him a few times, but had never seen him in action before. Ben had always seemed a bit bloodless for Lacey's taste. A bit too pale, a bit too smooth. Yet as a lawyer, he was reputed to be sharper than glass. He had to be, to hold his own with his sister, Brooke. Lacey was very glad to see him.

Benjamin was forever finishing up Brooke's legal briefs and grunt work to pay her back for something or other. But brother and sister lived by the Code of the Bartons, and they never squealed. Brooke was big on codes, like the Pink Collar Code, which required fealty to one's female friends.

"I simply mentioned your sterling record of assisting the police in various other murder cases, leaving out how you did it with your—*fashion clues*. I also pointed out," Ben continued, "that you couldn't be helpful behind bars. And that jailing reporters for any reason is always trouble, especially in election years. I guaranteed the sheriff I would make sure it was *much* more trouble than it was worth. It's like arresting the First Amendment."

"That's good. Can I quote you?"

"No. No quotes without clearance. I am your attorney now. Anything you tell me is under attorney-client privilege. And vice versa. Now, I must ask. Are you all right?" He frowned. "You were kidnapped, is that right? By an acquaintance. Were you harmed?"

"Depends on your definition. Abducted, yes. Publicly humiliated, yes. And forced to ride a horse two days in a row, after not being in a saddle for about seven years. But I am fine. Better now that you're here and I'm out of there." She took Ben's arm and headed for the exit, watching for T-Rex at every turn.

"Let's not rule out posttraumatic stress syndrome. I think we should contact a physician."

She laughed. "Benjamin, the only thing I'm suffering from is the no-hot-shower syndrome. And the dumb-ass county sheriff syndrome." Lacey was acutely aware of her general state of dishevelment beside her very crisply tailored attorney. Luckily, everyone in the Justice Center seemed to be familiar with *eau de cheval*.

He sniffed delicately. "You're sure?"

"It's the horse," she explained. "Now, why are you here, Ben?"

"You have to ask?" He had a funny expression, bordering on a smirk. "Brooke issued an edict. Here I am."

"So you owed her one. What does Brooke have on you?"

"After this? *Nothing.*" He pulled out a smartphone that looked like a *Star Trek* communicator and aimed the camera lens at Lacey. "Smile."

Lacey covered the thing with her hand. "You will take a picture of me this way on pain of *death*, Benjamin Barton." He put the phone away.

"I'd say under oath that you look pretty great. Under the circumstances. Brooke just wants to know that you're okay. She wants evidence."

"You can take photos for Brooke later. After I scrub the horse off."

"Very well. Brooke promised me this would be a colorful place. She was right."

Ben seemed oblivious to the interested stares from the female deputies and secretaries. In Washington, Ben might turn heads with his looks and his razor-sharp style, but he was still just another lawyer in the world capital of lawyers. In Sagebrush, Colorado, he was as exotic as a movie star.

"How did you know I was in trouble, and how did you get here so quickly?"

"Her Majesty Queen Brooke contacted me as soon as she heard you were taken hostage. She's very plugged in, you know. It's killing her not to come here and impose her iron will on the unsuspecting natives. For once, she had to stay and work on an important settlement."

"Must be super important."

"Too many zeroes to count, Lacey. She couldn't escape this time." Ben straightened his tie. "And I was already packing to go skiing in Aspen later this week. The timing worked out."

"You bring a three-piece suit on a ski trip?"

"Not usually, but Brooke told me to dress to impress. However, perhaps I should have toned it down a bit."

"No, you definitely impress. I'll talk to the paper. Maybe *The Eye* can pay your fee." She didn't want to even think about how expensive this could be.

He waved his hand. "The firm of Barton, Barton and Barton is pleased to represent you pro bono."

A chill ran down Lacey's spine. "Pro bono. Oh, dear. Why? What's the catch?"

"You're a friend. This is a high-profile case, and I'm the firm's criminal defense specialist now. I'm your man."

"I'm not a criminal."

"I didn't say you were, Lacey. But with your unexpected involvement, anything may happen, and I'm betting this case has potential for more media attention. Your abduction even hit *The Washington Post*." He frowned. "Not the front page."

"Metro section?"

"Sorry." He shook his head. "Style section, inside. Under an ad."

"Figures. They would never put an *Eye Street Observer* story on the front page."

"Just two paragraphs, but still." Ben looked at his watch. "I'm here to help and see how things work out. At least until they catch your missing cowboy, or I go skiing. I'm flexible."

"Flexible enough to represent Tucker?"

"Cole Tucker, the suspect? Tell me more."

Lacey stopped Ben with a hand on his arm. "Benjamin, you must understand one thing. Cole Tucker is not a killer. I'd stake my life on it."

"Again? Sure. I'm your attorney, so let's say I accept your theory of the case. Provisionally."

"Tucker's attorney is fresh from the bar exam. And there's something very funny about the evidence they've got."

"Funny how?"

"It's based on an anonymous tip to a deputy. Ben, there's no such thing as an anonymous tip in this town. And the same deputy unlocked Tucker's restraints."

"Excuse me?"

"Right in front of me. Anyway, you have to think about Tucker."

"This suspect is really innocent? I must tell you, that almost never happens. It's all right, though. Even the innocent have the right to a strong defense."

"Brooke is really going to owe you. Not to mention how much I'm going to owe you." *And I'm going to owe Brooke, big-time.*

"Don't mention it. After we debrief—"

" 'Debrief'? I hate that word. Can't we just say catch up?"

"After we *catch up,* I thought I'd check out the spring skiing in Steamboat Springs. It's closer than Aspen. You're not planning to get into any more trouble for a day or two, are you?"

"Funny, Ben. Very funny. I'm glad this is both business and pleasure for you. But sure, go skiing. Where are your skis?"

"At that awful motel. Brooke said there were no luxury hotels out here closer than Steamboat Springs. I'm distressed to find she's right."

Ben opened the door into the lobby, where Lacey's family promptly swooped down on her. *Not another family reunion!* Other women might have wanted their families with them at this moment, but all Lacey really wanted was a hot bath and some privacy. And Vic Donovan. She was swept up into a family huddle. Her sister, Cherise, was wearing her new nine-hundred-dollar cowboy boots, which made Lacey pause. If some killer was after women in fancy cowboy boots, Lacey wanted her sister safely in running shoes. Or combat boots.

"Have they mistreated you here, Lacey?" Rose asked.

"The décor crushed my spirit, but I'm fine, Mom. I just need to get out of here."

"Of course you do."

"You didn't tell Dad—"

"Tell your father about your being kidnapped? Good Lord, no! But it's been all over the news." She checked her watch. "He should just be getting settled in Taiwan. Thailand. Wherever. We'll talk to him later tonight."

"Mom, I told you she'd be fine," Cherise said, her eyes filling with tears. Then she saw Benjamin Barton and her attention swayed slightly. She dabbed at her eyes and threw Benjamin Barton her most dazzling cheerleader smile. "Hi, I'm Cherise Smithsonian. I'm the sister who *doesn't* get into trouble. And you must be?"

Ben seemed a little dazzled himself by the charms of a pretty blond former cheerleader. He held Cherise's hand perhaps a beat too long. But not too long for Cherise.

"Cherise, nice to meet you. Are you staying in town?"

"Oh, yeah! At that funky little motel. And I thought maybe I'd hit the slopes over at Steamboat. Now that Lacey is safe. She doesn't ski, you know. But I do. Do you ski?"

Benjamin beamed with pleasure. Lacey whispered in Cherise's ear, "You are such a flirt, sis. Careful with my lawyer. I might need him again."

Lacey looked beyond her mother, who was still talking. An exhausted Vic Donovan was leaning by the front door. Their eyes met and Lacey ran to him. He caught her in another crushing embrace.

"I didn't want to get between you and your mother," he said softly. "We have to talk, darlin'. Away from here."

"Oh, Vic," she whispered. "Could I possibly talk you into rescuing me?"

"I'd like nothing better. But you've got quite an entourage. Is that really Brooke's brother?"

"Can't you see the resemblance?"

"Now that you mention it. But he seems lucid and normal."

Rose Smithsonian interrupted the moment. "Vic's been worried to death about you."

"I've aged ten years," Vic said.

"What about Cole Tucker?" Cherise asked. "Where is he?"

"Silence." Ben Barton hushed them all and hustled them out the front door of the Justice Center. "No more chatter about anything related to the case, especially in earshot of the press. We must talk, Lacey. Privately."

A mob of reporters and photographers was hanging around the entryway, and suddenly Dodd Muldoon was front and center. There were flashing cameras and calls of "Lacey! Lacey! Is it true— Can I have a quote— Lacey, look over here!" Muldoon's voice cut through the babble.

"Welcome home, Scoop. *The Daily Press* is going to be the first on this story."

"You'll never have the whole story, Muldoon. That's mine." Lacey shot back. Someone stuck a microphone in her face. She cut through the mob, her bodyguards, Vic and Ben, clearing a path for her. Her mother and sister trailed behind.

Ben said in her ear, "Lacey, my best legal advice is that you stay out of trouble."

"Good luck with that, Ben," Vic said. "That's always my advice to Lacey too."

She glared at both of them.

"Don't irritate or engage the media," Ben continued, "and stay available for the sheriff. Don't say anything, but be polite. Now, I know it's not what Brooke would do. She'd think of something completely cockeyed and land you both in jail, and in the headlines."

"That's my cockeyed best friend you're talking about," Lacey pointed out, smiling.

"And my best sister. Cockeyed and, no doubt, brilliant. Forever skirting the letter of the law. I'd rather keep my clients out of jail than grab a headline."

"I don't care what happens as long as I can get cleaned up first. And rescue my rental car."

Cherise and Rose caught up with them. "What's going on?" her mother demanded.

"I'm taking Lacey back to her motel," Vic said. "You may consider me her personal bodyguard until we leave Sagebrush. And after that too." He stepped between her mother and sister and pulled Lacey to him.

Rose patted Vic on the back. "You've got your hands full," she said.

"Thanks, Mom," Lacey said.

"I didn't say you weren't worth it. But you were always a handful."

Lacey exchanged a look with her sister. Cherise took her mother's arm. "Okay, Mom, Lacey's got a bodyguard and the motel's got a bar. Let's go."

Ben took hold of Cherise's other arm. "Did I mention I'm a member of the bar?"

chapter 21

"Chief Donovan?" A careworn middle-aged woman approached Vic. She barely glanced at Lacey.

The woman's eyes carried so much sorrow that Lacey thought about stepping away from Vic's rented Jeep to give her some privacy, but he held her close. Behind the woman, a big man put his arm on the woman's shoulder.

"Chief Donovan?" the big man said. "Can you tell us what's going on with the search for Cole Tucker? The sheriff's office won't tell us a thing."

"Mrs. Fowler." Vic grasped the woman's outstretched hands. "Call me Vic. I'm not police chief here anymore, you know, not for a few years now. I'm a private investigator back East."

Lacey realized this must be Rae Fowler's mother. Kitty Fowler grabbed Vic's hand like a drowning victim reaching for a life raft. But she wasn't crying. She was dry-eyed and purposeful.

Lacey looked past the woman's shoulder. A knot of reporters was bearing down on her, with Muldoon bringing up the rear. Someone pointed a camera at them.

"Not here," Vic said. "We need to get away from these vultures."

Excuse me. I'm one of those vultures. But she too had no desire at this moment to be quoted or photographed. Vic and Lacey followed the large man, who turned out to be the woman's husband, Herb Fowler, to their green and white camper parked at the far end of the lot.

"It's a little small," Herb Fowler said, "but it saves on

motels. We don't know how long we'll have to be here in town."

Inside, there was room enough for the four of them to sit around a small built-in table. The camper, though cozied up with white ruffled curtains at the small window, felt closed in by grief.

While Rae had been pretty and round faced, her mother was plain and gaunt, with dark circles under her eyes. Kitty Fowler's lackluster, pale hair was streaked with gray and pulled back into a messy chignon at the back of her neck. She wore a navy blue knit jacket over matching slacks that hung on her frame. The thin woman had a hungry look, but Lacey suspected it had nothing to do with food. She was starved for justice and had left vanity behind.

"They let Cole Tucker escape," she said. "How could they do that? I want that monster caught."

"They'll catch him," Vic said. "Just a matter of time."

Herb Fowler made an effort to smile. He was balding, with a neatly trimmed sandy red mustache, and he wore a blazer over slacks. Herb had been in the army and had the air of a man who knew that life went on in the face of disaster.

"Our son wanted to come with us, but he's in college and—and this is such a sad business," he said.

Kitty smiled for the first time. "He's in his sophomore year. He makes all As."

"A little different from Rae. She wasn't much of a student." Herb grasped his wife's hand as if he could pour his strength into it. "Our son's in pre-med."

The son was the good child, while the prodigal daughter would never come home again. Kitty looked happy for a moment, but then she remembered why she was here, and her smile turned down. Not a day would go by for the rest of her life when the mother wouldn't think of her daughter's untimely death, when she wouldn't wonder what might have been. Would Rae have straightened out, gone to college, gotten married, had babies? She turned to Lacey, a question in her expression.

"He let you get away?"

"Yes. He let me go and put me on a horse." Lacey found it hard to keep her gaze, but she wouldn't turn away.

"Why did he let you live?" She closed her eyes for a moment and a tear squeezed out. "Did he talk about Rae? Why he did it?"

Lacey shook her head. "We talked about who might have set him up."

"And you believe that?" Kitty asked.

"I do. I don't believe Tucker could kill anyone. And I'm alive."

"But the police can't be wrong. They have the evidence!"

"Kitty," her husband said, "we want them to be right. But we don't know —"

"There is a big gaping hole in my life that nothing can fill," she continued. "As much as I dreaded Rae's future, I never expected this." Kitty's eyes filled with tears.

"Rae caused us a lot of heartache," her husband said. "But we loved her."

Kitty choked back a sob. "She ran away before. She was in such a hurry to grow up. You couldn't tell her being an adult was no bed of roses. That you have to answer to your boss and pay your rent. I never imagined what would happen to my little wild child."

"You can't blame yourselves," Vic said.

"We don't," she said. "Not really. We've talked it through, over and over, with our pastor. Rae was on a collision course her whole life. I always asked myself, what did I do wrong? Should I be harder? Should I be more lenient? But nothing could stop her. She was on a path to destruction."

Herb put his arm around his wife. "Don't torture yourself, Kitty."

"May I ask you a question?" Lacey asked.

Kitty looked Lacey in the eye. "Go ahead."

"Do you have any pictures of Rae? I'd like to see what she was like." Lacey refrained from saying she wanted to know what kind of *shoes* the girl wore. She knew that would sound tone-deaf to the seriousness of the situation.

"Sure do." Kitty squeezed out of the booth and opened a cabinet. She pulled out a photo album bursting at the seams with photos of her daughter. "Here she is. Here's our little Rae."

Lacey leafed through the pages from the beginning. Rae was a pretty child. Every snapshot seemed to vibrate with her energy. But Lacey wanted to jump to the end to see how she became the rebellious girl who ran away from home. She looked for a picture of Rae wearing cowboy boots.

"I've heard things about you, Ms. Smithsonian," Kitty said.

"We've read about your investigating those murders," Herb added.

Lacey braced herself. She never knew how people would react. "I'm just a reporter." Vic raised one eyebrow, visible only to Lacey. "Sometimes I notice when things don't add up."

"She does that," Vic said. "And sometimes, the plain truth is cops don't see everything. I should know."

Lacey turned a page in the album and paused. *There. Right there. Rae Fowler, maybe six years old, posing in a pair of pink boots.* She took a deep breath.

"Kitty, do you have any idea what kind of shoes Rae might have been wearing when she—went missing? You might not know."

"But I do know," Kitty said. "At least I'd bet money on it. She was wearing those silly boots."

"Boots?" *Don't get your hopes up.*

"She had this pair of cowboy boots," Herb Fowler said. "Real fancy. We couldn't get her out of them."

"I was afraid at first that Rae stole them," Kitty went on. "She came home from her babysitting job one day—this was back home in Denver—wearing this crazy pair of boots. Rae was just fifteen, I think. I'd never seen anything like these boots. Black with silver leather cutouts. Lightning bolts. And silver trim around the toe and around the heels."

"Filigreed silver?" Lacey asked, barely daring to breathe. "On the heels?"

"Filigree, yeah, whatever they call it. Looked real delicate. They must have cost a fortune. Rae said Mrs. Hurst, the lady she babysat for, *gave* them to her. God forgive me, I didn't believe her, and we had a big fight. Rae said I never believed her, and I guess I didn't."

Herb picked up the story. "She had this thing about being like a cowgirl. Even when she was a little girl. Don't know where she picked that up. We bought her a pair of pink cowboy boots when she was, oh, six or seven. There's pictures in there. She was still trying to wear them when her feet grew too big."

"Was Rae telling the truth about where those fancy boots came from?" Lacey asked.

Kitty nodded. "I called Mrs. Hurst. Sure enough, she said she gave them to Rae. Mrs. Hurst had them special-made somewhere. Well, she had the money, didn't she? Said her feet had grown so much after she had her babies, and Rae saw them and just went nuts over them, so she was glad to give them to someone who would appreciate them. Appreciate them. My goodness, Rae adored those boots! How she would polish them."

"Is there a picture of Rae in those boots?" Lacey tried to sound as neutral as possible. Vic pressed Lacey's arm as a warning not to go too far, but he didn't try to stop her. There hadn't been time to tell him what she'd found up at Thompson's cabin.

Kitty nodded and took the album from Lacey and flipped through a few pages. "We would have buried her in those boots. They found her barefoot. I don't know if you knew that. She loved them so much. But—"

"If they turn up," Vic said, "I'll make sure you get them back."

"There," Kitty said. "Oh, she was so pretty."

The photograph was of a teenage Rae grinning and posing triumphantly, just the way she had posed at seven or eight, the cowboy boots front and center, one turned to the side with a good view of the heel. Lacey couldn't be *exactly* sure the silver bootheel she'd found came from the boots in the picture, but it looked like it could.

But if one smart-ass reporter said the heel and photo were a match, Sheriff T-Rex would be sure to say they *weren't*. Lacey slumped back, feeling hot and feverish, her limbs heavy with exhaustion.

"Kitty, would you please show this photograph to the sheriff? This exact picture," Lacey said. "No, wait, not the sheriff. Take it to Agent Firestone with the CBI. He's probably still in the Justice Center. Vic, do you have a number for him?"

Vic nodded, a little puzzled. He took out one of his own cards and wrote a phone number on it.

The Fowlers looked at each other. "If it will help," Kitty said. "If we can get the picture back."

"They can make a copy," Vic said.

"Tell Agent Firestone what you told me," Lacey said. "About Rae's favorite pair of cowboy boots. That she might have been wearing them when she disappeared. Show him this picture. Please. It's very important."

"This might be something? Because she was found barefoot, you mean?"

Lacey hesitated. "I can't promise anything."

"The CBI is interested in any information that will help solve the case," Vic said. "This could be critical."

Thank you, Vic, she thought, *for backing me up even though you don't know what I'm up to.*

"Don't talk to anyone but Firestone, and tell him I sent you," Vic continued. "That's my card. And don't worry—they're going to catch Cole Tucker."

"If it's important—" Kitty clutched the photo album in both hands. "We'll go right now."

Herb Fowler opened the camper door. The reporters lounging in the parking lot snapped to attention. Muldoon must have gone to file his story, and Lacey didn't recognize anyone else.

The media made way for Kitty as she was helped down the steps by her husband. Lacey and Vic followed, and Herb locked the camper. "Now, back off, all of you," Herb ordered. The reporters seemed torn: follow Lacey or Kitty Fowler? Grieving parents of a murder victim, or the kidnap victim of the alleged murderer? *Tough call.*

Kitty and Herb were swallowed up by the mob of reporters.

"Give it up. I'm not talking to you guys," Lacey said to the journalists who stayed to shout questions at her. She marched to Vic's rental Jeep. He waited to speak until he and Lacey were buckled in and the engine on.

"All right, what's this cowboy boot business all about? You think the killer, if it wasn't Tucker, was swiping their boots?"

"Vic, I have so much to tell you I don't know where to start."

"Doesn't matter. Start anywhere." He put his hand on her knee and gently squeezed.

"Two of the victims wore unusual cowboy boots. Corazon liked to go dancing wearing her favorite boots."

"Tucker offered this information willingly?"

"No, I beat it out of him. The boots were the only thing he remembered about what she wore. That and short skirts."

"You interrogated him about her clothes?"

Lacey smiled slowly. "It's what I do, now, isn't it?"

"I gather you've concocted some sort of fashion clue theory, because that's also what you do." Vic turned the Jeep toward their motel. "Did the good sheriff appreciate your special talent?"

"You bet. Now, the Fowlers just told us about Rae and her favorite silver-heeled cowboy boots. Taking the victim's shoes? It wasn't just to keep them from running away, despite what all you manly lawmen think. And I'm not saying it was a boot fetish, per se, but some killers keep trophies, don't they? Why not cowboy boots? Especially strikingly unusual ones?"

"Point taken. Anything else you're not telling me? Okay, anything you haven't had a chance to tell me *yet*?"

She waited a beat. "I found a heel in the cabin where Tucker took me." Vic just stared at her. His eyes narrowed and he opened his mouth to speak, but Lacey rushed on. "A black stacked leather cowboy bootheel, wrapped in silver filigree. Looks like it matches the photograph of Rae's fancy boots." She took out her camera and showed him her shot of the heel. "T-Rex wasn't impressed, but he made me leave it with him anyway."

"About the cabin Tucker took you to . . ."

"But I do have photos of the heel." She smiled, pleased with herself. "Lots of photos, every angle, and comparing it to the heel on my boots. Same size."

"Okay, we'll talk about the cabin later." Vic picked up her camera and clicked through the shots. "Now, you told Firestone you took these photos, didn't you?"

"Didn't come up in the conversation. The heel was jammed in a loose floorboard under an old sofa in the cabin. Tucker wasn't very impressed, honestly. And for the record, neither was your old buddy Rico Firestone. But he hadn't seen Kitty Fowler's photo. Vic, darling, is that one heck of a fashion clue, or *what*?" She noticed the glazed look in his eyes. "You're not impressed either? What's a girl gotta do?"

Vic whistled. "Who said I'm not impressed? If that heel turns out to be Rae Fowler's, then she was in that cabin. Or her boots were."

"At least for a time." Lacey leaned across the console to kiss him.

"It's a theory. One hell of a theory. Firestone is a good guy. It was smart sending the Fowlers to him instead of T-Rex. He'll listen to Firestone. And Firestone will listen to Kitty Fowler. If she IDs the bootheel, T-Rex'll change his tune, sweetheart. He just won't tell *you* about it."

"Cole Tucker is still in love with you," Vic whispered into Lacey's hair as they lay on the bed in the motel room.

"I love *you*, Vic darling, but please shut up."

Lacey had spent a long time under the shower's wonderful steam. She changed into clean clothes for dinner, but then she made the mistake of sitting down on the bed. It would take heavy equipment to move her. She flopped down and dragged the pillow over her head.

"A man doesn't do a crazy thing like he did unless he's in love," Vic persisted.

"Maybe he's just crazy," she said from beneath the pillow. She peeked out. "Are you saying you'd pull a stunt like Tucker?"

"If I had to." Vic was mock-sulking.

"For heaven's sake, Vic, what's your problem? I'm fine, I'm back, we're together. No harm done. At least not much."

"I should have been with you, not Tucker."

"Yes, dear." *But we never would have found that cabin and that heel.*

"You know we're supposed to meet up with your lawyer and the home team tonight?"

"Of course, dear. Why don't you come over here and hold me for a while?" She inched over. "I forgot to tell you something else. Douglas MacArthur Jones and Tony Trujillo are coming to town, and my nightmare will be complete."

He was silent for a moment, smoothing her hair away from her face. "You're beautiful, you know that?"

She smiled and kissed him. "Aw, shucks, Detective Donovan. After a day like today, that's mighty nice to hear." Lacey closed her eyes and Vic snuggled next to her. "And I don't even smell like a sweaty palomino anymore, do I?"

"You're *my* sweaty little—"

She laughed. Lying there, wrapped tightly in Vic's warm arms, with a thousand responsibilities, an innocent man hunted for murder, and far too many people expecting her presence far too soon, Lacey Smithsonian fell asleep, as if, for that one moment, she had not a care in the world.

chapter 22

"You're late," Rose announced as Lacey and Vic arrived at the Blue Ox restaurant. Rose looked like she had just awakened from her own long nap.

"But I'm alive," Lacey said, kissing her mother's cheek. "And isn't that the important part?"

"Vic called to say you'd be late," Cherise said. "We've only been here ten minutes. You crazy kids probably needed a little time to yourselves, didn't you?"

Lacey just smiled. The décor at the Blue Ox was down-at-the-heels, the drinks weak, and the steaks barely passable. But it was seldom crowded, which was why Vic picked it. Dodd Muldoon knew Lacey had sworn never to set foot inside the place. The local and out-of-town media would most likely be at the Italian or Mexican restaurants downtown. Under the circumstances, it was almost private.

"I've been in contact with your fan base back home," Ben Barton noted.

"Did you mean back home on Planet Earth," Lacey asked, "or on Brooke's Conspiracy Planet?"

"My sister thinks those are the same planet. I promised you'd ring her tonight. Stella will be there too. If you don't call first, they'll conference-call *you*."

"You have the nicest friends, Lacey," her mother said. "You really should call them."

Ben hid behind his menu. "And you might want to check out Conspiracy Clearinghouse."

"What did that maniac Damon write now?" Lacey

sucked in a deep breath. According to Brooke, Damon was in a slump. He needed a fresh story.

"'Lacey Smithsonian, wearing her pink spurs, kidnapped by the very accused-mass-murderer-cowboy whose innocence she had trumpeted, makes a daring escape and rides bareback on a winged pink unicorn to the Old West hamlet of Sagebrush, Colorado, to fight for truth, justice, and the American way.' I paraphrase," Ben said.

"Damon is deranged," Lacey said.

"Damon is hilarious. I'd love to see your pink spurs, sis," Cherise said. "They'd go with my blue boots."

Ben set his menu on the table. "It is unfortunate that he believes everything he writes, and that he is dating my sister. The funny thing is Brooke is brilliant and lucid in every other respect. Well, nearly every other."

"Where's Smithsonian?" a booming voice interrupted the table. "I'm here to retrieve *The Eye Street Observer*'s missing scribe."

"Mac. Imagine seeing you here." Nothing would surprise Lacey at this point.

Douglas MacArthur Jones had arrived from Washington, D.C., and he was ready to play cowboy in his sweater vest and corduroy pants. Behind him, Tony Trujillo was dragging a couple of extra chairs to the table. At least Trujillo looked at home on the Western Slope, in his jeans and ever-present cowboy boots. Today's pair were tooled burgundy cowhide.

"How did you find me?" she asked.

"It wasn't because you answered your phone." Mac scowled.

"I turned it off," Lacey said.

"Mac Jones," Rose said, "my daughter was worn out. She needs rest."

Mac pressed on. "So Trujillo and I asked around about where all the reporters were hanging out. Figured you wouldn't be giving them any tips. We looked for the places they wouldn't go. Blue Ox was number one on the list."

"What's the story, Lois Lane?" Trujillo said, pushing

his chair between hers and Vic's. "Safe and sound? Leads on the escaped cowboy? Has he been in contact?"

Lacey shook her head. "No. He doesn't know my number. Or that the cops retrieved my cell phone, after he threw it out the car window."

Trujillo was jotting down notes in his slender reporter's notebook. "Tucker really threw your phone out the window? Some friend. And the cops really gave it back?"

"Lacey, you can't comment on an ongoing investigation," Ben cautioned.

"Sure I can. Do you think I'm going to let those other media monkeys steal my story? I can tell part of it."

Ben rolled his eyes. "You're as bad as Brooke."

"Of course they gave it back," Mac said. "She answered my call. Before she turned it off. I'm sure she's going to turn it back on."

"I heard he stole some funky car," Tony said.

"*Borrowed*," Lacey amended. "That's what Tucker says. Tasso Petrus's bakery truck, an old Jeep Cherokee with antlers on the grille. Can't miss it. Tasso probably has it back by now, unless the sheriff is holding it for evidence."

"Cool. I'll try to find a picture of it. So, Lacey, how did Tucker do it anyway? How'd he manage to get out of the shackles and overpower the deputy and grab you *and* escape from a courthouse crawling with cops and spectators and media? I'm having some trouble with this. You help him?"

"Don't be ridiculous, Tony. It all happened so fast." Lacey's blood pressure was rising. "And it's *my* story."

"It's *our* story," he said.

"You have enough for now, don't you?" Lacey asked him. "Smithsonian safe and sound, details to follow."

"Get pictures!" Mac ordered Trujillo.

Tony opened his canvas messenger bag and took out a big digital camera, a Nikon DSLR. "Hansen gave me a loaner. He says hey, by the way."

There was no way to get out of a photo for her own newspaper. Lacey flashed an obligatory smile and gave him two thumbs-up.

Rose and Cherise jumped in behind Lacey. "I want copies of those pictures! I just wish your father were here. I don't know when we last had a family photograph."

"Possibly under happier circumstances," Cherise said.

"What could be happier than finding out your daughter is alive and well, after being kidnapped?" Rose said. "And the whole family together? Almost. We can Photoshop your father in later."

"Just like real life," Cherise said.

"And Dad will only get the abridged version of events, right?" Lacey said.

"I don't know, Smithsonian." Tony frowned at her. "You look pretty good for going through such a grueling ordeal. Can you look a little more abducted?"

"You don't want her to look defeated, do you?" Mac said. "*The Eye Street Observer* is not defeated! Our Smithsonian is not defeated!"

"Okay, okay." Trujillo put the camera away. "I'll go file my story. I'll be back for drinks."

"What's good here?" Mac flipped open his menu.

"Nothing," Lacey said.

"On the plus side," Vic commented, "it probably won't kill you."

"Fine. I'll take the meat loaf," Mac decided.

Lacey felt a breeze. Someone new came into the dining room. She turned around in her seat to see CBI Agent Rico Firestone at the door. She got to her feet.

"I'll just be a minute," she said to curious stares. Vic followed Lacey into the lounge where Firestone sat at the empty bar and ordered a beer.

"Rico, are you looking for me?"

He cleared his throat. "Lacey. Howdy, Vic. Thought you'd like to know Mrs. Fowler identified that bootheel as belonging to her daughter."

"I knew it!" Lacey rejoiced, but sadness immediately followed. She and Rae had been in the same cabin. A cabin Tucker knew about.

"Their photograph cinches it?" Vic asked him.

"Looks like a match. New evidence." He nodded to Lacey. "We're taking a team to go over that cabin tomorrow, see if we can find anything else."

Lacey leaned against Vic. "You know where it is?"

"Cabin with a dead coyote on the fence post?" Rico Firestone smiled briefly. "T-Rex said he knows which one it must be. Let me caution you, this doesn't go anywhere near exonerating Cole Tucker. Fact is, it might go the other way. But it'll help us get a better idea of how and where those women spent their last days."

"Who knows about the heel?" The thought nagged at Lacey: If the killer caught wind of it, he'd destroy the evidence ahead of the cops.

"I can't plug all the holes in the wall." Firestone leaned against the bar. "The official word is that we're going to search the cabin where you were held by Tucker just to get a bead on where he went. We're not releasing any information on that heel."

"You taking the posse?" Vic asked.

"No way. Forensics is CBI's show." Firestone picked up his beer mug. "That heel? Turning up all the way out near the Sand Wash like that? When the victims were dumped closer to the city? Just plain weird. Good find."

"It's nice to be noticed," she said. *Fashion clue!*

"What are you writing?" Firestone wanted to know. Lacey shrugged and smiled. "I'd appreciate it, Lacey, if you wouldn't reveal the information. Not till we get a chance to process the cabin ourselves. Don't want a lot of souvenir hunters trampling a possible crime scene." He sipped his beer.

"My story won't appear until tomorrow online and in the paper after that." *The CBI better get cracking.*

He nodded slightly. "By the way, I just talked to an old friend of yours."

"An old friend?" *I can hardly wait.* "Really? Who?"

"Guy named Broadway Lamont."

"The big man himself." Firestone must have called the D.C. homicide detective for a reference. "Did he vouch for me?" Lacey knew that could go either way.

"Sort of. He also said you could be a real pain in the, um, the neck. And he alleged—how did he put it? 'Smithsonian's got a murder mojo.' That true?"

"No." She sniffed. "What can I say, Rico? It's good to have friends."

Lacey and Vic turned to go, but the mirror behind the bar suddenly showed another face at the door, one that looked remarkably ducklike. Lacey jumped. Grady Rush stared at her. She imagined it was with malevolence.

"You all right, sweetheart?" Vic said.

She spun on her heel and headed back to their table, but she couldn't help but pass Grady. He was halfway between the bar and the dining room, standing in the narrow passageway.

"Hey, Lacey. Glad to see you're okay." Grady's eyes were bloodshot, as if he'd already downed a few drinks. He grabbed her arm. His fingers dug into her flesh. There would be a bruise. "Cole could have killed you, you know. Like those other ladies. Man like that's got no conscience."

"Bull. You know Tucker and you don't believe that." She shook off his arm and backed away. It seemed to her that Vic should be with her, but she looked behind her and saw he was with Agent Firestone. They were watching. *Do they want to see how I react to Grady, or how he reacts to me?*

"We're going to get Cole Tucker and bring him back here. You can depend on that, Lacey." His voice rose. His breath reeked of liquor. "After what he did to me, I'm going to get him. Dead or alive."

She stared him down. "Who was it that called you about the evidence on Tucker's property, Grady?"

His eyes took in the room, as if he wanted to make sure who was around to hear his answer. "An anonymous tip. I brought it to the sheriff. Just doing my job."

"And you don't know who it was?"

"Like I said. Anonymous."

"I don't believe you. Who set up Cole? Was it you?"

Grady's answer took a few seconds longer than necessary. "We got Tucker dead to rights."

"And what did you tell the sheriff about Tucker's escape? Did you tell him that you unlocked the shackles because Tucker asked you to?"

"Tucker knocked me out somehow, and took the key." He put his face way too close to her. "Maybe you helped him escape. Maybe I should tell that to T-Rex." Grady glared at her, his little duck eyes narrowed.

"T-Rex will eat you alive. You're not a good liar, Deputy," Lacey said. "But you are a liar."

His nostrils flared. He was about to say something but decided against it. He was the first to walk away, head down, hands in his pockets. Lacey watched him take a seat at the far end of the bar, far away from Rico Firestone.

Vic caught up with her and put his arm around her. "You okay?"

She was trembling. "You and Firestone enjoy the show?"

"Firestone held me back. He's keeping his eye on the deputy. It looks bad to let a suspected murderer escape on your watch. No one is sure about Grady Rush."

"I'm sure about him."

"The consensus is Grady's dumb as a bag of rocks. But a rock is just a tool. Whose tool is he?"

Where's Tucker now? Lacey wondered. *Is he safe somewhere, hiding out in one of the other line camps? Is there a dead coyote hanging on a fence wherever he is tonight? Will his cowboy way of thinking save him? Or hang him, like that coyote?*

"I knew something like this would happen," Brooke said during the three-way phone call later that evening.

"All's well that ends well, right, guys?" Lacey was flat on her back on the bed, her battered cell phone at her ear, trying to keep her eyes open. She gave up and kept talking with her eyes closed. Vic was at the desk with his laptop, catching up on business in Virginia, and Colorado.

"Ha! I nearly died of anxiety, Lace," Stella chimed in. "I was so upset I had to cancel appointments! Imagine what I might have done to someone's hair!"

"So that's on my head too, I suppose," Lacey said, running her fingers through her hair. It felt dry.

"Exactly. And speaking of your head, don't forget to condition. I'm not there to watch you."

"How's Ben doing? Is he being nice to you?" Brooke asked.

"He's fabulous. I never expected to see him here, marching to your orders," Lacey said. "Thanks for sending him, Brooke. I understand the balance of power shifted, and you'll be in his debt after this."

"Not for long. I adore Benjamin, but our relationship is like a game of chess and I'm the grand master. He thinks he has me in check, but he's wrong. Silly boy. Just take good care of him."

"Cherise took one look at him and decided to be his personal assistant and tour guide. She said something about taking him skiing in Steamboat. Oh, and helping him buy new duds so he'll fit in."

"But Ben fits in everywhere. He's a Brooks Brothers boy. Suitable for every occasion."

"She was talking about a little Western camouflage. Maybe some Levi's."

"Benjamin? In jeans?" Brooke sounded dubious.

Lacey assumed both Brooke and Ben were born in little lawyer suits. While most babies were wrapped in pink and blue blankets, the Barton, Barton & Barton progeny were tucked into tiny pin-striped gray flannels. With little regimental ties. Briefcases instead of baby bags, and a Burberry check baby tote bag.

"Relax, Brooke," Stella said. "If Benny's as uptight as you are, he could use a little relaxation. Lacey's little sis is totally cute, remember, and she's not as, like, *backwards* as her big sis, if you know what I mean. You know?" Lacey groaned.

Brooke ignored the comment. "Listen, Lacey, just make sure he keeps you out of a twenty-four-hour hold."

"Ben's a tiger," Lacey said. "The minute the sheriff saw him, he knew it was all over and let me go."

"Good. We want you back in one piece."

"Don't worry. Ben is my barrister, and Vic is my personal protection professional. I'm covered." Vic tweaked her toes without turning away from his computer, and Lacey smiled.

"What about your cute cowboy?" Stella asked. "Looks not guilty to me."

"Tucker's not guilty." Lacey saw Vic shake his head. "No way."

"So tell us about this cowboy. What's the situation? Cole Tucker takes one look at you and decides to snatch you out of the courthouse and make a break for freedom? *Swoon!* Am I right, Brookie?" Stella cooed. "Is that totally swoonable or what?"

"Hey! It wasn't exactly like that, guys."

"It's, like, *totally* the most romantic thing I ever heard of!"

"Stella, are you demented?" Brooke broke in. "It was unbelievable, a wildly irresponsible act of desperation and madness. Only a madwoman would think that was romantic. But you have to admit it has a *slight* air of romance."

"Like I said. It took chutzpah, for sure. But what a gesture," Stella insisted, still under the spell of her upcoming nuptials to Nigel Griffin.

"It's not romantic," Lacey said, noting a puzzled scowl on Vic's face. "It was awful, uncomfortable, the most embarrassing moment of my life." She thought of crossing the snowy wastes of Yampa County on horseback, and the fear that ran through her like an icy trickle the entire time she was with Tucker. And the indignities of having to use an outhouse in the snow and, worst of all, exiting the courthouse slung over Tucker's shoulder. She shivered all over again. "At least there's nothing on YouTube."

"Not yet, anyway," Brooke said. "We're monitoring the situation."

"I'll keep checking," Stella promised. "If there is, I'll e-mail you the link."

"Don't you dare, Stel. I'm safe and sound, and I've got the handsomest bodyguard you ever saw."

Vic's scowl turned into a grin. Lacey said her goodbyes to her friends and turned her phone off for the night.

Why couldn't Tucker have thrown this damn phone a little farther?

chapter 23

"Smithsonian. Smile!" Mac held up a copy of *The Sage-brush Daily Press,* the one with the cover story on Lacey's abduction, and another with a CBI picture of Lacey mounted on Buttercup, being met by Tucker's brother, Kit, and the sheriff. The headline read: SHE'S ALIVE!

"Like Frankenstein," she said.

"Or Laceystein. I picked up extra copies for the newsroom back in D.C." Tony fanned out his collection of newspapers.

Lacey growled. "Give me that." She grabbed one of the copies, emitting groans and snarls as she read. But at least, she reflected, she was back in town and off that horse. Today she was clean and comfortable in her dark-wash blue jeans, forest green turtleneck sweater, and a vintage green wool jacket that nipped in at the waist. It wasn't an exact match for her green and brown cowboy boots, but they went together nicely.

The three of them were sitting at the Amarillo Café, relatively empty at ten in the morning. Laptops ready. Vic had reluctantly left her to meet with Mac and Tony without him. She had asked him to kindly go away, and he'd arranged a briefing with Agent Firestone before the CBI team headed out to find Lacey's lost cabin.

The rest of the media were nowhere to be seen. With Cole Tucker having vanished into the backcountry, and Lacey relatively safe and sound—and obviously hoarding her own information for an *Eye Street Observer* exclusive—the other news jockeys were sniffing out other leads to follow. Lacey was big news yesterday, but it was a day later and the world had turned to other events. Except for *The Sagebrush Daily Press* and Dodd Muldoon, who felt slighted that she hadn't graced him with an interview. She wasn't speaking to him, so Muldoon had milked Lacey's past as a local reporter with the intensity of a fever dream.

"I ran into that Muldoon character." Mac opened the paper to the jump. "Said he taught you everything you know." He chuckled.

"This gets better and better," Tony said, reading *The Daily Press.* "What a wacked-out little paper. I'm selling these to the guys in Sports. And Wiedemeyer, he'll love it."

"What did Muldoon say?" Lacey wasn't comfortable around Muldoon anymore. He was after Tucker's land, and he'd had a fling with one of the victims, Ally Newport. He knew too many of the town's secrets. Did he know about the silver heel?

"That fool said you were going to give him an exclusive. You never said that, did you?" Mac glowered at her.

"Don't believe a word he says. When I left town, Muldoon told people I was on vacation and I'd be back in a couple of weeks. He was still saying that a year later."

"He speaks fondly of you too," Tony piped up. Lacey rolled her eyes.

"Don't blame him for trying to weasel a story out of you," Mac said. "No one in this biz wants the out-of-town papers, the big guns, to come in and scoop you. Isn't that right, Scoop?"

"Don't call me Scoop." *If it's the last thing I do, I'll get Dodd Muldoon.* Lacey picked up her cup. It was empty.

"If the scoop fits," Mac said. He turned to his battered black ThinkPad. Lacey stared. She had never seen her editor use a laptop. "You come up with any fashion clues out there on the range, way out west of Purgatory?"

"Purgatory is a ski resort south of here." Their waitress was nowhere in sight.

"You know what I'm talking about. Or have you lost that special ability of yours, Smithsonian?"

She glared in response. "I'd hate to let you down, Mac." She helped herself to the unprotected coffeepot and refilled everyone's cup.

"She's got something." Tony scooted his chair closer. "Lois Lane always gets that smug look when she's bogarting a fashion clue."

"Spill, Smithsonian. Tony's got a hunch." Mac picked up his half-eaten cinnamon roll and took a bite.

"The women were all found barefoot," she began.

"Shoes," Tony said, propping his black snakeskin boots on a nearby chair. "Chicks are obsessed with shoes, high heels, flip-flops, flats."

"Not like *you*, Trujillo?" Lacey eyed his footwear.

She picked up her tote bag to grab a fresh pen. Instead her fingers touched upon something she'd forgotten in the rush: the years-old article about Ally Newport. Lacey unfolded it and stared at the yellowing article. In it, Ally was still blond, still perky, still alive, wearing her bartender apron over jeans and a crisp white shirt. And there was something else about the full-length photograph, something Lacey hadn't noticed earlier, because it was before she found the silver heel, before she heard about Corazon and her cowboy boots. In the picture, Ally Newport was wearing cowboy boots. Boots with chevrons up the side.

Three for three? Now Lacey knew all the victims owned and wore unusual cowboy boots, even if that didn't prove they were wearing the boots when they were abducted or killed. *Get a grip, Lacey. Everyone wears cowboy boots up here!*

"We're waiting, Smithsonian." Mac sipped some coffee.

"Right here. This is a clue," she said, handing the article to Mac.

Tony pulled the article out of Mac's hands. "She's wearing cowboy boots."

"That's it," Lacey said. "That's the fashion clue. If the boot fits, wear it."

The handsome police reporter made a sour face. "Come on, that's not fair. She wore boots? So what? So do I." He lifted up one booted foot as a visual aid.

Lacey lowered her voice. "So maybe I found a fancy bootheel in that cabin. Maybe it belonged to the first victim. Maybe there's a photograph that proves it. Maybe the CBI is checking out that very cabin today for more evidence." They stared at her, open-mouthed. She had them at "bootheel."

Mac cleared his throat. "Start writing, Smithsonian. Doesn't need to be long. Victim's bootheel is enough to knock their socks off today. Tomorrow I want you to start writing your personal account of everything from the courthouse to the cabin. We can run it in installments. And, hey, you got a Fashion Bite for me?"

"You want a pint of blood to go with that, Mac? And what's Tony working on?"

"Trujillo writes police interviews."

"I spoke with Agent Rico Firestone." Tony flipped through his notes. "He had no comment. The cops aren't talking. Transporting prisoners is not their gig, so they're just laughing their asses off at the sheriff losing a prisoner. The chief of police is out of town. Nobody seems to be in charge there at all. And the sheriff's not talking either. They really call him T-Rex? Good name for him. He said he'd had enough of out-of-town reporters, and he didn't much care for the ones in town."

"You call those interviews?" Lacey asked. "No comments all around?"

"When do cops ever want to tell us anything?" Mac said. "If they won't talk to you, Tony, work that angle. 'Local law enforcement clamps lid on story! What are cops hiding?' Find out what they're doing at that cabin where Smithsonian was held. Let's go, people. We've got a deadline. Remember there's a two-hour time difference. I want your stories by noon—that's two p.m. in D.C. Call this *The Eye Street Observer West*."

"Why so soon?" she asked.

"I got a mission for you, Smithsonian."

The sour-faced waitress finally made an appearance, stared at the trio and her purloined coffeepot, and muttered darkly to herself, "This place ain't been the same since we got Wi-Fi."

Hey There, Annie Oakley, It's Western Wear, Not a Costume

Yes, *you*, city girl in that fringed leather skirt, those boots, and the turquoise bangles. When you don a Western look, you're wearing an American classic, a little piece of the frontier, of the Wild West, and the wild imagination as well. Not a Halloween costume.

Forged out of the Old West, when desperados were dandies wearing dusters and carrying silver-tipped canes, many of these iconic Western styles are still embodied by the cowboy, and cowgirl. You can borrow a bit of that swagger for yourself. But be careful, because in the city, a little swagger goes a long way.

Sure, you can slip on boot-cut Levi's and Wranglers. But there's more to frontier fashion than jeans. Western Wear—hats, shirts, boots, and jeans—is made with a healthy dose of myth added to rugged functionality. It's clothing that works hard and captures the imagination while doing so. That's not fashion; that's style. A style that's embodied in movies and TV and music, and cultural phenomena as exotic as rodeo and as country as the Grand Ole Opry. And by *you*, Miss Twenty-First-Century Annie Oakley.

Take the Western shirt, with its distinctive yoke, which is made to fit and flatter a trim torso. The snap-front shirt was designed as a safety feature. Those pretty pearlescent snaps open quickly with a yank of one hand. They're made that way so a cowboy's shirt won't get caught on a fence post or

hung up on the horns of a bull—and take the cowboy with it. But why pearl snaps? That's where
practicality meets style.

The boots are made so a rider caught in the
stirrup can slip his foot out and escape being
dragged. Though coming home safe from a day
on the cattle range is not always a concern, there
are American designers in love with the frontier
fantasy, who draw on it time and again in their
collections. See how Ralph Lauren's designs ram-
ble from his polo field style and back to the ranch.

Real cowgirls can wear what they want: ker-
chief, fringed chaps, the works. It's their life and
their lifestyle. But full Western regalia is rarely
seen, except perhaps at rodeos and stock shows.
If you're not a cowboy or cowgirl, you should stop
at one or two pieces.

The key is to know what pieces to choose, not
the entire Sedona Arizona collection. Remember,
nothing screams *outsider* as much as putting on
the whole little dogie. You don't want to look like
an extra in a cowboy film. Unless, of course, you
are an extra in a film.

And watch the Native American jewelry. Over-
doing the silver and turquoise, with the belt, the
heavy squash blossom necklace, the bracelets, ear-
rings, watchband, and collar points, is too much of
a good thing, and a sure sign you're an outsider.
Turquoise is like the spice in a dish. Use it to add a
dash of clear blue color, not to add a couple of
pounds to your outfit.

So wear Western with a clear head and a clear
idea of the tradition behind it. You want to evoke
the cowboy or cowgirl. Not the rodeo clown.

chapter 24

"What's Lois Lane get to do that I don't?" Tony asked Mac.

"You two are worse than children, you know that? My hair is turning gray because of you," Mac complained.

"You don't have much hair left, Mac. How can you tell?" Lacey contemplated her screen and willed the words to come, haunted by thoughts from her day and night with Tucker. She had to start with Rae Fowler's boots. After that, for the longer piece, she could start from the beginning. *We had a history, Cole Tucker and I . . .* She looked up. "Mac. You said you have a mission for me?"

"Yes, a mission. Something important." Mac looked worried.

"About the story?" Lacey was feeling mentally drained. Nothing had turned out the way she planned on this trip. And she certainly hadn't expected her editor to show up with the police reporter in tow and bring the newsroom to her. Luckily her mother and sister were occupied: Cherise was taking Ben to Steamboat, and Rose was checking out the shopping in Sagebrush, which meant Wal-Mart. *Mom loves Wal-Mart.*

Lacey needed to find out more about Ally's boots. Were they as unusual as Rae's and Corazon's? She wanted to talk to Muldoon about his fling with Ally and why he was after Tucker's land. Was he capable of killing? She wanted an update on the status of the Tucker manhunt. Cole was never far from her thoughts. Neither was Vic. "My brain is full, Mac. I've got too many missions already."

"This is mission critical. We've got to go—shopping."

Lacey stared at him. "Excuse me, did you say *shopping*?"

Mac's wardrobe was an indictment against shopping. His clothes were an afterthought. Wrinkles and rumples and mismatched colors were his signature style, along with heavily pilled sweater vests. Lacey suspected Mac's wife, Kim, sometimes allowed him to dress himself particularly badly, perhaps when she was too irritated with him to edit his random wardrobe selections. A wife's silent payback: *Go ahead, go to work looking like that, see if I care.*

"We got a shopping mission, Smithsonian."

"A mission for what?"

"Jasmine and Lily Rose want—cowboy boots." He shrugged helplessly.

"Oh, Mac. I don't know. I've just about had my fill of cowboy boots." Her editor looked crestfallen. His bushy eyebrows made sad frowns over big brown puppy-dog eyes. She sighed. "Okay, okay. If it's for the girls."

Jasmine and Lily Rose, Mac and Kim's soon-to-be-officially-adopted daughters, had Mac wrapped firmly around their little fingers. Lacey and Mac had both played parts in rescuing the mixed-race daughters of a murdered Asian mother and a long-missing black father from a hellish life of homelessness. Mac was of mixed parentage himself, black and white, and Kim was Japanese American. They understood the girls' struggle to find their place in the world.

Lacey remembered the night they had come to an understanding: Mac and Jasmine, face-to-face and glower to glower. Though Lacey couldn't hear what they said, she would never forget the moment she saw fierce little Jasmine nod and then place her small hand in Mac's large one. She was the big sister, "totally almost thirteen," who had to protect her ten-year-old sister, Lily Rose. In that moment, Jasmine decided she could trust Mac to help her carry that burden.

The girls instantly fell for Mac's wife, Kim, and she for them. Kim had always wanted children, and the girls were her ready-made family.

But after so much deprivation, Jasmine and Lily Rose were enjoying having a mom and dad who would cave in to nearly their every desire. They were good girls, happy and well behaved, and not quite spoiled rotten. But possibly, Lacey suspected, drunk with girl power.

"I'm glad they didn't ask for a pony. Do you know what sizes they wear?"

"Here, got it somewhere." He fumbled in his pockets and came up with a crumpled paper. He handed it to Lacey.

"Why cowboy boots?"

"No idea. They were really worried about you going out in cowboy country, Smithsonian. I was telling them about how cool cowboys were, so they wouldn't worry so much—you know, the Code of the West and all that stuff—and well, one thing led to another."

"Tony is the boot expert." She could just see Trujillo preening in his boots du jour. "You should make him go shopping with you." Tony gave her a look of horror.

"Yeah, but you're the *girl* expert," Mac said. "Trujillo can come along too."

"Cowboy boot shopping? You and Lacey?" Trujillo asked with interest. "You know a good boot place?"

"A legendary boot place, but we'll have to go to Steamboat Springs. Mac can buy us a decent lunch there too."

"Don't press your luck," Mac said.

"No lunch, Mac, no boots. Now, do you know what the girls want? Color and style preferences?" The girls had been on a major pink and blue kick, but that mania might have run its course. They might be into yellow and lavender this month.

"Cowboy boots. That's all I got. Those are my marching orders."

"Why don't you call and get some more specifics?" Lacey suggested.

"Right. I'll see if I can catch them. They've got some

sort of teacher workday, so the kids are out of school."
Mac pulled out his cell phone, called, mumbled a few
words, and handed the phone to Lacey. The girls were on
speakerphone.

"Lacey! We heard you were kidnapped," Jasmine
yelled at the phone. "Did he hurt you? Were you scared?"

"Are you okay, Miss Lacey?" Lily Rose chimed in.
"We said prayers for you."

"You did? I'm sure that helped. Everything is fine,
girls," Lacey answered. She eyed her grumpy editor.
"Well, at least back to normal. You don't have to worry
about me."

"We could have helped," Jasmine insisted. "We wanted
to come with Mac! But he said we had to go to school."

"And we're not even in school today!" Lily Rose giggled.

"I'm sure you could have helped me." Lacey was
smiling. "But you have to go to school tomorrow. Listen,
we're calling because Mac says you need some new
boots."

"Cowboy boots," Jasmine emphasized. "They have to
be *cowboy* boots."

"What color?"

"Any color, really, it's okay. Just cowboy boots."

"I want mine *exactly* like Jasmine's," Lily Rose piped
up in the background.

Jasmine sighed. The kind of sigh that only a big sister
can sigh, deep and world-weary. Lacey knew that sigh.
She had sighed that sigh. "She copies everything I do!"
Lacey heard giggling in the background. "You *do*, Lily
Rose, you *do*."

"Please, Lacey," Lily Rose said. "Please! Pretty, pretty
please! Exactly like Jasmine's." She started to giggle
again. She was in the giggling stage.

Lacey put her hand over her mouth to keep from
laughing out loud. She knew how insistent little sisters
could be. Especially when it came to things like copying
big sis. "Would it be so terrible, Jasmine, if they were the
same? Or similar?"

"They could be exactly *similar*, but not exactly the *same*. Lily Rose is such a little copycat."

"I'm not a copycat!" Lily Rose protested. "I just want cowboy boots like hers. 'Cause Jasmine has *excellent* taste!"

"What if there aren't any excellent boots that are exactly the same?" Lacey asked.

"Well . . . then maybe they could be similar," Lily Rose agreed. "But *exactly* similar."

"Are you gonna go shopping with him, Lacey?" Jasmine asked. "Because Mac is really smart, but he doesn't exactly understand about clothes and everything, you know? Our dad needs a little help with style. You know our dad."

Lacey felt herself tearing up. Mac was suddenly alarmed. His eyes narrowed.

"Smithsonian, what's the matter? What'd she say?"

She sniffed back the tears and whispered, "Jasmine just called you 'dad.' "

Mac grinned. He coughed to cover his own emotions. "Yeah, they've been doing that a lot." Mac looked fit to bust with pride.

The world is a mysterious place, Lacey thought. *And sometimes wonderful.*

"Yeah, Miss Lacey," Lily Rose piped up. "Our dad is the best ever, but Mom says he is a fashion *disaster*!"

"Get enough shopping, you boys?" Lacey smirked. "Are Sundance Jones and the New Mexico Kid ready for a style showdown at ten paces?"

Lacey turned around in the passenger seat to observe Mac in the back, under a load of boxes and bags. He couldn't quite wear his new black cowboy hat in the backseat. It was too tall. He was admiring it in his hands. He had a silly grin on his face.

Tony was driving their rental SUV back to Sagebrush. He had succumbed to two pairs of boots, one in Colorado rattlesnake hide and one in Burmese python. He might not get the chance to shop at the legendary F. M.

Light & Sons again, he said, and a man couldn't have enough really good boots, could he?

"I gotta hand it to you guys. I am impressed. And they say men aren't interested in shopping." Lacey looked at Mac's hat again and snickered. She already knew that Tony Trujillo was a proud male peacock, with his never-ending selection of exotic boots, but Mac Jones? Shopping for Western jeans, hats, and boots, and actually having fun? Mac had untapped sartorial potential. He was well on his way to becoming a dude. All hat, no cattle.

At first, Mac had stood rooted to the wooden floor, staring at the wall of cowboy boots at F. M. Light & Sons in Steamboat Springs, the historic Western wear outfitter, famous for its ancient yellow and black signs along Colorado roads, and for its Wall of Boots. The boots stretched from the front of the store to the back, marching in neat rows nearly from floor to ceiling, and there were hundreds of pairs. So many choices. Mac had picked up a pair and grunted at the price tag, but he couldn't resist all that craftsmanship. And the smell of exotic leather.

And Trujillo had been a seductive Pan, piping a Western song of boots and saddles. Lacey doubted that Mac had ever spent so much money on clothes in his life. He was sporting his new black cowhide boots with his baggy old corduroy pants. But in his shopping bags he had black jeans and blue jeans and a couple of Western snap-front shirts—and in his hands, that handsome black cowboy hat.

Lacey had talked Mac into buying at least one thing for Kim. He settled for a women's navy blue Western-style shirt, with pink piping and pearl snaps. Lacey steered him away from the garish red and black ladies' shirts with embroidered red roses along the yoke and sleeves. She was sure Kim would never wear something so loud, but she thought the girls might like their mom to wear the blue and pink shirt—it matched their new pink and blue cowboy boots. Pink boots with navy blue embossed tulips for Jasmine, and their reverse, navy boots with pink tulips for Lily Rose. "Exactly similar, but not exactly the same," as the girls had requested. Lacey also eased Mac away from the bolo ties with their gaudy silver and turquoise slides.

"Nothing like that place in D.C.," Mac said, his voice filled with awe. "So how come you didn't buy anything, Smithsonian?"

"How could I? I had to watch your every move, to prevent a fashion disaster." Lacey had examined the Wall of Boots to see if there were any like Ally's. There was no exact match, but Lacey was pretty sure they'd been expensive. The boots on display didn't tell her anything. She didn't know if it was the boots that drew the killer, or something else about the victims and the boots were simply trophies.

"We could have turned you into a true cowgirl, Annie Oakley," Trujillo said.

"See? Disaster averted," Lacey said. "Besides, I do my serious shopping *alone*."

chapter 25

Free at last. Lacey escaped from Mac and Tony just before four, in time to meet up with Vic at the courthouse. As she breezed into the lobby, he was waiting for her, with his buddy, the prosecutor.

"Here comes trouble." Owens thought he was being clever. Though ordinarily crisp and combed, Brad Owens looked weary and rumpled. He flinched a little when he saw Lacey. She was a visible reminder that his career-making murder case had escaped before he could try the suspect.

"Hello, Brad," she said.

"Lacey, long time," Owens said, making it clear it hadn't been nearly long enough for him. "How are you bearing up after your ordeal?"

"Never better," she lied.

"I'd recommend you talk to someone about posttraumatic stress." She laughed in his face. "And don't worry. The sheriff is going to catch Cole."

"T-Rex will catch hell from the voters before he catches Cole Tucker." Lacey wanted to get the pleasantries out of the way.

Deputy DA Owens wanted the easy way out, but the resolution of the Cole Tucker case would now be anything but easy. When Tucker was found, it wouldn't be a feather in Owens's cap. With the enormous amount of local media attention to the murders and the daring courthouse escape, a change of venue was almost a certainty. Tucker would be tried in some other town clear across the state, like La Junta or Pueblo, where the prosecution would have no home team advantage.

"There's a reward out now. *The Daily Press* is putting up ten thousand dollars."

"Muldoon is putting up that kind of money?" Muldoon putting up even a dime was odd, even suspicious.

Owens smiled for the first time. "Some of the energy companies are supposed to pony up some more."

"I guess everyone wants Tucker caught," Vic said.

"Looks that way." Lacey hoped Tucker wouldn't do anything stupid. "By the way, where is the present chief of police? What's his name?" She had never met Vic's replacement, who seemed to be missing in action.

"They call him Chief. And he's ice fishing in Minnesota," Vic said. "He checked in, said he's got no plans to cut short his vacation."

"I like a man with priorities," Lacey said.

"Doesn't matter if the chief is here or not," Owens said. "Not his jurisdiction anyway. The victims were found out in the county. Life goes on. The law goes on. Someone is going to turn Tucker in, and when they do, you'll have to testify. I'll call you to the stand."

"Works for me. I'll tell the jury he didn't kill anybody." Lacey made a show of pulling out her notebook. "Is there anything else you'd like to tell me?"

"No one was supposed to release the information about the silver heel. And now it's all over the Web. Nice going. You may have compromised our case."

"I may have made your case, Brad. Against the real killer. And you'd have a real First Amendment problem trying to keep evidence out of the news when a reporter finds it. Finders, keepers. I have a duty to share with my readers. Anything else?"

"No comment." Owens nodded to Vic. "Donovan, we'll talk later." Lacey watched him stomp wearily down the polished granite floor and out of sight.

"I love that First Amendment. Works like a charm, doesn't it?" She tucked her notebook back in her purse.

"You had to go out of your way to irritate him?" Vic asked.

"Wasn't out of my way at all." Lacey flashed her most inviting smile and put her hand on his chest. "Vic, honey—"

"What am I going to regret agreeing to now?"

"How about the Little Snake Saloon?"

He made a face. "That place is no kind of bar for any law-abiding citizen. Or you."

Lacey unleashed The Look in warning. "But it's where Zeke Yancey hangs out."

"I never should have mentioned Zeke Yancey. That's why you want to go, isn't it? He's your prime suspect in these murders?"

"He used to be your prime suspect. Along with Muldoon."

"Times change. Now my favorite suspect is Cole Tucker," Vic said.

"Zeke Yancey has been warming bar seats there since I was in Sagebrush. And Ally Newport worked there."

"She worked at nearly every bar in town. What do you expect to get out of it? Other than a warm beer?"

"I'm not psychic, Vic. I just want to ask him a few questions about Ally. That's all I ever do, ask questions."

"Yeah, right. It's all business as usual until it's time to pull out the scissors and stab somebody."

"I hardly ever do that."

Vic jammed his hands in his pockets and headed toward the door. He grumbled under his breath. Lacey followed him.

"I could go alone, or I could get Mom and Cherise to come with me."

"Why not just unleash a bazooka down Sundance Way?"

"Sometimes you have to bring out the big guns," Lacey said to his grumbles. "Besides, the Little Snake is the only place where people won't think to find me. My family, Mac and Tony, Dodd Muldoon."

"Promise? Even Muldoon?"

"Muldoon wanted us to have a newspaper staff meeting there years ago, to try to sell them some advertising. I refused. I told him it was nothing but a scummy hole-in-the-wall. He'll never look for us there."

"It's probably even scummier now."

"Duly noted, Chief Donovan. I know where it is. See you later." She scooted ahead of him.

"Not without me." Vic knew when he was licked. He caught up with her and took her arm.

"Yancey may not even be there." Lacey ducked under his arm. "Buy me one drink at the Little Snake, Vic, and then you can take me wherever you want. How often does a guy get an offer like that?"

The Little Snake Saloon was a forbidding windowless barnlike structure, just off Sundance Way behind a taxidermy shop. Inside, the décor was straight from a hangover, with dark and dingy smoke-stained wooden walls that hadn't seen any care in a decade or more. The bar was an oak plank scarred with hand-carved graffiti.

An ancient mirror backed shelves of liquor bottles. Adding a touch of color behind the bar were neon signs advertising Canadian Club whiskey and Coors beer, and a forlorn string of Christmas lights with old-fashioned bulbs that had hung there since before Lacey left Sagebrush.

A hand-lettered sign over the bar warned: ANYONE CAUGHT DEFACING THIS PROPERTY WILL BE BARRED FOR LIFE. THAT MEANS *YOU*! THAT MEANS BARRED FROM THIS BAR AND THE BARTENDER WILL TENDER YOUR ASS OUT!

"The place just oozes class," Vic commented as they found their way through the gloom to the bar. A hardbitten woman, who looked ancient but was probably only middle-aged, approached them. She stared at her new customers.

"Why, Chief Victor Donovan, as I live and breathe."

"Hello, Aggie. Nice to see you. But I'm not a cop anymore."

"You still look like one to me. Better looking than the one we got now. He's missing all the excitement."

Aggie Maycomb, the proprietor of the Little Snake, looked about the same as Lacey remembered her. The woman was as wrinkled as a raisin and grayer than granite. Her small bright blue eyes, hawk nose, and receding chin were the same. Her smile was missing a couple of teeth. Aggie swore she never opened beer bottles with her teeth, people only *said* she did.

"And you." Aggie turned her gaze to Lacey. "I've seen you before." Her eyes squinted in concentration, then opened wide. "You were some girl reporter or something at Muldoon's rag."

"That's right," Lacey said. "I'm still a reporter, Aggie, and my name is—"

"Don't tell me. I got it. Something funny, like a building. Like a museum or something. Smithsonian. Something Smithsonian."

"Lacey Smithsonian."

"Ha!" Aggie's face beamed with satisfaction. She tapped the side of her head. "See? Still works. Why, you're the one Cole Tucker took a-running from the courthouse. Over his shoulder, I heard. Like Tarzan the Apeman or something. You were his girlfriend, long time ago? Weren't you? Now I'm putting it all together. Wish I coulda seen that." She cackled with laughter. "I'd like to see the surprise on old T-Rex's face at that. Stiff-necked old jackass. Like to see his face when you and Cole Tucker a-run out on him like that. Ha!"

Lacey squirmed on her barstool. She was glad the place was so dim. No one could see her red face. "I think I'll have—"

"Wait a minute. You the chief here's lady friend now? Ain't life strange!"

"Strange indeed." Vic's expression told Lacey this was the last place he wanted his business discussed.

"You don't need me to fill in the gaps," Lacey said.

"Yeah, I'm good at knowing things," Aggie bragged. "I never did think that Tucker killed them women. But then, I never figured he'd steal a woman right out of the courthouse under T-Rex's nose. You don't look any worse for wear, I tell you. Bet you got some crazy tales to tell." Her eyes glistened at the thought of being first to be able to spread some hot new gossip around her bar. "But look at me jabbering away. What can I do you for?"

"Dos Equis," Lacey said.

"Make it two," Vic added.

Aggie reached back into the cooler and brought forth a couple of beers, and she even added glasses, to demonstrate what a top-drawer joint it was.

"If memory serves, Chief, you was here when this whole murder spree began, when the little Fowler girl went missing. Pity, that." She picked up a rag and ran it down the bar to greet some new patrons.

Vic poured the amber liquid into his glass, and Lacey did likewise. The cold dark Mexican beer tasted good, not warm as Vic had threatened. She gazed around to see if her quarry was there. There was only a handful of customers at the Little Snake that early in the evening. With a nod to Lacey, Vic indicated a man at the far end of the bar.

Zeke Yancey looked like the proverbial forty miles of hard road. His face was pitted with old acne scars and a few scars from old fights. With his bleary eyes, he resembled a bear just awakening from hibernation, or possibly returning there. Yancey had four days' worth of black stubble on his face and hair that hadn't seen a barber in a while. His red flannel shirt and jeans were stained with what looked like motor oil. About forty-five, Lacey guessed, but he could have been ten years younger.

He might have been a handsome man once, Lacey thought, cleaned up, sobered up, and with about fifty pounds of lard melted off him. But Zeke Yancey had given up on being a better man, it was plain to see.

Zeke picked up his head as if he knew he was being watched. He stared at Lacey and Vic and slowly sidled down the bar. He stopped one barstool short of her and stood with one greasy boot propped on the rail.

Aggie stepped back a bit, enough so she seemed out of the way and out of their business, but close enough to hear what was going on. She liked to be in the know, and then she could say Muldoon's "damn newspaper don't know half of what goes on in Sagebrush, Colorado," and she would be right.

"Donovan," Yancey said, in guttural whiskey-washed tones. "God damn. Slumming it?"

"Zeke. Been a long time." Vic kept his hands on his beer.

"Who's your pretty lady friend?" He turned toward Lacey, beer gut out. "We don't get a lot of ladies like you in the Little Snake."

"I'm a reporter."

"You're a good-looking reporter, I'll say that for you." His eyes glittered from the Christmas bulbs and too much alcohol. "You the one, ain't you? The girl in the courthouse Tucker ran off with." Yancey started to shake with laughter. "Man, I bet Grady Rush is sorry he ever set eyes on you."

"You're friends with Grady?" she asked.

"Not hardly. Grady and me, we have some beers from time to time."

"Jail talk on Saturday nights?" Vic asked.

"No beer in jail, Chief. But Grady's a talker. Some of the crazy-ass stuff he's into, it's a wonder he's still working for T-Rex."

"Oh, really? What kind of crazy stuff is Grady into?" Lacey tapped her fingers against her beer.

"Ah, you know." Yancey realized he might have said too much. And maybe he didn't care. "Socializin' with people like me. Sheriff T-Rex don't like me much." His guttural laughter was as pleasant as the rest of him. "Still, I can't feature Grady being so dumb as to unlock the shackles on someone like Cole."

"Someone like Cole?"

"Oh, Cole's all right. I'm speaking of him as Public Enemy Number One around here. Looks bad for Grady. He wouldn't a-done that for me." He gurgled a laugh again. "Brick shy of a load, Grady is. No lie."

"What makes you say Grady unlocked them?" Lacey said.

"He had to, didn't he? You can't do it yourself. Unless you're some kind of Houdini. And Tucker can rope 'em and ride 'em, but I don't think he can unlock waist shackles."

"Do you see a lot of the deputy?" Vic inquired. "Does he hang out in here?"

"Wouldn't say a lot. Here and there. And when I'm a guest at the T-Rex Motel, the one with bars on the windows. You threw me in there once or twice, didn't you, Chief?"

Vic just smiled and tipped his beer at Yancey. Yancey took a long slurp, and wiped his mouth with the back of his hand.

"Have you seen Grady since the, um, incident?" Lacey inquired.

"Nope. He hasn't even come in here. Pretty damn embarrassing, losing a prisoner like that."

"You got that right," Vic said.

"Guess you came back to look at Cole Tucker 'midst his troubles. Ain't that right, Chief? But ain't she supposed to be Cole's old girlfriend?" Zeke drained his beer and tapped the glass on the bar. "Hey, Aggie? Sweetie? Baby?"

Aggie efficiently removed his glass, wiped the counter, and drew a fresh Coors from the tap. He nodded with appreciation. "Man, that's good. You ever take that tour? Over at the Coors brewery in Golden? Mighty fine. You get yourself some beer straight out of that Rocky Mountain springwater tap? Coldest beer I ever drank." He smacked his lips loudly. Lacey decided a little of Zeke went a long way.

"Do you think Tucker killed those women?" she asked.

He considered her question through bloodshot blue eyes. "I never woulda thought it. But let me ask you this. You think I coulda done it? 'Cause that's what your buddy Donovan here thought. Chief here had his eye on me for that murder. Little Rae Fowler, Little Miss Silver Heels."

"What did you call her?" Lacey snapped to attention. Vic tensed, but Yancey didn't seem to notice. It was the first time anyone else had mentioned the silver bootheels.

"Silver Heels. That's what Grady called her. She wore the prettiest boots you ever saw. Sexy. Little Miss Silver Heels thought she was something else." His voice rose. "Too good for the rest of us. I hate them snobby girls. But what do you think? Am I a damn killer?"

Vic stood up. "You tell me, Yancey. Are you?"

Lacey realized she was holding her breath. She reached out for Vic's arm.

"No, I ain't no killer. I just like having a good time. I never hurt nobody, 'less they're throwing a bottle at me. I never killed nobody. Not Little Miss Silver Heels, not anyone."

"Do you know anyone who did hurt her?" Lacey asked.

"You got yourself a murder suspect already. Cole Tucker. That's all I know."

A younger version of their crusty bartender plopped down heavily on the barstool next to Zeke Yancey. Jillie Maycomb's resemblance to her mother Aggie was fierce, though she was large and slow while Aggie was skinny and fast. Jillie had the same facial profile, small eyes and receding chin, though none of the bright-eyed energy. Her hair was dishwater blond and she'd made a stab at makeup, but a heavy hand on the black eyeliner managed only to make her look like she was bruised. On closer examination, Lacey realized Jillie *was* bruised. She had a crescent-shaped bruise on her face, inexpertly covered over with makeup, and only made worse by the Cleopatra eyes.

Zeke hung one arm around her shoulder. *Are they a couple again?* Lacey wondered. Neither one looked very happy about it.

Aggie pulled a Diet Coke out of the cooler for her daughter. Jillie smiled vaguely at Vic as if she were trying to place him. She gazed at Lacey with more curiosity. Her jaw suddenly dropped open.

"Damn, girl! You the one Tucker hauled out of the courthouse, ain't you?"

It's going to be a long night, Lacey thought.

"Your mom can catch you up on the details, Jillie. I want to ask you about something else. About Ally Newport. She worked here, didn't she?"

"Ask Aggie," Zeke Yancey said. "She's the boss lady."

Aggie heard her name and rematerialized with her wet rag. "Ally worked here 'bout a year before hauling ass over to the Red Rose, 'cause she said they had a better clientele. Hell, it's the same damn clientele. They just come here already drunk after the Red Rose closes down for the night, so they can get a little drunker. And some of them are drunk before the Red Rose even opens." She cast a sidelong glance at Yancey.

"Hey, it's not my fault I'm always here, Aggie. The plant cut my hours, and I don't go to the Red Rose no more. Their beer costs too much anyway. Bunch of damn snobs with their noses in the air over there."

Lacey was unaware that there were snobs in Sagebrush, but anything was possible. "But Ally worked here for a year? Were you friends, Jillie?"

"'Bout a year. We weren't friends. She was real popular." Jillie looked glum. "Always flirting with the guys. She didn't have so much interest in female customers, you know. Thought she was the only woman in the room, when it came right down to it."

"I found an article about Ally," Lacey said, pulling the story and photo from her bag.

"That damn Muldoon and his *Daily Press* would write stories about dirt," Aggie said. "'This here dirt's been in town for twenty-five years. Fell off'n a dirt truck passing through on its way to a dirt farm in Vernal, Utah. But it's been real happy dirt, making a home here in Sagebrush, home of all the best dirt in Yampa County.' " Aggie laughed and wiped the bar. Lacey winced. There was nothing more painful for a reporter than a slow news day, and there were many days in Sagebrush when she felt she was writing stories about little more than dirt.

"You ought to be a comedian, Aggie," Yancey said. "Open up one of them high-class comedy clubs."

"Maybe I will," Aggie said. "The Little Snake Saloon and High-Class Comedy Club." She took the article from Lacey and looked it over, nodding her head. "Ally was real proud of that thing. 'Best Bartender.' Readers' favorite. Ha! Had it framed and put it behind the bar here. Took it with her when she went to the Red Rose."

"Did she have a lot of boyfriends?" Lacey asked.

"Usual number, I guess." Aggie handed the clipping back.

"The 'usual number'?" her daughter asked, apparently feeling slighted. "Just what the heck is that supposed to mean? If Ally had the usual number of boyfriends, what about me? How many would I have, Mama? The usual number?"

"Now, Jillie, I guess I'd have to say you have had yourself a few boyfriends. The usual number. And then there's Zeke here, of course. Not sure he counts, usual or otherwise."

Lacey waited for the mother-daughter fallout to subside. She too wondered what the "usual number" of boyfriends might be.

Zeke put his arm around Jillie and kissed her with a loud smack. "Don't let your mama get your goat, Jillie. You and me, she just probably means, we're like old married folks."

"But we ain't married! We ain't nothing." She glowered at Zeke and at her mother. Aggie rolled her eyes for Lacey and Vic's benefit.

"I guess you could say Ally lived up to her name," Aggie said. "Alley Cat. That's what we called her. She wasn't a bad sort. She just had a lot of boyfriends, you know, maybe a little *more* than the usual number. She wasn't a stick-to-'em kind of gal. She told me once she didn't like to be alone. New boyfriends all the time. Met a lot of 'em right here at the bar, or at the Red Rose."

"Maybe that's why she turned up dead," Jillie shot at her mother.

"This picture of her." Lacey showed it to Jillie and tried to get the conversation back on track. "Did she dress like this all the time?" Jillie shrugged and sipped her Coke.

Aggie studied the picture. "Pretty much. That's Ally all right. Big smile. Customers like a big smile. Secret of my success," she said, baring the many gaps in her smile. "Try telling that to *some* people." She cocked her head at her daughter.

A few customers filed through the door and Aggie hustled off to pull more drafts, saving Lacey from hearing another mother-daughter set-to on the importance of smiling.

"Did Ally always wear jeans and boots?" Lacey asked Yancey.

He looked as baffled as if she'd asked him a math question. "Far as I remember," he said. "Everybody wears jeans and boots." His gaze lingered on Lacey. "You got some tasty boots on yourself."

"Stick to the question, Zeke," Vic said.

"These are pretty nice boots Ally is wearing in this picture," Lacey said, trying to get back to her subject.

"Oh, Ally had a big thing for cowboy boots," Aggie cut in again from behind the bar. "All she ever wore here. You ain't catching me in no cowboy boots back here, standing on your feet all damn night and day. I wear me some running shoes, because I run my ass off working here."

"Do you remember these boots, Aggie?"

"Yep. Red and white, they were. She had others, but I think these were her favorites. That's why she's wearing them for the picture, even if it was only *The Daily Press*. Not every day you get called best bartender in town. Even in that rag. Nobody ever called *me* that, I can guaran-damn-tee you."

"Now, Aggie," Vic cut in, "I bet you can out-bartend anyone around here."

"Did she wear any other kind of shoes?" Lacey asked.

"Nope. Just cowboy boots. She was no cowgirl though. Just playacting."

"What are you doing in here, asking us all these questions 'bout Ally all of a sudden?" Yancey asked, his voice rising. "And boots! What the hell is all this stuff about Ally's boots and Little Miss Silver Heels' boots? You writing a story, Miss Reporter? Didn't you get enough stories from Tucker? I heard you spent the night with him. Mighty cozy. Why don't you go ask him what happened to Alley Cat?"

Vic stepped between them and looked down into

Zeke Yancey's bleary eyes. "I don't think you meant any disrespect to Ms. Smithsonian," he said quietly. "I'd hate to think you did, Zeke. Convince me you didn't."

Yancey's shook his head, and backed away unsteadily, spreading his hands in surrender. He draped his arm around Jillie and they wobbled together toward a dark booth past the pool table. Vic put some money on the bar for their beers and escorted Lacey to the door of the Little Snake.

This interview was over.

chapter 26

"Happy now, darling?" Vic looked bemused. "Did you get what you wanted? Because I can't remember the last time I enjoyed the Little Snake quite so much."

"Testy, isn't he?" Outside the Little Snake Saloon, the sun was sinking behind Vic in the west, turning him into a looming silhouette. The air was rapidly cooling. Lacey zipped her jacket, but she still felt chilled. "Zeke Yancey gives me the creeps. But is he a killer or just a creep? He makes a good suspect though, don't you think?"

"Suspecting is not proving. I wonder how tight he really is with Grady. That's troublesome, even in a town as small as this."

"And Silver Heels?"

"First time I heard that." He looked unhappy. "You get what you wanted?"

"Just more questions. Could Zeke be the killer?" She wrapped her scarf around her throat.

"You confirmed that cowboy boots are one common thread among the victims."

"Not just any cowboy boots, Vic. Beautiful, eye-catching ones."

"The question is, where are the boots?" Vic zipped his own jacket and turned toward Sundance Way.

"The killer has them. Find the boots, you got your killer. Or vice versa."

"That's what you get from watching cop shows on television. Remember, darlin', other things were missing from those women. And no, I don't know what all the sheriff found on Tucker's ranch. But the boots? Killer might have burned them or buried them where we'll never find them."

"Maybe, maybe not," she said.

They marched past storefronts that were closing for the evening. Lacey stopped in front of the Westward Ho Realty. A green and white sign over the front window proclaimed Virgil Avery was the real estate agent and Homer Avery was a notary public. Decorating the window was a miniature Conestoga wagon drawn by plastic horses. A large man sat at a small desk absorbed in some task. He didn't seem to be aware of Lacey and Vic looking in the window.

"He must be the brother Tucker told me about," Lacey said.

"Can we go to dinner?" Vic asked. "I'm tired, I'm hungry, and you are too."

Virgil Avery came into view and spoke with the large man. Lacey opened the door, and a bell jingled.

"This will just take a minute, okay?" Lacey said. Vic groaned and followed her in.

Virgil straightened up. He smiled and his eyes crinkled. "Lacey Smithsonian. To what do I owe the pleasure?"

"Just passing by and saw your sign. You're not out with the posse?"

"No, but I'm always ready if I'm needed. Sheriff Rexford seems to think Cole Tucker's left the state. He's called back most of the posse. They're staking out some of the back roads along the state line."

"Where do you think he is?"

"No idea." Leaning against a desk, Virgil appeared relaxed. He stretched his legs out and crossed them at the boot-shod ankles. He was wearing a khaki outfit similar to the one she'd seen him in the day before, his personal uniform that showed Lacey a desire for order. Or a lack of imagination. He tapped his fingers on his brother's desk. "How're you doing there, Homer?"

"Don't distract me, Virgil. Now I have to. Start again," Homer said, in a slightly halting voice, as if he had once had a stutter. Homer was dressed in a blue paisley button-down shirt with red suspenders and brown slacks. He was middle-aged and his short brown hair was thinning, slicked back with a sharp part. Where Virgil was angular, Homer was pudgy. Even sitting down, he looked large, broad as well as tall.

Homer also wore a pair of dark brown cowboy boots. *This is ridiculous*, Lacey thought. Everywhere she turned, men, women, and children were wearing cowboy boots. Well, not *everyone*. Dodd Muldoon, for example, was a local good old boy, but he fancied himself a city boy, and he never wore cowboy gear.

"Homer is very particular about his work. But he is never wrong with numbers," Virgil explained.

"That's right." Homer barely looked up. "I'm never. Wrong."

Lacey didn't know what Homer was working on, but it seemed to involve numbers, graphs, and maps showing the surface features of the land. She recognized the outline of Yampa County.

"Why are you stopping by at this time of night, if I might ask? Most everyone's closed up by now. You interested in relocating to Sagebrush?" Virgil pulled out a brochure and offered it to her. "We got some mighty fine properties here. I'm sure you know what a nice place this town is. For hunting, fishing. Raising a family."

Another comedian. "Actually, no. I saw your lights on, and I remembered the sheriff spoke highly of you and all your work with the posse." Everyone liked to be flattered, and Lacey was betting Virgil Avery was no different. *Okay, Lacey, take one for the team, even if it makes you gag.*

His chest seemed to swell a bit. "Just doing my civic duty."

Lacey couldn't believe what she was saying, but maybe she could ease into what she really wanted to ask. "It's good to know there are people willing to volunteer their time and leave their jobs to hunt for an escaped prisoner."

Homer finished his work and put it in a folder. "I'm finished, Virgil."

"That's great, Homer. Now I want you to meet our visitors. This is Lacey Smithsonian, used to be a reporter here, and you might remember our former chief of police, Vic Donovan."

Homer stood and put his large hand out. Lacey took it and squeezed a little, but he didn't react. She said hello. He didn't meet her eyes.

As if reading her thoughts, Homer stared down at Lacey's feet. "Those are real nice boots. You. You got there. I like that stitching. Intricate. My boots are plain, but good boots. Darn good boots. Steel shanks. They'll last a good. Long time. But yours are real pretty. Beautiful. Aren't they, Virgil? Like a work of. Of art."

"They sure are, Homer," Virgil agreed. He squinted at her boots and smiled. "Mighty fine boots."

"They're years old," Lacey said.

"I like them. They're nice. You don't wear them. Much?" Homer said.

"No, I don't." *I may never wear them again.* "But that's not what I came to talk about. Virgil, I heard you've been trying to buy the Tuckered Out Ranch."

"You must've heard that straight from the horse's mouth." Virgil didn't seem surprised. "Tucker tell you that when you two were—on the run?"

"Lacey was not on the run. She was a hostage," Vic said.

"Poor choice of words. I apologize. It's no secret I've had some interest in that ranch. Me and many others. It's a fine piece of property. Good bottomland along the Yampa, lots of grazing land, been a profitable ranch for more than a century."

"But you don't want to ranch that land, do you?"

He grinned, but didn't look amused. "It's not a crime to speculate in all the economic possibilities this God-given landscape affords us."

"It's a prime. Piece of property," Homer said, still not making eye contact. He seemed to be looking either to the right or the left of Lacey's head, but never at her. His gaze kept returning to her boots. Or maybe just the floor.

"That's enough, Homer," Virgil cautioned his brother.

"It's all about the mineral leases, isn't it?" Lacey asked.

"I'd love to chat about what Cole Tucker told you about our offer, but now is not the time. We're about to close up shop here. You see him again, maybe you can talk him into selling. He won't be doing much ranching when he's in prison."

"Not much ranching. In prison," Homer repeated.

"Homer?" Virgil said warningly. "I do apologize, but we have to draw this conversation to a close, Vic, Miss Smithsonian. We have a prior commitment."

"That means we have. A meeting," Homer said, trying to be perfectly clear.

Lacey stalled. *Let's see how much of a hurry they're really in.* "I see. I'm just writing an article and I, um, thought I'd include something about the posse. Maybe you could tell me—"

"That's mighty nice of you," Virgil said. "Maybe tomorrow we could—"

A door opened and Mitchell Stanford emerged from the inner office. "Come on, Virg. It won't hurt to answer a few questions. We can give 'em a few minutes." Stanford carried a big fat cigar in his pudgy turquoise-ringed fingers and lit it, creating a cloud of noxious smoke. "Hi, guys. We met yesterday, Lacey. And I remember you, Chief Donovan. Call me Mitch, everyone does."

The foul smoke gave Lacey an instant headache. Wherever Mitchell Stanford was from, he'd gone thoroughly native. His jeans were cinched under his ample belly with a tooled leather belt, its silver belt buckle inlaid with turquoise. A matching silver and turquoise watchband covered his wrist. Nothing, however, could erase the strains of New York in his accent.

"We'll leave you to your meeting," Vic said, taking Lacey's arm. She delicately disengaged and pulled out her notebook.

"Mitchell Stanford? Spelled like the university?"

"Cute. Sure. You must have been scared to death, out there with that serial killer," Stanford said. "I can't imagine why he didn't hurt you, or worse. It's a miracle you're still alive. And what's all this about finding a little silver bootheel in that cabin?"

"You must have seen my story," Lacey said. "The Web edition."

"That right?" Virgil seemed a little more interested. "You found a heel? So what?"

"They say it belongs to that dead girl. The first one," Stanford told him.

"Someone must have. Lost the heel," Homer said. "The silver heel. You said it was the silver heel."

"That's right, Homer."

"Rae Fowler's parents identified it," Vic said. "It's with the CBI crime lab."

"I heard the CBI was going to tear that cabin apart today," Virgil said. "If Firestone takes command of things, T-Rex and the local boys won't like that."

"CBI has the expertise to process a location like that," Vic said. "No one else up here does. The sheriff and the posse sure as hell don't."

"I suppose you're right. Did you know the place, Lacey?" Virgil asked.

"Not the street address," Lacey said. *I'm supposed to ask the questions.*

"What did it look like? Was it a house, barn, cabin?" Virgil pressed.

"It was dark." She smiled, hoping to look guileless.

"Chalk it up to the idle curiosity of a real estate man. A thing like that could affect property values. No worries, Lacey. It'll all come out eventually. Small town like Sagebrush, impossible to keep a secret."

Here's hoping, she thought. "Why did you join the posse to search for Cole Tucker?"

"Well, it was my duty, wasn't it? We all have a duty to do what we can to bring some justice to those girls. And bring the killer back for punishment."

"Who knows?" Stanford gestured with his fat cigar. "Might be even more unfortunate women out there that he killed."

"Do you know something about that?" Vic stepped into his face. "Are there more women missing?"

Stanford shrugged and waved the cigar. "You'd have to ask the sheriff. Sagebrush is a transient kind of place. I'm just saying."

"I can't imagine why Cole would take you there," Virgil said, "to the same place he killed another girl."

"Cole Tucker didn't kill anybody," Lacey said. "Did you know the victims?"

Virgil stood. "Homer, will you put that file on my desk, and make sure everything is shipshape before we lock up?"

"Okay. Shipshape." Homer lurched to his feet and picked up the file. Still not quite meeting anyone's eyes, he walked stiffly into the inner office.

"I don't like to upset him," Virgil said. "Homer's a bit different from the rest of us. He's real sensitive."

If that's what you call it. "About the women who died?"

"Can't say I did know them," Virgil said. "This town is not as small as you might think."

"What about Ally Newport?" Stanford prodded. "She was that real cute bartender. You remember, Virgil, the one with the big smile."

Virgil nodded slowly. "Oh, sure. Ally used to work at the Red Rose. She probably made me a drink or two over the years." He dismissed the thought with a flick of the wrist.

"And you, Stanford?" Lacey lifted her pen.

"Sure. I knew Ally Newport to say hello," he replied. "The others? Don't know whether I'd have had the chance to meet an underage runaway."

"Her name was Rae Fowler. And Corazon Reyes?"

Stanford made a show of searching his memory. "Corazon. She was the real pretty one, wasn't she? Saw her picture in the paper. I might have seen her around. But you know, I can't be sure."

"You're also a member of the posse?"

"Sure am," Stanford said. "So tell me, can we expect to see more of your Cole Tucker stories, Lacey? Don't know how you could write so much. I'd think you must be worn out after spending the night with a killer."

Lacey ignored him. "And you, Virgil, did you know Corazon Reyes?"

"Like Mitch said, I might have seen her around."

Virgil was taking direction from Stanford. And he'd sent his brother out of the room when she started asking about the women. *Why?*

Vic stepped casually between Lacey and the men. "It's time for us to let you get to that meeting." His hand was back on Lacey's shoulder. "Sorry to bother you."

"No bother at all," Virgil said. "Always a pleasure, Chief."

Lacey put away her notebook and smiled as graciously as she could through Stanford's cloud of cigar smoke. *Hey, isn't it illegal to smoke in the workplace?* "I'd be happy to discuss the posse tomorrow."

Vic half turned at the door. "I suppose you'll make an offer for Tucker's land and mineral rights again, now that he's going to be needing a defense fund."

Lacey thought she saw the barest flicker of surprise on Mitch Stanford's face.

"Heck, it's no secret we're buying land and leases. Energy is what moves this country. My companies are spending millions searching for new reserves. Believe me, we're going to be heroes when this is all over. Cowboys like the Tuckers can say no all they want, but they can't stand in the way of progress forever, all high-and-mighty on horseback."

"That will be something to see," she said. *Whew, we finally got these guys riled up.*

"Let me tell you something, Lacey Smithsonian," Stanford said. "And you can tell this to your buddy Cole Tucker. We're going to get those leases on the Tuckered Out Ranch. There's a little thing in the state constitution, it's a little bit like eminent domain, where we can force something called 'pooling' on the Tuckers and include their land in our drilling plan. By state order." He took a breath. "We tried to play nice with those cowpokes, but that time is coming to an end. And there is nothing they can do about it."

"And I suppose you know something about the evidence they found on Tucker's land, the evidence that set him up?" Lacey asked. *You bastard.*

"Why, not a thing. Drop by anytime." Stanford smiled broadly. "It's been a pleasure."

Virgil opened the front door for Vic and Lacey, just as Homer returned.

"Everything is shipshape, Virgil," Homer said. "All shipshape."

chapter 27

"Now, sweetheart, you're going to tell me *everything*. Everything you haven't told me up to now," Vic said as soon as they were outside. His voice was deceptively calm.

"I don't even know where to start. Can you believe those bastards? Mitchell Stanford is just going to try to *steal* those mineral leases from Tucker."

"I'm tired of playing catch-up. I want to hear what Tucker told you. Every last detail. Including any and all crackpot theories of his, and yours, as to who really did the killings. Because I'm thinking that's why we were in there gasping for breath, chatting up these stinking oily lizards. Or am I wrong?"

Sean Victor Donovan seemed taller when he was irritated. Lacey wouldn't go as far as saying he was cute when he was mad though. He had his cop face on. But it wasn't her fault she hadn't told him *everything*. It had been a busy couple of days.

"Everything, Vic? Everything Tucker said didn't exactly come up before now. I was exhausted last night and I had to work today. You know. Shopping with my editor."

"I just hope you'd come to my defense like you're coming to Tucker's. And I came to yours." He sounded grumpy.

"Do you have any doubts?" Lacey said, turning her blue green eyes on him and opening them wide.

He grumbled and tugged on her arm, but she lingered on the sidewalk in front of the Westward Ho real estate office until Virgil Avery locked the door, lowered the shades, and turned out the lights.

The street was as empty as if they'd actually rolled up the sidewalk at dusk. Whatever was happening in Sagebrush wasn't happening on Sundance Way. It was in the bars and restaurants, and the new Wal-Mart. And wherever Stanford and the Avery brothers were having their mysterious meeting.

"What's up, Lacey? Don't leave me hanging on the ledge like this. Don't tell me it's because you are fascinated with posses or mineral leases."

"But don't you see, the leases may be why Tucker was framed."

"*If* he was framed. Big if, darlin'. Why bother, when Stanford thinks he can sweep up the mineral rights with a state order anyway?"

"Hold that thought." The light was on at *The Sagebrush Daily Press*. Lacey made a spur-of-the-moment decision. "I have to see a man about a horse."

Vic scowled. "Now what?"

"Muldoon." She tried the front door. It was locked. She headed down the side of the building to the back door. "I have to see Muldoon."

The back door was unlocked, as she remembered it always was. She walked in like she owned the place. But she paused a moment to look at the old web press, docked like a proud iron ship in the back bay. The smell of the ink and the sight of the giant rolls of paper called to her.

The Eye Street Observer was sent out to the suburbs to be printed in some giant printing plant she'd never even seen. Here she could see the heartbeat of her old newspaper, a sight she once saw every day. It was quiet now, but when it roared and papers rolled off the press, it was magnificent: the pumping, throbbing heart and bloodstream of the news business. She inhaled the scent of metal and paper and ink and took another hit of the heady aroma of a free press. Even if it was just a crazy small-town, no-account press. Run by a maniac.

"You having some kind of special moment with this place?" Vic inquired. "Should I leave you two alone?"

She squeezed his hand. "It's not the place, it's the press, the simple mechanics of printing a daily paper." Lacey kissed his cheek. "Silly, I know, but right now that ink is like a kind of perfume for me. Unfortunately, I also have to deal with the stench of Muldoon's dirty dealings."

"What are you talking about?"

"I love you, Vic, but don't cramp my style here. I will explain everything. I promise." She inhaled deeply once more before heading up the stairs to the offices. "Please, stay out of sight."

"I reserve the right to play hero."

Dodd Muldoon was in his office, which was, if possible, even more crowded with papers and files than Mac Jones's office back in D.C. He was stacking piles of paper on a dangerous tower of newsprint when he noticed her standing in the doorway.

"Well, well, well. Look who's come home to *The Daily Press*." His baggy face lit up like a bleary-eyed sunrise. "You came up with quite a scoop, didn't you, Scoop, for that East Coast rag of yours. And you didn't share." She waited for him to continue. "Lucky I could confirm your story with my own well-informed sources."

"You don't have any sources. You just rewrote my story, didn't you?"

He grinned like the jackal that he was. "Imagine you finding a silver bootheel belonging to poor little Rae Fowler. Sheer dumb luck. Not many people would pick up a dirty old broken heel and put it together with a dead girl."

"Dumb luck?"

"What are the odds Cole Tucker would take Lacey Smithsonian to the same cabin where Rae Fowler was killed? You think that was coincidence?"

"Was she killed there, Muldoon? I only know that her boot was broken there."

Muldoon clapped his hands together and rubbed them. "If she was killed there, Tucker killed her! It's logical, isn't it? She couldn't run away with a broken heel, now could she? Looks bad for your Tucker. You suppose he returned to the scene of the crime, like in the books? Took you along for the ride?"

"So why do you think I'm still alive?" She pulled a copy of the latest edition of *The Daily Press* from a pile by the door. It had another bad picture of her in it.

"I figure you got nine lives, Scoop. What are you doing here anyway? You got a story for me? Guaranteed front page. No hard feelings. Well, maybe a few."

"No. I have questions for you." Lacey stepped into the cramped office. It was paneled in the same cheap wood she remembered from her first day on the job. Vic listened in the hallway, out of sight, letting her take this wherever she wanted.

Muldoon wore his own familiar uniform: slacks, polo shirt, and the ever-present cardigan sweater, which he equated with being a newspaper editor. The very picture of a professional newspaperman, but still a relaxed good old boy who would listen patiently to all your stories. He set himself apart from the town; he didn't sport Western wear. He was above all that. His clothes told Lacey a lot, but it didn't tell her whether Muldoon was a killer.

"You have questions?" Muldoon leaned back in his chair and propped his shoes on his desk. "Some things don't change."

"Did you have an affair with Ally Newport just before she died?"

"Where'd you hear that?" He stretched out and put his hands behind his head.

"Around."

"Ally was sociable. But don't go believing everything you hear."

"Is that like not believing everything you read in the newspaper?"

Muldoon laughed. "Since you left, no one else here has had your kind of spunk. God, you come in here and ask the boss if he had an affair!"

"You are not my boss. Did you have an affair? Ally was the kind you like, young and friendly and none too bright. Remember, Dodd, I *knew* you."

"Oh, hell." He put his feet on the floor and sat up

straight. "We had a little fling, no big deal. She was a friendly gal. I am a friendly guy. And I'm a free man, since my divorce came through."

"Was your affair going on when Ally disappeared and ended up dumped on one of those lonely roads?"

"Matter of fact, it was well over. She saw other guys. Lots of them. Alley Cat, they called her. Did you know that, Scoop?"

"Did the cops question them? Did they question you?"

"I ask the questions in this town. I may have had a chat with the sheriff about Ally, but that was an interview for *The Daily Press*!" The color was rising in Muldoon's face. "Nobody knew who killed Ally, until Tucker was arrested."

"After evidence was planted on his land. You know anything about that?"

"Just what I read in the paper. Come on, next question."

He's a newspaperman, all right, Lacey thought, *albeit a piss-poor one.* Journalists always want to stick around to the bitter end of an interview, just to make sure they don't miss anything, even when they're the ones being grilled.

"I heard you made an offer for Tucker's ranch."

"You must have had quite a chat with Tucker out there in the wilderness. Must have been cozy, the two of you back together again. I'm flattered you had time to think about me, Scoop. I'd think you'd be too busy catching up on old times. But I'd be happier if you wrote a story for *The Daily Press,* for old times' sake."

I'd rather kick you in the head. "You knew about the potential for mineral leases, Muldoon, before anyone else did. You made a grab for his land."

"Grab, schmab. I made him an offer. Tucker turned it down. Big deal."

"But now that Tucker's been arrested, it might take selling the ranch to buy him a decent defense."

Muldoon paused. "There's a thought. Think I should make another offer?"

Swine. She wanted to slap the smug look off his face. "No, I'm saying Tucker was set up. Framed to squeeze him and his family out of his land."

"By me?" Muldoon looked astonished. "Me, set him up? Why, to frame him, I'd have to have the evidence that was found on his property. Things that belonged to the dead women. If I'd found any damn evidence, you'd have read about it in *The Daily Press*!" The wheels were beginning to turn. "Or you think— You can't possibly think I had anything to do with their deaths."

"Can't I? Muldoon, I suspect you of everything from lousy proofreading to the Great Train Robbery." She leaned against the doorjamb. She could feel Vic's presence next to her, out of sight, in the dark hallway. He touched the fingers of her hand that lingered outside the door.

"Sure, I wanted to make some money off those mineral leases," Muldoon said. "But I didn't set Tucker up. If he was set up. Good story though. Front page stuff." Muldoon scratched his head. All this thinking must have made it itch. "I didn't even know Rae Fowler. Saw her around a time or two, strutting on those silver heels like she was a big, grown-up girl. Playing dangerous games."

"What kinds of dangerous games?"

"Working in bars like the Little Snake when she was just a baby. Flirting with big bad boys."

"Did you know Corazon too?"

"Small town. You don't see many as pretty as her in Sagebrush. Corazon Reyes was kind of snotty though. Reminded me of you. Now, listen to me, Scoop. I am seriously hurt. I gave you your first job. I was good to you. Taught you everything you know."

"All you taught me was to get the hell out of this town." She threw the newspaper on his desk. "And I'm not convinced you didn't have something more to do with those women's deaths."

He jumped up suddenly and moved around the desk. Lacey took one step back into the dark hallway. Muldoon loomed in the door. He stopped when he saw Vic.

"I've had it with you, Scoop. Let me tell you one

thing. You ever mention me in print, except in a good way—in a positive light—as a public-spirited citizen of this town—I will kick your pretty little ass from here to the Wyoming line."

She laughed in his face. "Keep reading *The Eye Street Observer*, Muldoon."

"Start talking," Vic said.

Lacey waited until they had ordered their pepperoni, artichoke, and black olive pizza. They were in a new little Italian restaurant she hadn't seen before, a block off Sundance Way. They were tucked into a corner where they could talk.

"If Tucker's criminal defense runs to hundreds of thousands of dollars for his trial for murders he didn't commit, the family will have to sell the ranch."

"So how is just making an offer for the Tuckered Out squeezing the family, and just how does this frame work?" He smiled at her. "Call me skeptical. And I don't like the way Muldoon stormed after you."

"Good thing you were there. I'd have had to kick him where it counts. Anyway, Tucker believes someone, possibly the killer or someone who stumbled onto the killer's cache of the victims' property, planted evidence on his ranch and gave the anonymous tip to Grady, to force Cole's arrest."

"It's a stretch. In that case, the killer could have framed anyone." Vic sipped a glass of Chianti. "And the cops must have looked for DNA on those women's belongings."

"Cole did go out with Corazon, so there might be some kind of physical evidence from him. Somewhere."

"Are you saying someone might have targeted her *because* she dated Tucker and then killed her?"

"God, I didn't think of that. That's horrible." Lacey leaned back in her chair. "At any rate, now they can make an offer to buy the ranch when the family gets desperate and can't turn it down."

"Or wait for the state to take the rights."

"Maybe there's some reason to hurry. In any event,

that's bad public relations. Maybe someone knows the killer and wants to get the heat off him now."

"The family could simply lease the mineral rights on the Tuckered Out Ranch," Vic pointed out. "Or are you saying that wouldn't be enough money?"

"I don't know. The Tuckers turned down every offer. Cole said they have this crazy idea that you should own the land all the way up to Heaven and down to the center of the Earth, including the water rights and the mineral rights, not just the surface."

"Most ranchers out here feel that way," Vic said. "But in order to frame Tucker, Avery or Muldoon, or even Stanford, would have to be involved with the crime, or somehow luck into the evidence. And then there is Zeke Yancey. He doesn't seem to be after anything but his next hangover. But then there're his cracks about 'Little Miss Silver Heels.'"

"And Zeke seems to be friends with Grady. What if someone knew Yancey was a killer and was keeping souvenirs?"

"What if? Lacey, I know you've got that famous instinct of yours. Cops have gut instincts too, but they still have to go on the facts. Hard cold facts."

"You want to hear me out, or are we just here for the lecture?"

"Lacey, darlin', we're here for the pizza. I have not yet begun the lecture part of this evening. Believe me, you will know it when it happens, because it's going to come complete with charts and graphs."

"I may want to take notes."

He rolled his eyes. "Okay. Who did it, who killed those women?"

"I don't know."

"Who do you suspect?"

Lacey blew out her breath. "Everybody."

"The Averys?" She nodded. "Virgil's the slick one. And Homer, he's unusual. Maybe a high-functioning autistic. He knows things, in spite of appearances, whatever his ability or disability might be."

"He was way too interested in my boots. And Virgil?"

Lacey shook off the chill traveling down her neck. "I don't know. Creepy. Don't trust him, don't like him. Now maybe we should consider Deputy Duck."

"You're talking about Grady Rush?" Vic asked. "The way you ladies talk."

"Deputy Rush caught the anonymous tip about evidence on Tucker's land."

"Yeah, Owens told me that."

"Okay. Has Grady come up with a reasonable explanation for how and when he got this tip? Is there any proof there was an anonymous tipster?"

The pizza came steaming to the table. Vic put a slice on Lacey's plate and helped himself. "You're mentioning Rush because?"

"He knows something, Vic. I really think he does. Maybe he knows something about Yancey. Maybe something about the Averys, or that cigar-chomping, turquoise-wearing carpetbagger, Mitch Stanford. And something else. Grady was at the Amarillo yesterday, even though he had to know T-Rex would turn purple at the very sight of him. And last night when he showed up at the Blue Ox? I think he's afraid I'd tell he unlocked Tucker's restraints."

"That is just impossible to believe." Vic shook his head. "A lawman would never do a thing like that."

"A *dumb* lawman would! I saw him do it. Maybe he did it because he knew Tucker was being railroaded. A favor, so Tucker could kiss me or something. He didn't think Tucker would take off."

"All different breeds of weasel, I'll grant you that. But that is not enough to base a murder accusation on. And you, darlin', have to consider the possibility that Tucker might have killed those women." Vic dug into his pizza.

"Then why did he put me on a horse and send me back to town? Sentimental reasons?"

"I don't know, but I was so relieved I could've leapt tall buildings with a single bound." He put the pizza back down. "It slays me you were with Tucker all that time. I died a thousand deaths just thinking of you and him." She squeezed his hand, and he kissed her fingers.

"That's how I feel about Montana," Lacey said. "And Tucker never for a moment behaved like anything but my friend. He didn't hurt me. He didn't touch me. Except for hauling me out of the courthouse over his shoulder, where he may have single-handedly provided me with the most humiliating moment of my life."

And except for that, Tucker really didn't touch me—except for that kiss. But Vic didn't need to know about that kiss. It was only fair. She had never told Tucker about Vic's kiss on that long-ago New Year's Eve. *Why complicate things?*

"If we never see him again, Lacey, I'd be okay with that. But I don't think it's going to be that simple."

Lacey took a deep breath. He was probably tired of hearing about those boots. "You know, everyone's saying the killer kept the women barefoot just to keep them helpless. It took me a while to persuade T-Rex to even consider that the silver heel I found might have something to do with the victims. He thought it was crazy."

"I did too. I don't anymore. Okay. Is there anything else I should know?"

"Well—" The map in her bag was one more little thing she hadn't mentioned. But she couldn't be blamed; she'd almost forgotten about it. "After I found the heel, Tucker and I talked about where the women might have been taken. He didn't think the cabin where we stayed could have been a murder scene. Too many people use it."

"Maybe Tucker knows where the women were killed because he killed them."

"Will you give the poor guy a break for half a minute?"

"Okay! The guy who knows *nothing* about the murders has a prime theory."

"The cabin where we stayed was too busy. After the owner died a couple years ago, it apparently became a sort of teen hangout. A place to go party."

"Some of the cops mentioned that."

"Tucker said there are a couple of old line camps in the area, near the roads where the bodies were found.

But way off the road. And before you say something, everyone in the county knows where the bodies were found. It was in *The Daily Press*."

"And people have nothing better to talk about," he replied.

"Tucker drew me a map of where these other cabins are. One of them could have been the killer's hideaway."

"And you gave that to T-Rex?"

"Ha. Sure I did. After he mocked every word I said and called the amazing silver heel I found a bunch of baloney? You bet, I offered myself up for more humiliation."

Vic sighed and leaned back in his chair. "So you kept that back." He didn't look happy.

"I didn't tell him what I had for breakfast yesterday either. For the record, we had day-old bagels from Petrus's Bakery. They were in the Jeep that Tucker *borrowed*. I should probably stop by the bakery and pay Tasso Petrus for them. And thank him for the use of the Jeep."

"I wouldn't worry. Petrus'll probably dine out for the next year on that story. But tell me about that map. Where is it?"

"In my bag."

"May I have it? Please."

"I have to make a copy first." She retrieved the map and her notebook and sketched out a rough map of her own. It struck her that Virgil Avery was far too interested in the location of the cabin where she and Tucker spent the night.

"Have you finished yet? It doesn't have to be exactly high art." Before Lacey could retort, Vic's phone rang. He looked at the number. "It's Brad Owens. Hold on to that map. I better take this."

Lacey planned on listening in, but then her own cell phone rang. It was the voice of doom.

"Hi, Mom. What's up?"

chapter 28

Ladies' Night at Sagebrush's semi-famous Red Rose Bar was the place to be on Wednesday evenings. This particular Ladies' Night for Lacey meant sharing "quality time" with her mother and sister, after her plans for an evening with Vic fell through. After their pizza, Vic went to see the deputy DA and left Lacey defenseless against Rose and Cherise.

Nevertheless, the Red Rose suited her plans. Ally Newport had worked there, and it was likely all three victims had spent time there. *It's been such a fun night already, how could I pass up the Red Rose?*

For the first three hours of Ladies' Night, the bar was women only: No men allowed. The tradition had begun back when Lacey was a reporter and the male-to-female ratio in town was considerably more lopsided, nearly ten to one. Single women in Sagebrush had felt like they were the prey in a big game hunt. Ladies' Night gave them a half-price drink or a soda, a long-stemmed red rose at the door, and a little after-work conversation in a semi-civilized, testosterone-free zone: three precious hours.

It also allowed the Red Rose to corral the women for the predators when the men were finally let in, in a thundering herd of testosterone. Her first time at Ladies' Night, Lacey and her girlfriends from *The Daily Press* were blissfully unaware of this secret plan. At nine o'clock, the floor began to vibrate and the room began to rumble. It sounded like a buffalo stampede set to steel guitar. The doors flew open and suddenly, yee-hah, there were men everywhere, in their best snap-front shirts and cowboy boots and hats, pouring through the doors, mobbing the bar and the tables, dragging women onto the dance floor. After that, Lacey always made sure to leave early.

Sagebrush's boom times had gone bust for the moment, but the Red Rose Ladies' Night soldiered on. It had become a tradition. Women still arrived at six for the half-price drinks and the girl talk and the country band, featuring the only men allowed in early. The rest of the desperados still came at nine, hoping to get lucky.

"We won't be bothered here, Mom. Not for another hour and a half."

"Not even by that rude sheriff?" Rose asked.

"He's had a long day," Lacey said. "Trust me."

"You mean there aren't any men in here at all?" asked Cherise, still rosy cheeked from her day of skiing in Steamboat Springs with Ben Barton. The powder apparently had been *awesome*, and so had Ben. But the Smithsonian ladies were on their own for Ladies' Night.

The décor at the Red Rose, on a scale of wretched to divine, fell somewhere between a Victorian madam's bordello and a cowboy movie saloon. The red flocked wallpaper and red leatherette upholstered chairs, the chandeliers and fringed red velvet lampshades—it all would have worked in either setting. Old-fashioned movie posters of Western heroes and villains graced the walls, and the floor sagged from the weight of years of customers bellying up to the bar. The restrooms were labeled BUCKA-ROOS and COWGIRLS. It was the classiest bar in Sagebrush.

"Oh, my Lord, would you look at this place," Rose had said upon entering the bar. "Lacey, are you sure decent people come in here?"

"Nope, just us, Mom."

"It looks like that place on East Colfax in Denver. The place where they have those exotic dancers?"

"Even exotic dancers deserve a Ladies' Night out," said Cherise.

"Of course they do, sweetheart," Rose said. "But that

wallpaper. And the lighting. The feng shui is wrong, simply all wrong."

"It's Sagebrush, Mom," Lacey said. "They think feng shui is something you eat with chopsticks."

"I could never get the hang of chopsticks," Rose said. "But I'm here with my two girls, and you're both still alive and beautiful, so I've done my job. Of course, when I get back home, I'm planning a weekend yoga retreat to get my center back."

"Where did it go?" Lacey laughed.

"It went AWOL the second I heard you were kidnapped by your lunatic ex-boyfriend."

"It was intense, Lace," Cherise added. "I had to leave work and go home before Mom had a panic attack. And before you know it, she had me in the station wagon heading for Sagebrush."

"I talked to your father. He's in, um, wherever he is. He knows nothing. I'll fill him in when he gets back," Rose said. "The abridged version."

"I owe you, Mom," Lacey said. Smithsonian women always banded together to protect Even Steven from unhappy news. "You're sure there weren't any pictures of the whole courthouse drama on TV?"

"Unfortunately, no," Cherise said, no doubt thinking about the YouTube video memorializing for all time her infamous cheerleader kick. "I would have given a lot for that."

"Cherise, don't tease your sister."

"Who's teasing? I'm serious."

"No, there were no photos of you," Rose said. "Just one of the getaway car Tucker stole. The antlers on the grille. Nice touch, Lacey. Classy."

"Yeah, I begged him to take that one, thinking how cool it would look on the front page. You're still wishing I'd taken that reporting job in Glenwood Springs, aren't you?"

"If this had happened in Glenwood, I'd be swimming in the hot springs pool right now."

A soak in a hot springs sounded good to all three Smithsonian women. They found a table near the dance floor and Lacey waved to a waitress. Rose was deep in an imagined redecorating scheme for the Red Rose bar, mentally ripping down the wallpaper and installing new chandeliers. Lacey spied at the bar a pink angora sweater that was too tight for polite company and jeans that fit like wallpaper. *Uh-oh.*

"Hey, isn't that, um—?" Cherise paused, hunting for a name.

"It sure is." Lacey stared at the overprocessed platinum blonde. "Montana McCandless Donovan Schmidt."

"Vic's ex?"

"Not ex enough for me." *What is it about certain blondes that make men lose their minds?*

Montana was drinking at the bar with another cotton-candy blonde in a supertight, baby blue sweater.

"*What* is she wearing? Looks like a bandage. Do they shop in the children's section?" Cherise whispered. Lacey smiled. Sometimes family solidarity could be a comfort.

"What's going on?" Rose shifted her attention from the décor to the blondes. "What's that woman doing here?"

"I've got your back," Cherise said. "And my badass blue boots."

"Don't move. I just need to say hello. I'll call if I need you." It was time to face her fears. Lacey tugged off her leather jacket and tossed it to her sister. She squared her shoulders and marched over to the bar.

"Hello, Montana."

"Well, look what the cat just dropped off. On a horse, no less," Montana said. "You got more lives than a cat, don't you?"

"Gee, I'm fine. Thanks for asking. How are you?"

Montana's sister in blondness eyed her. "Is she the one? With your Vic?"

"She's the one."

The friend gave Lacey a quick once-over and exchanged a look with Montana.

"It's mutual," Lacey replied. "Shouldn't you be out with your new boyfriend?"

"Brad's with Vic, trying to decide what to do about

the mess you made with Tucker. They're, um, meeting Cindy and me here later."

"You and Cindy?"

"That's right. I think Brad will like Cindy."

"He's cute," Cindy said.

"And Vic?" Lacey was sure Montana had plans for Vic.

"He's mine."

"Really? What was that divorce all about, then?"

"Haven't you heard? Divorce isn't forever anymore."

"In your case, it is."

Montana narrowed her eyes. "When Tucker carried you out of the courthouse, I thought it was my lucky day."

Sometimes it's good to get the enemy on the record. "And you'd be there to comfort Vic, wouldn't you? That was the plan, wasn't it?"

"Who better than me? Believe me, I know how to comfort Vic. Tell me, Lacey. How'd *you* get so lucky? First, you rope Cole Tucker, the hottest cowboy this side of the Divide." Montana pouted. "And then you snare my husband."

"Ex-husband. The ex-husband before your current ex-husband." *The Las Vegas drive-through wedding-mill, doesn't-really-count ex-husband, you man-eater, you.*

"How do you do it? Keep roping other women's men?"

"I don't know, Montana. How do you keep losing husbands?"

Montana did a boil, momentarily at a loss for words. Her friend Cindy stood up and announced, "Ladies' room! Now." Montana swallowed her beer and followed her friend, grabbing her jacket.

"Now why'd you have to go and ruin their little pity party?" the bartender cracked.

"I have a certain talent for it," Lacey said with a smile. She watched as Cindy and Montana veered away from the ladies' room and headed for the front door.

"You ought to teach a course in it. Now, something I can get you?" She appeared to be in her mid-forties. She had black hair and eyes with crow's feet, indicating that she smiled a lot.

"Please." Lacey grabbed a barstool and ordered a virgin Bloody Mary. "And do you mind if I ask you a question?"

"You're that D.C. reporter? Writing a story?"

"That's right."

"I'd think you'd be all done in, after that wild ride with Cole Younger Tucker. But go ahead. Name's Effie, just spell it right." She produced a copy of *The Daily Press* with the photo of Lacey mounted on Buttercup. "You mind signing this for me?"

"As long as I can send you a copy of the story I'm writing." Lacey signed her name above the photo.

"Deal." Effie grabbed the autographed paper and set it aside. "I never even heard of *The Eye Street Observer*, but I found it online. I'd love a copy. Now shoot."

"Okay. Did Ally Newport have a steady boyfriend?"

"Sure, every couple of weeks. Steady like clockwork. That girl was an eternal optimist. Always looking for Mr. Right."

"What happened to all the Mr. Wrongs?"

"This and that. She had a list of requirements. They never quite measured up. Didn't slow her down though." Effie pursed her lips. "Never figured she'd wind up dead the way she did."

"And barefoot," Lacey offered.

"Wasn't that a curious thing," Effie said. "Ally'd hate that. Mean thing that, taking those boots from her. She set great store by her boots."

"How many pairs do you think she had?"

"Six, seven maybe, but she was no cowgirl."

Same thing Aggie Maycomb had said. "What did men see in her?"

"A good time. Ally was just a good-time girl. Until she wasn't anymore." Effie fixed Lacey's drink as she talked.

"So she was a party girl? Or just playing the field?"

"Ally wanted to get married," Effie said, with a wave

of her hand. "Her clock was ticking. Like a time bomb. But her good-time reputation kind of got in the way."

"Wasn't there anyone special, different?"

The bartender laughed. "She thought she had one hooked, but he just got rid of one ex-wife, he wasn't about to get hooked again. Dodd didn't like her demands."

"Dodd Muldoon?"

"Thought that would get your attention. He loved the way she looked in those little skirts she wore and those pretty boots. I heard his line of manure at the bar. To be honest I hadn't thought about that before I read your article online, about finding the heel of Rae's boot."

"What do you think about that?"

"I think we got a monster in this town. And you might want to talk to *her* before you go." Effie indicated a young woman in her early twenties at the far side of the bar. "Name's Vonda McKay. She thinks her friend's in trouble."

Lacey followed Effie's glance. "Will do. Anything else?"

"Ally might not have been the best bartender around. But no one deserves what happened to her or those other poor kids." Effie turned her attention to a group of happy, thirsty Ladies' Night ladies.

Lacey tucked her notebook away and scooted down the bar. Vonda McKay had spiky, bright yellow hair, dyed at home and possibly cut with a lawn mower, and eyes ringed in black liner. Her miniskirt over black tights, red sweater, and cowboy boots completed her cowpunk look. But despite the tough-little-cowgirl camouflage, she looked like a good girl in bad girl's clothing.

"Hi, I'm Lacey Smithsonian. Mind if I sit here, and talk?"

The woman's eyes grew wide. "Oh, it's you! I read about you in the paper. I'm Vonda. Okay if we move? Bar gets so packed here."

Lacey sent her mother and sister an I'm-working-don't-bother-me look. She followed Vonda to a small table in the corner.

"Don't believe everything you read in Muldoon's newspaper," Lacey began.

"I read that Cole Tucker didn't hurt you and you think he didn't hurt anyone."

"That part's true." Muldoon had quoted Lacey correctly in his otherwise embarrassing story about her.

"You think the guy who killed them is still out there? Somewhere?"

"Yes." *Or here in Sagebrush.*

"That's what I'm afraid of." Vonda looked around the room warily. "I mean, I don't believe it was that Tucker guy either. He never bothered anyone."

"Effie said you're worried about a friend?"

"Yeah. I haven't heard from her in a couple of days." Vonda's eyes filled with tears. "Maybe she's dead too."

"Don't jump to conclusions. There was a missing girl in Wyoming a couple days ago, but she turned up. Why do you think she's missing? What's her name?"

"Emily. Emily Ogden. She isn't answering my texts or my calls. And we're *best friends.*"

Best friends. Lacey's best friends had led her on many little misadventures, but they would always be there for her. It was understood. Lacey touched Vonda's arm. "Where does she live? Could she just be sick, or visiting family, or a boyfriend?"

"She's got an apartment, but she's not there. I pounded on the door. No boyfriends right now. And she wouldn't leave town without letting me know." Vonda began to weep. "I know she wouldn't."

"What does Emily look like?"

Vonda sniffed and wiped the black liner running under her eyes. "She's the pretty one. Guys always talk to her first, you know? I kind of hate that, but then they'll talk to me too, so it's kind of nice. When I'm here with Emily, guys always send over free drinks. You know?"

Lacey remembered nights in Sagebrush when she couldn't pay for a drink, when the town was full of men who would try anything to meet a pretty single girl. The ones who stormed the Red Rose every Ladies' Night.

"Some things never change," she said. Vonda nodded, dabbing at her eyes.

Across the room, Rose was growing impatient. She picked up her wineglass and crossed the dance floor to Lacey, with Cherise trailing behind. They sat down without asking.

"Hello, I'm Lacey's mother."

"Hi, I'm Cherise. Lacey's sister."

"This is Vonda McKay." Lacey's expression said, *Don't interfere with this!*

"You seemed to need company," Rose said. "You can tell us anything you can tell Lacey. We helped her take down a killer one time."

"I used my cheerleader kick," Cherise added, suddenly proud of that curious lethal ability.

Lacey issued The Look. Again. "We're doing just fine by ourselves, Mom."

"What is it, dear? What's the matter?" Rose produced a fresh tissue and handed it to the weeping woman. Vonda wiped her eyes and blinked at the table full of Smithsonian women staring at her.

"Um, yeah. Thanks. Um. My best friend. Her name is Emily and she's missing and—and I know something terrible has happened."

"Go ahead, sweetie," Rose encouraged her. "You can trust us. What's she like, your friend?"

Thanks, Mom. Please go away. But instead of clamming up as Lacey had feared, Vonda seemed to take comfort in Rose's mothering.

"Emily is, like, about my size."

"Petite, then," Lacey said.

"Yeah. We're the same age. Twenty-two. She's got blue eyes and long blond hair, really light. That white-blond thing? That's the first thing people notice about her. Only it's natural—she doesn't dye it. She doesn't have to." Vonda pulled self-consciously at her own spiky locks. "My hair's hopeless. Anyway, Em's genuinely nice too, so you can't hate her for being so pretty." Vonda looked miserable. "She's gone and the killer's got her. I just know it. Right here." She thumped her chest.

"Who do you think has her?" Rose asked. "Do you think it was Cole Tucker?"

Vonda looked at Lacey. "No, no, no, it can't be him. 'Cause he, like, sent you back, right? I'm thinking she's been snatched by some weird guy who's been hanging around, bothering her. Us."

"Why would he take Emily and not you?" Lacey asked.

"Because Emily's too nice for her own good. If I don't want to be with someone, I let 'em know. Like, I go, Chill, dude! Back off! Not happening! You know?"

"That's very straightforward of you," Rose said. "I admire that, but some men don't take no for an answer, do they?"

"To hell with them." Vonda clenched her fists. "But Emily, she's different."

Cherise jumped in. "She never wants to hurt anyone's feelings, right?"

"Right. She'll be nice just to be nice and then these creepoids think they have a chance with her." Vonda stared at her beer. "Sometimes you just gotta be a bitch, like me."

"I wouldn't have put it that way, Vonda, but you have a point," Rose said. "For example—"

"And then there's this old jerk who always comes sniffing around her."

"Does this old jerk have a name?" Lacey cut in. *Dodd Muldoon? Zeke Yancey? Virgil Avery? Just for starters.*

"I don't know. To be honest, there's more than one. But this one, Emily doesn't like him, but she lets him buy her drinks. He's been after her, asking her out, a *lot*. And he's bad enough, but he's got these creepy friends he hangs with."

"Do you know their names?"

"Made a point of not knowing them. Now I wish I had. When I see 'em come in here, I go the other way. These guys weird me out."

"Can you describe them?"

Vonda rolled her eyes. "Older guys. I mean, like, *old*. Thirty-five or forty. Or even older."

Rose nearly choked on her wine. "That's old, all right."

"Can you describe the one who bought her drinks?" Lacey asked.

"Big guy, dumb." Vonda screwed up her face. "He reminded me of, I don't know. Like an old cartoon character? He's got all these teeth, crooked, and a really wide mouth, and, like, squinty eyes?"

"Yosemite Sam?" Cherise asked.

"No mustache."

"Snidely Whiplash?" Rose suggested.

"No whip."

"Elmer Fudd?" Cherise offered. *That might fit Homer Avery*, Lacey thought.

"No, like— I know. Daffy Duck. And all squinty-eyed? It's worse when he smiles. Makes him look demented."

Grady Rush. How many faces like that could there be in this town? "A demented duck?"

"Yeah. And then there was this super sleazy guy, ugh, who used to hang around, but Effie threw him out."

"What did he look like?"

Vonda cringed. "Dirty, black hair, bad skin, thought he was all that. Gross."

Yancey? "Have you called the police?" Lacey asked, already knowing the answer.

An expression of utter disbelief crossed Vonda's face. "No freakin' way! You don't know the cops in this town now. Freakin' bullies. And this guy, he works at the jail."

"So he's a sheriff's deputy." *Grady for sure.*

"That's it, a deputy! And those guys are just like cops, right? You think they'll listen to me if I tell 'em my number one choice for the bad guy is one of them?"

Their waitress returned and the conversation stopped. Vonda wanted the burger sliders, and Rose and Cherise ordered salads. Lacey had already dined with Vic, and the thought of one more missing woman made her sick to her stomach.

"When did you notice Emily was missing?" Lacey asked.

"Monday night," Vonda said.

"When I was with Tucker."

"I guess. We met for lunch Monday and then we were supposed to meet up at Wal-Mart after work. Just to see if there was anything new, you know? Something to do."

"Of course." There were days when Lacey used to wander for hours through the Kmart store in Sagebrush just to feel like she was in a real town, with real stores. Before there even *was* a Wal-Mart.

"Emily never showed up." Vonda caught her breath. "I called her. I texted her. I e-mailed like crazy. She hasn't even checked in on Facebook. I called her work yesterday and today. They said she hadn't come in. And she would never miss Ladies' Night. It's a big tradition. That's why I'm here. I thought maybe she'd show up. We call Ladies' Night at the Red Rose the Weirdo-Free Zone, long as you leave before nine." Vonda started to pick at the blue polish on her nails. "She's a secretary at the power plant. Talk about weirdos over there."

"What do you do, Vonda?" Cherise asked.

"I work at Wild Bunch Taxidermy over on Sundance. The place with all the elk and mountain lions in the windows? I just do phones and the paperwork. But they say they'll teach me taxidermy if I want."

"Dead animals? Gross." The former cheerleader opened her eyes wide. Lacey would have kicked Cherise under the table, but she was too far away. But Vonda didn't mind.

"You sort of get used to it. The guys I work for are, like, artists. They do amazing stuff. I mean, yeah, the animals are *dead,* but they look alive. Hunters bring them there for trophies, but they kind of live forever this way, you know?"

Vonda "kind of sort of" liked her job. Lacey suspected there was no dress code, the taxidermy guys were probably cute in that outdoorsy kind of way, and Vonda was free to express herself with her spiky yellow hair. *There are worse jobs. I've had them.*

"What about Emily's job at the power plant? Did she like it?"

"No way. It's totally boring, and she gets hit on a lot. Jerks."

"What about a boyfriend?" asked Cherise, the eternal romantic.

"She dated a guy from the power plant for a while. But he moved to Wyoming. It's not like he broke her heart or anything. He just went away. Hey, I Googled you the other day," Vonda confided to Lacey. "You've got, like, thousands of hits, you know that? Is it all true?"

"Is what true?" Lacey asked.

"That you figure out crimes by, like, looking at people's clothes?"

"That's an exaggeration—"

"No, it's not," Cherise said. "It's completely true! Lacey's like a fashion *dowser*. Some people find hidden water? She finds fashion crimes."

"We're talking about real crimes, Vonda," Rose clarified. "Not silly things like how high your heels are. Unless you use them as a weapon."

"Okay, I get that, but what about Emily?" Vonda asked. "What am I going to do?"

"This is going to sound crazy," Lacey began. "Does Emily wear cowboy boots?"

"Oh, yeah. We love our boots!" Vonda nodded. "We bought our boots together. Cost a fortune practically, but we wanted something different. Really special. For our, like, kick-ass punky cowgirl look."

Vonda swung her legs around to show her boots, buff-colored leather with inlaid turquoise and coral ornaments.

"Wow! So cute!" Cherise said, showing off her own pair of kick-ass cowboy boots. "Lacey has a cute pair too. Hey, sis, why aren't you wearing your boots tonight?"

Déjà vu. "What do Emily's boots look like?"

"They're white leather with a sunset design stitched across the top in different colors, blue and purple and green, orange and red and yellow. Like a blazing sunset. I thought they were maybe too much of a good thing. But Emily loves them."

"What's the matter, Lacey?" her mother asked. "And don't tell me nothing. I can see it on your face."

"What? What is it?" Vonda said. "If Emily's dead—" She started to cry again.

Lacey looked at the other faces at the table. They were excited, curious, worried.

"What I say here does not go beyond this table. I'm dead serious."

"How can you even ask?" Rose said, speaking for all of them. "It's between us, until you say different."

"The boots are a common thread among the victims. The killer has a favorite type."

"Of boots?" Vonda looked puzzled. "I don't get it."

Cherise was getting it. "You're saying those dead women all wore cowboy boots? But everyone wears cowboy boots up here! I thought I wouldn't be allowed inside the city limits without mine."

"Not just any boots," Lacey said. "Extraordinary boots, eye-catching boots, expensive boots."

"The murderer is attracted to their boots?" Rose asked. "That's depraved."

"Maybe. Maybe not just the boots, but the kind of women who wear the boots. Young, sassy, attractive. Kick-ass. Like Emily."

"It's disgusting," Cherise said.

"Like I said. It's a theory," Lacey said. "I have no proof."

"Oh, my God," Vonda said. "The creepy guy wanted to party with me and Em together. Said he'd meet us tonight. He kept talking about our boots. After Ladies' Night. Of course we weren't going to do it, but what if he—" She couldn't go on. Her voice was choked with sobs.

"Are you all right?" Lacey said.

Vonda put her hands on the table and staggered to her feet. "I'm going to be sick." She ran for the ladies' room.

Lacey ran after her. Inside the bubblegum pink and heavily mirrored COWGIRLS restroom, she found Vonda rinsing her mouth with water.

"What am I gonna do?" Vonda asked, her eyes filling up with tears.

Cherise stormed through the door, followed by Rose. "We've got to go to the police," Rose said.

"Absolutely," Lacey agreed. "After we make sure Emily is really missing."

Vonda wiped the runaway mascara from her eyes. "I just can't face the cops alone. Lacey, will you help me?"

Oh, this will be swell. Another cross-jurisdictional rumble, Lacey thought. Turning the Sagebrush cops, Vic's old crew, loose on the sheriff's department? The two overlapping law enforcement agencies had been rivals since long before Lacey and Vic ever set foot in town. The police department was no doubt still yukking it up over Tucker's escape, the sheriff's latest fiasco. Vic's cops used to tattle to Lacey on the sheriff's deputies, and the deputies told tales on the cops. *More déjà vu.*

"Yes. We'll do this together," Lacey told her. Rose handed Vonda a fresh paper towel for her eyes.

"Of course we will, dear," Rose said. "All of us."

chapter 29

"That's Emily's Beetle," Vonda said. "Right where she always parks it. So she must have got home from work Monday. But then after that— That's her apartment, on the second floor. The one that's dark."

Cherise was at the wheel of the turquoise Oldsmobile station wagon. Lacey rode shotgun, and Vonda and Rose sat in the backseat. All eyes looked toward a slightly battered red Volkswagen Beetle parked at the curb.

Cherise pulled up behind it and parked. Lacey opened her side door and jumped out. Vonda was right behind her. Soon the entire red-Beetle focus group was staring at it in the wagon's headlights.

"It's kind of a wreck," Cherise ventured.

"It's a beater," Vonda acknowledged, "but it always runs. Emily loves it." Vonda opened the driver's door. "Lock's broken."

"Don't touch anything else." Lacey peered through the window. It looked as if Emily's purse had spilled on the driver's side floor. There were coins, makeup, and what looked like an ID card for the power plant. *Was she yanked right out of her car? When she got home from work?*

Vonda nodded and slammed the door, which made the others flinch. "You have to slam it, or it won't shut," she said. "I told you it was a beater."

The shabby Beetle may have been a bright red badge of independence for Emily, but Lacey found the car's barely-getting-by vibe depressing. She didn't miss the poverty of her first after-college job. Lacey's first apartment in Sagebrush was the uninsulated top floor of an old bungalow on the verge of falling down. It should have been red-tagged by the building inspector, but at the time Sagebrush was booming and there was a serious housing crunch. Emily's apartment building was slightly more upscale, a squat and sturdy-looking two-story brick block not far from the Red Rose, with six apartments, three up and three down.

There was no answer at Emily's door, so they knocked on the manager's door. A thin bleary-eyed man of about fifty answered. He eyed them suspiciously. He'd been knocking back brews and watching the basketball game, still playing in the background. He smelled of beer and cigarettes. Lacey stepped back to avoid the reek.

"What's the crisis?" he belched.

"We need to get into Emily's apartment," Vonda said. "I'm her friend Vonda. Remember me? I'm over here all the time."

He stood there like a stump and looked at the four women. "Yeah? So what? I can't just go letting anybody into people's apartments."

"Have you seen Emily Ogden in the last couple of days?" Lacey asked.

"Can't say I have." He leaned against the dirty doorjamb. "Been real quiet here. But she's always nice and quiet. That's why I like her," he said, as if to imply the four women at his door were not so nice and quiet. He turned to close the door.

Rose was faster. She put her foot in the door so he couldn't shut it. "Listen, you. I am a personal friend of her mother's, and I promised I would check on Emily and make sure she's all right, living here on her own in this dump of yours. Her car is here, but she's not answering her phone. Now, if Emily is sick, or God forbid, *very* sick, I will hold you personally responsible."

Nice work, Mom! Lacey exchanged a look with her sister, who winked. Even Vonda looked impressed.

"Okay, okay, lady. Jeez, give a guy a break. Lemme get the passkey." He reached back into the gloom of his apartment, filled with the blue light of his giant TV screen. He handed Rose a key strung on a filthy white shoelace. "Go check it out yourself. Slip the key under my door when you leave."

"What if there's a problem?" Lacey asked.

He thought for a moment. "If it's a plumbing leak, lady, you call me. Anything else, you call nine-one-one." He slammed the door.

"He's always like that," Vonda said, leading the way.

Emily's apartment was eerily quiet. It was clean and well maintained, considering the location. There was a living room, kitchen, bedroom, and bath, all in a row, one after the other. The living room's ancient threadbare carpet was a grimy gold. The kitchen linoleum was gray with age, and the few battered pieces of furniture screamed *low-rent furnished apartment*.

Nevertheless, it was apparent Emily Ogden had taken pains to make it cozy. There was a handmade quilt on the wall, another one on the sofa. Fashion magazines were placed carefully on the scarred wooden coffee table.

"Vonda's prints are already here," Lacey announced. "So, Mom, if you and Cherise want to check out the fridge and the cupboards, use a towel or something."

"We have gloves, darling," Rose pointed out, pulling on her red kid leather gloves. She smoothed the fingers and marched toward the kitchen with Cherise.

Lacey waited for Vonda to flick on the bedroom lights. The bed was made up with a feminine light blue bedspread and matching dust ruffle. Perfume bottles stood on the dresser in front of a spotted mirror. There were some photographs tucked into the edges of the dresser mirror, including one of Emily and Vonda at a rodeo, with Emily grinning, wearing her fancy boots and a bright green Western shirt. She was just as pretty as Vonda had said.

"She's not sick and she's not here," Vonda said. "I knew it."

"We should take this picture with us. They'll need it to search for her."

Vonda sighed deeply. "Right." She slipped it gently into her bag.

"Someone recently bought groceries," Rose announced, walking into the bedroom. "Looks like Emily's coming right back."

"What does it feel like to you, Vonda?" Lacey gestured at the whole apartment.

"Like normal. Emily's really neat. Not like me."

Lacey stepped around the bed and peered into the small closet. The door was open, and Emily's clothes were hung neatly, simple tops and pants, a few dresses and hooded sweatshirts. Emily had a hard-core hoodie habit. There was one in every color. But Lacey didn't see what she was looking for. She got down on her hands and knees and looked under the bed and the dresser.

"What are you doing, Lacey?" her mother asked.

"Cowboy boots."

"They wouldn't be here," Vonda said. "Em leaves them by the front door in case they're muddy, and so she can see them. And she has this thing for only wearing socks or slippers in the apartment. Like her mom was a clean freak or something."

Rose pursed her lips. Lacey took a deep breath. She had to find out how the story would end. It was her curse.

"No sign of Emily," Lacey said.

"Oh, my God! He's got her. She's going to die," Vonda sobbed, starting to hyperventilate. "And I'm next. He's going to kill me!"

"Well, Lacey? What now?" Rose waited for an answer.

Cherise told Vonda, "Deep breaths! No one's going to hurt you. Not while we're here." Vonda abruptly sat down on the floor and started tugging at her boots. "What are you doing?"

"I got to get these cowboy boots off." She threw the right boot on the floor and started on her left.

"I'm making the call." Lacey strode into the living room with her cell phone. "Vic, honey, I need your help— Yes, I'm fine. But I need you this very minute—

No, they're with me. Listen, there's another missing woman. Yes, it's life or death— I *am* taking a breath. The missing woman's name is Emily Ogden—"

"There is no way Emily is at the same cabin that Tucker took me to, you know." Lacey tapped Vic on the shoulder. He seemed deep in thought.

"Not after the sheriff and the CBI were there today." He gazed at her; his green eyes seemed darker.

It was almost last call at the Lazy Day Motel bar, and Lacey was alternately typing on her laptop and sipping hot chocolate.

"Okay, Mr. Skeptical. Emily went missing the day Cole and I were out riding the range. If Emily is indeed another victim, I'm Cole's alibi, Vic. *His alibi.* Do you think T-Rex and Firestone and Owens and the rest of them really understand that?"

"I don't know, Lacey. Maybe if you'd told them another dozen times, or carved it in T-Rex's cowboy boots with a coyote jawbone, the way you said you were going to." Vic scowled, but he ruined the scowl by laughing. "Maybe then they'd get it."

She grinned. They were both sipping hot chocolate. Lacey didn't care if they were the only two people in the bar not getting drunk; she had a story to write. Her laptop was set up in the bar because she didn't trust herself to stay awake in the motel room. She knew she'd be out cold as soon as she saw the bed.

She and Vic and Cherise and Rose had spent nearly an hour and a half at Emily's apartment while every law enforcement agency in Sagebrush took Vonda's report, in exhaustive detail. Vonda had found her courage, with the Smithsonians and Vic backing her up. Vic refereed the various agencies and managed to make them play nicely together. Firestone's CBI team was still there, collecting prints and DNA.

Lacey's e-mail to Mac and Tony would bring them up to speed on Emily Ogden. She attached a rough draft of her story: ANOTHER MISSING WOMAN IN SAGEBRUSH, COL-

ORADO. Mac would change the headline anyway. Finally, she dashed off a quick e-mail to Benjamin Barton, backed up all of her notes to a flash drive, and closed her laptop. She stretched her shoulders and back, trying to work the kinks out. It felt like weeks since Monday and her visit to the courthouse to see Tucker.

"What about the other two cabins?" Lacey asked. "What did Owens say about Tucker's map? Did he tell you anything more on the phone just now?"

Vic kissed her lightly. "You are so not his favorite reporter. You heard him: He passed the map on to Firestone and T-Rex. They'll try to find those cabins tomorrow, with CBI in the lead. But the fact that you provided the map—even through me—really galls him."

"Glad to be of service."

"Vonda McKay's description of Grady Rush? That made an impression, I can tell you. Coming from that tiny little thing. Sounds like Grady has been one busy and very bad boy. Not too smooth with the ladies either."

"But is he working alone or does he have friends? I'm worried someone will tip him off to the search of the cabins. He must have buddies in the department." Lacey tapped her fingers on the table.

"Which is only a problem if he's involved with the dead women, or with Emily's disappearance," Vic added.

"You think Grady's not smart enough to be the guy behind all this? But he can still be in the loop. That's why he wants to stay close to the investigation. Do you think the cops and the sheriff and the CBI can find Emily Ogden in time?" Lacey closed her eyes and sipped her hot chocolate, trying to chase away the chill around her heart. The endorphins percolated through her bloodstream and right up to her brain. She didn't know what kind of *real* drinks the bartender at the Lazy Day could whip up, but his hot chocolate was stellar.

"Something must be good," Vic said. "You're making those *um* and *yum* sounds again."

"Good chocolate. Wish everything in this town were just as good."

"Sweetheart, Grady Rush is under a microscope right now. T-Rex would be happy to string him up by the gonads. He is not in the loop."

"But Vic, if Grady has even one friend in the department, he'll know about Tucker's map. And Grady will tell his buddies about the map. And something else bothers me."

"Just one thing?"

"Just one right now. Both Virgil Avery and Dodd Muldoon said that Rae was killed in that cabin. While that may be true, we don't know for sure. Neither one suggested that the others were killed there. Did they just jump to a conclusion? Or does one of them have Emily?"

"Where do you want to start, Lacey? Conduct a house-to-house and cabin-to-cabin and barn-to-barn search of the whole county? There's not enough manpower in all of Colorado." Vic put his hands on her shoulders and started to massage the knots in her muscles.

"Don't stop! There." Lacey sighed with satisfaction. "A little to the left. At any rate, the cabin where I stayed is too hot now. The killer couldn't take her there."

"Not only that, you've ruined it as a lover's lane motel. Teenagers in this town are going to hate you."

"The whole town hates me. They can take a number."

"I know your gut is telling you these are some seriously bad guys here, and I don't discount your gut feelings for a minute, sweetheart. But that's not proof, and it doesn't give us a starting point. Maybe Tucker's map does. We'll find out tomorrow." He stopped rubbing. She turned her neck and stretched.

"Vic, do you always have to talk like a cop? 'Move along, folks, nothing to see here, let the authorities do their jobs.'"

"Do you always have to talk like a reporter? You make this whole town sound like the devil's triangle."

"I like that. I'll be sure to use 'devil's triangle' in my next story. But now tell me: What did they find during the cabin search today? Besides the dead coyote on the fence."

Vic looked beat. "Hair and fiber. Lots of prints, lots of DNA, probably much of it from horny teenagers. Probably your prints. Tucker's too."

"Anything else?"

"I'm not supposed to tell you this, but what the hell: Firestone was impressed with you finding that bootheel. They don't know yet if Rae was killed there, but she *was* there, so it's their first break in tracking the killer's movements. It was crucial that Rae's mother ID'd the heel and had a picture of her daughter's boots."

"In other words, without Kitty Fowler and Rae's silver heel, the cops would think I was just a drama queen from another planet. Some planet back East."

"Not just a drama queen. A drama *empress*. With her own planet." Vic drained his chocolate, stood up, and offered her his hand. "Come on, Empress, let's get some sleep. We'll solve the rest of the world's problems in the morning."

Lacey took Vic's hand, and they didn't speak until they were back in the motel room. Then there was no need for words. Vic swept Lacey up into his arms. Coats, sweaters, and jeans went flying. Arms, hands, and legs entwined. Passions connected, flared, and caught fire. Kissing, holding, and touching, they forgot about everything but each other.

An ice chip that had lodged in Lacey's heart the first day she returned to Sagebrush was finally melting.

chapter 30

My dear Chantilly Lace,
I hope Buttercup treated you right on the way
home. There's one more line camp I want to tell you
about. I didn't think of it before, but somebody's put
new glass in the windows of an old cabin nobody
owns. . . .

The letter wasn't signed, but there was only one person who called her Chantilly Lace.

The note had been slipped under Lacey's door sometime in the night. At first glance she thought it must be
the motel bill, a day or two early. Lacey opened the door
and peeked out into the hall in the early-morning light.
Everything was quiet.

Tucker must have had Kit deliver the message, she
thought. *He wouldn't have chanced it himself. He's not
that crazy.*

"Lacey, what's up?" Vic was right behind her. His
breath tickled her neck.

"Tucker sent me a letter." *First ever.*

"God help him, that boy is a fool. Let me see."

Vic reached for it, but she dodged his hand. She
wanted to finish reading it before handing it over.

Tucker described this last line camp as "nearly forgotten." It had even slipped his mind. The land ownership
was unknown, and no one had occupied the place in
years, so far as he knew. It could only be reached via a
jeep trail or on horseback. Tucker had seen it a month or

so ago, from a distance, mounted on Ricochet. He said it looked like someone had fixed it up a little. Maybe to use as a shelter during hunting season. Maybe someone who just wanted to be left alone. Or maybe to hide sins away, he said.

Lacey turned the paper over. On the back was a rough map, with this note: *You have to hike in the last half mile from the jeep trail. Watch out for rattlesnakes.*

She handed it to Vic. "It could be some kind of trap," he said, reading it. "What if it's Tucker's own hideout, despite everything he says?"

"What if Emily is alive?" Lacey was willing to grab any bit of hope. "Besides, Tucker already had me trapped, and he lent me a horse. He even escorted me part of the way back. And he knows everything he tells me, I'm going to tell you. Does he expect to trap every lawman in Northwest Colorado?"

"Lacey, sweetheart." Vic wrapped her in his arms. "T-Rex and Firestone are going to check out both of those other cabins today. But now there's a third cabin? Nobody's going to like it if Tucker's playing us, leading us around by our noses on some phony scavenger hunt."

"Tucker just wants to go home. To his horses and his cows."

"Honey, you don't want to send these guys on a wild goose chase. They'll never trust you again."

"They don't trust me now! I don't trust them. But I trust Cole Tucker. If I couldn't trust him, I wouldn't be here right now. And I trust you."

"What do you want me to do about this?"

She waved the map. "Couldn't we just take a drive and check it out? Hit the jeep trail? Go see this third cabin for ourselves?"

"Not a good idea."

Lacey grabbed Vic's arms. "You can't think like a cop now. You're a private investigator, and PIs have to follow their instincts and protect their clients."

"Without doing anything explicitly illegal. And Tucker's not my client."

"How about me? I'll be your client. There is nothing

illegal about taking a drive in the country. Nothing illegal about this note. Especially not if it saves Emily
Ogden. And we are under no obligation to disclose the
contents of our mail to anyone. This note isn't even signed.
Call it an anonymous tip."

He sighed. Dramatically. "Okay, client. Maybe we'll
check it out. You up for a drive? I know how you love
the Yampa County countryside."

"I adore you, Vic," she said.

"I know." He kissed her, then considered. "No one in
his right mind would be fixing up an old cabin out in the
wilderness that they don't own. And the killer's taking
these women *somewhere*." He examined the map closely
under the desk lamp. "Huh."

"What now?" Lacey leaned over his shoulder.

"Tucker found a cabin *here*? This place is a lot closer
to Sagebrush than those other cabins. It's in some rugged country though. And what in hell is that idiot doing
still hanging around, riding the range, making a target of
himself, sending you love letters? Any self-respecting
outlaw would be out of the state by now," Vic grumbled.

"It's not because of me, Vic, dear. It's because he's
not an outlaw. Tucker's got an irrational affection for
this hard land and this hard life. He just wants to get
back to it."

Someone tapped softly at the door. They both froze.

"Who is it?" Lacey called out.

"Tony. I come in peace, Smithsonian."

Lacey cracked the door open and held her robe
closed. "Trujillo? It's a little early." She poked her head
out and looked up and down the empty hallway.

"I'm still on East Coast time, Lois Lane," Tony replied. "It's already eight-thirty back in Washington."

"Mac said we wouldn't start work till nine Eastern
time. Where's your evil twin?"

"He's having coffee. Mac couldn't sleep, so he woke
me at six. I've given you a big half-hour grace period.
But your presence is requested. Make that commanded.
Editorial meeting. About the latest missing woman. Café
near the lobby, next to the bar."

"Give me twenty minutes," Lacey said. "Order me some—never mind, I'll do it when I get there." Tony saluted and left.

"I'm going with you," Vic said, behind her. "To your meeting."

Lacey was surprised. "It's just work."

"You're not giving me the slip this time." He smiled grimly.

"Me? *You're* the one who had to go talk to Brad Owens last night."

"And you had to go to Ladies' Night at the Red Rose?"

"I don't have time to recycle this argument, darling. I'm getting dressed. We can start a brand-new fight later."

They each stomped off to their respective bathrooms for showers. Lacey put on jeans, silk thermal underwear, and a thick black turtleneck. Everyone looks good in black, and a woman can't have too many black sweaters: one of Lacey's style rules. Her old hiking boots: not beautiful, but practical and sturdy. She filled her leather backpack with her essentials: purse, notebook, pens, digital camera, batteries, extrastrength moisturizer, sunscreen, makeup, scarf. A couple of bottles of water, refilled from the tap. Granola bars for snacks. And a silent prayer for Emily's safety, for Tucker's, for her own and for Vic's. Then she was ready. Vic's gaze took in the jeans, the hiking boots, and the backpack. He whistled.

"You look adorable, mountain girl."

"Don't get used to it." She kissed him, admiring his faded jeans and dark green sweater that brought out the jade color of his eyes. Lacey always found the dangerous expression in them sexy and inviting, but she didn't have time right now. Her cell phone rang as she was sweeping a little mascara onto her lashes.

"You're late," Trujillo complained.

"On my way." Lacey clicked off. She gave Vic a quick kiss and headed for the door. "Give me half an hour with Mac and Tony and then drag me away, would you, sweetheart?"

*   *   *

"I see we've got the full-court makeup," Tony said from behind his laptop. "Goes well with the mountain-mama look."

"Standards are standards," Lacey sniffed, and pulled up a chair.

Mac wore his new boots and jeans and Western shirt. The cowboy hat had a place of honor on its own chair. *Thank goodness he stopped short of loading up on turquoise Indian jewelry too*, Lacey thought. *I'm to be congratulated.*

"Morning," Mac grumbled into his coffee.

"Well, if it isn't Hopalong Jones," she said. "You plan on rounding up some cattle, Mac?"

"Just reporters," Mac replied calmly. A smiling Trujillo wore his usual jeans, turtleneck, and cowboy boots. He was also exercising his usual Western charm on women, women who weren't Lacey. He'd already charmed the waitress, who had a big smile on her face, despite the early hour and the regrettable pea green uniform she was wearing. She came running over with a fresh pot of coffee.

Remembering keenly the last time she was out in the county without services (or breakfast) for fifty miles, Lacey ordered a serious breakfast of bacon and eggs, coffee and toast, home fries, and fruit.

Mac's eyebrows, the barometer that measured his mood, rose in semicircles of surprise. "If you're finished ordering a breakfast the size of Wyoming, give me an update on this Emily Ogden." Mac had a giant cinnamon roll on his plate. His laptop was already sticky with icing. He was hardly in a position to comment on her menu choices.

"You got my e-mail," she said.

"I've already checked with the cops and the sheriff," Tony said. "No sign of Emily in Sagebrush. CBI is still processing her car and apartment. The sheriff's department had no comment, said it was a 'city case.' Since when is this place a city? And this CBI agent, Rico Firestone? Couldn't get ahold of him. He's in the field, not answering his cell."

"Let me guess, Tony. You want a double byline?" She frowned, but there was nothing she could do about it.

"That's right." He grinned broadly. "We're ready to file. Partner."

"This Emily, you figure she's another victim?" Mac bit into the cinnamon roll and followed it with a slurp of coffee and a smacking of lips.

"Yes, that's how I figure it. Emily Ogden's best friend was frantic last night."

"Could it be a false alarm? Took off on a road trip, didn't tell anyone?"

Lacey's gut instinct hadn't changed. "I don't think so. Emily's car is parked at her apartment. Since Monday after work she hasn't contacted her job, her parents, or her best friend, who says they normally swap a hundred texts a day. I believe that's in there, in *my* story. I'd love to be mistaken. But I'm not."

"Just checking," Mac said.

"If the killer has Emily— Well, we don't know how long he holds them before— This is the most important part, Mac. She might still be alive."

Tony nodded. "The CBI thinks they were all held for at least a few days before they were killed."

"Damn," Mac said. "I hate to get out of D.C. and go off to a quiet corner of the country and see the same twisted stuff happening."

Turning heads as he walked into the café, Vic Donovan joined the party.

"Donovan. Joining the staff?" Mac asked.

"Better get used to me." Vic gestured to the waitress and pulled up a chair next to Lacey. "I'm not leaving Lacey's side today. When I do, things happen."

"Things?" Tony egged him on. "What kind of things?"

"Strange things. Dangerous things. Things that don't happen to other people."

"But newsworthy things," Mac added. "There's an upside to everything."

"You guys are easily amused," Lacey said. "And Mac, I'm supposed to take a few days off. Personal leave, remember?"

"I suppose you're going to tell me you're suffering from posttraumatic shock?"

Everyone else has suggested it. "Not at the moment. But it could strike without warning."

"Unless you're dying, all personal leave is revoked due to breaking news. And remind me to pick up some Maalox," Mac said. He liked to reach for that little blue bottle of bliss when Lacey made his stomach flip over. When Lacey was breaking news that came with a sidebar of danger.

"Who's minding *The Eye*? You said you could barely afford to let me take leave. Then you show up in Sagebrush with Tony, like the East Coast cavalry. It's pretty weird."

"You were abducted! *The Eye Street Observer* isn't going to close its eyes when that happens to one of our own. Good golly Moses, Smithsonian. And did you check out our stories online? Courthouse drama, fugitive on the run, silver bootheel. It's golden! Got a ton of hits."

"Beat out the congressional budget story," Tony said.

"I'll print it out for my scrapbook, Mac. But I'm safe now."

"That's why you brought your bodyguard?" Lacey gave her editor The Look. He laughed. "Not a bad idea, you having a bodyguard. I'm just asking. Don't worry about *The Eye*. Claudia's manning the news desk."

"Claudia Darnell?" If the publisher of *The Eye Street Observer* herself was pitching in, times were strange indeed.

"Had an unhealthy gleam in her eye. Said she missed handling copy, and I'd rather not witness her in action." Mac paused for effect. "She's also got this *idea*."

"You'll love it," Tony piped up.

"What kind of idea?" Lacey was curious but wary. Big bosses with big ideas usually spelled trouble.

"True crime books. Publish them ourselves," Mac continued. "You know the kind of story, one where we've got a reporter on the scene, or inside the scene. Like this one. This story's got it all, Smithsonian. Multiple murders, kidnapped reporter, fugitive from justice, even a posse, for crying out loud. Maybe *The Eye* could make some money for a change."

"You can't be serious!" Lacey didn't think she could be shocked, but she was.

"We're trying to think of ways to save the newspaper."

"Come on, Lois Lane," Tony said. "You know the stuff, sensational but accurate. What we do best. Three-way byline."

"Three-way byline?" This was really too much. Lacey wasn't willing to fracture her byline any further.

"You, me, and Mac. We slam it out in six weeks. It'll be half written already. We're doing all the legwork right now anyway. We compile all our news stories, write some narrative, add witness sidebars, throw in some analysis, wrap it all up in a lurid eye-catching cover. E-book edition too." Tony flashed his dazzling smile.

That snake-oil smile only means trouble, and lots of work.

"But nothing's settled yet!" Lacey protested. "The story's still in motion. Cole Tucker is still out there. And Emily might be—" She closed her eyes, as if that could block everything out. Working on a book with Tony and Mac? There would be untold numbers of fights. Not to mention late nights slogging through copy.

The waitress scooted over with Lacey's plate and a fresh pot of coffee. She took Vic's order for waffles and sausage.

"At any rate, we'll be here at least a couple more days," Mac said. "Anything we can do to help find this missing woman?"

Lacey dug into her breakfast. She tapped Vic's boot under the table. "Um. Probably not. Just let the authorities do their thing," she said.

"That doesn't sound like you," Mac said.

"Oh, they have some leads."

"What kind of leads?" Tony pressed. "And how do you know this? Don't bogart the facts, Lacey."

"Leads. They always have leads. You know. Anyway, I

can't hang around here all day. Vic and I have some — errands to run."

"Smithsonian," Mac rumbled ominously. "Errands? We have brainstorming to do. This is an editorial meeting. *Eye Street West.*"

"Don't you trust me, Mac?"

He chuckled. "Trust a reporter?" He laughed louder and helped himself to more icing on his cinnamon roll. "Trust a reporter. Ha. You slay me, Smithsonian."

Lacey and Tony exchanged a meaningful look. It wasn't like reporters ever trusted their editors either. She took a bite of succulent bacon. Vic concentrated on his coffee, scanning the room out of habit and training. He saw them first.

"There she is!" Lacey heard Cherise yell. She spun around in her chair and saw her mother and sister in the doorway. They had Vonda McKay in tow, and Benjamin Barton brought up the rear. *The parade is starting early today.*

"You invited the whole tribe?" Mac looked pained. "Your family got a song and dance act too? Well, I got one thing to say: Keep your mother out of my hair."

"I wouldn't worry about my hair if I were you, Mac." *How am I going to slip away with Vic without getting hijacked by Mom and Cherise?*

Rose's eyes were shadowed from her late night, but she still had her trademark sparkling enthusiasm — and her preppy-parent outfit of gray slacks, white shirt, and burgundy V-neck sweater, and finished off with penny loafers. Cherise was truly her mother's daughter, full of energy, bouncing around in her jeans, purple sneakers, and a petal pink V-neck sweater, a big smile on her face.

This morning, even Vonda had been transformed. Her hair was combed, she wore a lavender V-neck sweater of Cherise's, and her Goth eyeliner had been left in the shower. She wore a pair of pink sneakers. No boots. Vonda looked younger and more innocent — and less afraid — than the night before.

With all those matching V-neck sweaters and healthy complexions, the trio looked ready for a family photograph. Ben Barton, in crisply pressed jeans and a red and white Nordic ski sweater, rested a friendly hand on Cherise's shoulder. With a start, Lacey realized he too would fit right into that family photo. His blond good looks complemented Cherise's nicely.

Obviously, Lacey thought, *Baby Lacey had been dropped on the Smithsonians' doorstep by gypsies. Gloomy, world-weary gypsies.* She lifted her coffee cup to her lips and tried to open her eyes very wide. *Be perky!*

"Lacey, you look tired, dear," Rose said. "You need rest, and what are you eating? You should be having whole grains, like oatmeal."

"Protein, Mom, lots of protein." She took a bite of bacon, a simple reward for being alive. *Yum.* "Brain food. Oatmeal and carbs just make me hungry."

Her mother sniffed. "Vein-clogging cholesterol. No wonder you're dragging."

The waitress waltzed past Rose with Vic's huge platter of waffles and sausages.

"We're taking Vonda to Steamboat Springs, and keeping her out of boots," Cherise said. "She spent the night on my spare bed. Isn't my sweater cute on her?"

"I still don't know if it's the right thing to do," Vonda began. "I want to help find Emily."

"We want you safe. We'll all feel better if you get away from here," Vic said. The killer knew Emily, so he had to know Vonda: where she hung out, where she worked, where she lived. Vonda might be the next target in the killer's crosshairs. The Sagebrush cops had agreed the night before: Getting her out of town was a good idea. "We'll do everything we can to find Emily."

"Well. I guess. If there's nothing I can do to help here," Vonda said. "I'll stay with my aunt and uncle in Steamboat. The guys at Wild Bunch Taxidermy said I can take time off with pay. A week or so anyway."

"That sounds like a plan," Lacey said. *A very good plan.*

"God, I hope Emily comes home safe."

Tony stood up and turned to Vonda. "Tony Trujillo, with *The Eye Street Observer* in Washington, D.C. Do you have time for a few questions? About your friend Emily?"

"I told Lacey everything already."

He smiled and steered Vonda to a nearby table. Tony could be sensitive with sources that needed a gentle touch, and he was a good reporter. *For a source-stealing, byline-grabbing snake in the grass.*

"Want to come along, sis?" Cherise asked. "We're heading over to Vonda's place to pack, then Steamboat. And shopping!"

"Sounds great," Lacey said. "But we have things to do." She checked her watch.

"Mr. Jones, all work and no play is *not acceptable* here in Colorado," Rose warned Mac. "A balanced life is the key to good health. And that doesn't include that disgusting half-eaten thing on your plate. Sugar, white flour, and fat are a lethal combination. I can just imagine your arteries."

Mac took another bite of cinnamon roll. "I appreciate your concern, Mrs. Smithsonian. Have a nice day." He returned one sticky hand to his sticky laptop and proceeded to peck at the keys. "We got work to do."

"That man is going to have a heart attack," Rose observed.

"But not today," Lacey assured her. "Thanks for the offer. Take good care of Vonda and I'll call if anything happens."

Lacey liberated Vonda from Tony and herded her family toward the door. Cherise and Ben shared a hug, but Ben stayed behind.

"I thought you were heading back to the slopes," Lacey said encouragingly. "Steamboat? Skiing? Powder to die for, and all that?"

"Not just yet." Ben took her aside. "Brooke is unhappy. She feels neglected, left out of the loop. We had a long conversation last night."

"Ben, I haven't had a lot of spare time to stay in touch with her, or Stella either." Lacey noticed Vic was hovering over them. "How unhappy?"

"I'm supposed to monitor your every move today.

She's convinced you're still in danger. Legal, if not mortal, and perhaps both. And I have to say I concur. Especially with this latest disappearance."

"Your sister is a doll, but really, Ben, I'll be fine. I'll be with Vic. Your skis are calling you. Hear them? 'Oh, Benjamin! Come ski with us!'"

"Yeah, she said you'd be evasive. So to recap, I'm up to speed on Emily Ogden and her friend Vonda McKay. Cherise is taking Vonda under her wing, and that's very helpful." Ben looked to the spot where Cherise had stood and a goofy look came over his face. "She's really sweet, your sister, isn't she?"

"Cherise? Sweet? Oh, yeah. Very." Lacey felt her eyes roll. It seemed Cherise didn't need a lethal cheerleader kick to fell a man. *She smiles and men fall at her feet, and then they compliment her boots from down on the ground.*

"What's really on your agenda for today, Lacey? It's something important, or you'd be speeding to Steamboat with them, interviewing Vonda along the way."

"Brooke said you were smart."

"*Smart* is such a pale word. Now, your plans?"

"I suppose Brooke wants a full report." She caught Vic smirking behind Ben's back. "Vic and I are going for a drive. *Alone*. In the country." *Nobody said it would be easy.* Tony slipped up behind them.

"And when you say take a drive, you mean *what* exactly?" Ben persisted.

"Get in the car! Drive! Take the scenic route. See the sights."

"I recognize that look," Tony said to Ben. "It means something's up."

"What look is that?" Vic stepped forward. "I'm curious."

"That lone-wolf-ditching-the-rest-of-the-pack look," Tony said.

Vic was nodding. "Sure, I recognize that look."

"Is that true, Smithsonian?" Mac had finished his cinnamon roll and was on his feet and ready for action.

"What is this, Pick On Lacey Day?"

"Every day is Pick On Lacey Day," Mac said. "Now, where are you two headed?"

"Wild goose chase," Vic said under his breath to Lacey. "And now we've got this whole flock of geese tagging along."

"You got room in that Jeep?" Mac closed his laptop. "I feel like a ride myself. Break in my new hat."

"And I have it on good authority that you shouldn't be going anywhere today without your attorney," Ben said. "In fact, Lacey, I believe you should always have an attorney present."

"Lacey wouldn't head out on the range without her posse, now would you, Annie Oakley?" Tony grabbed a piece of toast from her plate. "Better deputize me. Because if *they* go, *I* go. Have pen, will travel."

She was trapped.

"Are you going to tell them, or should I?" Vic asked.

"I knew it wasn't just a walk in the park," Tony said. "I knew it!"

"We can talk now or in the car, Smithsonian," Mac said. "Your choice. But you are going to talk. You can't sequester this scoop, *Scoop*."

"This is so unfair," Lacey said. She could feel the map burning a hole in her purse. "And don't call me Scoop."

"Nobody said life was fair," Mac said.

"Or editors."

Lacey understood *how* the Three Musketeers had invited themselves to the party, but she didn't understand why Vic allowed them to tag along. He could have just said no and made it stick. It was his rent-a-Jeep, after all. Maybe because he didn't believe anything would come of it. She asked him when they went back to their room to collect their supplies for the road, her backpack, his duffel bag.

"Maybe I think there's safety in numbers," he told her. "Maybe I think Mac needs the exercise. Maybe the only way to get them off our backs is to take them along."

"You don't think we're going to find anything, do you?"

"Doubt it. I hope we don't. But you never know." He unzipped his duffel bag and pulled out a handgun case. He checked the fit of his shoulder holster over his sweater, took it off again, loaded his stainless .357 Magnum revolver and slipped it in, then tucked it all back in the bag. Lacey's jaw dropped as she watched all this.

"It's that serious?"

"Better to be prepared." He flashed a smile. "Like a Boy Scout."

"A Boy Scout with PI papers and a permit to carry."

He lifted her backpack to test its weight. "You're bringing along a lot of stuff. Computer? Fax machine?"

"I like to be prepared too." She threw in extra hand wipes.

"You know, Lacey, if we screw this up, we'll never be able to show our faces in this town again." He frowned, but she grinned at him and he started laughing.

"You promise? Vic, honey, that's the best news I've heard all week."

Ten minutes later, they were on the highway heading north out of Sagebrush. Lacey knew there were just a few big ranches and a barn or two all the way to Wyoming. Vic drove and Lacey rode shotgun with Tucker's map in her hand. Ben, Mac, and Tony filled the backseat. Vic's duffel bag, Lacey's backpack, Mac's hat, and Ben's ski poles were piled in the back of the Jeep. Ben said the poles could double as hiking staffs.

"Hey, that sign is full of bullet holes!" Mac sat up straight and pointed.

"Welcome to Yampa County," Vic cracked.

"People don't shoot road signs in D.C.," Mac grumbled.

"No, they just shoot each other," Lacey said.

"By the way, Lois and Clark, where are we headed? Or is it *Lewis* and Clark today?" Tony asked. "Is it still a secret?"

"North and northeast," Lacey said. "We're going to check out an old line camp, a cabin where cowboys used to stop while they were driving cattle across the range. We may have to hike in a ways. Half a mile or so."

"We have a map, so that's something. We may even see some wild horses," Vic said. "And pronghorns! On your left, people, pronghorns at nine o'clock."

"So those are pronghorns?" Mac leaned back and stared out the window. "Beautiful day in the country. But as a matter of curiosity, Smithsonian, who drew this map, and what are you looking for? And don't tell me wild horses."

"It's a long shot," Lacey began.

"What's a pronghorn?" Ben wanted to know. "Will my iPhone work up here? *Why* are the road signs all full of bullet holes? And is whatever we're doing legal?"

"An antelope." Lacey took his questions in order. "Try a tin can and string. Because it's the West and that's how we roll. And what we're doing is not *illegal*."

"I get it. We're rendezvousing with Cole Tucker?" Tony was excited. "I want an exclusive."

"Wrong. Traveling with you guys really is its own punishment," Lacey commented. She prayed this wouldn't be a bust. *At least there are no Western wear stores where we're going.*

Vic tapped Lacey's arm. "You want to tell them now or later?"

Lacey sighed. "We might be on the trail of Emily Ogden."

chapter 31

"This is closer to Sagebrush than I thought," Lacey said as the Jeep bore down on its target.

"Don't get too excited. We've still got a ways to go," Vic cautioned them.

The Jeep turned off the highway, then down a maze of county roads through sagebrush flats and into hillier up-country with a few scattered trees. The snow had blown off here and there, and the barren landscape was muddy and brown. They crossed posted BLM land on a ruler-straight single-lane dirt road. It was a patchwork quilt of land, public and private. They passed through rolling private ranchland, through barbed wire fences with hand-made gates they opened and shut themselves, and finally onto another narrow dirt road, heading across a little ravine and through dense cottonwoods.

The Jeep bumped along ruts and climbed in and out of pits that would put D.C. potholes to shame. The two-track trail was soon passable only by Jeeps or ATVs and mountain goats, and a few pronghorns. The hillside fell away steeply from the trail in places, and Lacey was afraid the ground might open up and swallow them.

"I don't think we're on a road anymore," Mac said as he jostled around in the backseat. "Is this on that map of yours?"

"You wanted to join the party," Vic said. "This is the fun part."

After their teeth were sufficiently rattled, their spines shaken out of alignment, and Lacey's stomach knotted like a crocheted doily, Vic wheeled off the trail into a small clearing in the sagebrush. He parked the Jeep in a slight depression where the brush was taller and the vehicle couldn't be seen from the trail. Opening the hatch, he retrieved his holstered revolver from his duffel bag. He strapped it on over his sweater and under his jacket.

"Guns? You think we need guns?" Mac asked, his eyes wide.

"Just a precaution," Vic answered, strapping on a fanny pack filled with his water bottle, handcuffs, phone, and spare ammunition.

"It must be like having an umbrella, isn't it?" Ben offered. "Or a lawyer. Bring one along and you won't get rained on."

"Exactly," Vic said.

"When I think of taking precautions, I think of handing out condoms in high schools, not guns," Mac countered.

"Cheer up, Mac, there might be an unprotected road sign to blow full of holes," Tony said.

"Anyone who thinks this is too dangerous doesn't have to go," Vic said. "Stay in the Jeep. Keep warm. Read the paper. Play the radio, if you can find a station."

"Didn't say that," Mac protested. "I just haven't handled a gun since I was in the military." All heads swiveled toward Mac.

"Military?" Lacey asked. "You?"

"What? A couple of years in the army, long time ago," Mac said. "No big deal."

"Must be where you got that soothing way of barking at people," Lacey cracked.

"I don't bark!" Mac barked.

"Yeah, you're a lamb," Tony said. "You got a gun for me, Vic?"

"Nope. There's only one gun out here, so far as we know. Mine."

"Brooke will hate missing this." Ben smiled. "She loves guns. You don't really think anything is going to happen, do you?"

"No, I don't," Lacey said.

Ben pulled out his ski poles and handed one to Mac to use as a staff. "Now what?"

"We walk. Half a mile or so." Vic glanced at the map. He showed it to Lacey and the others before folding it up in his pocket.

Lacey bundled up, put on her ear warmers and her scarf, and slung her heavy backpack over her shoulders. The sky had turned an unpromising shade of gunmetal gray. The air smelled like snow and tickled her nose. The men turned their jacket collars up, and Vic pulled two ball caps from his duffel bag, one for himself and one for Tony. Vic's was a souvenir from out of the past. It read SAGEBRUSH COLORADO POLICE DEPARTMENT. Mac looked ready for action in his enormous black cowboy hat. Ben pulled his fleece ski hat, sky blue with white snowflakes, down around his ears.

It was a desolate spot. The main roads lay far behind them, and only jeep and horse trails lay ahead. The nearby bluffs were striped in peach and white stone. Silver green sagebrush poked through patches of crusty snow, but most of the muddy path had been blown clean by the wind, which was picking up.

It was a tricky walk up the slope toward the bluffs, and slower than Lacey liked. All talk ceased as the group concentrated on not falling. Lacey stopped for a break, and she and Vic shared their water bottles with the less Boy Scout–prepared members of their party.

Vic forged ahead. He spotted the cabin around a bend in the trail before the others saw it. There was no sign of activity, but he signaled them to stop. He directed the group back around the bend, out of sight of the cabin.

On the bluffs, a half-dozen wild horses stood watching them with curiosity. They all turned to admire the animals. They watched the horses watching them.

"Wow! Got to get a picture of that for my girls," Mac said, handing Lacey his small camera. She took several shots of Mac grinning in the foreground in his new hat with the horses posing on the ridgeline behind him. Tony also snapped photos, and Ben asked him to e-mail cop-

ies. Vic waited patiently for the photo op to conclude;
then he told them to wait there while he and Lacey went
on ahead.

They stopped when they caught sight of a weathered
log structure about fifteen feet by twenty. The cabin
looked decades old. A rusted stovepipe rose at a rakish
angle through its sloping roof. The logs had long since
turned a silver gray, but the chinking between the logs
held against the snows, and there were no obvious gaps
in the roof or walls. Still, the cabin was sagging slightly to
one side and it looked like a heavy wind might knock it
down. Not far away, an ancient outhouse was visible,
leaning down the hillside, downwind.

The cabin was a lonely interloper in a harsh land. It
was too far from the roads to be anyone's home year-
round, and clearly had no electricity or plumbing or running water. Yet it had once been a welcoming temporary
home on the range for cowboys moving cattle to the
good grazing land near the bluffs.

But something was odd about this cabin. Set into the
old logs on the front side of the structure was a brand-
new wooden door, no windows. And in the long wall fac-
ing them someone had set a new window, high up, with a
clear pane of glass.

Vic told Lacey and the others to wait out of sight. He
quietly worked his way through the sagebrush, clear
around the cabin and back to her side.

"Appears empty," he whispered. "There's a small window on the back side, no other doors. Some muddy footprints, but no one around. But fresh glass? New door?
That's just weird. Somebody's been making themselves
at home."

"I'm coming with you."

"No, Lacey, wait here till I give the all clear."

She watched him from her cover behind a large sagebrush. Vic stepped silently to the front of the cabin and
flattened his back against the log wall, next to the doorknob. With one boot, he kicked back hard on the door,
the sound echoing against the bluffs. There was no answer. He turned the knob, his revolver drawn. The door

wasn't locked. Vic carefully opened it without exposing himself and let it swing into the cabin, slowly. It squeaked on its dry hinges. Not another sound. He slipped quietly around the corner of the cabin to the far wall, the wall Lacey couldn't see.

She saw Vic slide around the corner to the open door and roll right through it in a crouch, leading with his gun. He turned to call her, but Lacey didn't wait. She was already through the door right behind him.

Despite the open door and the two windows, the light was dim inside the cabin. The air was dank and it smelled of—what? She couldn't quite place the odor. Sour beer and sweat? And something else. Fear.

As their eyes began to adjust, Lacey stopped short. A huge rack of elk antlers was nailed high on the far wall. Cowboy boots were impaled upside down on the antler points. Four pairs: eight boots. Their leather was decorated, embroidered, and tooled. One small pair, with a boot missing its heel, was trimmed in filigreed silver. Lacey gasped. They had to be Rae Fowler's boots. A length of heavy rope hung looped over the rack of antlers, ending in an untidy noose. It swung slowly as the wind blew in through the door.

Before she could say anything, she heard a muffled sound coming from the far corner. Something was huddled on the floor under a metal cot.

The hair rose on the back of Lacey's neck. Vic spun around with the .357 at the ready, but Lacey put up her hand to stop him.

"Emily?" she said through dry lips. "Is that you?" Lacey inched closer, holding her breath. Vic let out a slow whistle, the only hint that he was as stunned as Lacey.

She bent down to see a young woman, barely more than a girl, shivering in a fetal position beneath a filthy quilted covering that looked like an old sleeping bag. Shaking with fear, the captive was making sounds that might have been screams, if she weren't already hoarse from screaming. Her long white-blond hair—the hair Vonda had described to Lacey—streamed out against the dark floorboards. She shrank farther back in the shadows against the wall as Lacey lifted the light metal cot and approached her.

Vic checked the rest of the one-room cabin. Satisfied, he holstered his gun. Mac, Tony, and Ben stood in the open door watching, as still as toy soldiers lined up in a row.

"It's all right, Emily. My name is Lacey. I won't hurt you." She sat on the floor next to Emily, who was whimpering like a hurt animal. "Vonda told me about you. Your friend, Vonda." Lacey didn't know if the woman understood her. "She was worried about you when you didn't show up. We all were. We've been looking for you. You are Emily Ogden, aren't you?"

Emily nodded and tears leaked from her eyes. She put her hands up to her tearstained face and sobbed. Her wrists were handcuffed and her blackened eyes were as wild as a cornered animal's.

"Water." Lacey slipped off her backpack and grabbed a bottle. "Here, drink this." Lacey uncapped it for her and Emily struggled to sit up, her shaking hands reaching for the bottle. She drank greedily, water dribbling down her chin. "Better?"

Emily nodded. She drank more and then leaned against the wall, panting, watching the men warily. She screeched when Vic came near her. He backed away, his hands turned up to show her they were empty.

"We have to get you out of here," Lacey said.

"Can't." Emily's voice croaked. She pointed to her feet.

Lacey lifted the sleeping bag. Emily was dressed in nothing but a short skirt and a thin top. Wrapped around one of her bare ankles was a length of metal chain, as heavy as a tow chain. The steel links were padlocked to the cot with just enough slack to reach a nearby chamber pot and an empty water jug, or to stoke the now-cold stove. Her ankle was scraped raw.

"Oh, God, Vic, she's chained. And handcuffed."

"Let me see." Vic knelt to heft the chain. Emily sobbed helplessly as Lacey wrapped her in her arms.

"He won't hurt you, I promise," Lacey said, her own eyes misting up. "Trust me." She found it hard to breathe, Emily was holding on so tight. Lacey took in the cabin with a turn of her head.

The meager furnishings of the cabin included a table, a few chairs, and several coils of the same heavy rope as the noose hanging over their heads. There was more chain, coiled in a rusty bucket, and Lacey could just make out things that looked like bullwhips hanging on the smoke-stained log walls. Battered Styrofoam coolers, pizza boxes, and empty beer and liquor bottles littered the floor in the gloom. She saw shreds of fabric so torn up they were almost unrecognizable, perhaps remnants of women's clothing. A pair of ripped black tights lay near the cot.

Lacey saw a fleece-lined jean jacket hung tauntingly out of reach on a nail on the wall. "Is that your jacket?" Emily nodded. "Tony, hand me that jacket." He tossed it to Lacey and she draped it over Emily's shaking shoulders.

The air was frosty. Vic found a kerosene lamp on the table and lit it. "We may have to break this cot apart to get her out," he said. "There's a hell of a big padlock on this chain, and the cot's chained to the wall." Emily shivered in Lacey's arms and wouldn't look at him.

"It's almost over now, Emily," Lacey said. "I promise."

"Emily, my name is Vic." He crouched down to her level. "I'm going to help you. Do you know if there are keys for these padlocks?" She shook her head no without lifting her face from Lacey's neck. "Okay. At least we can take these cuffs off."

He fished out his standard police-issue handcuff key, and Lacey used it to release Emily's wrists. They were chafed and bleeding from trying desperately to work her hands free. Lacey helped her slip her arms through the sleeves of her jacket. She rubbed Emily's cold hands.

"Phones!" Lacey said. "Anyone got a signal up here?"

The four men checked their cell phones, including Ben's new ultrasmart smartphone. No one had service.

"Mac, Ben, see if you can get a signal outdoors," Vic ordered. "Here, take mine too. Try down the hill out in the open, or up on top of the bluff. Stick together. If you get a signal, call nine-one-one. Tell the dispatcher you're with me. We're on the lower western slopes of Black Mountain. You got that?" Mac frowned. Ben nodded eagerly. "Tell them we have Emily Ogden and she's alive. Alert Firestone and tell him a helicopter would be nice. Or they can meet us with an ambulance back at the highway. Now go."

Ben and Mac headed out the door. Vic turned to Tony. "We're going to tear this cot apart, you and me. See if you can find us a pry bar, a piece of pipe, a big stick, anything for leverage." Tony nodded and started pawing through the cabin's litter.

"Vic, her feet are nearly frozen," Lacey said. "Can we get a fire going in here?"

Vic shook his head no and took one of Emily's feet. "Might signal the wrong folks."

Emily flinched at first but then she relaxed while Vic gently massaged one foot to get the circulation moving, then the other. He kept at it until Emily's feet were warm enough she could flex her toes. She relaxed her grip a little on Lacey.

"Boots," she said. "My boots. Please. That bastard took them." Emily was beginning to recover her voice, but it was still a whisper. She pointed to the rack of antlers on the wall.

Tony reached up. "Which ones?"

Lacey knew. Vonda had told her. "The white ones, Tony. The ones with the sunsets. Wait. Get photos first."

"Already got 'em."

Tony handed the boots to Lacey, who hesitated a moment before asking Emily, "Do you want your tights too?"

Emily shook her head. She wiped tears away with the back of her hand and hugged her beautiful boots. Lacey reached into her backpack with one hand.

"You hungry? I have a granola bar." Emily nodded. Lacey ripped it open for her and Emily took a big bite.

Whoever had left her chained to the cot hadn't left her anything to eat. Lacey pawed through her pack and finally pulled out a pair of socks. She handed them to Emily, who tried to put one on, but she grimaced with pain as she bent over.

"Oh, God. I think he broke some of my ribs."

"Don't try, Emily. I got it." Lacey took the socks and gently tugged them onto Emily's bare feet. The chain around her ankle was just loose enough to snug the sock under the links.

"Socks? You brought socks, Smithsonian?" Tony gave Lacey an incredulous look.

"Extra socks. My feet get cold." Lacey didn't mention she also had a pair of clean underwear in her backpack, sealed in a plastic baggie. She didn't expect them to understand. It was a girl thing. They were guys. *Clean underwear, clean socks, a little lipstick and mascara, what do guys care?*

"We'll get you out of here," Vic said to Emily. "Promise."

Tony gave up on the trash in the cabin and went outside to look for a pry bar.

"We'll bust the bed," Vic said to Lacey. "Emily will still have that chain on her ankle. We don't have anything to pick a lock with, or cut the chain. She's in no shape to walk very far, and a ride down the mountain in the Jeep would be agony for her with a broken rib."

"We'll have to stay here, Emily. Just for a while." Lacey didn't like the thought of spending any more time there than necessary. Vic obviously didn't either.

"You two sit tight for a minute. I'll see what's up with the phones." Vic pulled the door shut behind him.

"We have to get out of here now!" Emily tried to get up, but the effort was too much. "He said he was coming back! For some more—more—"

Lacey drew a deep breath. "Who's coming back?"

"The bastard! I hate him, I hate him, I hate him! Hope a rattlesnake bites him in the balls."

Lacey appreciated Emily's flash of spunk. She was going to need it.

"Does he have a name?" Lacey asked.

"Mitch. That's all I know. His buddies call him Mitch. Bunch of creeps who hang at the Red Rose. But he wants me to call him Daddy. He says, 'Call me Daddy, baby.'" Emily sneered, her eyes flaring with anger. "He calls me baby. And then he makes me—" She gagged.

"Mitch Stanford?" Lacey felt a little sick.

"All I ever heard was Mitch. I was getting out of my car after work and suddenly there was something over my head and around my throat and everything went dark." Her panic was growing. "We've got to get out of here, Lacey. Now! He said he's bringing his friends back with him so they can all *party*. They're gonna kill me. And now they'll kill you."

"No, they won't. You're safe. With us. We're all going to be safe," Lacey said, and tried to believe it. "Can you stand up?"

Lacey helped her to her feet, but Emily was breathing hard and hugging her ribs. "It hurts." Emily collapsed onto the cot. "He's going to kill me. Just like Corazon. I saw her boots up there on that rack and I knew." Emily hung her head and sobbed. Lacey had to wipe her eyes. *Keep it together, Smithsonian. Reporters don't cry.* "I kept thinking, is this it? Really? This is my whole life? That's all there is of it? I never got to do anything I really wanted. Oh, God."

"But you didn't die. You hung on. You're alive. And we're going to get out you of here." Lacey pulled a comb from her purse in her backpack and tried to untangle Emily's pale blond hair.

"I want him to die," Emily said. "You don't know the things he did to me, the things he said he was going to do." She gagged again. "I want to see the life pour out of him like a flat beer in a filthy gutter. Him and his filthy cigar."

"You could never punish him enough," Lacey said. "But we'll make sure someone does."

Emily shook her head. "Why did you come here? You're not the police. How did you find me?"

"The short version is—" Lacey sighed. There wasn't a

short version. "Your friend Vonda. I met her at the Red Rose. She was really afraid for you. We told the CBI and the police. Then Cole Tucker sent me a map showing where there was an old cabin that had a new window, and he said we should check it out. And I just had a feeling—I had to try."

"That's crazy," Emily said.

"I know. I'm a reporter. I have this problem with curiosity. Occupational hazard."

"But how did you know that creep had me? Vonda didn't know—nobody knew."

"Cowboy boots."

Emily peered into Lacey's face. "You're the one Cole Tucker took from the courthouse, aren't you?"

"That's me."

"I heard it on the radio that day. Petrus's truck and all. But Cole didn't kill anybody. Mitch the pig did all that."

"I know." Lacey felt relieved to hear someone else confirm it.

There was a sound of stamping feet. Mac and Ben opened the door in triumph. Vic was right behind them, and Tony followed with a yard-long piece of rusty metal pipe.

"I got through!" Ben crowed. "We had to go all the way up on the bluff to get a signal."

"Those wild horses just stood there and watched us," Mac said. "Then they followed us around till we started back down!"

Lacey cleared her throat. "Excuse me. And?"

"Oh, right. We finally got through to nine-one-one," Ben said. "Firestone's on his way here with the CBI team. Got the GPS coordinates off my phone. So we're supposed to just sit tight, stay warm, and keep Emily still. That's my best legal advice."

"Oh, my God," Emily cried out. "Is it really almost over?"

"I think so." Lacey finally smiled and reached out both hands. Emily hugged her tight.

With their improvised crowbar, Vic and Tony attacked the cot Emily was chained to. Tony held it down while Vic levered the pipe. The rivets popped right out of the flimsy aluminum frame like buttons popping off a vest. Vic handed Emily the now-free end of her ankle chain. She took it from him and stared at it, dazed.

There was a sound in the distance, a sound like an engine. More than one engine. They froze.

"It's too soon for the law to arrive, isn't it?" Lacey asked.

Vic took a quick look outside. When he came back in, he shut the door behind him and drew his revolver.

"Everybody get away from the windows. We've got company."

chapter 32

"Who is it?" Lacey asked.

"It's him! He's coming back to kill me." Emily was on the verge of hysteria.

"Our friendly neighborhood real estate agent, Virgil Avery. He's got friends," Vic said. "The others were too far away to make out. They're on ATVs. They came up a different way than we did."

"Mitch Stanford too?" Lacey asked.

"Something tells me you haven't shared everything you know, Smithsonian," Mac said. Lacey ignored him.

"How many are there, Vic?"

"Four men. Three ATVs."

"What are they doing here?" Ben said.

"Quiet," Vic commanded. "Somebody blow out that lamp." Mac snuffed the light. Vic latched the door and Tony upended the wooden table across it.

There was an uneasy silence in the cabin while the group inside listened to the men approach. The engines whined to a halt and stopped outside the cabin. They heard boots scuffling in the mud, then raised voices. There was an argument that became clearer the closer they came.

"You dumb son of a bitch." It sounded like Virgil Avery. "How're we supposed to clean up another one of your messes?"

"Just like the other ones," came the smooth response from Mitch Stanford, with that hint of New York sneer. "T-Rex will blame Cole Tucker, and a jury will send him

to prison. Or death row. What are you worrying for?
He's on the run, they'll find him, he takes the fall. Any
luck, they'll shoot him first."

"Your luck's going to run out." Virgil Avery sounded
angry.

"Hasn't so far. And Grady here told the sheriff how
Cole turned into a vicious madman when he knocked
him out. I still want to know how he did that little trick.
What'd he do, Grady, tickle you behind your ear? A little
coochie-coo and you just drop like a sack of—"

"Shut up!" The new voice belonged to Deputy Grady
Rush.

"You're forgetting Tucker let that snotty reporter go,
and she's been asking questions," Virgil complained. "She
found that silver heel. That was sloppy, Mitch."

"Oh, hell, who cares! We'll get around to Smithsonian
too. Meantime you're gonna like this little bitch I got up
here now, Virgil," Stanford said. "She's special. She's
young and blond, and she's a fighter. I know you like it
when they put up a little fuss. And I'll bet Homer here
just can't wait to hang up a new pair of pretty boots on
his work of art. Ain't that right, Homer?"

"I like the boots." Homer Avery's was the fourth
voice. "But I don't like it when they. When they scream.
You always make them scream and I don't. Don't like it.
It's not right."

Lacey felt the urge to vomit and sucked in her breath.
Emily was frozen like a frightened deer, her fist in her
mouth to keep from making a sound. Drops of sweat
flecked her forehead. Lacey put an arm around Emily's
shoulders.

Vic motioned for everyone to get down on the floor
against the windowless front wall of the cabin, next to
the door. There was no place to hide inside the cabin,
but the walls were made of thick logs, tightly chinked.
Vic stood with his back to the wall by the door, his gun
ready.

"This one's all screamed out, Homer," Stanford said.
"She won't be doing any more screaming, so don't you
be worrying your tender ears, little boy."

"Shut up, Mitch." Virgil Avery again. The footsteps stopped again. "It was never supposed to go this far."

"I didn't know you were gonna kill them," Grady said. "I thought it was all just gonna be, you know, *partying*."

"Things happen." Stanford chuckled. "I may have snapped their pretty necks, but you all partied with these girls. That's the thing, boys. You're in this just as deep as I am. And you're all having a good time, right? So what's the problem?"

"I didn't do any. Partying," Homer said. "It's wrong."

"Poor Homer! You're still in this thing. You all are. Might as well have a good time."

"Why don't you just shut up for a damn minute," Virgil said.

Stanford apparently liked to hear himself talk. "You covered up for me, 'cause you're greedy bastards—we all are." Emily was shaking, crying silently. The footsteps came closer, but Stanford carried on. "There are certain things you can count on in this life. Death and taxes and greed. You two want a piece of the mineral lease money, don't you, Grady? Virgil? You stick with me and you'll be rolling in mineral money. You too, Homer. By the way, that was a brilliant idea, Virg, Tucker taking the fall."

"Listen, Mitch, we got to get out of this," Virgil said. "You've got to leave Sagebrush."

"I don't think so. Relax. You'll get what you want. The land and all those beautiful oil and gas leases. Just hang in there and do it my way and—"

"Someone's been. Been here," Homer said.

Inside the cabin, everyone held their breath. The footsteps stopped.

"Yeah, *me*, you idiots. I've been here." Stanford sounded irritated at the very suggestion. He was right outside the door.

"You're wrong. Mitch," Homer said haltingly, in his simple declarative way. "Someone's been. Up here. Footprints. Big ones and little ones. Lots of them. See?"

"Those are *my* prints! The little ones are hers. You

dumb-ass, Homer—"The doorknob turned and stopped. Vic had locked the door. Lacey could almost see the surprise on the men's faces. A boot kicked the door, hard, and it shook in its frame. Stanford was still laughing, but his tone darkened. "She locked the door on me, can you believe that? Must've pulled the cot across the floor. Open up, Emily baby! Time to party! Daddy's home!"

Just inside the door, Vic held up his hand for silence.

Lacey heard a *click-click*. A gun fired and a bullet slammed through the door of the cabin, the table too, and struck the back wall. So loud it made her jump. Emily whimpered and quaked like a leaf.

"Stay down," Vic warned in a whisper.

Another bullet came flying through the door. The six people inside the cabin sat on the floor very still.

"What are you waiting for?" Lacey whispered.

"For him to empty his weapon," Vic whispered back. "And see if anybody else starts shooting. So far, so good."

From outside, Stanford laughed, a harsh and horrible sound. "Playing games with Daddy, are you? I'll show you *games*, baby."

Vic moved close to Lacey. She held his free hand. There was another *click-click,* another gunshot. "Three shots," she said.

"That's good." Vic took a breath. "Lacey, sweetheart, I know this isn't the best time. But I'm not sure there will ever be a right time for— Well, this is a good time. I have to ask you something."

"What? Why is three shots good?" She gazed at him. If these were going to be her last moments, she wanted to be looking at him.

Vic seemed to be intent on saying something. But it was difficult. Lacey didn't know whether it was because of the gunfire or if he was nervous about something else. His eyes seemed to be an especially deep shade of green, and that dark pesky curl fell over his forehead. He was listening to the silence.

"Hear that? That pause?" Vic said. "Three rounds and a pause. I figure a bolt-action rifle, three in the well, big scope, a little slow to reload. Probably a magnum, otherwise he'd have four rounds on tap, or more. But he only has three."

"Stop babbling about guns, Vic. What do you want to ask me?"

"From the sound, it's something like a seven mag, the hot elk round out here," he said. "Now Stanford's reloading. But he probably only has three more rounds on him."

"'Probably'?" Trujillo whispered. "A maniac with a seven magnum, and you're betting the farm on *probably*?"

Vic shrugged. "Elk don't shoot back, Tony. Most hunters don't fire three rounds all season."

"Butt out, Trujillo. Vic, you were saying something?" Lacey said. "Something *not* about guns?"

"Lacey. Yeah, I was." Vic gazed at her and drew her closer. "This is not how I wanted to say this. I wanted to have flowers and music and take you to a five-star restaurant in Paris or maybe somewhere on a beach at sunset, someplace beautiful, someplace worthy of you."

There was another gunshot. Outside the cabin they heard jumbled voices and Mitch's laughter. Emily jumped and clutched her side, tears running down her face. Lacey turned toward her. "I'm okay," Emily choked.

Vic cocked his head. "One. I was right, three rounds and a reload."

"What are we doing?" Mac asked. "We got a plan, right, Donovan?"

"Vic?" Lacey opened her eyes wide. Another bullet hit the back wall of the cabin. *That makes two.* "Was it something important?"

"God, yes, it's important." He took another deep breath. "Lacey, will you marry me?"

"What?!" *Did I hear him correctly?*

"Marry me, Lacey. Sickness, health, richer, poorer, all of it. For as long as we live, though that might not be very long. In danger and in safety, though I'd really like to know what that *safe* part might look like with you around. Hasn't happened yet, but in any case, our marriage will never be boring. But will you? Please?"

"Marry you?"

"Marry me."

Lacey's heart was beating like a jackhammer, but everything seemed to be moving in slow motion. She felt dizzy. She willed herself to forget the others for a moment, which was difficult. They were all staring at her. Even Emily seemed to forget her pain. She nodded to Lacey encouragingly. They all waited for an answer.

"If I say yes, will you still take me to that restaurant and that beach?" Lacey's fingertips smoothed his curl off his face.

"Flowers and music? Yes. Do you love me, Lacey?"

"Oh, Vic. I have loved you for the longest time."

"So it's yes?"

"Yes! Yes, yes. Of course, it's yes!" Lacey said, and Vic kissed her.

"Are you freaking kidding me?" Tony said in a stage whisper. "Guys with guns are trying to kill us and you two are playing kissy-face?"

There was another shot. Very close to the door. *Three.*

Vic was instantly on his feet. In command mode. "Stay away from the door. Grab anything you can for a weapon. Lacey, darlin', take care of Emily."

The men sprang up from the floor. Emily tried to get up but she seemed dazed and in pain, hugging her ribs. Lacey held her tight. "Everything is going to work out," she whispered. "We're going to make it."

"Alive?" Emily asked, on the verge of tears again. "Please. So you can get married?"

"I promise." The silence on the outside was menacing. *What are they doing now? Are they still out there?*

"Stay out of sight until I say *clear*." Vic kicked the table away from the door and yanked it open. Behind him, Ben hefted one of his ski poles like a spear. Mac took the other one, holding it like a club. Lacey picked up two of the coiled ropes. She threw one to Tony, who hung it around his shoulder while he readied his "crowbar" and his camera. Vic stood in the open door, covering all four men with his revolver.

"What the hell—?" Lacey couldn't see through the

crowded doorway, but it was Stanford's voice again. "God damn! If it ain't Chief Donovan. Join the party, Chief. We're just, uh, having a little — ah, target practice."

"Drop the rifle, Stanford." Vic's voice, very calm. Lacey listened for the sound of a rifle being dropped. She didn't hear it. She peered out the door over Mac's shoulder. All eyes were on Vic. No one moved for a moment.

Lacey played nervously with her coil of rope. It was something to do. As she watched the standoff, she tied a honda at the end without looking, securing it with a stopper knot, and slipped the rope through it, forming a loop, which she held in her right hand. She coiled the rest of the rope in her left, slipping it over her shoulder, like Tony.

"You're not top cop anymore, Donovan," Virgil Avery was complaining. "I don't care what it says on your hat. And you're trespassing on private property."

"Not going to matter when they see Emily Ogden here," Vic said. "Hands on your heads, gentlemen, or I'll drop you all where you stand. Stanford, drop your weapon. Everyone on the ground. Now." Vic took a big step toward the killer. Lacey saw the rifle land in the mud.

"Now, Donovan, let's be reasonable men," Stanford blurted. "Maybe we can work something out? I can make you a mighty rich man—"

"Don't give me a reason to blow your head off, Stanford. On your knees, all of you. Hands behind your heads."

"Rush him!" Stanford yelled. "Get him! We can't let him live."

Lacey's heart leapt in fear. Homer was still kneeling as he'd been told, but Virgil and Grady were rushing toward Vic, while Stanford, the big talker, was running hard the other way, away from the cabin and the ATVs. Vic sidestepped Virgil, kicked Grady aside, and followed the escaping Stanford, who was already disappearing into the sagebrush. Mac, Ben, and Tony burst out after Vic. Lacey pushed Emily safely out of sight, her rope at the ready. She tried to keep her eyes on Stanford, and on Vic in hot pursuit, but there was a brawl happening right in front of her.

Mac and Ben were going after Virgil and Grady with ski poles. Virgil swung a fist at Ben and Ben knocked him down with his pole.

"Homer, help me," Virgil yelled from the mud.

"But he. He told me to get down. On my knees," Homer explained patiently, his hands behind his head. "He has a gun, Virgil. He's a. A policeman."

Virgil bounced back swinging and brought his fist up into Ben's face. Mac sliced the air with his pole like a saber, holding Grady off, but the deputy was younger and faster. He grabbed Mac's pole and they struggled over it, like a tug-of-war gone very wrong. Tony dropped his rope and whacked Grady across the back with his metal pipe. Grady staggered and let go of the pole. Mac went down in the mud and took Grady with him. Mac and Grady rolled in the mud, trading punches.

Tony looked for an opening to impale Grady with his pipe. Grady rolled away and Tony impaled the mud instead. The pipe was stuck fast, so he switched to his camera and started snapping away. Mac connected a beefy fist with Grady's jaw and stretched the deputy face-first into the mud.

Although he got a few good licks in, attorney Benjamin was taking a beating from Virgil Avery. Lacey saw Vic turn back from pursuing Stanford, who was clearly running the wrong way. She figured the pudgy oil man would soon have to turn around if he meant to grab an ATV and get away. Vic leveled his revolver at Homer's brother.

"Let him go, Virgil, or I shoot."

Virgil twisted out of Ben's grip and spun toward Vic, but he slipped in the mud. Vic took his best shot, but as Virgil fell he turned to the side and took the bullet in his right buttock. He toppled and rolled in the mud in pain, clutching his butt with both hands.

"My God, Donovan, you shot me in the ass! What the hell!"

Homer tentatively took his hands off his head. "Are you okay, Virgil?"

"Hell no, I'm not okay! He shot me in my damn ass!"

"I don't think you can die from. A butt shot." Homer

put his hands back behind his head. Vic looked disgusted. It wasn't the shot he had planned.

Ben got to his feet, breathing hard. He was going to have quite a shiner, but he had a silly grin on his face.

"Chief Donovan. Can I get up? To help my brother?" Homer asked plaintively. "He says he's been shot. In the ass."

"No, Homer, you stay right where you are," Vic replied evenly, "or I'll shoot you in the ass too."

"Yes, sir." Homer stayed on his knees. Vic fished his backup handcuffs out of his fanny pack for Grady, and sent Tony inside for the pair Lacey had taken off Emily. They would do for Homer.

The brawl seemed to be over, and the good guys had won. Vic was busy cuffing wrists and roping up the losers. Tony, Mac, and Ben were covered in mud and blood, trying to catch their breath.

But where's Mitch? Still out there running toward the bluffs? Away from the ATVs? What is he thinking? Lacey wondered. *He's going to climb those bluffs? He's out of his mind!*

Just then, Stanford emerged from the sagebrush not twenty feet away, muddy and scratched and sweating like a pig, but still trotting pretty fast for a fat man. He'd circled around the cabin, heading for the ATVs, his only chance for a getaway. He looked at Lacey. She looked at him. He skidded in the mud and ran the other way. Lacey shouted for Vic and took off running after Stanford, rope in hand.

She wasn't a cowgirl, and Mitch Stanford wasn't a calf. Still, she had the lasso in her hand, she knew how to use it, and she was chasing a killer. It felt good to be taking action, any action, after waiting in the cabin for the shooting and fighting to stop. Stanford looked over his shoulder to see her closing in on him. He stumbled in the sagebrush, sprawled, and dropped his hat. He staggered to his feet, which gave her one precious extra moment.

Lacey stopped, lifted her arm, and swung the rope over her head, preparing to throw the lariat. She held her breath, opened her hand, and let the rope go, keeping her arm and wrist straight, the way Tucker had taught her years ago. She willed it to land where it was supposed to land, around Stanford's chest.

To her complete astonishment, the rope met its target, and took Stanford by surprise. He tried to shrug it off, but Lacey tightened the rope and pulled out the slack as he struggled to get out of the loop. She was unprepared for what happened next.

Stanford stood up and ran away, jerking the rope taut. It was the same reaction a startled calf would have had. Lacey held on tight even though she was skidding on her bottom, heels first, through the mud and snow and sagebrush, pulled along by the big man. Until Vic caught up with her. He grabbed the rope with her, his hands on her hands, planted his heels hard, and together they brought Stanford down.

"I had him, you know," she said, huffing and puffing.

"Course you did, sweetheart. I'm just helping." Stanford was rolling in the mud, clawing helplessly at the rope and cursing a blue streak, when Lacey heard a horse snuffle somewhere off to her right. She looked up and over the sagebrush.

"That was pretty good ropin', Chantilly," Tucker called out.

It wasn't a wild pony. It was Ricochet and his rider. Cole Tucker dismounted rodeo-style, no hands, tipped his hat, and took the rope from Vic and Lacey. The fugitive cowboy reeled in a swearing Mitch Stanford and trussed up him professionally, like a stray cow on the Tuckered Out Ranch. Lacey stared open-mouthed.

"Nice timing, Tucker." Vic caught his breath. "Riding in for the big finish *after* we dogged him down."

"Heck, if you'd let him run a little farther I'd have roped him myself." Tucker grinned wide. His voice softened, all the mocking gone. "Chantilly Lace, you'll make a cowgirl yet. Where you been practicing?"

"Cole, where on God's green earth have you been?" Lacey asked.

Tucker shrugged. "Here and there. Ricochet and I been nosing around. Didn't know if you got my map.

Thought I'd give this place another look. When I heard the gunshots we came as fast as Rickie could run."

"God damn!" Stanford cried. "You can't leave me here, tied up like an animal." He kicked and rolled and stamped and swore, but the rope held fast. He made it to his knees, but he couldn't struggle to his feet.

"Sure we can." Lacey was so angry she was practically spitting. "That's what you did with those women, before you killed them. Isn't it?"

"Ricochet will be happy to drag you back to Sagebrush on the end of a rope, Stanford," Tucker said to the roped man on the ground. "Might not be much left of you though. Just enough to hang."

"We don't hang them anymore," Lacey said.

"Technicality."

"I appreciate the offer, Cole, but the CBI ought to be along here pretty soon," Vic said. "Firestone or T-Rex will trade that rope for some cold metal handcuffs. For now, let's just drag him back to the cabin."

Tucker pushed his hat back off his face. "So this is the animal who killed Corazon and Ally, and poor little Rae?"

"He murdered them, but he had friends." Lacey suddenly wondered what was going on back at the cabin. She turned to see Trujillo and Mac standing in the door, dusting themselves off. The Avery brothers and Grady were neatly tied up just outside the door. Mac was scraping mud off his new boots and hat.

Emily had pulled on one of her cowboy boots and she was leaning against the doorjamb, holding on to the other boot, the ankle chain trailing on the floor. Trujillo gave her his arm. Ben was making his way toward Lacey and Vic.

Tucker pulled tight on the rope, toppling Stanford into the mud on his face. The man on the ground screamed in pain and outrage. "You deserve more than I can give you," Tucker said. "Corazon didn't deserve to die." He tightened the rope again. "None of them did."

"You can't do this to me," Stanford managed to say between painful breaths. "You'll take the rap for those girls! Not me! Not me!" Tucker pulled back his foot for a kick, aimed right at Stanford's soft gut.

"That's enough." Vic stopped Tucker. He squatted next to Stanford and pushed the oil man's face back into the mud. "You're lucky to be alive, Stanford. If I'd had a clear shot, I'd have killed you and saved the state the trouble. I'd let Tucker here hang you on a fence like a dead coyote. Not a living soul would miss you." Stanford shut up.

Tucker put his hand on Lacey's shoulder. "You figured it out, Chantilly. Girl, you impress me."

Vic stepped casually in between Tucker and Lacey. "I'm just glad she's safe."

"Emily is alive because of you, Tucker," Lacey said.

"And because you wouldn't give up, darlin'," Vic said.

Lacey studied each man's face. Cole, the sun-bronzed, windblown cowboy with the Western, aw-shucks-ma'am charm. Vic, the Western cop turned Eastern private eye, with those disarming green eyes and unruly dark curls, who moved back East to be near her, who had braved bullets for her.

Tucker taught her how to throw a rope; Vic showed her how to shoot a gun. She had such warm memories of Cole. But her heart skipped a beat for Vic. She reached for his hand, and he nuzzled her hair.

There may have been a momentary pang that showed in Tucker's face, but he smiled and tipped his hat to her. "I'll never forget you, Chantilly Lace. You ever change your mind, I'll be here."

Ben reached the group and put his hand out. "I take it you're the famous Cole Younger Tucker, fugitive from justice."

"I'm Cole Tucker," Tucker said guardedly.

"Benjamin Barton here, criminal defense attorney with Barton, Barton and Barton, of Washington, D.C." Ben was smiling, his eyes glassy with excitement. He looked a lot like his sister right at that moment.

"You're a bit far from home, aren't you, Mr. Barton?"

"Yes indeed, Mr. Tucker, and you're going to need a good lawyer. Not for the murders—it's clear those charges will be dropped—but there is that matter of escaping from a courthouse, evading arrest, obstructing justice, embarrassing the sheriff and the judge, and so forth. And of course you took physical custody of Lacey and hauled her out of the Yampa County courthouse without her permission."

Lacey nudged Ben. "I'm not pressing charges."

"That's good to know," Tucker said to Lacey. "And you won't hold that horseback ride against me, Chantilly Lace?"

"I didn't say that."

"Our firm would be happy to represent you," Ben announced. "Pro bono. To see justice done."

Tucker stroked his chin. "Well, my last attorney most likely quit. And I reckon T-Rex will still want my hide."

"Oh, he definitely will," Ben agreed enthusiastically. "I guarantee you are going to want Barton, Barton and Barton on your side."

Tucker laughed, and stared at Ben's shiner. "You look like a lawyer who's not afraid to take a punch. Think you can make this whole mess go away?"

"*Make it go away* is my middle name. Deal?"

"Deal." They shook on it.

Vic pulled Lacey aside. "So tell me, darlin'. What is all this 'Chantilly Lace' business?"

"Later, honey." She snuggled against him and smiled. A little touch of jealousy, she decided, could be a good thing.

A sound had been growing in the distance as they talked, and now it was filling the sky above them and echoing off the mountainside. Everyone looked up. It was the sound of helicopter blades chopping through the air.

The cavalry had arrived.

chapter 33

The chopper's propeller blades kicked up clouds of dirt and snow, giving Mitch Stanford something else to complain about, but Lacey couldn't hear him above the roar.

Relief left her feeling exhausted and giddy at the same time. She felt Vic steady her, and she held on to him. Trujillo was photographing the helicopter landing, Mitchell Stanford, the cabin, Emily, Tucker, everything he could get his camera lens on.

Virgil Avery and Grady Rush sat tied up together in front of the cabin. They were not happy about it. Homer Avery sat placidly handcuffed next to his brother, while Mac stood with his ski pole at the ready, making sure no one got any ideas to run. It looked like everyone was present and accounted for. Except Emily. Lacey started to run toward the cabin.

She ran past Virgil Avery and Rush and slipped between Mac and Homer into the single dim room, which by now was a little warmer. Mac had started a fire going in the woodstove.

"Emily? How are you doing?"

Emily was slumped in one of the chairs, hugging her broken ribs with both arms. "I saw what you did," Emily said, every word taking some effort. "With the rope. That was the coolest thing ever. I want to learn how to do that. I want to be a cowgirl."

Vic strode into the cabin, followed by Tucker, who left Ricochet by the door with Mac holding the reins. Lacey made introductions.

"Howdy, Emily." Tucker tipped his hat to her. She held out her hand and he took it.

"You all saved my life." Emily turned her baby blue eyes on Tucker. "Thank you, Mr. Tucker. I know who you are. Do you think you could show me how to do that thing with the rope someday? When I'm all healed up?"

Tucker flashed his cowboy grin. "Sure, Miss Emily. When you're ready to rock and roll, I'd be pleased to show you. Are you doing all right?"

"I'm feeling lots better." Emily smiled and closed her eyes against the pain.

"The helicopter is landing," Vic announced. "Medical team from the hospital."

A fresh wave of ATVs rolled up to the cabin. Sheriff T. Rexford jumped off one, Agent Rico Firestone another, and the CBI team was behind them. Firestone spared a curious smile for the trussed-up Mitch Stanford. T-Rex glared at everyone in his way, stopping for a moment to take in the bloodstained mud and snow.

"How do, Sheriff," Homer said. "My brother Virgil got his. Butt shot. That's what the blood's from. Can't die from a butt shot though. I think." Homer seemed sanguine about his predicament. "We're under. Arrest."

"There's been a big mistake, Sheriff," Virgil whined, but the sheriff cut him off.

"Save it." The sheriff glared down at his erstwhile deputy, Grady Rush, who hung his head and said not a word. T-Rex marched into the cabin. "Where is Emily Ogden?" He stared at Emily, still slumped in the chair, her eyes closed, her bruises bright against her pale skin. "Mercy, God in Heaven, girl. What did those animals do to you?" She just shook her head, and tears rolled down her face.

T-Rex looked over the cabin, side to side and up and down. His mouth dropped open as he eyed the rack of antlers on the wall, festooned with cowboy boots and a hanging noose.

"Cowboy boots! Damnation." He seemed mesmerized. He shook his head in amazement. He wasn't about to give Lacey the satisfaction of admitting she was right, not just yet. "What about Emily's boots? She's wearing boots. Well, one boot."

"We found them up on the antlers," Lacey said. "There are Rae Fowler's boots too. See the one with the broken heel? You know who the others belong to. Emily was barefoot."

"I wanted my boots," Emily said. "I was so cold. They took care of me. Especially her."

"She was chained to that cot over there," Vic said. "By the way, Sheriff, if your guys have some bolt cutters, that chain ought to pop right off."

T-Rex nodded. The helicopter was down and the prop was idling. Paramedics came running through the door with a stretcher and went straight to Emily. Everyone got out of their way. The cabin was filling up with people. T-Rex finally noticed the man he'd been looking for. "Cole Tucker, nice of you to join us. We got a warm cell waiting for you."

Tucker didn't say a word. He didn't have to. Benjamin Barton moved smoothly between them. "Hello, Sheriff. You remember me?" Ben's black eye was blossoming into a beauty.

"What happened to you? All I need is a fancy-pants East Coast attorney to get in the way."

"I'd hold off on that cell reservation for my *client*, Mr. Cole Tucker," Ben said to T-Rex. "He assisted in the apprehension of the real killer, Mitch Stanford."

Yeah, Cole Tucker and his wonder horse, Ricochet, Lacey thought. *And the rest of us.*

"Sheriff, I personally witnessed the apprehension of Mitchell Stanford and his accomplices," Ben continued. "And I believe there are photographs. Many photographs, taken by the media, soon to be seen nationwide. I'll be speaking with the county prosecutor immediately on our return about dropping all charges against my client."

"Hold on a damn minute—," T-Rex started. "He escaped from custody!"

"The way I hear it, from an *eyewitness*, your deputy let him go. But with your help, Sheriff Rexford, together we may be able to save Yampa County a great deal of expense and embarrassment. Lawsuits for wrongful imprisonment, defamation of character, loss of reputation, I could go on and on—"

The sheriff was turning that color of red Lacey had so admired, but he was listening to every word Ben said.

"Who shot Virgil Avery in the ass?" asked Firestone.

"I did," Vic said. "And I'd do it again. A little higher."

"Virgil Avery was trying to kill me," Ben said. "Vic Donovan shot him in defense of my life."

"His ass wasn't where I was aiming," Vic said. "I plead moving target."

Firestone ordered everyone but Emily and the medical team out of the warm cabin and into the frigid air, so he and T-Rex could question her while the EMTs tended to her. Homer still sat on the wet ground next to his brother, both of them slumped over with their wrists cuffed behind them.

"Does it hurt much to be shot in the. Ass, Virgil?"

"Course it hurts," Virgil said. "Dumb-ass."

A deputy and the EMT led Virgil around to the back of the cabin for some privacy to examine his wound. Lacey leaned down next to Homer to talk with him.

"Homer, what did you have to do with all this?"

He looked up at her with his sad brown eyes. "I don't like to stay. Home alone," he said, in his halting way. "Virgil said I could come along. If I stayed in the truck. Down the hill. But I didn't like staying. In the truck. I could hear the ladies screaming. Even out in the truck. I'm big so they made me carry the ladies. Down to Mitch's pickup."

"Were they alive when you carried them?"

"Not anymore. I think they were. Dead."

"What about the boots?"

"Mitch wanted to keep their boots. He liked the way those girls looked. Wearing them. He told me to do something. With the boots. So he could look at the boots. I put them up on the antlers in the. The cabin. I was making a tree full of boots. I was making art out of them."

"You know what they were doing was wrong, don't you, Homer?"

"But Virgil told me to. He's my brother. He said we

couldn't ever. Tell the sheriff. But the sheriff never asked me about it. You're the only one who ever asked me. Virgil didn't tell me not to tell you."

"Thank you, Homer."

"You're welcome, Lacey. Can I call you Lacey?"

"Yes, you can." She straightened up and leaned against the cabin.

Soon, Vic and Lacey watched as the EMTs carried Mitch Stanford's last victim out of the cabin on a stretcher and loaded her into the helicopter. She waved at them.

The chain had been cut from her ankle. Emily was wearing both of her cowboy boots.

"We could have been killed out here today," Mac said, back in the Jeep. His new cowboy hat looked battered and well broken in. "But we weren't. And that is outstanding in my book!" He seemed extraordinarily pleased, hopped up on adrenaline, survival, and a great story. But the light in his editorial eyes could mean only one thing for Lacey and Tony. *More work.*

"Vic, please turn up the heat," Lacey said, buckling herself into the Jeep. "I'm freezing, honey." Vic just smiled. Lacey smiled too. *We'll be turning up the heat later.*

She and the others weren't allowed back in the cabin of death. There was a tree of boots, and a crime scene, waiting for the authorities to process. But there were plenty of photographs for *The Eye Street Observer*.

"I blew through three camera batteries and a whole extra memory card," Tony said with a smug look. He was in the state of bliss reporters achieve when they've nailed the scoop. "I got it all."

"As I was saying," Mac said, "we weren't killed. Today was heroic, people. Epic. *Eye Street Observer* reporters— and editors, I might add—put their lives on the line to find this missing woman, the next intended victim of a serial killer. And his accomplices. Well, crew, we rocked it."

"You writing the lede, Mac?" Lacey said. "That's our job."

"I can still rock a lede," he said. "Now, I want you to

write up your stories as soon as possible, so we don't lose the immediacy, the energy. I want this on the Web this afternoon, just a teaser, and we'll hit print tomorrow morning. Front page."

"We can write a dozen features out of this day alone," Tony said. "We'll be up all night! Tucker's charges being dropped, the arraignment of the Stanford gang, trial coverage, the sentencing—"

Lacey leaned her weary head against the headrest and closed her eyes. "Why don't you just take the rest of my blood now? Or maybe a kidney."

Vic chuckled and kept his eyes on the jeep trail.

"We're going to play this for all it's worth," Mac was saying. "'*Eye Street Observer* Saves the Day!'"

"And what about the sheriff's official statement, that *they* rescued Emily themselves, with some assistance from former Sagebrush Chief of Police Victor Donovan?" Lacey asked.

"Whatever. Quote the sheriff for comic relief," Mac said. "We'll print our story, the *real* story. And the pictures. Let the readers decide how it went down."

"How about your old boss, Lacey?" Trujillo asked.

"Muldoon? He'll write whatever he wants to write, no matter what the facts are," Lacey said.

"I'm thinking we can turn this story into a book in five weeks, six tops," Mac said. "Our publisher is going to love this."

"That's insane, Mac," Lacey said in horror. "Pure lunacy."

"Come on, Smithsonian. Or should I say Scoop? It's not like you have to make up the plot. It's straight reporting. And how about this for the title: *Terror at Timberline*."

Lacey groaned. "How about *Lacey Goes On Vacation*."

Things happened in a hurry that afternoon when they got back to Sagebrush. Vic and Lacey, along with Mac and Tony, marched into the courthouse, mud and all. There was no time to change.

They got to witness attorney Benjamin "Make It Go Away" Barton performing his magic. By late that afternoon all the charges against Cole Tucker had been dropped, and he walked out of the Yampa County courthouse a free man. A free man who just wanted to get back to his family, his ranch, and his horses.

chapter 34

"You're alive." Rose Smithsonian hugged Lacey hard, then held her daughter at arm's length and inspected her.

"Yes, Mom. I'm alive."

"This time. What happened to your hands?"

Rose picked up her daughter's hands. Red rope marks scored Lacey's palms and the back of her hands, where she had held on to the lariat. They still stung. "It's nothing, really."

"I have some aloe in my room. We'll fix you up."

She and Cherise were waiting in the lobby of the motel when an exhausted Lacey and Vic returned from the courthouse. It felt later than it was. A chilly dark night had fallen, glistening with stars over Sagebrush.

Tony and Mac, still hopped up on adrenaline, were posting stories to *The Eye*'s Web site. Somehow Tony had managed to take a photo of the takedown of Mitch Stanford, with Lacey sliding in the mud and snow on her bottom, taut rope in hand. It would be on the front page. She would have to get even somehow.

"I'm fine, really," Lacey said.

"You don't look fine. You look beyond exhausted. Oh, Lacey, I can't believe you went off on this daredevil adventure without your home team, your posse," Rose lamented. "Out in the wilderness! With another crazy killer."

"But we had an army of people there, Mom. And I wasn't really ever in danger. Not really."

"Tell me another one." Rose's Look could humble Lacey's Look any day of the week.

"News travels even faster at this altitude," Lacey said, exasperated.

"No kidding," Cherise said. She grinned. "Did you know that crazy Muldoon put out a special edition of his rag?" Her sister produced a thin newspaper: DAILY PRESS ALUMNI REPORTER ROPES KILLER. There was a photo of Lacey with Sheriff T-Rex and Rico Firestone, taken the day she returned to town on horseback.

"It could be worse." Lacey grimaced.

Vic picked up the paper. "Another memento for the scrapbook." He started reading. And laughing. Lacey ignored him. She was eager to change the subject.

"You were on your own special mission today, you guys. Saving Vonda McKay. How did that go?"

"We had a nice lunch and got to know her. Met her aunt," Rose said. "Cherise called to let her know Emily is safe and all the bad guys are in jail."

"You also did a little shopping, didn't you?" Lacey stared down at the floor. "Boots! You bought boots."

A new pair of sleek mahogany brown cowboy boots with cream accents graced Rose's feet. She turned her ankle for the full effect. "It's not like I'll get back to F. M. Light in Steamboat anytime soon."

"And guess what?" Cherise said. "They cost more than mine did!"

"Don't tell your father." Rose winked.

Lacey and Vic finally escaped for a semi-intimate dinner for two at El Caballero Loco, the best Mexican restaurant in Sagebrush, where the sizzle of hot fajitas perfumed the air and the margaritas came in fishbowl-sized glasses.

They sat on the same side of the bench in a secluded booth. After the day she'd had, Lacey didn't want to be far away from him. She leaned her head on his shoulder.

"It was a little rough out there today," Vic said.

"This has always been a tough town. But you knew that, Chief Donovan." His proposal felt like a distant memory, punctuated by gunshots.

"I swear my heart stopped several times today," Vic said, lifting his margarita.

"And yet you look so alive. You were amazing. So when did this heart-stopping thing happen?"

"When the bullets started flying. And when I was waiting for your answer. You know, that question I asked you? That marriage thing. You did say yes, didn't you, sweetheart?"

Lacey snuggled closer and sighed. "After your incredibly romantic and creative proposal, how could I say no? Bullets whizzing over my head? Death stalking outside the door? Isn't that the proposal every woman dreams of?"

Vic ruffled her hair. "Today, when that idiot started blowing holes in the door, I suddenly realized *this might be it*. What if this really was it? What if this was all there was of it? And I knew I wanted to spend the rest of it with you. I can't imagine living without you."

It reminded Lacey of what Emily had said to her, only hours before. When Emily thought she was going to die, she kept thinking, *Is this it? Is this all there is of my whole life?* Lacey felt her own heart ache again, remembering Emily's words: *I didn't get to do anything I really wanted.*

Well, that *wasn't* all there was of it. Emily had her whole life ahead of her now, a chance to make a new choice. Redemption was all around. They all knew they had a second chance: Emily and Cole Tucker, and Lacey and Vic.

Life was short and often brutal, and always heartbreaking in some ways. But sometimes, if you were lucky, love was waiting around some corner. She wasn't going to pass Vic by, to run away from love the way she had in the past.

"I want to spend the rest of it with you too, Vic."

"I was biding my time, but today time almost ran out." He picked up her hand and kissed it. "I love you, Lacey Smithsonian. I had to ask you today. I couldn't wait another minute."

"Now that we've rehearsed that question, darling, I

remember something about flowers and moonlight? And a beach?"

"Maybe I'll surprise you." He picked up her left hand. "Now what about a ring?"

"If a woman's going to wear a ring every day of her life, she should like the ring. Not just *love* it. Really *like* it."

"You want to help pick it out?"

"You're so perceptive, Vic. If you don't mind."

"Got it. No surprise gumball machine ring. Take your lady out jewelry shopping. Keep proposing to her at random intervals. See, I'm making notes." He traced a ring around Lacey's finger. "Would your answer change if I asked you again? With moonlight and champagne, instead of boots and bullets?"

"No. It wouldn't change. I love you, Sean Victor Donovan."

He looked her in the eyes. "You ready to be engaged? To me?"

"To be engaged, yes." *To be married? Not so sure.* Lacey believed in long engagements. Long, *long* engagements.

"You don't feel like suddenly leaving town, do you? Like you did after the last proposal you got in Sagebrush?"

"This town? Oh, Vic, leaving this town is all I've been wanting to do ever since I got here. As long as you're leaving with me."

He kissed her long and slow, ignoring the waiter arriving with their fajitas. When they broke the embrace, Vic caught Lacey grinning. He grinned back.

"Now what?" he said. "Did you remember something?"

"Yes. I always wanted an unforgettable proposal, Vic. Today I pretty much won the lottery for unforgettable. And I won a lot more than that. I won you."